Titles by K S Ferguson

Rafe & Kama series:

Calculated Risk

Hostile Takeover

Family Owned

River Madden series:

Touching Madness

Undercover Madness

The Hellhound series:

No Place Like Hell

Stand-alone novella:

Puncher's Chance (with James Grayson)

Hostile Takeover

Contact the publisher: http://www.ksferguson.net

ISBN: 1-938179-20-X
ISBN-13: 978-1-938179-20-4

HOSTILE TAKEOVER

Rafe & Kama
Book 2

K S Ferguson

K S FERGUSON

ACKNOWLEDGMENTS

I would like to thank the many people who assisted with this novel. First, thanks to my daughter for her unfailing support and thoughtful suggestions. Thanks to James Grayson for his suggestions and assists with the action scenes. Thanks to my beta readers, Pam and Ellen, and Luke for his sharp editorial eye.

I would also like to thank my readers. Your support is greatly appreciated. If you enjoyed this book, please consider leaving a review at your favorite retailer or library site. Reviews help other readers find this work and keep food on the table so writers don't starve.

If you would like to be notified when the next book in the series is released, please sign up at http://www.ksferguson. net/sign-up-for-news.html. I won't sell your contact info to anyone for any reason.

1

---

18 March, 2040

Kama's gaze slid to the flyer's side window, and then down. The breath caught in her throat. A thousand meters below, a blanket of dense smoke obscured the ground. Hidden beneath the smoke, flames driven by a stiff breeze consumed endless hectares of noxious garraweed, the dominant life form on EcoMech's colony world, Harvest.

The heat of the updraft buffeted the flyer and jolted Kama against the passenger door. She tightened her seatbelt a notch and tucked her duffel firmly between her feet. Then she ordered herself to stop thinking about the raging inferno below. They were perfectly safe at this altitude.

She'd seen the garraweed up close when she'd arrived at Harvest's shuttleport. An ocean of two-meter tall golden stalks crowded the runways and buildings. With each gust of wind, billowing clouds of red dust spewed from the crimson flowers at the apex of the waving growth. The swirling haze of spores painted a spectacular blood red sunrise over Harvest's too-blue sky.

At the flyer's controls, newly appointed EcoMech CEO Rafe McTavish tossed her an apologetic smile. "Sorry about the bumpy ride."

He eased the controls back and boosted power. The flyer climbed into thinner smoke, and Kama got her first glimpse of River City, Harvest's only settlement, still ten kilometers ahead.

"Scorched earth," she said, choking back a cough. "Typical corporate approach. Do the eco-protesters storming your Mumbai offices know about this?"

He raised one eyebrow and cast her a cool look. "No, and I'd prefer to keep it that way."

His tone was light, but Kama heard the fatigue—and the warning. He'd sacrificed piloting his own company to take the job at EcoMech, all so he could pursue Leon Goldman's blackmailer undercover. He didn't need more complications.

Something mechanical screeched. Then a belch of oily black smoke puffed from the flyer's right front nacelle. The craft canted right and dropped two meters. The pitch of the fans in the other three nacelles increased, and the flyer corrected back to level.

"We lost a fan," McTavish said in a patently 'don't panic' voice. "Probably a bad bearing. We'll be fine running on three engines."

Kama released the death grip on her duffel strap, irked that he thought she needed reassurance—or that she didn't understand the mechanics of a flyer. Give her three hours with an industrial grade replicator and she'd design and build a four-passenger flyer that would run rings around this crate.

She'd expected McTavish to pick her up in something snappier, something more in line with his playboy reputation for flashy women and racy transport. Instead he piloted a staid corporate vehicle. He was a chameleon, rolling out whatever persona the situation required while keeping the true man hidden. She wondered whether she'd ever really know him.

The flyer bumped and jounced through the turbulent air over the fire. Kama gritted her teeth.

"This thing has worse aerodynamics than a pig," she said.

McTavish turned her way, and his blue eyes sparkled. "You've flown a pig?"

"In simulations," she replied.

He grinned and waited. She shifted in her seat and wished she hadn't said anything.

"It was a genetic engineering lesson meant to teach the limits of genome manipulation. The pig had to be flight capable while retaining its ability to produce high quality ham and bacon."

His grin broadened. "And did you succeed in creating such an animal?"

"That depends."

"On how you define flight?" he guessed.

She crossed her arms over her chest. "No, on how you define ham. It's simply appendage muscle infused with carcinogens. The source appendage shouldn't matter."

McTavish stifled a laugh and turned back to the controls.

Kama craned her neck to check the airspace behind them.

"Where's your security escort?"

"I don't have one. None of the executives use them while they're on Harvest."

Kama blinked at him. "Because like you, they're all secretly immortal?"

"If I tighten security suddenly, it may tip off our blackmailer that we're on to him."

"You'll have a tough time catching a blackmailer if you're dead," she muttered. "Traveling across the galaxy is less of an impediment to crazy stalkers and lunatic eco-terrorists than you might think."

McTavish seemed too occupied with the controls to respond. When he focused that intently on anything, it meant trouble. A ripple of tension swept over her.

"What is it?" she asked.

"Something isn't right." He frowned and jabbed the controls with nimble fingers.

When he scanned the ground, Kama's tension soared. He was looking for a possible landing site. They couldn't land in a sea of fire.

"If I'm going to die," she said, "I'd like to know why."

"It's not that bad," he replied, although his expression said otherwise. "The other fans are running hot, and the control system isn't compensating."

Kama swallowed a lump in her throat. "Pull the circuit breakers. Let them cool off while we lose altitude, then turn them on again to land."

"They aren't working." McTavish lifted his chin and sniffed. "Do you smell something burning?"

She clamped her jaw against a hysterical laugh. The planet was on fire, and he wanted to know if she smelled it?

His nose wrinkled. His eyes narrowed while he focused on whatever it was he detected. His head snapped around to the rear of the flyer.

"Battery overheat," he said, face grim. "The runaway fans are drawing too much power. If we can't shut them down, the battery will explode."

"There are redundant systems, checks and balances, lock-outs..." She looked at him with disbelief while her fear shifted into overdrive.

He tapped at the buttons on the control panel. When they didn't respond, he slammed his fist on the control housing.

"The system's been jumped." He glanced her way, saw her confusion, and said, "All those redundancies and lock-outs are grouped in the rear control cluster. It's possible to bridge them with a jumper cable and circumvent the safety equipment."

"Kali! Who'd be so stupid?"

A tinge of red crept up his face. "Sometimes kids do it to make a flyer run above the enforced safety limits."

"Options?"

He shook his head. "Cut power or die."

"Cut power *and* die, you mean."

Kama dragged her duffel from the floor and pawed through it, even though she knew its contents. Spare coveralls and computer hacking tools wouldn't get them out of this mess.

"What are you looking for?" McTavish asked.

"Something pointed and sharp."

He hiked up his trouser leg and drew a nasty little dagger from a sheath strapped to his calf. "Unless you go for your carotid, you won't bleed out before we explode."

Kama gaped at the knife. She snatched it and pulled her data cube from her duffel. The square black box was awkward in her hand, but then she hadn't designed it to be used as a sledgehammer.

"Prepare to lose power," she said.

"Hold on."

McTavish heeled the control stick over so they pointed upwind. The edge of the garraweed burn seemed an impossible distance away. The rear of the flyer dropped, and the nose angled toward the sky.

"Go," he said.

Kama shoved her duffel aside, placed the tip of the dagger against the floor between their seats, and smashed the data cube down on the handle. Pain erupted in her fingers and wrist. The knife sunk into the flyer floor two centimeters.

She slammed the data cube down again. The knife plunged to the hilt, but the fans droned on unabated. The smell of burning electronics overpowered the smell of burning vegetation.

"A little left," McTavish said.

Kama hammered the knife handle sideways, enlarging the slit in the floor enough to withdraw the knife. She tipped the knife at an angle and drove it down again. Sparks leaped from the slit, and she flinched back, the power conduit severed.

The fans cut out, leaving the boxy flyer at the mercy of the wind and updraft. McTavish clenched the steering control. A useless gesture. Without power, he could do nothing to change their course.

Sky was all she could see out the front window, but through the side window, the ground in the distance flashed by. Would they survive the coming crash only to burn alive in the wreckage? Her fingernails dug into the armrest, and her lungs refused to inflate.

"Brace for impact," McTavish said, voice strained. A sheen of sweat moistened his tanned face.

Kama curled over her duffel as far as the shoulder harness would allow. The wind whistled past outside. Impenetrable smoke hid the approaching ground. Her pulse drummed in her ears. Every muscle stretched taut.

"Vishnu, preserve us," she whispered through gritted teeth.

McTavish reached over and squeezed her hand.

They dropped into a wall of flames. Their aft end scratched across the burning garraweed creating an impressive cinder wake. The jolt when the craft contacted the ground drove her spine up through her head. They hurtled on.

The fire washed over them. Garraweed torches flailed the side windows. The cabin filled with smoke and the temperature spiked. The shoulder harness dug into Kama's flesh. She bit back a cry and thanked Lakshmi that they weren't dead already.

They plowed through the inferno, the flyer jerking and bouncing when it struck bumps and rocks. Metal tore with a shriek. A chunk of front wing and twisted fan flashed by Kama's window.

As they slowed, McTavish popped the release on Kama's harness and reached for his own. Acrid smoke swirled in the passenger compartment. The craft ground to a halt.

"Out!" he said.

McTavish shoved his door. It opened a dozen centimeters and stopped. Kama's door wouldn't release. Fresh panic raced through her veins.

McTavish leaned her direction, swiveled in his seat, and kicked his door with both legs, twice. It swung back enough for him to squeeze out. She hoisted her bag and scrambled to follow. Strong hands grabbed her arms and dragged her from the vehicle.

They stood on a ripple of fresh-turned dirt. Less than a meter away, a jumble of burning garraweed stalks created a knee-deep sea of flame. Unbearable heat burned against Kama's cheeks, and the dense smoke brought tears to her eyes. She held a sleeve against her nose and mouth and turned toward the front of the craft.

"This way." McTavish caught her hand and pulled her the opposite direction.

He must be turned around. She pointed. "Open ground is that way."

McTavish slapped at a spark smoldering on the right leg of his dress trousers. "Unless those are asbestos coveralls you're wearing, you'll never make it."

He jerked her along behind him, past the rear of the flyer and into the furrow it had dug in its rush through the field. The cleared rut shielded them from the worst of the heat but did nothing to aid their breathing. They stumbled over the rough ground, coughing as they jogged.

McTavish glanced back often. Of course, he was waiting for the battery to explode. She'd killed the power, but the fire would provide enough heat to finish the job a saboteur started.

McTavish spun her around in front of him so his body would shield her. She wrestled to reverse their positions. He wrapped strong arms around her and pulled her to the ground, landing on top of her.

The battery blew with a deafening boom. The smoke cloud was too dense for Kama to see the disintegration of the craft, but she heard the rain of debris over the crackling of the fire.

McTavish's breath soughed against her cheek, sending a warm glow lancing to her core. His chest pressed against her. Those cobalt eyes looked into hers, a lock of curling black hair falling over a forehead streaked with soot and dust. His lips moved closer.

"We can get up now," Kama whispered.

His eyes widened. Color flooded his cheeks. He rolled to her side. "Sorry."

She clamored up, still choking on dust and smoke, and slapped dirt from her coveralls. Her eyes ran over McTavish's lithe frame and ruined suit, ensuring that he wasn't about to become a human torch or otherwise injured by the falling debris. His embarrassed gaze met hers.

"Nice landing, McTavish."

A grin curved his lips. "Welcome to Harvest."

Kama shook her head. "Never a dull moment with you, is there? I hate to say I told you so, but if this wasn't an attempt on your life, then you ought to fire your maintenance manager."

Despite the flames raging around them, a chill crept over Kama. Watching CEO Rafe McTavish's back was going to be more challenging than she'd thought.

2

Rafe McTavish rubbed his eyes, still stinging from the smoke at the crash site, and considered how to tell Aaron Goldman that the man's plan to catch his dead son's elusive blackmailer sounded like madness. They'd set Rafe up as the next target. They needed to wait for the malefactor to come after him. He leaned back in the leather armchair and sipped his glass of chardonnay while he chose his next words.

"With respect, sir, we've made good progress. We want to be sure of our evidence."

Aaron hunkered forward over the massive oak desk that dominated the cozy study, his pale eyes flashing. "I'm not interested in securing proof for a court case. All I need to know is which of the bastards who wanted Leon's job thought he could manipulate his way to the top of *my* company. I'll ruin him."

"You don't have any idea what he used to blackmail Leon?"

"No." The chairman spoke a little too quickly, his gaze shifting from Rafe. Then he coughed, and his face stiffened with pain. He suddenly looked every one of his seventy-eight years. He reached in his sweater pocket and withdrew a pill vial.

Rafe jumped to his feet and poured water from a carafe on the desk into a crystal tumbler, which he handed to Aaron. The man's sun-darkened skin appeared ashen, and his wrinkled hands trembled.

"Should I call someone?"

"No, no." The old man waved him down. "I'm getting a transplant next month, and then I'll be good as new. At least the surgery will quash the dispute about whether I have a heart."

Rafe forced a smile. After five days as EcoMech's new CEO, he'd wondered whether Aaron had a heart, too. Had the man always been so ruthless, or was the death of his only child driving his hatred?

Or maybe it was their change in relationship. Before, Rafe had simply been the son of Aaron's oldest friend and business partner, Cullen McTavish. Now, he was an employee of the board.

Rafe glanced at his wrist. His nanocom flashed up 18:50, 18 March, 2040. Only it wasn't March here on Harvest. With its twenty-nine hour days and fourteen month years, Harvest was always out of sync with Earth.

Rafe rubbed gritty eyes and wondered whether he'd ever catch up on his sleep. Too many reports to read, too many meetings, too little time. But Kama was here now. The thought of her sent a jolt of energy through him—along with a ripple of apprehension. What would Aaron think of her?

Aaron eased back in his chair, and a hint of pink suffused his skin. "How far have you gotten on the financials I sent?"

Rafe ran his hand through his hair and resisted the urge to squirm. He wanted to pull the little rubber ball from his pocket, roll it in his palms, and improve his focus. But Aaron might find the behavior bizarre.

Instead, he roved his eyes over the mahogany bookcase stuffed with leather-bound volumes, the elaborate mini-bar set to one side of the room, and the oil portrait of Aaron's second wife, hanging in a place of honor behind the desk.

"Far enough. I hope it isn't as bad as it looks at first glance."

"It is." Aaron frowned. "Maybe worse. I should have done something sooner. EcoMech is six months from going under. Less if the stock price continues to drop."

Rafe's stomach tightened, and fear walked on cold feet up his spine. Millions of small investors counted on EcoMech stock dividends to support themselves. They'd be devastated by the loss of their investment. And if the company tanked while he steered it, his reputation would go, too. It was his job to save EcoMech, and right now, he wasn't sure he could.

"It's the blackmailer's fault," the old man said at last. "If Leon hadn't been pressured to deliberately make bad business decisions, EcoMech wouldn't be in such a hole."

The list of things Leon had done at his unknown blackmailer's behest didn't begin to account for the many monumentally bad choices the deceased CEO had made. But Aaron loved Leon. Rafe smoothed his trousers and considered how different his life would be if he'd had Aaron for a father.

Aaron sipped his water. "I've drawn up a recovery plan. It's in your mail. You'll need to implement a lot of unpopular measures to get the company back on track. I'm sorry to make you the hatchet man, but it has to be done. As long as you and I stand together, we control enough shares to force the board to go along. But whenever possible, give in to the board's demands. That'll earn you some credit when you have to make the hard cuts.

"Take this business with the contractors' labor council. At the board meeting tomorrow morning, they'll ask you to fire the council members, and you'll agree. It's a simple request that costs you nothing, but it will get you off on the right foot."

Rafe blew out his cheeks. "I'm not so sure, sir. It seems to me that labor issues will escalate if we retaliate. We need to meet with the council and let them air their demands. If we can agree to some of their requests, we can improve labor relations."

"That might have been possible before that bunch of ruffian contractors disrupted Leon's funeral service, but not now. Our share price dropped two percent overnight because of the bad press from that incident." Aaron's knuckles rapped on the desktop. "They have to be punished for that kind of loss—or we'll be seen as weak and ineffective."

"My understanding is that none of the council members were at the demonstration, and that the contractors who were are already on their way back to Earth. We have no justification for letting the council go."

"They're the ringleaders. We need to make an example of them. I know you think you have the board eating out of your hand because of this deal you made with Oasis Corp to build jump gates. They don't see it that way. You were in the job five minutes when you agreed to it. You should have run it by us first. Don't get me wrong. The board's grateful you stepped up. Share prices jumped when I named you CEO. But you're the new guy. Listen to your elders."

Rafe's cheeks warmed, and he tightened his grip on his wine glass. Leon had warned him that public corporations were a whole different beast from his privately owned company, Security Partners, but he hadn't understood what his brother-in-law meant. He'd committed to twelve years of stewardship until Aaron's grandson, Gabe, would be old enough to take over. Twelve years under Aaron's thumb acquiescing to the board's demands stretched like a life sentence.

"We'll need to abandon Harvest for the time being," the chairman said. "If we can, we'll find someone to sublease until we're into a recovery phase, probably a couple of years from now."

The room twisted around Rafe. "Isn't there a clause in our lease with Earth Authority that requires us to remain on-planet?"

Aaron gave him a grim smile. "Legal tells me that if we sublease and keep a token contingent here, we can get around it. Your company has done a fair amount of business with EA through your contracts with Earth Force. I'll be counting on you to call in favors, get them to look the other way."

The old man shifted in his chair and dropped his eyes to the desk. "Your father is the best salesman I ever met. Without his ability to close deals with the food consortiums, EcoMech would never have become the largest agricultural company in the galaxy. But as you're aware, he doesn't have a head for business. I haven't shared my plans with him yet. None of the board members are aware of how bad things are. I'll bring them into the loop later, when we've negotiated debt refinancing with the banks."

"What about our deal with Oasis to develop the new jump gate system?"

"We can't afford it. We'll stall as long as we can on signing any agreement, and then we'll cancel negotiations. We can't let news of our financial situation slip out."

What would Kama say when she found out he'd strung her along, let her believe EcoMech would participate in the Sharma Network, all the while having no such intentions? She'd never forgive him. He regretted again taking the reins of the company. The regret must have shown in his face.

"I should have told you about the situation here when I offered you the job. You'll do fine once you get your feet on the ground. For the time being, let me worry about the blackmailer. You focus on saving the company."

"The blackmailer worked for years to force Leon into failure so he could fill the position. He's been thwarted because you appointed me instead, and now he's sabotaged my flyer. You should have extra security here at the house."

"You said there was no evidence—"

"—because it was destroyed in the explosion," Rafe said.

"I've known Lars Svenson and Bert Gerlach for years. Lev Koslov grew up here on Harvest with Leon. Yes, they're aggressive. That's what makes them excellent executives. Any of the three might be tempted to cross the line to become CEO, but they aren't cold-blooded killers." Aaron eyed Rafe. "Your flyer had a maintenance issue, that's all. You should take it up with the maintenance manager, fire the person charged with servicing the flyer. There's no excuse for sloppy work."

"Let me talk to Alana, get her to post someone nearby, just as a precaution."

Aaron waved a dismissive hand. "No, no, EcoMech security officers are the worst gossips on the planet. If word gets back to the markets that we're beefing up security, we'll see the share price plummet again."

"Let me make a call. Security Partners can supply you with discreet bodyguards."

Aaron studied his forefinger while he ran it along the edge of his desk. "First Security has done some work for me previously. I'll arrange something with them tomorrow."

Rafe resolved to have a private conversation with EcoMech's chief of security, Alana Dzandarova. After the disturbance at Leon's funeral, it shouldn't be difficult to convince her that Aaron needed protection. The difficult part would be keeping Aaron in the dark about the increased surveillance—and Alana in the dark about his hunt for the blackmailer.

The doorbell chimed, and Rafe sprang from his chair. Aaron rose and walked into the hallway that served as foyer. Rafe wanted to rush past, but he followed politely behind the chairman. With agonizing slowness, Aaron opened the front door.

Kama stood on the welcome mat. At five foot ten, she rivaled Rafe's own height and had the beauty of an Indian goddess despite wearing no makeup. Her black duffel hung from her shoulder. A faint whiff of smoke still clung to it.

A wave of uneasiness washed over Rafe. He'd expected her to play the part of a submissive contract teacher eager for a job at EcoMech. Instead she'd changed from her Oasis Corp coveralls into EcoMech's standard contractor coveralls, attire inappropriate for a job interview with a potential employer of Aaron's stature.

She brushed back a stray wisp of thick brown hair that had pulled loose from the ponytail at the base of neck. Her chocolate eyes found Rafe's, but her expression remained impassive. His worry amped up.

"Yes?" Aaron said, drawing her attention.

"I'm Kamala Bhatia." At his surprised look, she added, "The tutor you hired for your grandson?"

3

The house wasn't what Kama expected. As chairman at EcoMech and one of the wealthiest men in the galaxy, Aaron Goldman could afford an opulent mansion bustling with servants. He'd chosen instead to occupy a comfortable two-story home in an upper-class neighborhood of River City and opened the door to guests himself. She didn't see any security guards, but maybe they were stationed nearby, observing the house via video feed. *Sloppy.* Oasis Corp would never leave their chairman exposed like this.

McTavish stood behind Goldman, clad in a handsome charcoal suit, white silk shirt unbuttoned at the neck, and loosened tie. His hands were thrust into his trouser pockets. He looked more like a pouty fashion model at a photo shoot than a dedicated executive.

Goldman lifted an eyebrow and ran his gaze from her feet to her head, his disapproval plain. He stepped back and waved her in.

"A pleasure, Dr. Bhatia. You come highly recommended." The old man's tone belied his words.

She smiled and offered her hand, which he accepted, his grip firm and brief.

"You know Mr. McTavish."

"We've met," she said.

At the same time, McTavish blurted, "We're old friends."

Goldman frowned and looked from one to the other, while McTavish flushed and rocked on his heels. *Moorhk.* If he didn't get himself under control, he'd give away the game. Kama noted that she hadn't been invited farther than the entry hall. Maybe she should have used the servant's entrance around back.

"Tell me, Dr. Bhatia, what's your plan for my grandson's education?"

So much for the small talk. McTavish went rigid. What did he expect? For her to say she'd have Gabe hacking secure computers within a week? Regardless, she'd need to put the wily old chairman in his place. She heard the suspicion in his voice.

"I'll begin with testing. I'll evaluate his knowledge base: where he's strong, where he has gaps. Then I'll set up lesson plans designed to fill those gaps and extend his learning. Of course, I'll share the test results and lesson plans with you. Does Gabe have a preferred learning style? Visual, auditory, kinesthetic?"

The question stopped Goldman cold, as she'd expected. He'd had little time caring for his grandson since the death of the boy's parents, and he probably knew nothing about learning styles. She'd asked purely to throw him off balance.

"And of course, I'll need to see the results of his assessment and meet Gabe before I can fully commit to being his tutor," she pressed. "My services are in high demand, and I take only the brightest pupils. Is he here?"

The old man took a step back, and she smiled to herself. McTavish wiped the surprise from his face and moved aside to let them both pass. His footsteps fell in behind her, the heels of his dress shoes clicking against the tile floor.

Goldman stopped beside a staircase. "Gabe, could you please come down?"

An instant later, a beautiful blond boy of eleven clattered down the stairs. *He had to be listening near the top, or he couldn't have responded that fast.* He dressed in casual navy trousers and a white button-down shirt, a miniature version of a businessman after hours. It put Kama's teeth on edge.

When he saw her, Gabe's bright blue eyes rounded, and she knew in a nanosecond that he recognized her. Her welcoming smile froze on her face.

"Gabe, this is Dr. Bhatia," Goldman said. "She's here to help us figure out your education options."

She never should have agreed to McTavish's dumb idea. *Moorhk!* What was she thinking? Gabe would tell his grandfather that when he'd seen her at the mining station in the asteroid belt, she'd been an Oasis computer technician, not a contract teacher. Goldman would have her arrested.

"Do you subscribe to the idea that a person's environment speaks volumes about who they are?" McTavish said, filling the sudden silence.

"I'm sure you'd find it enlightening to see Gabe's room. Gabe, take Kama up and show her around, won't you?"

He gave the boy a conspiratorial wink.

"Sure!" Gabe replied.

She brushed past Goldman and followed the boy up the hardwood stairs, her heart beating fast. He led her down a white-carpeted hallway to an open door at the far end, confirming for her that he'd been listening at the top of the stairs, not waiting in his room.

Gabe's room was a generously proportioned five by seven meters, furnished with an antique Queen Anne bedstead, matching dresser, and work station table. A Persian carpet covered much of the floor. White sheers filtered the intense Harvest sunlight coming through the two windows that overlooked the street beyond. Old landscapes and still-life oil paintings hung on the white plaster walls. It was a staid, elegant room in conflict with its youthful occupant.

"What are you doing here?" Gabe's eyes were alight, and his voice was a whisper.

"I'm your new tutor."

"You're one of Uncle Rafe's secret agents, aren't you? It's okay. I know all about you. Greg told me."

Kama stifled rising ire. "He did, did he? Then you know that I'm undercover here, and you mustn't tell anyone who I am, including your grandfather."

"This is about my father, isn't it? He did something bad, and now Uncle Rafe's trying to find out about it." The boy frowned and dropped his eyes to his shoes.

Leon had been an arrogant jerk, but he'd loved his son. The affection went both ways. She pulled him to the bed and sat down beside him.

"How did you know about your Uncle Rafe's investigation?"

The boy's pale skin shaded to brilliant red. "Sometimes I overhear things, like when Grandpa talks to people in his study and leaves the door open. The sound carries up the stairs."

She considered scolding the boy for his snooping, but that seemed like hypocrisy coming from her. Besides, he hadn't done any harm, and she needed him to keep up the tutor ruse.

"It's not your father we're investigating. Someone knew a secret about him and used that secret to make your father do things he shouldn't have. We're trying to find out the man's identity."

Gabe brightened. "Can I help?"

"This isn't a game. People died at the mining station."

His sweet face turned to granite, and his eyes looked into the distance. Kama cursed her thoughtlessness. He didn't need to be reminded of his part in the events at the station. He'd been a brave kid then, and maybe he'd be safer inside their operation than outside now that he knew about it.

"All right. You can help. But you have to do exactly what you're told, and you can't tell anyone, not even Greg. Do you swear?"

"I swear!" He bounced to his feet. "What should I do first?"

Having ears in the house might prove useful, and if he did some harmless eavesdropping, he'd feel like he contributed without being in any real danger.

"You'll be our inside man. Listen to conversations your grandfather has and report back."

The boy's brow drew down. "I heard you tell Grandpa that you'd stay only if I did well on my tests. What if I fail?"

Kama grinned. "Don't worry, you won't."

4

"With four PhDs, I thought she'd be older." Aaron frowned at his desk blotter.

Rafe nearly spewed his mouthful of wine. *Four PhDs?* What the hell had Kama put on her resume? Granted, she was a genius, but four seemed impossible at her age.

And what were she and Gabe talking about upstairs? He'd thought Gabe wouldn't remember her. The boy had seen her only once, and he'd been in shock then. He'd miscalculated. He hoped she could fix it. He needed her working undercover to help him find Leon's blackmailer.

"I assure you, she's the very best at what she does." He'd never encountered a better computer hacker and corporate spy—or even one who came close—during his nine years in the security business.

"She's dressed like a common contractor."

Rafe spread his hands. "We do specify what contract staff wear."

"Not household staff. Not in *my* household. I should get someone else."

He could only imagine Kama's response at being referred to as 'household staff.' More likely, the old man resented the complete lack of deference in her tone and body language. Kama bowed to no one.

"Gabe responded well to her. Maybe you should give her a chance before you decide?"

"There is that."

Rafe would have a private conversation with Kama about her attitude toward Aaron. It wasn't a discussion he looked forward to. Aaron represented everything Kama hated most about capitalism and corporations. Was she a good enough actress to be deferential? He couldn't picture it.

Goldman regarded him with narrowed eyes. "Gabe needs a father figure in his life—a big brother he can relate to. I'd like you to be that man."

Rafe squirmed. "He has you."

"I'm an old man. He needs someone of your generation, someone who can play soccer with him, listen to his girl troubles. Someone who'll raise him if anything happens to me. You don't have to decide now. Just think about it."

Footsteps echoed in the hallway, and Gabe led Kama into the study, a huge smile splitting his face. Such a radiant boy. He made Rafe's heart ache for his own lost children. Did Kama want a family? One more thing he didn't know about her.

"Well?" Goldman rose from his desk.

Kama patted Gabe's shoulder. "He's very bright. I'll begin testing in the morning if that schedule works for you."

The old man studied the boy, who gazed back at him with hope and longing.

"Be here at eight sharp. Human Resources has arranged quarters for you at the contractor housing compound. The information should be in your mail. Now if you'll excuse me, I have business to take care of. Gabe will show you out."

Rafe jumped up. "My car's outside. Can I give you a lift?"

After a moment's hesitation, she gave a curt nod. The boy beamed up at Kama and led her away. He followed.

"Rafe," Goldman called.

He stopped at the study door and faced the chairman, new energy coursing through him.

"As you know, Leon was something of a womanizer. The press ate it up. EcoMech can't afford any scandals, and you have a certain reputation of your own with the ladies. Naturally I don't expect you to be celibate. But with all this trouble between management and the sub-contractors, it wouldn't do if word got out that you were..." Goldman nodded toward the hallway. "Try to limit your recreation to the full-time staff."

☠   ☠   ☠

Rafe clenched the steering wheel, his back stiff, his mind churning. *Of all the—*

First Aaron suckered him into being the fall guy who would do the onerous tasks necessary to save EcoMech. Then he'd been told to lie to Kama and Oasis. Now the chairman wanted to control his private life. He should tell Aaron to take his job and go to hell.

"Maybe you want to spit it out." Kama lifted an eyebrow. "Before you choke on it?"

"It's nothing." But it wasn't. He couldn't betray Kama's trust and still expect her to marry him, not that she'd agreed yet. He couldn't face twelve years under Aaron's control without her. He checked the navigation com for directions to the contractors' housing compound. After fourteen years away, so much had changed in River City that he didn't recognize the place.

"How'd it go with Gabe?"

"What exactly did you tell Greg about me?"

He glanced over at her before making a left onto a wide boulevard lined with upscale houses sporting rolling lawns of Harvest-adapted bluish green grass and manicured hedges. He dialed up the tint on the car's windows, blocking the glare from the over-bright sun and inhaled the fragrance of her lavender-scented shampoo.

"Nothing. Why?"

"Rumor has it I'm an undercover operative for Security Partners."

"Ah." He sighed. Trust his teenage nephew to fill Gabe's head with spy stories. "I'll have a word with Greg."

They drove on, the quiet hum of the electric engine filling the silence. They'd had a business-like exchange of messages about the blackmail case the past few days since he'd left the mining station, and little else. He wanted to know everything about her, but he didn't know where to start. He didn't know how to tell her about Aaron's plans.

"Your resume was a tad over the top, wasn't it? You're what, twenty-four?"

"Twenty-five." A little crease formed between her brows.

"*Four* PhDs by twenty-five? You didn't need to exaggerate. My recommendation was enough to get you the job."

"Seventeen." She turned her attention to the passing scenery.

"Excuse me?"

"I was seventeen when I finished the fourth PhD." She shifted her duffel between her feet. "What did Goldman have to say?"

"He doesn't like how you dress," Rafe said, reeling from his faux pas over her credentials. No one earned four PhDs that quickly, even a genius. He glanced at her and swore smoke rose above her head.

"EcoMech mandates how contractors dress. If he doesn't like me in prison attire, then he should get his company to change their barbaric rules. *You* should change the rules."

Did she expect him to change EcoMech's dress code? He thought about the battles ahead with EcoMech's board over the company's dire financial straits and laughed. "Sure, why not?"

"You're laughing at me."

"At *me*, not you. At this whole crazy, impossible mess."

He wouldn't ask her be more deferential toward the elder CEO. She'd never pull it off. He'd just hope they found Leon's blackmailer before Aaron fired her.

"Aaron plans to set traps for our key suspects."

"What? How?"

"He's going to leak bogus stories to them, a different story to each one, the kind a blackmailer might try to leverage. Then he'll wait to see which story comes back to him with a request for a payoff."

"You told him that's insane, right?"

He snorted. "He's my boss now. You don't tell your boss his idea is crazy."

"Crazy and dangerous." She chewed her lip, sunk in thought. "I can't believe his security is so lax. Why doesn't he have better protection?"

"He won't allow it because he thinks he's safe here—and he thinks that if word gets out that he's increasing security, it will be a sign that management can't maintain control."

"Varun doesn't like being escorted by an entourage of agents, either, but Samir doesn't let that stop him from doing the job properly."

"He's hiring private agents. Or at least he assured me he would."

Mention of her step-father, Varun Sharma, Oasis' chairman, brought his uneasiness swimming to the surface—as did her boss's name, the shady and dangerous Samir Ganguly. He thought about the commitments he'd made to help Chairman Sharma build a new transportation network. He had to tell Kama that EcoMech couldn't afford to support that dream anymore, but he didn't know how.

"I'll speak to EcoMech security, get them to keep an eye on Aaron, and hope he doesn't notice."

"What will you tell them?" she asked.

"I'll have to bring Alana Dzandarova in. She needs to understand the danger."

From the corner of his eye, he caught the stiffening of her posture.

"The more people who know, the more chance that word gets back to the suspects. We can handle this without her involvement. I'll watch Aaron," she said.

Worry nibbled at his conscience. Putting Kama in the crosshairs as a bodyguard for Aaron didn't seem like a good tradeoff, but it would only be temporarily. She was right. If he told Alana about Leon's blackmail, the security chief would want to launch her own investigation. If he didn't tell her, she'd be unlikely to go against Aaron's wishes regarding protection.

They drove in silence for a minute. He had to tell her about Aaron's decision to abandon Harvest.

"Join me for dinner?"

She threw up her hands. "I'm undercover, remember? I'm not supposed to *know* you, never mind have dinner with you. I shouldn't have accepted this ride—or the one this morning. And if you don't stop grinning like the village idiot when I walk in the room, the whole galaxy will know we're working together."

He thought about Aaron's warning, and his anger returned. He wanted to take Kama to River City's best restaurant and flaunt their relationship in front of everyone, contractor prison garb and all. It felt too much like the oppressive days of his youth when Cullen McTavish, Aaron Goldman, and George Tanaka, the three founders of EcoMech, arranged the marriages of their children and set them all on a path to destruction.

5

McTavish had gone silent, and Kama wondered why. He had that stormy look again. Old pain echoed in his eyes. Returning to Harvest after fourteen years must be tearing him apart.

Did the ghosts of his dead wife and children haunt his dreams? He'd been just sixteen when he'd fled their slaughter. Too young to be married with three kids on the way. Much too young to be a widower.

But that's how it was after the ice flu epidemic, when Earth Authority slapped the corporate colonies with population quotas they were forced to meet or give up their leases. Children birthing children, all so greedy corporations could escape bringing disabled workers from Earth.

Kama chewed her lip and watched suburban River City slide past the window. Ahead, the middle-class residential neighborhood's cookie-cutter houses squatted in tiny plots of dead grass like tombstones in a giants' graveyard. They gave way to a complex of four massive, ugly buildings.

The off-white concrete structures rose thirteen stories into the deep blue Harvest sky, their sides punctuated by hundreds of narrow, tinted windows. Each building ran fifteen meters wide and nearly two hundred meters long. Packed red dirt separated them, not a sprout of vegetation in sight. A two-meter chain link fence topped by razor wire surrounded the complex. All it lacked were manned guard towers to complete its resemblance to a prison.

McTavish rolled up to the double gates blocking the road, and a uniformed security guard stepped out of the pillbox guard house to greet them. The guard, a slender man not much older than McTavish, bent down by the window. He eyed them both.

"No vehicles allowed in the compound."

"I'll get out here." Kama opened the car door, and blistering heat washed over her. She hated Harvest already, and she'd been here only a few hours. Good thing she didn't plan to stay.

"I'll walk you in." McTavish popped his own door. He peeled off his jacket and tossed it inside. The tie followed. Then he unbuttoned his cuffs and folded up his sleeves, all the while taking in the complex. He slammed his door.

"You can't leave your vehicle here," the guard said. "You're blocking the gates."

McTavish grinned, an evil glint in his eyes. "Doesn't matter if I block the gates. No vehicles allowed inside, right?" With that, he strolled toward a small gate next to the guard house.

What's up with McTavish? He always played the diplomat, turned on the charm, and got his way. The last thing she wanted was to attract attention, but he seemed determined to make a scene. She trailed behind the guard, who hurried to get in front of the CEO. A big bruiser whose gut hung over his uniform belt stepped out of the guard house to block the gate.

"Let's see some ID."

"Kamala Bhatia." She raised her right hand and pulled back her sleeve to reveal an ID bracelet locked on her wrist. McTavish frowned at the bracelet, and then returned his attention to the complex, the frown deepening. The guard waved his nanocom over the bracelet, read the screen, and nodded.

"Where's yours, buddy?"

"Must have left it in the office," McTavish said, tone surly, weight shifting to a loose fighting stance.

Kama stepped toward the gate. "He's Rafael McTavish, your new CEO. It's hot out here. You want to let me through?"

The big man's eyes opened wide. He tapped at his nanocom, and she made out an image on the tiny screen, which he checked against McTavish.

"Sorry sir, I didn't recognize you." He opened the gate to let her pass but pulled it closed behind her.

"I can't let you inside, sir." The guard ducked his head. "Not without a security detail."

McTavish stared, eyebrows raised. "Why?"

"We have fifteen thousand contractors in residence, two-thirds of them inside right now." The guard gestured toward the buildings. "If something starts, we can't protect you with two stunners. I'll have Chief Dzandarova send an escort squad, but it'll take some time. You can wait in the guard house where it's cool."

"Fifteen thousand live in there?" McTavish wheeled toward the buildings. His hand ran through his hair. Then he spun back, and drew himself up. "I'll go where I damn well please. Now stand aside. And don't even think about calling Dzandarova."

Kama sucked in a breath. The guard melted away under his new CEO's ferocious glare, and McTavish stomped through the gate, not bothering to close it behind him. He trudged toward the buildings, head down, shoulders tense. She fell in beside him. Worry gnawed at her stomach. Had the power of leading one of the galaxy's largest corporations gone to his head already?

He glanced back at the guards.

"Sorry." He jammed his hands in his pockets. "I don't know what got into me. He's just a guy trying to do his job."

"I'm in Building C." She looked up at the three-meter high black letters painted on the windowless end walls and veered right.

Red dust coated their shoes and little clouds of it disturbed by their footsteps rose in the still, hot air. The sun burned against her head and back. She marveled that anyone would live in this when they could opt for a nice climate-controlled orbital station or underground facility. And yet Earth Authority sold planet leases at premium prices while potential colonists cheated, bribed, and even murdered their way onto waiting lists to emigrate.

McTavish pulled open a cracked glass door to Building C, and they walked into a stuffy, low-ceilinged lobby dotted with faded plastic couches and chairs. Linoleum covered the floor, its pattern worn through and unrecognizable. Most of the overhead lights were out, leaving the place dim and hot. Sweat and dust tainted the air. Half a dozen men and women dressed in green coveralls lounged around the room, the murmur of their voices echoing off the bare concrete walls. They glanced at McTavish, their expressions ranging from curious to openly hostile.

Kama approached an unmanned desk on the far side of the lobby. A ragged, grimy sign taped to the desktop proclaimed that someone would return at 10 a.m. The sign looked like it had been there for decades.

"I can find my way from here." She wanted him to go, before word got out that she was a corporate collaborator. "You should get some rest."

McTavish's brow furrowed and his eyes swept the lobby. "I'd like to see the place."

With that, he strode down the hallway, headed toward the sound of children's voices raised in song. Kama trailed behind, brushing back wisps of hair that stuck to her sweaty face.

They passed doors marked 'Maintenance' and 'Laundry' before coming to a dining hall that occupied the full width of the building and ran thirty meters down its length. Light filtered through narrow windows at each side.

At the dining tables, children sat in groups sorted by age from toddler to teen, fifteen or so per group. Each group had an adult in attendance. The singing came from toddlers practicing their ABCs. From the youngest to the oldest, everyone wore green coveralls.

"Who're these kids?" McTavish asked.

"They're the children of contract employees."

"Why aren't they in school? Or at a daycare facility?"

"Contractor kids aren't allowed in EcoMech schools. Schools are considered a benefit if they're provided by a corporation, and contractors can receive benefits only from their contract agency, not the agency's client. It's all in the info packet EcoMech gives contractors. Maybe you should read it."

"And the ID bracelet you're wearing?"

"Anyone who applies for a contract position or is hired as a contractor is required to wear one. They provide access to buildings. They also make it possible for security to track every move a contractor makes." She headed back the way they'd come.

He trailed behind her. "That's an invasion of privacy. They shouldn't have to wear them off-duty."

"Corporations can require anyone on corporate property to carry corporate ID, and all of Harvest is considered corporate property. There's a curfew, too. All contractors who don't have assigned duties on campus between 20:00 and 6:00 are confined to this compound. The full-time employees are treated like humans. Contractors are little more than low-cost chain-gang labor."

Kama punched the button between two lift doors. They waited in silence but saw no lights, heard no whirring of equipment. She sighed and crossed the hall to a door marked 'Stairs.' In the heat and the heavier than Earth-normal gravity, it was a tiring climb to the sixth floor.

The smell of too many sweating bodies washed over her when she reached her level. She found 617 near the end of a long, central hallway. The door stood open, as did many they'd passed. She glanced inside.

The room was four meters deep and three and a half wide, with one narrow window centered in the outside wall. Bunk beds stood against the side walls. The top bunk of one was occupied by a woman sleeping in a tank top and shorts. A small blonde woman sat on the bottom bunk reading something on her nanocom. She nodded a silent greeting, putting a forefinger to her lips and pointing up at the sleeper.

A pink comforter with giant red poppies covered the other bottom bunk. The remaining top bunk supported a thin, bare mattress. A portable clothes rack and temporary shelving filled the wall spaces on each side of the door.

Kama made to step in, but McTavish grabbed her arm and drew her back.

"You can't stay here," he hissed in her ear, revulsion tainting his voice.

She gave him a wry smile. "You're the CEO. If you don't like the conditions, *change them.*"

And if he didn't, she'd take her own steps.

6

Aaron Goldman sat at the head of the conference table in the cool, spacious boardroom, his face calm and confident. Morning sunshine filtered through the expanse of tinted glass behind him, forming a halo around his white hair and spilling onto the table to reveal the golden stripes of the wood grain. Beyond the windows, stunted trees dotted the open spaces between the corporate campus buildings, shiny glass and concrete pillars rising twelve stories into the cloudless sky.

On Aaron's right, Rafe's father leaned forward and glared down the table to the opposite end where his son sat. His fierce blue eyes drilled into Rafe. Angry pink tinged his tanned cheeks and clashed with his flame-red hair. His strong jaw flexed. On each side of the table, the other members of the EcoMech board watched the duel and took their measure of their new CEO.

A fire bomb had exploded in Rafe's stomach the moment he entered the room. He kept his hands flat on the table to minimize their shaking. He'd spent the night tossing in his bed and running scenarios about his first encounter with his father after fourteen years. In the end, he took the coward's way out and arrived at the last minute, avoiding any chance for a personal conversation.

He didn't expect to be welcomed with open arms, although some small part of him wished it might happen. Rafe had to work with these men, had to follow Aaron's plan to save EcoMech. And perhaps if he did, his father would see that he'd changed. He was no longer a destructive, hyperactive kid. He'd grown into a man his father could be proud of.

The meeting had rocketed downhill from the start. As Aaron predicted, the board grumbled about the Oasis jump gate venture, not because it didn't have merit, but because he hadn't informed them before committing EcoMech.

From there, they complained about EcoMech's stock price, although Rafe's acceptance of the CEO post had lifted it to a high it hadn't seen in a year. They whined about quality issues with the new line of harvesters shipped last month, and excoriated him over cost overruns for the building of a billion-credit orbital manufacturing station Rafe was convinced EcoMech didn't need.

No one—including Aaron—addressed the corporation's impending bankruptcy. Rafe alternated between suppressing hysterical laughter at their folly and fighting off a growing sense of doom.

His father leaned forward. "What do you intend to do about these contractor riots?"

"I wasn't aware we'd experienced riots." Rafe immediately wished he hadn't said it. And what did they matter anyway? In a month or two, EcoMech would fire all the contractors as part of the move back to Earth.

"Don't play semantic games with me." His father's voice, low and threatening, shot down the table. "Contractors breached security at Leon's funeral for God's sake. The leaders should be sacked, and Alana, too, if she can't do her job better."

Breathe, think, speak. Address the issue, not the man. "Security here on Harvest has been systematically gutted to pay for increased security at EcoMech's headquarters in Mumbai, where we're at risk from eco-terrorists unhappy with our policies as well as organized contractor protests.

"To compensate for Harvest's decreased security force, we instituted draconian constraints on the contract staff. The consequences have come home to roost. Instead of having fewer incidents, we've had more, and we'll see them increase as long as we continue to treat our contractors like prison labor. None of that is Alana's fault. She's doing the best job she can with the resources she has."

"You've been in the job six days and already you know everything?" His father turned to Aaron. "I told you he was a mistake. We should have selected a new CEO from inside the company, someone who understands EcoMech's priorities."

Aaron leaned back in his chair. "He's something of an expert on security, Cullen. Maybe we should hear him out. What do you suggest, Rafe?"

He stifled the urge to tell them they were little better than slave traders the way they abused their workers. "Let the contractors air their concerns. Improve conditions for them in ways that don't cost us anything but make them feel they have dignity and a voice."

"You're rewarding them for their bad behavior," his father said. "That's unacceptable."

Rafe moved his hands to his lap and balled them into fists. He wondered if his father had ever visited the contractor housing. His skin crawled when he thought of Kama living there.

Mild disappoint settled on Aaron's expression as he corrected what he undoubtedly saw as Rafe's blunder. "First we make it clear their previous behavior was unacceptable. We let the council members go, and then Rafe can implement his ideas for improvements. If they don't cost anything, what's the harm in trying them?"

His cheeks burned. He felt like a little kid who'd failed a test and now faced his parents' ire. He needed to suck it up. He'd promised Aaron he'd see the job through, and that meant following the chairman's orders. He didn't have to like them, he just had to follow them like an obedient soldier.

"A good compromise, sir." Rafe choked on the bitter words.

The chairman checked the time on his nanocom. "That's it for today."

Like the rubber-stamp automatons they were, the other men around the table took their cue and rose. Rafe joined them, one more drone in Aaron's army of robots. He bolted out the door ahead of them all, before Aaron or his father could stop him. As he strode away, he planned his own act of sedition.

7

"Thumbprint here." The middle-aged woman flopped a filmie on the counter.

Kama applied her thumb and scooped up the access chip next to it. She'd wanted one of the sleek two-seater car/plane flyer hybrids, with their four high-powered swiveling fans mounted on stubby wings at each corner of the car-like body. But Goldman had reserved a four-passenger hulk with dinky fans that probably wouldn't do more than ten clicks an hour on the top end.

"You ever operated one of these?" The woman raised a thinly plucked brow and stared at Kama's coveralls. "I ask because contractors generally aren't allowed to use flyers. Full-timers only. Especially on a day like today."

"I can fly anything." If someone as dense as the flyer rental shop clerk could handle one, it couldn't be too hard.

She hadn't seen anything about a flyer restriction in the contractor manual. Maybe someone forgot to update it. The rules changed weekly, getting more repressive with each modification. McTavish needed to fix that.

Before she'd come here, she'd thought EcoMech wasn't a bad place to work. Now she saw Harvest as little more than a slave-labor camp. Maybe Oasis shouldn't have partnered with EcoMech on the Sharma Network project after all. She'd bet humanity's future on McTavish. She'd better be right about him.

McTavish needed to step up. He had to make EcoMech a shining example of how corporations should treat their employees. In the current competitive hiring market, it would help EcoMech attract the best people. Dedicated employees meant EcoMech could build the Sharma Network faster.

"I should verify your authorization."

Kama gave the clerk a phony smile. "Be my guest. I'm sure Chairman Goldman will take your call."

The woman's eyes widened. She looked again at the rental form. "I didn't realize this was for Mr. Goldman."

"What's so special about today?"

She'd spent the morning testing her new pupil. Then Goldman came back to the house and suggested she and Gabe go to the countryside tonight to enjoy a meteor shower. She thought watching streaks of light in the sky was a complete waste of time, and driving into the country even more so. If this were to be a teachable moment, they should have watched the telemetry readouts from the comfort of a climate-controlled monitoring station and studied the formulas used to predict meteor trajectories.

But when Goldman ordered a flyer instead of a car, the trip gained appeal. If only the rental company delivered instead of making her take a stuffy, crowded bus to retrieve it.

"They fired that contractors' council this morning. Shipped 'em out an hour ago. Harvest is on high alert. You'll be lucky if they let you take the flyer across the city, since you're one of them. It has built-in crash prevention systems, in case you try something stupid."

Kama blinked. *Fired the council?* She'd listened to the contractors talking last night. The council had nothing to do with the flap at Leon's funeral. They'd advised against the demonstration. But McTavish fired them anyway?

The contractors planned to hold a ten-minute candlelight vigil on campus if their council was let go. But if they did, EcoMech would use the ID bracelets to target those involved and fire them, too.

Someone had to even the odds. Someone had to show EcoMech management that they couldn't abuse their contract workers. If McTavish wouldn't do it, she'd take matters into her own hands.

8

"This is a non-disclosure agreement. By signing it, you agree that you won't reveal the terms of your dismissal to anyone. It also binds EcoMech from discussing your dismissal. Should the terms become public, you'll forfeit your severance pay and face jail time for revealing sensitive corporate information."

Rafe scanned the faces of the eight members of the contractors' council who gathered in the conference room. One by one, they placed their thumbprints in the box at the bottom of the page, resignation in their expressions.

He passed packets of filmies around the table. "These contain the details of your severance. You'll receive two months' pay for early contract termination. You'll each find three job offers from Earth-based employers for positions that start immediately. Should none of those appeal, you'll also find a personal letter of recommendation from me, which you can share with any prospective employers you apply to. My contact information is included in case they want to verify the authenticity."

Resignation turned to disbelief as the council members checked with one another.

Rafe nodded to reassure them. "Just remember that you're bound to secrecy."

9

Kama leaned against the fiberglass body of the flyer and pointed into the night sky. "There goes another one."

"Wow!" Gabe said. "They're beautiful. This is the best meteor shower ever."

"You've watched showers before?" Goldman hadn't mentioned that when he'd pushed her to take Gabe on a field trip. Maybe he didn't know.

"Every year. Dad and I would spend all night..." His voice trailed away.

Kama's heart ached. She'd lost her own father when she was a little younger than Gabe, dead from the complications of ice flu, complications that could have been cured if he'd used his money to save himself instead of buying passage to Oasis for her and her mother so they could escape the pandemic. Fifteen years later, she still missed him.

She stifled a yawn. "What's your grandfather been up to today?"

"Making calls with the door closed. Mr. McTavish came by right after you left to get the flyer. It took you a long time."

Kama ignored his remark. After she'd left the rental shop, she'd parked a block away and hacked the EcoMech network. She'd drilled her way through to the ID tracking system and planted a package, set to activate shortly before the vigil began.

"What did your uncle want?"

"Not Uncle Rafe, his dad. He and Grandpa went in the study and closed the door. I heard shouting, and then someone pounding. A few minutes later, the door opened, and Mr. McTavish came out. Before he left, he yelled, 'You'll regret this, Aaron.' Then Grandpa closed the door and made calls."

"You didn't hear any of those?"

"No. I think he arranged for someone to come over tonight."

An uneasy feeling fluttered in the pit of her stomach. "What makes you say that?"

"He asked Chona to fill the ice in the mini-bar before she left for the day. He does that when he's expecting company."

Kama had heard the request, too, and thought nothing of it. She hadn't put it together with visitors. Goldman's innocent suggestion that she take Gabe to the country suddenly seemed less innocent. The old fox had taken precautions to get Gabe out of the house. Was he baiting his trap tonight?

"Time to go," Kama said.

She made sure Gabe buckled up, and then she revved the flyer's fans, sending the craft surging upward until she swiveled them back and raced toward the glow of River City.

☠ ☠ ☠

As they came in over the bluffs to the north, smoke and flames leaped into the sky from a location near the river that bisected the city. Her breath caught in her throat. The sprawling corporate campus rested on the north river bank, and McTavish lodged in the penthouse rooms of a posh hotel a few blocks south on the opposite bank. From this distance, she couldn't tell what burned. Downtown stood in darkness. She tapped her nanocom and listened to the news, hands stiff on the controls.

The reporter told of widespread rioting driven by a terrorist who'd broadcast a message telling the contractors they could take to the streets with impunity because the ID tracking system and all security cameras had been disabled. What started as a candlelight vigil by a few hundred protesters on the corporate campus had quickly grown into a mob that smashed windows and set fire to two campus buildings. Then they'd spilled into the city streets, setting shops and a hotel ablaze while the fire brigade battled to get through the rioters.

Kama programmed the Goldman house coordinates and set the flyer to autopilot. She grabbed silky black VR gloves from her duffel and unfolded a square of metallic cloth on her lap. She tapped her nanocom into programming mode, jammed the gloves on, and began rapid hand movements. Code spewed down the cloth. Gabe watched, wide-eyed.

"What are you doing? I've never seen anything like that before."

"Trying to fix things." No time for elegant hacks. She used McTavish's login, pilfered from him by dropping code onto his Security Partners' account after she'd stolen his credentials at the mining station.

Something must have gone wrong with her package. It was timed to last thirty minutes, in a window that bracketed the planned demonstration. It should have shut down the ID system and the campus cameras, no more. She hadn't programmed any power failures, nor had she made any announcements encouraging rebellion or promising immunity. What the hell was going on?

She found no trace of her incursion on the system. Her clean-up bot had done its job and removed the evidence. But the security systems remained inactive. They should have rebooted an hour ago. Her commands to restart were ignored. She delved deeper into the system and found the culprit: a tiny piece of code spinning out unsolvable equations that gobbled all the processor threads. Whoever planted it knew what they were doing—they'd hit both the primary and backup systems. She isolated the section, deleted it, and rebooted.

As she looked toward downtown, lights flashed, defining the streets and businesses. She turned her attention to the power control network, although she was probably too late. She started a system dump, sending the files to a folder on McTavish's corporate account and loading another clean-up bot to erase her tracks. Moments later, the flyer settled on the street in front of the Goldman house, and she stashed her equipment.

Lights shone from the other houses along the block. Nothing moved on the empty street. The upstairs of Goldman's house remained dark. Dim illumination came through the drapes covering the study window, but no glowing porch light welcomed them.

Rising fear kicked her in the stomach. She'd assured McTavish that she would watch over Goldman. But the crafty old chairman had gotten her out of the way all too easily. She'd been a fool.

"Wait here." Kama got out of the flyer. Halfway across the lawn, she could see the front door ajar. Where was security? She retreated to the flyer and punched McTavish's connection into her nanocom.

While she waited for him to respond, she grabbed three high-end hacking devices from her duffel, equipment disguised as innocent computer tools. With the press of a few buttons and some twists and taps, she broke them down into component parts, which she reassembled into a neat little stunner. Gabe stared.

"Kama?" McTavish said at last, the shouts of the rioters and the roar of a fire in the background. "Where are you?"

"Goldman's. We just got back. There's something wrong here. I'm going in."

"Wait where you are. I'll have security there in ten."

"I'm leaving Gabe locked in the flyer." She cut the connection.

Gabe unbuckled his seat belt. "Shouldn't I go in with you? What if Grandpa needs help?"

"Lock the doors and don't open them for anyone except me or your

Uncle Rafe."

She sprinted across the lawn and flattened herself to the wall by the door. The stunner slipped in her sweaty hand. She gritted her teeth and gave the door a push. It swung back unobstructed, squeaking on its hinges. She dropped into a crouch in the doorway.

The dark hall stretched toward the back of the house. A square of faint light from the partially opened study door shone on the floor. An unreadable scrawl defaced the wall opposite. She listened, but all she heard were the rustling of shrubs by the door and the wail of distant sirens.

She stepped inside. Nothing moved. She edged forward until she reached the study doors. From here, she could read the writing spray-painted on the wall. 'Contractors revolt' it said, only the 'l' wasn't complete, and the 't' was missing. Her stomach rolled. *My fault.* Her fingers touched the incomplete letter and came away wet.

She pushed open the study door and stepped in, stunner sweeping the space. A knocked-over lamp cast grotesque shadows around the room. Goldman slumped across the desk, eyes still and dead. The water decanter lay on its side, spilling its contents over the blotter. More writing defaced the wall. A quick glance told her the filmie under Goldman's hand contained a list of contractor demands required before he'd be released. So, it was a kidnap gone horribly wrong.

A squeak sounded from the hallway. She bolted for the door and peeked out, wishing she'd brought her work light. She tiptoed toward the darkness at the back of the house, holding her breath.

At the base of the staircase, she glanced up into pitch black. Her pulse pounded in her ears. The kitchen door stood closed three steps ahead. Inside the kitchen, a door led out to the side drive. To the right of the staircase, another doorway opened into a dining room. From there, French doors offered escape into the backyard. Which way first?

Down the hall, the front door creaked. She whirled around, pointing her stunner. Light flashed behind her, and searing pain ripped along her muscles. The floor jumped up to meet her, its brutal slap adding to her agony. Then everything went dark.

10

"I have questions, Mr. McTavish. I expect answers."

Alana Dzandarova turned dark eyes on Rafe where he fidgeted in the back seat of the security flyer. "Let's start with why this contractor called you instead of us."

The security chief was a short, squarely built woman, all steely gaze and calm menace. She had a reputation for incorruptibility, something of a rarity in the world of corporate power. It didn't make her any friends.

But she didn't report solely to EcoMech's chain of command. She also represented Earth Authority law enforcement on Harvest. Right now, she watched Rafe with an expression he imagined she reserved for contract workers caught peddling drugs.

"She's probably aware of the impact more negative news would have on EcoMech and wanted me prepared to counter it."

Alana's eyebrows lifted. "A contractor concerned about EcoMech's share price?"

He flinched. How much more difficult would his job be in the aftermath of the riots? That's what he'd thought about while he watched the chaos from his penthouse balcony. He'd come on board to maintain status quo at EcoMech for twelve to fifteen years until Gabe took over. He hadn't signed up for the negativity—the animosity—that guiding the failing company as Aaron's puppet promised. No one liked the hatchet man.

Now his worry for Kama and Gabe consumed him. Neither of them answered their nanocoms. He fished his ball from his pocket and rolled it between his palms.

"What's your relationship with her?"

She'd already decided they must be sleeping together. After all, as Aaron said, he had a reputation. No point telling her they hadn't even kissed.

He stared down at the blocks of suburban homes that rolled by under the flyer and squeezed the ball in his fist. Maybe he should tell her the truth, the whole story of Leon's blackmail. He should have requested extra security for Aaron, especially after hearing Aaron's daffy plan.

"I recommended her to Aaron."

The pitch of the fans changed, and they sank to the street in front of the Goldman house. Rafe leaped from the security vehicle and ran to the rental flyer. Kama's duffel lay on the driver's seat, disassembled electronic equipment strewn across it. So she was armed at least.

He didn't see Gabe. Where was the boy? He charged for the house.

Alana's armor-clad security forces stood at the open door, their rifles pointed into the dark hall, night-vision goggles active. He tried to muscle his way past, but Alana snagged his arm and dragged him back. He checked his impulse to deck the security chief and waited, impatient, on the porch, aware of the dim outline of a body sprawled on the floor by the staircase.

"We need a med evac," a tense voice said over Alana's nanocom. She acknowledged the officer and relayed the request to the hospital.

Another flyer came down behind them, and security officers ran down the sides of the house toward the back yard. Minutes ticked by before a guard emerged and declared the house clear.

Lights came on inside, and Rafe stepped through the door, his heart in his throat. Kama lay on the tile at the other end of the hall. A guard bagged a stunner next to her hand.

He trotted down the hall and knelt beside her. His fingers found a strong pulse in her neck. *Stunned.* Only then did he take in the surroundings. Two ambulance attendants maneuvered a gurney through the study doors. He hurried to it.

Inside, an EMT read a med bracelet strapped to Aaron's wrist, shook his head at Alana, and cleared the way for the attendants. Rafe's eyes swept the room, the devastation, the spray-painted slogans.

He didn't see Gabe.

He pushed through the clog of people in the hall and knelt again over Kama. She groaned and rolled onto her side, her eyes fluttering open. He placed a hand on her shoulder.

"Kama, where's Gabe?"

She blinked and raised a hand to her head. "Outside. In the flyer."

"Don't get up." He rose to face Alana.

The security chief frowned at him. "You're contaminating a crime scene. Get out."

"Gabe Goldman's missing. Get your people searching the neighborhood. Put up roadblocks, and ground all air traffic."

"With all due respect, sir," Alana said, her ruddy face darkening, "you're the CEO, and I'm the security chief. Now get the hell out of my crime scene and let me do my job."

"You two." She waved at a couple of guards. "Out the back. Search the yard. Stay off any soft areas that might give us footprints. The rest of you, spread out, search the adjoining yards. Go door-to-door. Ask whether anyone saw anything."

"Try for a lock on his nanocom." Rafe ran a hand through his hair and silently cursed Leon Goldman's mismanagement and his own decision to follow Aaron's orders. Now Aaron was dead and Gabe missing, all because he hadn't given a damn about doing the job right, only about avoiding confrontation with Aaron and the board.

Kama groaned behind him, then sucked in a sharp breath as she sat up. Despite his order to stay down, she drew her legs under herself and tried to rise. He caught her arm and slung it over his shoulder, steadying her as she swayed.

"What were you doing with a stunner, Ms. Bhatia?"

"Not now, Alana." He dragged Kama past her toward the front door.

"Goldman's dead." Kama's voice broke.

"You've been stunned. You need to clear your head." He hoped she'd heed his advice and stop talking before she said something she shouldn't.

They continued through the front door into the warm evening air. Lights from the security vehicles blazed in the yard, casting grotesque shadows against the house. Rafe took her to the rental flyer, opened the door, and eased her onto the seat.

Kama looked around, and panic lit her eyes. "Where's Gabe? Isn't he with you?"

"We're looking for him." Tension laced his voice.

"Shit. Not Gabe, too. I have to find him."

She tried to get out, but he blocked her. "Sit tight, get your bearings, and then tell us what happened."

Alana stood nearby, supervising events while she observed them. Rafe didn't like the way she looked at Kama. All too easy to blame the contractor found in the house and sweep everything that didn't fit under the rug. He'd seen it happen before. He couldn't let that happen to Kama.

He heard the patter of feet, and Gabe burst out of the darkness, one of Alana's security officers following. The boy dashed to Kama and stopped in front of her, his breathing heavy, cheeks and forehead flushed. He must have run away from whatever happened inside the house. Rafe couldn't blame him, not after what he'd been through recently.

"Found him down the block," the guard said as he walked up.

"Are you okay?" Gabe asked Kama.

Kama hugged the boy to her, tears threatening to spill from her eyes. Then she pushed him to arms' length, and her brow drew down.

"I told you to stay put."

Before Gabe could reply, a sleek red sport flyer purred up the street to join the mob of vehicles at the curb. The driver's door opened, and Rafe's father stepped out, lean, elegant, commanding—the last person Rafe wanted to see. Standing six foot two, clad in slim black pants, a black mock turtleneck, and black linen jacket, he looked larger than life and filled with self-importance. Hooded eyes raked the group, and he stalked to Alana.

"Where's Aaron?"

Rafe sucked in air, his chest tight, and forced himself to join them.

"Mr. Goldman is dead," she said.

His father froze, lips parted, eyes widened. When he recovered, he took a step closer to Alana.

"How did it happen?"

"The investigation is in the early stages," Alana said.

"I want to see him."

His father took a step toward the house, but Alana barred his path. "This is an active crime scene. I can't let you in."

"Crime scene?"

"A person or persons unknown broke into the house, and Mr. Goldman died. Those are the facts as we know them."

The man's jaw worked back and forth, and he jerked his head toward Rafe. "What's he doing here?"

"I called him." Kama joined Rafe. Gabe clung to her hand and half hid behind her. Rafe wondered if he'd known his grandfather was dead, or had it come as a surprise? He looked more frightened than shocked.

His father turned his attention on Gabe. "This is no place for a child. I'll take him to Shannon's."

The kid pressed against Kama. "I want to stay with her."

"Sorry," Alana said. "She's coming with me. You go with Mr. McTavish."

His father stepped forward, and Gabe jumped back. He darted to Rafe, refusing to look at the elder McTavish. "I don't want to go with him."

Rafe put a protective arm around the boy's trembling shoulders. "You can stay with me while we get things sorted out."

"You?! Absolutely not," his father said, voice fierce. "He goes to Shannon's."

"Seems to me he's already made his choice." Kama stepped between his father and the boy. "Maybe you should stop frightening children and pick on someone your own size."

His father towered over her, his face darkening, but Kama didn't flinch. Rafe's stomach churned. In a minute, she'd hit him, he just knew it. The situation was already in the toilet. He didn't need her to flush.

His father's eyes shifted from Kama to Rafe and back. A smirk formed on his lips.

"You're his little trollop, aren't you? And he hides behind your skirts. What kind of man does that?"

Rafe's fists bunched, and he stepped forward. Alana jumped between them, hands up.

"We've had enough violence for one night, gentlemen. Now get the hell off my crime scene before I arrest you both for obstruction."

His father glared at him a long moment before directing his attention to Alana. "If you want to keep your job, you'll have the murderer in custody by morning. I'll expect a full report by eight."

He spun on his heel and strode to his flyer. With a roar of the engines, the little craft leaped into the sky, disappearing over the rooftops.

"In your dreams," muttered Alana. She turned to Kama. "Ms. Bhatia, I'm taking you into custody."

"You can't do that. On what grounds?" protested Rafe, aware of his own trembling as adrenaline drained away.

"On the grounds that I'm running a homicide investigation, Mr. McTavish, and I have the right to question her. She's a contractor out after curfew, and I have a city in flames and a dead chairman. I want to know where she was and what she was doing this evening, and I'll be damned if I'll ask your permission to do my job."

He should have decked her at the door when he had the chance. Then his eyes caught the fear lingering on Gabe's face. He took a deep breath, and another. In her place, he'd ask the same things. He looked at Kama, and she made a tiny nod.

"Sorry, Alana. I was out of line." He gave her a quick smile. It bounced off. "As one security professional to another, would you permit me to observe the interrogation? I might be able to fill in some gaps."

"Don't worry, Mr. McTavish, you'll have plenty of opportunity to answer questions."

11

It seemed like they'd spent the whole night at the security center answering Dzandarova's questions, but when Kama checked her nanocom, only three hours had passed. She thought McTavish might fold and tell the security chief about their real mission, but he didn't.

Dzandarova agreed to release her into McTavish's custody, provided he stayed the night at his sister's house so the security chief would need less protective staff to cover the family. Kama had seen the distress on his face, seen the internal battle play out in his eyes before he'd acquiesced. He'd done it to keep her out of a cell. It left her with crawling guilt.

They streaked across the city in the rental flyer, headed for Shannon's, McTavish as black and silent as the night around them. A security escort flew close behind. What did Dzandarova think? That the contractors intended to kidnap the CEO in midair? No, she just didn't trust McTavish, Kama decided, and wondered why.

Cullen McTavish was a piece of work. How could a man treat his son so cruelly? No wonder McTavish left and never looked back. But that wasn't true. The son might have run away; he hadn't broken free. She could see it in his face when he confronted his father. He still wanted—still hoped for—love and approval. She fumed, thinking of what she'd like to do to Cullen.

Then her thoughts drifted to Aaron Goldman, the slogans scrawled on his walls, and the riot. If she'd contributed to his death, she could never forgive herself. What would Gabe say if he knew she might be responsible? She'd have to tell McTavish about her hacking. And she'd have to take responsibility for not providing the man better protection.

She needed to look into the files she'd downloaded, hack back into the corporate network to see what other evidence she could unearth before the network security team muddied the waters. She'd wasted hours already going over and over the same useless ground with the security chief.

They came in over a peaceful residential neighborhood populated by long, low ranchers set on oversized lots. Most of the houses sported the same expanses of lawn and over-pruned hedges evident in Goldman's neighborhood.

By contrast, the Nighthorse house looked like a Spanish hacienda set down in an orchard. Red tile graced the roof, white stucco covered the sides, and a stone walkway led to carved wooden doors held in place by black cast-iron hinges. Fruit trees grew in a double row down one side, enveloped a wide garage, and disappeared in a sweep around back. A grape arbor and vegetable garden flanked the opposite side of the house. She caught a glimpse of a jungle gym erected behind the garden. Soccer goal posts stood at one property line, and a chalk-line penalty zone striped the well-trampled front lawn.

As they touched down, the front door opened, and Shannon Nighthorse stepped onto the porch. McTavish stared out the window at his sister, tension showing in the tightness around his eyes. Kama squeezed his hand. He gave a sigh laden with resignation and got out of the flyer. She shepherded Gabe up the walk behind him.

Shannon had Cullen's red hair and pale skin, but her eyes were a striking green. She wore no makeup. Her tan polo shirt hung over worn blue jeans smudged with dirt on the knees, and her sneakers boasted more of the same.

"Rafe." A brittle smile rounded her cheeks but never reached her eyes.

"Shannon." McTavish ducked his head. "I'm sorry to show up on your doorstep like this. Alana insisted..."

Shannon crossed her arms and gripped her elbows. Silence stretched between the siblings. *Vishnu, we'll still be standing here at sunup.* Kama walked around him and stuck out a hand.

"Kama Bhatia. Thank you for sharing your home with us."

Recognition sparked in Shannon's eyes. "You're the woman that Greg talked about—from the mining station."

Kama sighed. "Any stories you may have heard about me being a secret agent are the figments of an overactive teenage mind. I'm just a computer technician. And teacher."

Shannon's gaze traveled from Kama to her brother and back, and she smiled, bright and warm. "No stories about secret agents."

Then what the hell *had* Greg said? Shannon's attitude change worried her. McTavish hadn't told Greg he'd proposed, had he? He couldn't be that stupid. Or maybe he could. *Men.*

"The kids are in bed." Shannon ushered them inside. "Ben's gone on a water survey, and Greg's still on Earth."

They entered a spacious living room, obviously the center of activity in the house. A vid screen occupied one wall, a long, well-used couch opposite. A loveseat and armchairs bracketed the couch. The open floor plan gave a view into an informal dining room and a cheery kitchen beyond. Family photos covered the walls: birthday parties, picnics, school plays, sporting events.

"Gabe, I'm sorry to hear about your grandfather," Shannon said, voice soft. "Rosie's at a sleepover tonight. I've made up her room for you. I don't have any pajamas your size, but I put one of Greg's t-shirts on the bed for you. It's the second door on the right. The bathroom's the next door along."

"I'll give him a hand." McTavish slipped off with Gabe.

"Would you like something to drink?" Shannon offered. "I have lemonade or ice tea."

What Kama wanted was to get started on those files.

"And chocolate cupcakes," Shannon added.

Chocolate. Kama's mouth watered. When had she eaten last? "Maybe just one. And some ice tea."

Shannon flashed her own version of the charming McTavish smile and led Kama to the kitchen where she directed Kama to a barstool at the counter.

"Have you known Rafe long?" Shannon poured tea into a tall, ice-filled glass.

Damn. Cupcakes, tea, and interrogation. How could she take this conversation some other direction?

"Nine days? We met at the station."

"While you were fixing their computers? Or were you teaching there, too?"

No teaching. Just a top secret mission for Oasis. Probably best if she didn't tell McTavish's sister that.

"Teachers are grossly underpaid. I supplement my income with the occasional contract job."

"I see." Shannon placed a cupcake on a plate and put it in front of her. "Then you don't know my brother well. But he got you the job here, teaching Gabe."

Kama swiped a finger through the soft, red frosting and sucked it off her finger. *Raspberry. Heavenly.*

"We're not sleeping together, if that's what you're wondering."

Pink climbed Shannon's cheeks, but she made a fast recovery.

"Separate rooms then."

Kama eyed the woman, and they both laughed.

"You can use the guest room. It's next to Gabe's room." She poured herself a glass of tea. "You like him though."

"He's handsome, charming, prone to throwing himself under the bus for others, and infuriatingly dedicated to his family no matter what it costs him. What's not to like?"

Shannon blinked at her. "He hasn't spoken to any of us in fourteen years. I don't call that dedication to family."

"Then why is he here? He had everything in Mumbai. He didn't need or want what EcoMech has on offer. At the mining station, he came within a whisker of dying for your son. He stood unarmed against a mob that beat him senseless with lengths of pipe, wrenches, hammers, while Greg escaped. *Kali*, Leon slammed the hatch in his face. But he still promised Aaron he'd look after things for Gabe because Gabe is *family*."

Shannon's face paled. Kama suspected that Greg hadn't told his mother about his close call or his uncle's sacrifice. Did the family have any idea of who McTavish had become after he left them behind? It was time for them to find out. McTavish needed their support.

"He's crazy dedicated to you people despite the abuse his father's heaped on him. When McTavish most needed his father's love and support, Cullen accused him of murdering Youko and the children."

"Rafe said that?" Shannon asked, her tone sharp. "Dad accused him to his face?"

Shannon stared at the counter, eyes unfocused, while Kama scarfed the cupcake and drained her tea. A few minutes later, McTavish joined them. Sizzling anger replaced the awkwardness he'd displayed earlier.

"Gabe's asked for you to tuck him in," McTavish said, voice strained. "And then I'd like a word."

Kama slid off the stool and headed to Gabe's room, curious about what had caused McTavish's mood swing. Had he overheard her conversation with Shannon? Resented them discussing him?

Rosie's room fit its namesake. Rose print curtains fluttered in the breeze coming through the open window, and a matching rose print spread covered the bed. A row of stuffed bears, tigers, and horses lined one shelf above the bed, toys and games another. Pink hearts ringed a bulletin board on which pictures of other girls and mushy love-notes had been pinned. No question that a child occupied the space, unlike Gabe's bedroom at Aaron's.

Gabe lay under the blankets, a worried frown turning down the corners of his mouth. Kama sat on the bed beside him and brushed his hair back from his forehead. She'd been so absorbed with finding the hacker that she hadn't thought about how Goldman's death must have hit the boy.

"I'm sorry about your grandfather," she said. "I should have done more to protect him."

"Uncle Rafe said it was his fault because he didn't order extra guards." Gabe's bleak stare focused on the blankets.

Of course McTavish would take the blame, but she was the one who convinced him she could do the job. She felt sick about it.

"You want me to tell you a story?" she asked.

"I'm too old for stories." He fought back tears. "What's going to happen to me now?"

He didn't have any living relatives, Kama realized. No family would come forward to claim him. McTavish was related to the boy by marriage only. Would he step up?

"I'm not sure. I know that isn't much comfort, but we don't know what's in your grandfather's will. He may have arranged for someone to become your guardian if anything happened to him." It seemed a distant possibility given the short amount of time Goldman had between Leon's death and his own, but she didn't know what to say.

"Would you adopt me?"

"In a mad minute, but I don't know that I'd be allowed to."

"Would Uncle Rafe?"

"I don't know. I'm sure Shannon won't mind if you stay here until we get everything sorted." She gestured around. "It looks like a great place to be a kid."

"Uncle Rafe's mad at me for getting out of the flyer."

And rightfully so. Had he taken it out on the boy? Gabe seemed unnaturally quiet—and worried.

"Why did you do it?"

The boy's worry deepened. "I thought the bad guy might see me."

His answer sounded hollow, off. She ruffled his hair and waited, but he didn't say anything more.

"We all get scared sometimes, and that's okay," she said.

Gabe squirmed under the covers and focused his attention on the bulletin board. "If someone said something bad about your dad, would you be mad at him?"

Kama straightened. "You mean if he were being mean and said bad things about my father?"

"No, if he said stuff that was true, like if your dad did something he shouldn't have and this person told on him, would you be mad at him?"

Did Gabe overhear Aaron and the blackmailer talking? What was he so reluctant to talk about? She took a deep breath and kept her voice casual.

"Did someone say something about your dad, about something he did?"

"No." Gabe scanned the room, eyes brimming, reply too hasty. "I just want to go home. I miss my dad."

Kama scooped the boy into her arms and hugged him tight while tears rolled down his cheeks. "I know, Gabe."

She held him until his crying stopped, and then she tucked him in again. He was a child adrift. She'd talk to McTavish. He needed to comfort the boy and reassure him about the future.

12

"Do you want something to drink?" Shannon asked.

"No, thanks. I might break the glass," Rafe quipped.

Fourteen years since he'd seen her, and that was the best he could do? Remind her of all the accidents, the clumsy, inattentive mistakes? What the hell was wrong with him? He wasn't a kid who couldn't control his mouth anymore. He'd left all that behind. He'd led troops into battle, grown into a successful businessman, learned to compensate for his attention problems. But at every turn, his mutinous tongue betrayed him.

"How long will you stay?"

Rafe shrugged. Another five minutes seemed too long. He had a headache and a stiff neck, and he wanted to give Kama a piece of his mind, not make small talk with his sister.

"This was Alana's idea."

Shannon set Kama's plate in the sink and wiped crumbs from the counter. "Would you ever have come on your own?"

He thrust his hands in his pockets and didn't answer.

"When Dad kicked you out, we took you in, gave you a home. You could have come to us when Youko died."

"So you could say, 'I told you so'? When I announced the engagement, you told me what a mistake I'd made. You refused to come to our wedding. As I recall, we weren't speaking when Youko died."

"You were a sixteen-year old kid marrying a crazy woman for all the wrong reasons. I wanted to protect you," she said, heat in her words. "But you didn't want to hear it."

"Feel better now you've said it?" He instantly regretted his words.

Shannon turned her back and busied herself placing dishes in the dishwasher. "I'm sorry for the loss of your children."

He should thank her for her concern, but the words stuck in his throat.

She wiped her hands on a towel and turned to face him. "Kama says you risked your life to save Greg. Thank you. He worships you, you know."

Rafe rubbed his stiff neck and shuffled his feet. "Better if he didn't, since I'm brain-damaged."

Her face flushed. "I didn't say you were brain-damaged."

"No? Well that's what he heard." Rafe glanced into the dining room and wondered how long it took to tuck in an eleven-year old. If he kept talking, Shannon would bounce his sorry ass to the curb, and then he'd have Alana on his case.

"ADHD isn't brain damage exactly. Besides, you've obviously grown out of it, or you wouldn't have done so well for yourself. Aaron wouldn't have asked you to be CEO."

He drew his ball from his pocket, walked it across his knuckles, and laughed. "Aaron would have hired an imbecile if his name and face lifted the stock price. Maybe he did."

Shannon frowned at the ball and then at him. "What will happen to Gabe?"

"I'm sure opposing armies of lawyers are prepared to argue that end-lessly—or at least until the money runs out."

She drew back. "Don't you care about him?"

Shame crept over him. "Aaron had heart surgery coming up. He asked me to be Gabe's guardian in case anything happened."

"You?" Shannon put a steadying hand on the counter.

"Thanks for the vote of confidence."

"It's just—" She crossed her arms and fell silent.

"It's just that I'm a colossal screw-up, the black sheep of the family, and you can't imagine me raising a kid."

"That's not true. But I did think Aaron would want Gabe in a... fam-ily home. You're unsettled, a different woman on your arm every week. You can't raise a child like that. Gabe needs stability, a mother figure, not a parade of one-night stands."

Rafe wished he'd asked for a drink. Then he could throw the glass across the room, or smash it against the counter. Shannon had no idea what his life in Mumbai had been like, but she was quick to judge it wanting. He'd been an idiot to think he could change anything here.

"What do you suggest?"

"Ben and I can raise him. Now that Greg's grown, Ben misses having another 'man' around the house. Of course he loves the girls, but fathers don't Indian wrestle with daughters."

"Can you love Gabe despite your hatred for Leon?"

Shannon turned stormy eyes on him. "I won't blame the son for the sins of the father."

They glared at each other in cold silence.

"If Aaron wanted you to raise Gabe, he would have asked you."

"Did he ask you because he thought you'd be a good father, or to ensure you'd hand over EcoMech to Gabe when the time came?"

Rafe saw the events of the past few days with new eyes. The crafty old man didn't care one whit about Gabe's home life. All he wanted was continued Goldman domination of EcoMech. Ever the sharp business-man, Aaron had purchased insurance by asking Rafe to be the boy's surrogate father.

Thank God he hadn't agreed yet. He was every bit the fool his family thought him. All he wanted to do was go home to Mumbai and run his own company.

"Fine. If you petition for legal guardianship, I won't fight it."

13

When Kama returned to the kitchen, McTavish looked like a man who'd taken a beating. Maybe he'd vented his anger on Shannon. If he had, he'd gotten as good as he'd given. And now she had to tell him about her own part in EcoMech's contractor woes.

"Let's step outside," McTavish said when he saw her.

They exited onto a stone-paved patio behind the kitchen. McTavish slid the door closed behind them and walked to the far edge of the space. Kama followed, working up the courage to tell him what she'd done, how she planned to set things right. She'd start with Gabe.

"Gabe's frightened about what will happen to him. He's looking to you for support. This isn't the time to chastise him for getting out of the flyer."

McTavish's eyes smoldered. "Why did you tell Gabe he could be a spy? Didn't you think about the danger you'd put him in?"

Kama opened her mouth, closed it.

"He got out of the flyer to be your backup. He thought that's what he ought to do as part of your super-secret strike force." McTavish scowled at her. "You should have waited for help like I told you. You should have kept Gabe safe."

Is that what Gabe had told him to assuage his anger? Or was it the truth? Had Goldman died because of her? Had she put Gabe in danger by leaving him alone? The doubts tied her stomach in a knot.

"Someone hacked EcoMech's system and disabled security tonight," she blurted, off-kilter from his unexpected assault.

"Of course they did. That's why we had a riot, and why we'll never catch the contractors who murdered Aaron during their botched kidnapping." He paced the stones, his ball bouncing with each step. Then he stopped and looked hard at her. "You were in the system."

Her face heated. "I knew the contractors planned a vigil tonight to protest the council's firing, and I wanted to be sure the protestors didn't get fired, too. I dropped a piece of code that shut down the tracking and the cameras during the time of the vigil."

McTavish goggled at her. "You *what?*"

"You fired the council, and you shouldn't have. EcoMech has to understand that it can't treat the contractors like slaves. They have rights, too."

His fists bunched, and his neck muscles corded as he clenched his teeth. She took a step back. He spun and strode away across the lawn, headed for the side of the house. Kama ran after him.

"McTavish! I'm sorry." She grabbed his arm and pulled him to a halt. "I don't know what happened, but I'll find out."

"Haven't you done enough?"

She flinched and dropped her hand from his arm. "What about those contractors you let go for no reason? They'll never work again. How will they take care of themselves, their families?"

"I expect they'll use the salaries from the new jobs I got them. Did you honestly believe I'd just chuck them out? Is that what you think of me?"

Kama pulled back. "I didn't know."

"Because you never asked. You just charged in alone to do what *you* thought was right. By firing them, I got Aaron to agree to let me make changes, to improve the contractors' situation. That's how change happens in a civilized society, by negotiation—and teamwork.

"But there won't be any change now. After the riots, the board won't even *consider* relaxing restrictions or improving conditions. Are you happy? Or do you intend to singlehandedly burn down the rest of EcoMech before you go?" McTavish stormed away around the corner.

Pain stabbed like a mugger's blade in her chest. *Go?* He wanted her to leave? How could things have gone so wrong? She stumbled back to the patio and stared into the darkness, arms wrapped around her ribs.

☠ ☠ ☠

The wan light of dawn streamed through the living room window as Kama tiptoed to the door. Her shoulders ached, and her eyes burned. She'd spent all night combing the EcoMech system for any clue to the identity of the hacker who'd disabled security. It beat tossing sleepless in bed and flogging herself for her stupidity.

McTavish had shown his true colors. He wouldn't stand up to the board and change EcoMech. He couldn't accept her for who she was, and he didn't even know the worst about her. No doubt he regretted his marriage proposal. She'd expected as much. She didn't want a relationship anyway. Why let his words bother her? But they did.

She'd trace the hacker back to the kidnappers. They were the ones responsible for Goldman's death, not her. She repeated the words over and over, but she still didn't believe them.

Kidnapping Goldman. How did that make any sense? EcoMech's Harvest colony consisted of one city of a hundred thousand and a few minimally staffed research outposts. It wasn't like Earth where kidnappers had a whole planet to hide. EcoMech security would find the culprits in hours. Besides, McTavish would never negotiate for the old chairman's freedom.

Whoever had done it was a potential threat to McTavish. What if they came for him next?

She'd keep McTavish safe even if he didn't approve of her methods, and show him... what? That she cared about him? She didn't. She needed EcoMech to partner in the Sharma Network, that's all. What he thought of her didn't matter. Another mantra she repeated endlessly.

She turned the doorknob slowly and silently, and then pulled the door open. Two steps took her onto the porch. As she drew the door closed, she heard his voice, raw and throaty.

"You don't need me at the press conference." He spoke to someone on the other end of a nanocom connection. "My father can represent EcoMech's position."

He sat hunched on a lawn chair on the porch and glanced up while he listened to a reply. His clothes were rumpled, his face drawn, his beautiful blue eyes bloodshot. An empty wine bottle lay on its side next to the chair. His rubber ball walked the knuckles of his right hand.

"I don't recommend that he release information about the investigation. That's Alana's job. Let her do it when she's ready." He paused again while whoever he spoke to rattled on about liability.

Kama hitched her duffel and strode down the path to the street as though she didn't care if he saw her.

"EcoMech employs an entire department of lawyers. Get one of them out of bed to vet the statement."

She heard the rattle of his chair, and then he said, "Where do you think you're sneaking off to?"

She kept walking. "The contractors' complex."

"Did you say goodbye to Gabe, or are you ducking out on him, too?"

She stopped and turned. Pain lined his face and hung like a mantle from his shoulders. Concern for him warred with her anger.

"You told me to go. Now you accuse me of slinking away?"

"Aaron's dead, a fireman lies in critical condition, shops and offices were destroyed." He stepped down from the porch, his posture stiff and his eyes narrowed. "Do you feel any remorse?"

She took a step back. "EcoMech treats its livestock better than it treats its contractors. I had to help them."

"Because I didn't." He threw his hands in the air. "You have no idea how corporations work. You think that because I'm the CEO, I can change any damn thing I want with the snap of my fingers. Well not anymore. I resign. I'm leaving this hell hole and never coming back."

"You can't resign," she stammered. "What about the Sharma Network? What about the millions of people who will remain trapped on Earth without it?"

His mouth pulled into a hard line. "You never cared about me at all, did you? You just wanted to be sure your precious Sharma Network got built, and I was the means to the end. You used me, just like Aaron used me. I was nothing more than a puppet for either of you."

Her hands trembled on the duffel's straps, and her breath came in short, fast gulps. "It was your idea to come to this godforsaken sand pile, not mine. Now you'll let Aaron's killer run you off?"

McTavish snorted. "What makes you think my father will let me stay? He'll be the new chairman. Replacing me will be his top priority."

"And instead of standing up to him, you'll cut and run, just like before."

He winced and stumbled back. Kama clenched her teeth, regretting her words.

Behind him, the door opened and a sleepy-eyed Gabe stepped onto the porch, still wearing Greg's over-sized t-shirt over his grey slacks and bare feet. His gaze traveled from her to McTavish and down to the empty bottle.

Fans whined in the street, and Kama shielded her eyes while she watched a security flyer settle behind theirs. Dzandarova and a guard got out. The security chief arrowed up the walk to stop in front of Kama.

"Kamala Bhatia, I'm arresting you for the murder of Aaron Goldman."

The world spun to a halt while Kama waited for McTavish to say something, come to her defense. He just stood there, silent.

Dzandarova flagged the guard forward. He drew out handcuffs and secured her hands behind her back.

"She didn't do it." Gabe bolted down the walk to confront the security chief. "Mr. McTavish killed Grandpa. I saw him."

14

Another betrayal. Rafe passed a hand over his tired face. His arm felt heavy and unresponsive while his head floated in the growing morning heat.

He was trapped in a nightmare, once again accused of a crime he didn't commit, facing the daughter of the security chief who'd been all too eager to arrest him last time. But this time, Aaron wouldn't intercede on his behalf.

"I was at my hotel when Aaron died. You had security guards outside my door."

"Wait a minute," Kama said. "Gabe, which Mr. McTavish do you mean?"

The boy turned sad eyes on him. "Your dad."

Rafe stared, open-mouthed. *My father murdered Aaron?* He couldn't take it in. Gabe must be making it up to protect Kama. Then he thought about Gabe's behavior the previous night, how he'd cowered away from his father.

Alana eyed the boy. "Maybe you better come down to the station and tell me more."

"Hey, buddy, go get your shoes," Rafe said.

The boy darted into the house.

"Maybe you want to rethink your arrest," Kama said.

Alana grudgingly nodded to the guard, who released her hands.

"Since you're his legal guardian, Mr. McTavish, I'm required to have you present during questioning."

He held up his hands. "I'm not his legal guardian."

"According to the terms of Mr. Goldman's will you are. I contacted the lawyers this morning. You get custody of Gabe and the estate. Your father gets proxy control of the stock until he's eighteen."

"But I never agreed. I don't want him."

Behind him, the door banged closed. He looked down into Gabe's pained eyes. The boy walked to Kama, head down, shoulders slumped. She put an arm around him and tossed Rafe an angry glare.

"Mr. McTavish, you can ride with me," Alana said. "Danny will bring them in the other flyer."

Rafe watched the guard load Kama and Gabe in the rental flyer, and reluctantly climbed in beside Alana. He wanted to order her to drop him at the shuttleport, and he'd take the first ship back to Earth. His thoughts slid away from Kama's uncomfortable accusation that he was running out on his duty.

"Your PR department called me this morning." The security chief adjusted their course. "They want a statement. I'm not prepared to give one."

"They aren't *my* PR department. Tell them to go to hell."

Alana glanced sideways at him. "I did. They keep calling back."

Rafe laughed. "Yeah, they've been calling me every five minutes all night. Bunch of assholes."

"I heard you did some favors for those contractors you let go." She chuckled at his sharp look. "I have my sources. Maybe if more people had known about your generous severance terms, we wouldn't have had riots. Or maybe those generous terms were payment in advance for the murder of Aaron Goldman."

He snorted. "Why would I want to kill Aaron?"

"When Mr. Goldman named you as the new CEO, your father gave me the file on your wife's death. He thought I ought to know what you'd done."

Anger boiled in his gut. So his father had kept a copy of old Chief Dzandarova's real investigation report, one that described the bloody double homicide/suicide instead of the official lie of a fatal miscarriage in late pregnancy.

"Once a killer, always a killer. Is that what you think?"

Alana took a deep breath and let it out. "I think it's a big leap from being a wise-ass kid who pulls practical jokes and joyrides in stolen fly-ers to murdering three people in cold blood. Kill your wife, maybe, in a moment of passion. But the surrogate mothers? The mutilation of the fetuses? Your wife, however, had a history of mental health issues."

Memory flooded over him: the yellow coverlet soaked in blood, the coppery tang in the air, the carving knife used first to cut his unborn daughter from the womb, and then embedded in her tiny chest. He squeezed his hands into fists, but they shook anyway.

"Your father seems convinced of your guilt. Maybe you hold a grudge against him because of it. Maybe you had your contractor friend, Ms. Bhatia, murder Goldman.

"Or maybe you just want to take over EcoMech, hold all the power. If Aaron's dead and your father's in prison, that leaves you to do what you like with the company. And the money."

"I don't *want* the damn company," he muttered. "Or the money."

"Then why'd you come back?"

Rafe examined her profile as she piloted the flyer across the city. This was the question she really wanted answered. All the rest had just been warm-up. He gave her points for interrogation technique.

Why *had* he come back? He thought it was to repay a debt he owed Aaron, but his subconscious whispered that was a lie. He'd accepted the job to force his father to acknowledge that he was an honorable man, not a murderer. It would never happen, and he didn't understand why. He'd taken up a career in law enforcement, built his own successful company. What more could he do to prove to the old man that he was wrong about his son?

"Leon Goldman had been blackmailed for years by someone bent on taking the reins of power at EcoMech, but we don't know who. To thwart the blackmailer's plan, when Leon died, Aaron asked me to step in."

Alana swung her head toward him, eyes wide. Then her face closed down. "If they wanted control, you'd be the next target."

He shrugged. "That was the plan."

"But they went after Goldman instead."

"When we didn't make as much progress as he wanted, Aaron decided to flush them out his own way." Rafe ran a hand through his hair. "I should have set up a surveillance detail as soon as he told me."

"'We'? You mean Ms. Bhatia and you?"

He turned away to watch the city steam past under the flyer.

"She's a Security Partners' operative?" Anger colored Alana's voice. "And you didn't think you needed to share that with me last night?"

Should he tell her the truth? If he hadn't allowed himself to become snarled in a web of lies and subterfuge, Aaron might still be alive. Maybe if as Alana suggested, he'd stood up to the board and refused to fire the contractors' council instead of easing them out behind the board's back, there wouldn't have been a riot. Maybe Kama wouldn't have betrayed him, and his future with her wouldn't be in ruins.

"She's a corporate liaison from Oasis. We're entering a partnership with them to build a new jump gate system. It hasn't been announced publicly yet."

And it never would. A downsized version of EcoMech might survive the impending bankruptcy, but it wouldn't have the kind of resources required to build the Sharma Network. By betraying him first, Kama saved him the pain of her disappointment. It seemed small comfort.

"Oasis," Alana said, thoughtful. "They do software. Think she can help us with our hacker problem?"

☠ ☠ ☠

They sat in Alana's cramped office, the security chief behind her battered metal desk, he and Kama opposite her, flanking Gabe.

"I peeked in the front door." Gabe told his story to Kama and avoided eye contact with Alana or him. "You turned around, and he stunned you. He came down the stairs, and that's when I saw him. He went through the dining room and out the back."

"He didn't see you?" Rafe asked, the hair on the back of his neck rising. If the killer knew Gabe had seen him, the boy could be in jeopardy.

The boy shook his head. "I ran around through the side gate. He jumped the fence into Mrs. Marley's yard and ran through to Thurston Street. I almost lost him because I couldn't get over the fence. He ran really fast.

"The street light is out on Thurston, and I couldn't see him very well. He was all dressed in black. He turned the corner onto Maple. When I got there, he was getting in that red flyer of his, the one he drove when he came to the house."

"You're sure it was Cullen McTavish?" Kama said. "You saw his face?"

The boy nodded, his dejection plain in his body language. "He was parked by the street light."

"Gabe, will you wait in the lobby, please?" Alana paused while he slipped out. "Do we believe him?"

Kama glared at the security chief. "Why would he lie?"

"People lie for lots of reasons, Ms. Bhatia."

"What was the cause of death?" Rafe asked. Despite his determination to leave Harvest, he wanted to understand how Aaron died—perhaps so he could torture himself with guilt later.

"Heart attack brought on by stunning." She sent an unfriendly smile Kama's direction. "Which is why I liked you for the crime. You had that illegal little stunner. That, and your tracking bracelet made you the only contractor within kilometers of the house."

Rafe gave the security chief a puzzled frown. "I thought the security system was down?"

"It came back on just before Ms. Bhatia called you. The techs can't explain why. Nor do they know why it went down in the first place. It was unresponsive to all commands one minute, working the next. They thought they'd have to reload from backup. That would have taken another hour."

Kama stiffened in her chair and refused to look at him. Another dilemma. Should he report her? Of course. But would he? He drew his ball from his pocket and rolled it between his palms. *Focus.*

"It doesn't track. My father would never be CEO of EcoMech. Why kill Aaron?"

"They argued earlier in the day," Kama said. "Gabe overheard them while I was away renting the flyer. If he wanted you fired, and Aaron wouldn't agree..."

He bounced the ball at his feet. Would his father murder Aaron to be rid of the son he hated? His mind shied away from an answer. "All we have to go on is Gabe's testimony."

"Not quite." Alana eyed the ball. She tapped a filmie on her desk. "We found a whiskey glass in the dishwasher. It has your father's fingerprints on it. The maid said the dishwasher was empty when she left for the day, so he was there while Gabe and Ms. Bhatia were gone. We didn't think anything of it because we assumed contractors killed Mr. Goldman."

"Goldman prepared for company. I should have realized..." She slumped in the chair and chewed her lip.

Weighed down by her guilt perhaps. Dark rings colored the skin below her eyes. Did she really think him a coward?

"Have you checked Aaron's calendar to see if he had appointments scheduled with anyone?" he asked, dragging his exhausted mind back to Aaron's murder.

Alana nodded. "Nothing in his calendar for last night."

Kama leaned forward. "Gabe said that after his argument with Cullen yesterday afternoon, he stayed in his study making calls. Who did he contact?"

The security chief tapped her nanocom. "Four outgoing calls, one each to Lev Kozlov, Bertold Gerlach, Lars Svenson, and Cullen McTavish."

With the exception of his father, the names matched their list of blackmail suspects.

15

Inside the interrogation room, Cullen McTavish picked a speck of lint from his trousers and looked around the small, gray room, mild annoyance drawing his mouth down. Kama watched him on the monitor and wondered how long the security chief would keep him waiting.

Beside her, McTavish shifted in his chair. He rolled his ball between his palms, his eyes glazed and distant. He must be in shock, learning that his father had murdered Goldman.

"What will happen to Gabe?" she asked.

McTavish flicked her a glance, then returned his eyes to the monitor while the ball wove between his fingers. "He'll live with Shannon and Ben."

She'd seen the way he'd comforted Gabe at the mining station. She didn't understand why he'd grown so cold toward the boy now. Maybe being saddled with a child would crimp his playboy lifestyle. She chided herself for her uncharitable thoughts. He'd been devastated by the loss of his own children.

Her worry shifted to the Sharma Network, raising a little niggle of guilt. As McTavish said, she wanted it built. Without it, no new colony worlds would open, and the current colonies didn't have the capacity to embrace the kind of large-scale emigration Earth needed before industrial and agricultural contamination doomed anyone too poor to buy a place on a colony.

If McTavish abandoned EcoMech, Varun might rethink his acceptance of EcoMech as a Sharma Network partner. He'd invite Caligo Corp to replace EcoMech, and Kama couldn't allow that at any cost.

The man on the monitor was the key. Cullen was the one chasing his son away from the duty he'd shouldered at Goldman's request. Prove the old man guilty of Goldman's murder, and McTavish could step in as chairman instead of CEO.

The security chief entered the interrogation room and took the chair across the table from the elder McTavish.

"Thank you for coming," Dzandarova said.

"I don't know why we couldn't do this by nanocom." Cullen glowered at her. "We're in the midst of a crisis, and I have a board meeting to attend."

"I'll try to keep this brief."

"Good. Get on with your report."

Kama laughed to herself. So he thought he was here to get an update on the investigation. Clever of Dzandarova to lure him in that way.

"We're trying to reconstruct Mr. Goldman's day, and we thought you might be able to help us. When did you last see him?"

Cullen frowned and turned his gaze on his hands where they lay in his lap. "At the board meeting yesterday morning."

Kama sucked in her breath. *A blatant lie with his first statement.* But it didn't surprise her. He'd killed Goldman without thinking things through.

"You didn't see him later?"

"I had a busy day."

"So you don't know what he might have done, who he might have talked to after the board meeting?"

"I was his friend and business partner, not his personal assistant. Check his calendar. Did you arrest that contractor you found in his house? I understand you caught her red-handed with the murder weapon."

"And where did you hear that, Mr. McTavish?" Dzandarova was all toothy smile and good cheer.

Cullen checked his nanocom and stood. "If that's everything?"

The security chief jumped up to block his path. "Not quite. Please take a seat."

He frowned down at her, but she didn't give a centimeter. She kept her smile in place and pointed to his chair. Pink crept into his face but he sat.

"We checked Mr. Goldman's call records. He called you in the afternoon. What was that about?"

Cullen's face reddened further. "I'd forgotten. We had a brief conversation about who might make the best candidate for the CEO position."

Alana's eyebrows twitched up. "Mr. Goldman planned to replace your son?"

"Yes. I warned Aaron that Rafael wasn't up to the job. The board meeting yesterday proved my point. Aaron intended to let him go as soon as he had a commitment from a suitable candidate. It wouldn't surprise me to discover that contractor woman murdered Aaron at his behest. You've seen his file. You know what he's capable of."

Kama looked to McTavish, but his face was unreadable. The ball rolled smoothly between his palms and his tired eyes squinted at the monitor.

"And that's the last time you spoke to Mr. Goldman?" Alana asked.

"Yes. May I go now?"

Dzandarova rose and stepped back from the table. "Thank you for coming in. You've been very helpful."

"She can't let him go! He murdered Goldman."

McTavish chuffed out a breath. "She has no more evidence against him than she has against you."

"She has an eyewitness!"

"An eleven-year-old witness who chased a man dressed in black down a dark street."

"But he lied about going to Goldman's."

McTavish slid back his chair and left the room. Kama trailed behind, mind churning. The hacker had been a distraction, Kama realized. Nothing more than window dressing to support the fiction of kidnapping by contractors and to keep security busy. With Goldman dead, Cullen could fire McTavish and do whatever he wanted with the company.

Had Cullen chafed while he watched the Goldmans dominate the company he'd helped start? Did he hunger for the power and recognition that had been Aaron Goldman's? If Kama could find the hacker and make the miscreant talk, she could expose Cullen.

They met Dzandarova in the corridor.

"I know you're stretched," McTavish said, "but Gabe needs protection."

"You want me to lock him up? Because that's what I have resources for."

McTavish ran a hand through his hair. "Take him to Shannon's. Make sure you keep security on the house. Do you have someone who can give him a ride?"

Kama wanted to slap him. Why was he acting like such a bastard? He couldn't just dump the boy like that. But perhaps if she delivered the boy to Shannon's, she could swing by the Goldman house first and search for his backup files. They might reveal the secret that Leon had been blackmailed over, and that might help net Cullen McTavish.

"I'll take him." She stared at McTavish, daring him to say no. When he didn't, she turned to Dzandarova. "He'll need some clothes. Is the crime scene clear?"

The security chief nodded. McTavish checked the time on his nano-com and walked away. Kama stared after him. He was in denial. Let him believe what he wanted. She'd prove Cullen had done it.

☠   ☠   ☠

Kama guided the flyer down to the street in front of Goldman's. She supposed she ought to return it to the rental agency. No one had called her on it yet, and it beat using the River City bus system or walking.

"Are you okay with this?" she asked Gabe. "I can get your things while you wait out here if you'd rather."

Gabe's lips flattened into a hard line. He opened the flyer door and scuffed up the front walk. Kama followed.

The house was cool and dim. The study door stood open, and she glanced in as they passed. They continued upstairs, where the search of a hall closet netted them a suitcase. She opened it on the bed and crossed to the dresser.

Gabe grabbed her wrist. "I can do it."

Kama gave him a smile and patted his shoulder. "Okay, but don't forget your toothbrush. I'm going to look around downstairs."

Kama returned to the first floor. She walked down the hall and into the study. McTavish didn't believe his father murdered Aaron. That didn't make it so. But he knew the justice system. If he thought Dzandarova didn't have enough evidence for a conviction, then probably she didn't.

Kama wouldn't find anything incriminating in the study. Security had gone over it already. The hacker might provide the key, though. Cullen must have hired the hacker to create a diversion while he killed Aaron. If she could find the link between the hacker and Cullen, she'd have all the proof a court needed.

Besides, she had a personal score to settle with the hacker. He'd made McTavish's life hell, and for that he'd pay.

Where did the blackmailer fit? McTavish would never believe Aaron's murderer and the blackmailer were two different people unless she showed him he was wrong. To do that, she'd have to find the blackmailer. And if McTavish took over as chairman, he'd need a CEO loyal to him, not some crook grasping for more power. To keep McTavish safe, the blackmailer had to be found.

Her eyes traveled around the room. They'd taken Aaron's body, and with it, his nanocom, something Kama wanted access to. They still didn't know what the blackmailer had on Leon, although McTavish said he thought Aaron did. Perhaps somewhere in the chairman's records, she'd find a clue.

She began a systematic search of the desk, which turned up nothing, its drawers empty. It didn't surprise her. Antique desks like this were designed for an era when people needed a place for office supplies. Nanocoms and reusable filmies eliminated the use of sticky notes, staplers, and reams of paper. Old men like Goldman clung to the useless furniture as a symbol of their power. Bunch of brainless dinosaurs.

Where would Goldman keep backups of his business records? Not on a corporate server somewhere. He seemed too crafty and too paranoid for that. She prowled along the shelves scanning the leather-bound volumes, all of them in new condition, and wondered why he kept books if he never read them. Another token from a generation long past.

She stopped in front of the oil portrait behind the desk. The subject was a middle-aged woman with flowing chestnut hair, brown eyes, heavy cheek bones, and a strong chin. She could see the resemblance to Leon Goldman, and a check of the brass plate on the frame confirmed that this was his mother, Goldman's second wife, dead fifteen years, a victim of ice flu.

Kama tugged at the picture frame, and it swung back, revealing an old-fashioned safe with a handle and dial. She ground her teeth. She'd expected to find a digital lock, one she could open with relative ease. Without the combination, she'd need dynamite to crack this archaic monstrosity.

"What are you doing?"

She jerked around, every nerve tingling, and saw Gabe watching her from the doorway. "Don't you know it's not polite to sneak up on people?"

The boy hung his head.

"Sorry. You startled me. I'm looking for your grandfather's backup records. They might help us figure out who blackmailed your father."

She chewed her lip and eyed the safe. She'd read Oasis' files on the Goldman family. In a moment, she spun the dial to enter Goldman's birth date. The handle didn't budge. She tried every date she could think of: Leon's birthday, Goldman's wedding anniversary. None of them worked.

"What am I missing?" she muttered.

"Did you try 12, 15, 19, 9, 8?"

"Why that?"

"December 15, 1998 was the day Grandpa incorporated EcoMech. He told me a bunch of times it was the most important day of his life."

Of course the old man would value his business more than his family. She spun the lock entering the numbers, and when she tried the handle, the door swung open.

Inside, she found a handful of stick drives. She grinned and swept the lot of them into her duffel.

☠   ☠   ☠

Kama made a smooth landing in front of the Nighthorse house. A security car was parked at the curb, but it was empty. On the front lawn, a gaggle of kids played a rowdy game of soccer. Gabe showed little interest in them.

"Uncle Rafe hates me because I told on his dad."

She put a hand on his shoulder. "He doesn't hate you."

"Then why do I have to stay here?"

She had no answer. When she'd met McTavish at the mining station, he'd been kind, selfless, willing to stand up for what he thought was right. Now he kowtowed to the board members while sneaking behind their backs to undermine their directives, and he treated Gabe like so much extra baggage. His confrontation with his father seemed to have deprived him of his backbone.

Shannon and Ben Nighthorse weren't related to Gabe by either blood or marriage. McTavish had no business off-loading his responsibility for Gabe to them. Most importantly, it wasn't what the boy wanted. But there was little chance McTavish would listen to her. She'd work on Shannon instead.

"Your uncle has a lot going on right now. Give him some time," she said.

Inside, they found Shannon serving iced tea to a uniformed security guard. She gave the man a hard stare. Gabe was an eyewitness to a murder. He should have a full protection detail, not just one lazy officer lounging in the cool of the house instead of on duty outside.

The officer finished his tea before putting the glass on the counter, thanking Shannon, and strolling out.

"Gabe, I've given you the guest room. When things settle down, you and I can figure out how you'd like to decorate it. Do you want to put your clothes away?"

The boy gave Kama a mournful look and left. Shannon frowned at his back.

"Is it true that Gabe claims to have seen my father murder Aaron?"

"He saw Cullen stun me and slip out of the house. Since Goldman died only moments earlier and no one else was in the house, it follows that Cullen killed him."

"That's impossible. Aaron was his best friend."

"Your father lives fifteen minutes away by flyer, yet he arrived at Goldman's minutes after Dzandarova contacted him. How do you explain that?"

Her forehead creased, and her mouth drew into a firm line. "He has friends. Maybe he was visiting in the neighborhood."

"He denies he was anywhere near Goldman's house all day, but Gabe saw him there earlier. Why say that if he didn't have anything to hide?"

Shannon chewed her lip. "I expected Gabe to have issues from losing his parents. I didn't think he'd tell such outrageous lies. He'll need to see a psychologist immediately, before he causes more trouble."

Kama raised her eyebrows. "Why do you think he's lying?"

"I can only assume he's doing it in a misguided attempt to help Rafe take revenge against our father."

"You don't believe your father is a murderer, but you think your brother would use a distraught eleven-year old to frame him? What kind of crazy family is this?"

Color rose in Shannon's cheeks. "Thank you for seeing Gabe home. I think it's time for you to leave."

Kama ground her teeth and walked away. Gabe couldn't stay here. She had to get McTavish to see that. A tall order if they weren't speaking. A fresh wave of regret washed over her.

She found Gabe in his new room, sitting on the bed beside his unopened suitcase.

"Hey, Gabe, I have to go." She drew his arm to her and punched her contact information into the boy's nanocom. "That's my hi-pri channel. If you need me, you call, okay?"

He threw his arms around her and squeezed. "I'll miss you."

"I'll miss you, too." She fought back tears. Shannon's words about seeing a psychologist rang in her head. "About last night, I believe what you said about seeing Mr. McTavish. Don't let anyone make you change your story."

Outside, the sun beat down, any hint of cool morning air burned away. Her thoughts turned to the broken cooling system at the contractor compound and how unpleasant it would be going through Goldman's files in the stifling heat. But the sooner she found the blackmailer and proved Cullen guilty, the sooner she could leave.

The rental flyer was gone. The security car still stood at the curb, engine purring. Kama stormed over to it. Before she reached it, the officer got out.

She gestured to her empty parking place. "Where's my ride?"

"The rental agency came for it. It was overdue. Besides, contractors aren't allowed to use flyers," he said with a smirk. He opened the back door of the security car. "Get in. Chief Dzandarova wants to see you."

16

My father a murderer? There had to be another explanation. Despite what he'd told Kama, he'd seen convictions won on less evidence. Maybe it was karma. The old man would find out what it was like to stand falsely accused, just as he had. Regardless, it wasn't his case to pursue. Alana could sort it out.

Rafe straightened his tie and ran a hand through his hair. A smoky odor clung to his suit jacket, and he wrinkled his nose. His room had been spared, but smoke from the fire in the hotel lobby had tainted everything in his building. He still wore yesterday's shirt and tie, the only clothing he had that didn't reek like a bonfire. He hoped no one noticed.

Then he remembered that the impression he made on the board no longer mattered. He'd deliver his resignation and be on his way, back to the people who cared about him, back to his home and life in Mumbai. He wondered if he'd ever see Kama again, and fresh pain stabbed at him.

Taking a deep breath, he stepped into the boardroom. His father sat in the chair previously occupied by Aaron. The other board members lined each side of the table, and their faces all turned toward him as he slipped into his own seat.

His father glared at him, then turned his attention to his nanocom. "Your presence isn't required."

Rafe's face heated. *Fine.* He'd write a letter of resignation on his way to the shuttleport and send it before liftoff. He pushed his chair back, preparing to rise.

Alberto Cobo, a short, swarthy middle-aged man lifted a hand to stop him. Rafe glanced around the table. The other board members exchanged uncomfortable looks, and that surprised him.

Cobo cleared his throat. "I believe the board would like to have Rafael present today. As Aaron pointed out, he's an expert on security, and we need to safeguard River City against further violence."

Heads nodded agreement, although no one met his father's gaze. A chill settled over the room. What was going on? He pulled his chair back to the table.

"Let's get started," his father said. "We'll take the official vote on the chairmanship first."

Another round of uncomfortable looks circled the table. Cobo, the group's de facto spokesperson, rubbed his finger on his upper lip.

"I think we'd prefer to postpone naming the next chairman. It would be unseemly to select a replacement so quickly following Aaron's death."

His father drew back, fire in his eyes. "You didn't think it unseemly when Aaron named Rafael CEO within hours of Leon's death."

"That was different. No questions surrounded Leon's death."

"No questions surround Aaron's death. He was murdered by that contract woman Alana found in the house."

More looks, and then another of the board members said, "There seem to be other... persons of interest."

So Gabe's accusation had leaked. EcoMech couldn't afford the scandal if his father was arraigned after he'd been made chairman. Rafe shifted in his chair, uncomfortable with the turn in conversation and uncertain what he should do about it.

"Who?" his father demanded. A vein throbbed at his temple.

Cobo eyed Rafe, and Rafe stared back. They didn't expect him to answer, did they? He wouldn't be the one to stick the knife in.

"You think Rafael is a suspect?" his father asked, his eyebrows lifting and a grim smile touching his lips. "Did you think you could wheedle a confession from him here at the meeting? He's too clever a liar for that."

Cobo cleared his throat. "Rafael isn't the subject of the investigation. We understand questions have been raised about your involvement."

Slow realization crawled across his father's face. For the first time, the man's arrogant confidence faltered, and Rafe felt sympathy for him. The other board members straightened, perhaps emboldened by the display of weakness.

"We think," said Cobo, "it would be best if you stepped away from the board for a time."

His father's stricken expression paled. Part of him wanted to rejoice that his father had finally received his just rewards. Part of him was sickened that he'd had the thought. He'd sworn he'd never be that kind of person. Everyone deserved a fair trial based on facts, not a lynching driven by rumors, innuendo, and incorrect assumptions.

"Gentlemen," Rafe said, drawing everyone's attention, "in my experience, it's best to reserve judgment until the investigation is complete. Frequently, information gathered in the early stages is out of context and misinterpreted. Only when a crime is exposed in its entirety can observations and actions be explained."

"Rumors or truth, they all affect the share price," Cobo said. "The board feels that distancing ourselves from the matter is our safest strategy."

His father's face hardened, his hands curled into fists on the table. How many years had his father served with these men? Now they turned on him like wolves on an injured deer. And for what? What benefit would they receive by barring his father from the chairmanship?

In a flash of intuition, Rafe saw Leon's blackmail and Aaron's murder from a new angle. What if driving Leon to make bad business decisions had been part of a larger scheme to ruin the company, not just an attempt to take over the CEO slot? Aaron would have found a way to counter the downturn—had a plan already—and so he had to go. Now his father was under suspicion and being pressured to give up his position. Like dominos falling, someone was removing the key players.

Who would be next? The Madison Trust controlled nearly thirty percent of EcoMech's stock, and Rafe controlled the Madison Trust. But could he count on being targeted before the rest of his family? What if they went after Shannon first? Or Gabe? He could never forgive himself if harm came to them and he could have prevented it. He had to stay—at least until he'd unmasked Aaron's killer and assured his family's safety.

"I assume you intend to name someone as interim chairman," Rafe said examining the sharp, ambitious men gathered at the table with an investigator's eyes.

"Yes, of course," Cobo responded. "We can't be seen as disorganized and unable to govern the company."

"No, you wouldn't want to look disorganized." Rafe said. He needed to put a crimp in the plans of anyone trying to grind down the company. He needed to remain in control. But how to do that?

"Of course, anyone named interim chairman might be seen as someone who had a motive to remove Aaron Goldman, particularly if the heir apparent for the position has suddenly been... removed from contention."

Cobo's eyes widened. "No one would dare make such an accusation."

"Certainly no reasonable person would. But the press are so rarely reasonable. They'll latch onto any rumor they think might sell copy. In such an atmosphere, they're bound to start digging into closets looking for skeletons." Rafe put on his most charming grin. "How's your closet, Alberto?"

Cobo's dark brows inched up his forehead, and he looked around the table. A few of the gathered men made eye contact. Most averted their eyes while they straightened their ties or picked lint from their sleeves. Good. They'd understood his threat.

"What do you suggest?" Cobo asked, voice wary.

Rafe steepled his fingers and did his best to look thoughtful. He avoided glancing down the table, but from his peripheral vision, he could see the surprise on his father's face.

"Give people what they expect. The PR department has a statement about Aaron's death ready. It's innocuous enough. Let my father read it, and then let the PR folks and Alana handle any further communications."

"And if the press ask about Aaron's replacement?" one of the others asked.

"Alberto's initial response will suffice. It would be unseemly to name Aaron's replacement without first memorializing him. Agreed?"

Cobo gave a grudging nod, and others followed. Awkward silence hung over the group.

"You mentioned security concerns?" Rafe prompted.

"Alana's incompetent. I—" His father glanced at the others. "*We* order you to replace her immediately."

"She's understaffed and doing the best she can in the circumstances." His hands knotted on the table. So this was to be his thanks for preserving his father's dignity and place of importance.

"We can't have more riots," Cobo said. "They're hurting our share price and disrupting operations, to say nothing of putting everyone on Harvest at risk. The contractors have to be controlled and EcoMech property protected."

Cullen slapped the table. "Fire the lot of them. Bring in new workers, people thankful to have jobs, ones who won't complain endlessly."

"Replacing our contract staff would take months and seriously impact our ability to keep the place running."

"Then hire more security," said another.

Rafe thought about the sea of red ink drowning the company. Where did they expect him to get the budget? He didn't think they'd be willing to pay for it out of their fat salaries.

"Properly trained and equipped security forces are expensive. It would be less costly and more effective if we addressed the contractors' concerns, met with them to—"

"Nonsense," his father said. "I've been contacted by Total Security. They've offered us very good rates on additional forces. They have trained investigators prepared to take command of the inquiry into Aaron's death."

"They're bargain basement rent-a-cops," Rafe protested.

"If their rates are affordable and we'll have additional boots on the ground to protect EcoMech property, then I think we should accept their offer," said Cobo. "Unless you can find a company willing to do the same work for less."

Rafe looked around the table and saw that hiring Total Security was a foregone conclusion. He might be able to win this fight, but if he did, it would emasculate his father, whose position was already tenuous.

His objections stuck in his throat. "I suggest that for continuity, we leave Aaron's murder in Alana's hands. If she's relieved of the day-to-day security operations, she'll have the time and resources necessary to expedite the investigation."

A humorless grin twisted his father's lips as the man savored his victory. "If she doesn't have a suspect in custody by end of day tomorrow, I think we should turn the matter over to Total Security."

The men nodded again. Rafe wanted to pound his fists against the wood. Instead, he clenched his teeth and nodded with them.

☠   ☠   ☠

Rafe hung his smelly jacket over the back of his leather desk chair. *Leon's chair*. His office at Security Partners had been a quarter the size of this one, a bare room with a plain desk, a fabric chair, and no windows whose view might distract him. He could host a meeting of twenty in this office, and it wouldn't seem crowded. Expensive paintings graced the walls, and equally costly sculptures stood on shelves or tables. Maybe he could sell them and hire *real* security forces.

His executive assistant, Bob, bustled in across the soft carpet. The heavenly aroma of hot coffee steamed from the cup in his hand. The mousy, affable man raised eyebrows at Rafe's appearance, but only for a moment. He'd survived two years as Leon's assistant, something of a record for the mercurial former CEO known to fire workers for the tiniest of transgressions. He'd proved himself invaluable helping Rafe navigate management processes at EcoMech.

If his father wanted someone else in the CEO position, he ought to consider Bob, even if he *was* a contractor. The little man knew more about running the company than anyone on the planet. He also made a damn fine cup of coffee.

"Morning, sir." Bob set the cup on the desk. "Very sad to hear about Mr. Goldman. I've rescheduled the two early meetings you missed to this afternoon."

"Thanks. And you can drop the 'sir'. I'm just another EcoMech peon, like you."

"Yes, sir." Bob flashed him a smile and placed a stack of filmies on his desk. "Would you like me to get you a change of clothing, sir?"

"What's left in my closet isn't in any better shape than what I'm wearing. It all needs a trip to the cleaners." He dropped into his chair and took a sip of coffee.

"Leave it to me, sir." His assistant scurried out.

Before attacking the mountain of filmies accumulating on the desk, he scrolled through his messages. There were hundreds of them, all people wanting a few minutes to meet with him. He didn't want to meet them. What was the point? Once he bagged Aaron's killer, he'd return to Mumbai. Better not to see the faces of the thousands unknowingly facing layoffs.

At some point after he solved Aaron's murder, he'd have to bring his father and the board up to date about the state of EcoMech and share Aaron's plan for saving it. Then his father could have whomever he wanted for CEO, assuming he could find anyone foolish enough to risk their reputation on a lost cause.

Without Aaron's clout, the company would never win refinancing from the tight-fisted bankers, and without refinancing, EcoMech had no hope of surviving. In the meantime, he needed to keep the corporation's financial state under wraps.

Bob knocked and entered, showing two people in. One was a short, round middle-aged fellow of Indian subcontinent origins who introduced himself as Raj Bose from Caligo Corp. The other was a petite, striking Chinese woman dressed in a red silk jacket and skirt that set off her shiny black hair, dark eyes, and red lips.

"I'm Ivy Tang." She offered a hand with long red nails that matched her dress and lipstick.

"A pleasure." Rafe showed her to one of the visitor chairs that faced his desk. Bose took the other chair. Rafe wanted to be rid of them as quickly as possible.

Ms. Tang lowered her voice to a somber tone. "A terrible business, this murder of Aaron Goldman."

Bose nodded his agreement, lips pursed. "And coming on top of your labor strife and Leon Goldman's death, you must have your hands full. Not an auspicious start to your tenure as CEO."

Rafe shrugged, annoyed by their deferential attitudes. "We all have our crosses to bear. What can I do for you?"

Tang and Bose exchanged a glance, and then Tang turned a radiant smile on him. It caused another twinge of annoyance. Given his reputation, both his business foes and those seeking favors used beautiful women as their weapon of choice against him. His defenses rose.

"Caligo Corp would like to make EcoMech a business offer. Over the past eighteen months, EcoMech has fallen on hard times. Stock prices continue to slide, your latest release of harvesters has been plagued by quality issues that have alienated customers, and a growing number of analysts have changed their recommendations from 'Hold' to 'Sell.'

"Quarterly reports paint a dismal outlook for the company. Earnings are projected to drop, costs skyrocket, and profit margins... well, profits are almost non-existent. Dividend payments have been cut to the bone."

Rafe struggled against the urge to fidget. They weren't telling him anything he didn't already know, but they were using precious minutes he needed to spend finding Aaron's killer so he could go home.

"I'm aware of the issues facing EcoMech. You mentioned a proposal?"

Bose leaned forward. "Caligo is in a strong financial position. Profits are high, debt low, outlook rosy. All we lack are the right kind of investment opportunities in which to sink our profits. We believe that EcoMech may be such an opportunity. We propose a merger of Caligo and EcoMech."

"A merger?" Rafe rocked back in his chair. "Caligo is a healthcare and pharmaceutical company, and EcoMech is focused on agricultural equipment manufacturing, development of genetically modified plants, and food production. How does a merger between the companies make any kind of sense?"

"We have more in common than you think," Tang said. "We both engage in genetic research, for example. We're both in the colony business, and we both struggle to meet EA population growth mandates for our colonies. Caligo needs technical assistance to increase food production on Bliss—which has proved resistant to our terraforming efforts—and EcoMech can supply it. EcoMech must accept more health-challenged workers to fulfill EA-required population quotas for your colony. Caligo can provide medical support to make them productive."

It still didn't make sense. Maybe he was just too tired.

"Do you have something specific you can leave with me?"

Bose pulled a stick drive from his pocket and placed it on the desk. "We'd prefer that our negotiations remain confidential. If word of our discussion leaks out, it could have a profound impact on both our stock prices."

"I understand." Rafe rose.

"We'll need a firm commitment within seventy-two hours." At Rafe's surprised look, Bose gave a deprecating smile. "I'm sorry, but we have other opportunities that require an immediate decision."

He shook their hands and showed them out. Then he plugged in the drive and looked at their proposal.

No one put a deal like this on the table with a seventy-two hour deadline for a response. He'd have to run it by the board first, and then the lawyers would want a week at least reading all the fine print. Once they'd finished, the accountants would begin their analysis.

Was Caligo's proposal the salvation EcoMech needed? It wouldn't save the company for Gabe, but it would ensure the livelihood of thousands of workers and the funds of millions of investors. Kama would get her wish. Oasis could partner with the new, merged company and develop its gate system.

He'd be freed from his obligation to Aaron without leaving EcoMech in the lurch. He'd be rid of his family and back in Mumbai heading his own company again without appearing to have cut and run.

Rafe spun his chair to look over the sun-washed corporate campus, pulled out his ball, and rolled it in his palms.

Or was this the next move by someone bent on destroying EcoMech? An offer from one of EcoMech's competitors, perhaps Ag Intergalactic—or a bid from one of the more aggressive investment consortiums—made more sense than this proposal from Caligo. Was Caligo part of a conspiracy to take down EcoMech, or just a savvy corporation looking for investment opportunities, as Bose stated? Maybe he was seeing conspiracies where none existed.

He crossed to the door, swung it open, and addressed Bob.

"Get hold of Bert Gerlach, Lev Kozlov, and Lars Svenson. I want to meet with each of them in their offices this afternoon."

"Yes, sir. Mr. Kozlov may be a problem. I think he's at the orbital station supervising construction, but I'll check."

"The appointment I had with Bose and Tang, was that something originally scheduled with Leon?"

"No, sir. I was contacted yesterday morning by the executive assistant for Caligo's CEO and asked to arrange the meeting." Worry furrowed Bob's brow. "Would you have preferred that I check with you first? With the call coming from that level, I assumed…"

"You did the right thing." Rafe turned to go, and then stopped. "See if you can find out when Mr. Bose and Ms. Tang arrived on Harvest, please. But do it quietly."

Bob's eyebrows twitched. "Yes, sir."

Rafe returned to his desk. Unbidden the image of dominos falling rose in his mind. He could stop the whole sequence if he could just prevent his father's domino from toppling. To do that, he needed to know the truth about his father's movements the previous night. With a guilty backward glance at the pile of filmies awaiting his attention, he strode from the office.

⚝ ⚝ ⚝

Rafe's father stood behind the podium in the main room of the conference center, thirty or so reporters gathered in the space designed for two hundred. It would have been better to hold the conference in a smaller room, one with side exits. *Never give reporters an opportunity to waylay you when you've finished speaking.* Rafe lingered by the glass wall at the opposite end of the space, trying to remain unnoticed, hidden by the glare of Harvest's harsh sun streaming through the tinted windows. He'd interview his father after the press conference.

He asked himself again whether his father was capable of murder. Gabe seemed so sure. He couldn't reconcile the two. His chest grew tight at the thought of confronting the old man. He shrugged his shoulders and drew in a couple of deep breaths trying to relax. It didn't work.

His father leaned into the microphone. "Ladies and gentlemen, I have a statement to make."

The crowd quieted. They reminded Rafe of a school of piranha, teeth bared in anticipation of a juicy meal. His father needed to convince the reporters the story of Aaron's death didn't have legs. He should exude calm control and stick with the script prepared by the PR department, avoiding any questions about EcoMech's labor issues.

"As you've heard, Aaron Goldman, co-founder and chairman of EcoMech died in his home last night. We're all saddened by his passing. His contributions to EcoMech are well-documented and too numerous to list. We'll honor his memory by closing all EcoMech offices galaxy-wide for one hour beginning at 12:00 Harvest time today. The investigation into his death is ongoing, so of course I can't comment on that. But I assure you that EcoMech is in capable hands and will continue to prosper."

His father should leave now and turn the conference over to the PR department spokesperson who hovered at his shoulder, before the feeding frenzy started. Thirty hands went in the air, and reporters shouted a cacophony of questions.

"Please." His father waved them down. "One at a time. We'll begin with you."

Rafe groaned inwardly. The last thing EcoMech needed were off-the-cuff comments from someone rumored to be involved in Aaron's death. He resisted the urge to rush forward and shove his father away from the microphone, even though that's what he would have done with any of Security Partners' clients who were in the same situation.

The selected reporter grinned. "Can you tell us how Aaron Goldman died?"

"The investigation is ongoing. Chief of Security Alana Dzandarova will have a statement in a few hours."

"Is it true he was murdered in a home invasion?" another reporter shouted.

"Yes," his father snapped while Rafe gritted his teeth. "Next question?"

A woman in a bright yellow dress flapped a hand. "Are there any suspects?"

"No comment. As I said, the investigation is ongoing."

"I heard that EcoMech Security had you in for questioning this morning," the woman persisted. "Do you deny that?"

His father glared down at her while the PR manager fidgeted behind him. "Aaron Goldman was a dear friend of mine. I offered my assistance to help our security chief trace his movements before his death."

More lies. Hadn't his father learned his lesson about prevaricating in a murder inquiry? Rafe debated taking the podium. He would only anger his father if he stepped forward. He reached in his pocket for his ball, but it was empty.

"I see a lot of burned-out businesses across the street from the campus," a man in the back row said. "Is that from the labor riots? What's the damage estimate?"

"We're still working on the estimates," his father said. "But rest assured that the perpetrators will be punished. We have no tolerance for all this demonstration nonsense. The contractors should be grateful we give them jobs. Anymore violence and we'll replace them all."

Rafe shook his head and thrust his hands in his pockets. What the hell was wrong with the PR man? He should have shouldered in by now, before his father sank the company for good.

A scruffy, pot-bellied man in a rumple shirt and pants pushed to the front of the group. "I heard an eye witness puts you at Goldman's house at the time of the killing. What do you have to say about that?"

His father's face flushed. "We track all our contract workers, and I can say irrefutably that one of them was in the house at the time of Aaron Goldman's death. She's the one you should be questioning. She's typical of the contract riffraff we get these days. We're forced to track their every move or they'd rob us blind."

The woman in the yellow dress pushed the rumpled reporter aside. "So you're saying all contractors are thieves and killers?"

Rafe sucked in a breath while his father fumbled for a reply. If they didn't have contract riots start within the hour, it would be no small miracle.

"Where's your new CEO, Mr. McTavish?" another reporter asked into the silence. "Doesn't he want to share a podium with someone known to be a 'person of interest' in a murder investigation?"

Rafe plastered a smile on his face, pulled his hands from his pockets, and hurried forward. By the time he'd reached the back of the crowd, his father's brows were pulled so low his eyes could barely be seen. The man's body had gone rigid.

"Sorry, folks," Rafe said while pushing through the crowd.

He mounted the dais and slipped between the podium and his

father, blocking him from the microphone. "Sorry to be late. Guess I got turned around. It's a big campus."

He added an endearing grin and a sheepish nod. Chuckles rose from the crowd. To his left, his father looked thunderous. To his right, the PR spokesman heaved a sigh of relief.

The rows of chandeliers overhead winked twice and went out. Sunlight streamed in the glass at the far end so they could still see, but with the lights off, the reporters lost their network connections to EcoMech's light-based computer network. Groans and complaints rose from the group.

"To clarify," Rafe said, sure it was too late to get his platitudes included in any reports, "we value our contract staff. Regretfully, a few have engaged in unlawful acts, but most of our staff are hard-working men and women who make it possible for EcoMech to operate successfully. We wouldn't be the company we are without them, and we appreciate how they've focused on their jobs despite the disruptions we've had."

Cullen shoved in. "That doesn't mean we'll let them get away with murder."

Hot air flooded down from the ventilation ducts.

"Sorry," Rafe said pulling the microphone his direction. "We're having some maintenance issues. I'm sure they'll be resolved shortly."

The woman in the yellow dress smiled up at him. *A vulture masquerading as a canary.* He'd have to find out who she was. And the scruffy guy, too. They knew far more than they should about the investigation.

"We're surprised to see you two on the same stage," she said. "We'd heard you hadn't spoken in years. Is it true there's bad blood between you?"

"Have you seen what EA charges for intergalactic calls these days?" Rafe quipped. "How can a family afford to stay in touch?"

The giant view screen that covered the wall behind them lit up, and a litany of demands appeared: equal rights for contractors, schools for contract children, open housing, an end to the curfew. At the end of the list, 'CONTRACTORS REVOLT' scrawled across the panel in blood-red letters. Reporters held their nanocoms up to capture the screen. The lights flickered on. They punched in connections, sending their video to news outlets around the galaxy.

"What the hell's going on?" his father growled. "Damn contractors! I'll have them all arrested."

Alana trotted past outside the glass wall, following an employee in a maintenance uniform. A security guard, Kama, and two employees wearing dress shirts and ties trailed in the security chief's wake. Rafe frowned before remembering where he stood. He changed his expression to a careful neutral.

What was Kama doing here? How dare she continue her sabotage. Did she think he wouldn't press charges? Or did she believe she'd covered her tracks so well that he could never prove she was the hacker?

"To wrap this up, I'd like to thank you all for coming and express my deep regrets for the loss of Aaron Goldman. He was a man who—"

The ear-splitting wail of fire alarms shattered the air. Seconds after that, the overhead fire-suppression sprinklers came on, soaking everyone. The reporters stampeded to the doors. Rafe and his father ran after them.

Outside, the reporters trailed away, probably headed back to their hotels for a change of clothes. Rafe envied them. His father wiped water from his face with a jacket sleeve while cursing under his breath.

"You behaved like a fool in there," his father said. "Making jokes and pandering to those reporters. I was ashamed to be in the same room with you."

Rafe withered under his father's tirade, and his hands shook. It took two tries to get a reply out.

"I was trying to help."

"Everything was fine until you showed up. Now Leon's dead, and I've lost my best friend. Go back to your parties and your whores, and leave us alone."

His father stormed away across the grass.

17

Kama stepped out of the ladies room at the data center properly dressed in her gray Oasis coveralls and strolled down the empty hall to the control room. Inside, she tossed the wet EcoMech coveralls in the nearest trash receptacle.

The IT manager stared, open-mouthed. "As a contract worker at EcoMech, you're required to dress in clothing that meets company guidelines."

The security chief was desperate to catch the hacker, and the bozos in the IT department hadn't a clue. She'd been reluctant to get involved—until she'd gotten drenched at the conference center. While she didn't want an audience when she squared off with the hacker, she wouldn't put up with the hacker's insolence.

Kama arched an eyebrow at the manager. She pulled a filmie from her duffel and proffered it to Dzandarova. "Thumbprint in the box at the bottom."

Dzandarova dropped her towel on the desk and took the filmie. "What's this?"

"Standard Oasis consulting contract."

"But you're already on contract!" the IT manager protested. "We're not paying you twice."

"Fine. When's the next bus to the shuttleport? Or has your network marauder shut that down, too?"

The security chief glared at the manager, and then she applied her thumb to the contract.

The manager's hands clenched. "She's still a contractor. She has to wear appropriate attire."

"Section 23 of the contract says I wear Oasis' colors." She stashed the contract in her bag before the manager could grab it. "Now can we get on with it? Or maybe you want to debate how many angels can dance on an event horizon first?"

Kama scanned the data center. They were two stories underground, surrounded by thick concrete walls, and insulated from further chicanery by the hacker. The data center had its own power supply and fire suppression systems independent of the corporate network. At least EcoMech had gotten that much right.

On the far side of a glass wall, racks of computers talked to every building and every nanocom on Harvest through EcoMech's light network. On this side of the glass, computer technicians sat at workstations and watched helplessly as their network malfunctioned. No green coveralls in here. It was all trousers and dress shirts and imbeciles who didn't have any idea how to stop a criminal like the one they faced.

"I'll need a private room with a large vid screen. And access to a super-admin account."

"We won't give you access. That's against company policy. You can tell one of our people what you want done, and if we think it's advisable, we'll do it."

Kama laughed and stepped back into the hallway. Two doors down, she looked through a window into a conference room. A table for twelve ringed by chairs filled most of the space. A two-meter square vid screen covered an end wall. She went inside and set her duffel on the table. Dzandarova and the manager joined her, one of his underlings in tow.

"I need my stunner back." Kama dragged equipment from her bag.

The security chief crossed her arms. "I don't think so."

"What's that?" The manager pointed to a black device six by ten centimeters, and four centimeters thick.

"It's a nanocom." She pulled a similar unit out and stripped off the back. Half the guts were missing, currently part of her stunner that Dzandarova refused to return. She cross-wired it to the unusually large nanocom she'd placed on the table.

"And that?"

"A decrypter."

Next came her data storage, a black cube a third of a meter square. *Thank Lakshmi I didn't cannibalize this.*

"I suppose that's another nanocom," the manager sneered.

"Of course not. Any moorhk can see it's a data brick." She pulled on her VR gloves and spread the metallic cloth on the table. The manager wasn't idiot enough to ask about them. She flipped a thumb at the underling. "This the guy I'm giving instructions to?"

"This is Ricardo. He has admin privileges on the system. I will evaluate your requests, and if I approve, Ricardo will carry them out."

Kama smiled at the tech. "Okay, Ricky, bring up the network on screen."

The guy wasn't any older than her. His forehead glistened and damp circles formed under his arms. He tapped at his nanocom, and a network status report filled the screen. Alternating green and red text scrolled by as the hacker moved from system to system disrupting buildings across the campus.

"The red text is where we have malfunctions: false fire alarms, power cuts, network interruptions," Ricardo said.

Kama stifled a laugh. "Really? I did not know that."

Then she realized that the tech was probably speaking for his boss's benefit, not hers. Why did the incompetent ones always rise to the top? She dropped into the system via a hidden account she'd set up the previous night while hunting the nefarious interloper.

"Well?" the manager said. "Are you going to do something?"

"I already am." She kept an eye on the screen, but saw no pattern to the chaos. The disruptions had as much organization as a three-year-old child's finger painting. A clever hacker then. Not one she could easily predict.

She raised her hands and wiggled her fingers. The scrolling list shrank to a small box on the lower right corner of the screen. She divided the remainder of the screen into a dozen additional boxes, each displaying reports from different subsystems.

The manager crowded closer. "What did you do?"

"Ricky brought up the subsystems: HVAC, network communications, ID tracking, security cameras, and a few others."

Ricardo glanced at her and swallowed.

The manager waggled a finger at him. "You don't do anything unless I tell you."

Kama split the windows again, and code scrolled past at a furious rate in the bottom half of each window. She took it all in, getting a feel for how the invader operated. Then she waved her gloved hands, and code ripped down the metallic fabric.

Ricardo stared, his thick, dark brows drawn down. He looked up at her, and then continued reading the list of issues to his boss. She grinned, but only for a moment. The duel was about to start.

She loosed her bots into the EcoMech system, switched all the windows to scrolling code, and overlaid the screen with a transparent map of the campus buildings, each color coded according to their current malfunctions.

"Building 10, fire alarm, mark. Well, Ricky?"

"No, nothing going on in ten—oh, yes, there it is."

"Building 3, lights out, mark."

"Um... yes, power outage."

"Let the games begin," Kama muttered. "You can go now, Ricky."

"What?" The manager turned to his tech. "What's she done?"

"I don't know for sure, sir. She has access to everything, and I think maybe she loaded some code onto the system. She's predicting where the hacker will strike before he does."

"Chief Dzandarova, I want her under arrest now."

"Is that right, Ms. Bhatia? Have you illegally broken into the EcoMech network?"

"Building 4, HVAC offline; Building 5, power outage, mark. My contract stipulates that I'll have access to any necessary systems to analyze the nature of the issue, and I can load any software required provided it's legally licensed from the copyright holder and removed at the completion of the contract. It's in the fine print near the bottom. Back to Building 10. You like Building 10, don't you?"

She wished everyone would just get out of the way. She'd had no sleep the previous night and didn't need the distraction. Once she engaged her opponent, she'd need all her concentration.

"Have your people lock down every building. No one goes in or out until we nab the culprit. I'll have his location soon." Kama looked at the manager. "Bring me a cup of hot tea. Don't forget the cream and sugar."

The manager stormed out, followed by Ricardo. Kama grinned. *Good riddance.* She didn't need their help. She didn't need anyone's help for the task ahead.

Dzandarova eyed her. "You sure you can catch this guy?"

Kama clenched her fists and stared hard at the data scrolling across the screen. "Consider it done."

"What's it going to cost me?"

"I want my stunner back."

The security chief laughed.

18

Rafe glowered at Kama through the conference room window. "What's she doing in there?"

"I don't speak Hindi, but I'm pretty sure a lot of it's swearing. She's been at it for two hours." Alana stifled a yawn. "She said she could catch the hacker."

He'd be interested to see that, since Kama was the one who'd broken in to begin with. Why was she pretending to chase someone else through the system? To throw Alana off her scent? The screen at the end of the conference room showed a dizzying array of computer logs, code, and surveillance videos of buildings all over campus.

"I meant why is she involved in catching the hacker? What's EcoMech's IT staff doing?"

"Nothing as of ninety minutes ago. They tried to kick her out of the system, and she shut down the control room. She and the hacker are the only ones with full access now."

"Whatever possessed you to let her have access in the first place?"

The security chief frowned at him. "She came with you. Are you telling me you don't trust her?"

He'd thought in time, she'd open up, stop hiding secrets from him. He thought she'd display better judgment. But leopards didn't change their spots and criminals rarely changed their behaviors.

"Besides, the techs couldn't catch our guy last time."

He turned his attention on Alana. "Last time?"

"About a week ago, an anonymous mail circulated stating that if we didn't fix the climate control in the buildings at the contractors' compound, we'd have a network outage. Two days later, we had problems with the network in Building 6. IT assured me it was just a bad router. Our hacker took credit.

"Now IT admits they don't know what went wrong in Building 6, nor have they been able to trace the source of the mail. When the hacker struck again today, they also revealed that there *may* have been unauthorized intrusions dating as far back as a month ago."

Rafe's head spun, and he put a hand against the wall. What had he done? He'd been so tired last night, so stressed out by confronting his family, so guilt-ridden about Aaron's death that he hadn't listened. Kama's words came back to him now. *Someone hacked the network.* She'd been trying to tell him, trying to help, and he'd blamed her for Aaron's death. He'd told her to leave.

Alana took his elbow. "Are you ill? Should I call the medics?"

He blinked down at her. "No, I..."

He had to talk to Kama, had to apologize. He had to convince her to forgive him. He stepped to the door and twisted the knob. It didn't budge. Rattling it got him no further. He stepped back and gestured at the door. "Open it."

"I can't. When she locked the techs out of the system, the manager stormed down here to throw her out. The door wouldn't open for him, either." Alana cocked her head. "Is there something I should know about your girl?"

Rafe considered kicking down the damn door. Instead, he moved to the window and pressed a hand to the glass, hoping Kama would look his way. But her eyes never flickered from the monitor. Why hadn't he listened? More important, what could he do to make it up to her?

"Is there something you need, Mr. McTavish?" the security chief asked. "You seem... disturbed."

Rafe turned from the window. Alana watched him, her eyes telegraphing worry mixed with suspicion. How long had he stood there waiting for Kama's attention? He didn't know. Time had slowed to a crawl. He sucked in a deep breath but still couldn't get enough oxygen.

"I came here to tell you we're bringing in Total Security. They'll take over day-to-day operations. Your staff will focus on the investigation into Aaron's death."

Alana stiffened. "If you're not satisfied with my work, I'll hand over my resignation. You don't have to ease me out."

"This isn't about your performance. You need additional resources. Total Security is a stopgap measure until I can address the contractors' issues. Aaron's murder is the priority, which is why you'll work it."

"You aren't concerned that I might arrest your father? Or maybe that's what you want."

"I expect you to make an arrest based on solid evidence, not the whims of your boss."

Admiration flashed in her eyes, and a tiny smile curled her lips. "And your girl in there, do I let her keep chasing the hacker?"

Rafe looked in the window again. Kama sat cross-legged on the end of the conference table, waving her hands like some wizard drawing runes in the air. Even if he could read the code on the vid, the data moved too fast for him to so much as recognize the letters.

But Kama not only read it, she could recite back every line. He'd seen her do it at the mining station. If anyone had any hope of catching the hacker in real time, it was her.

"Give her anything she asks for."

☠ ☠ ☠

Rafe climbed the stairs of Building 14 by the light of the battery-powered emergency beacons. At least this building seemed to be having a respite from the ear-splitting wail of the fire alarms.

He puffed his way to the tenth floor and promised himself he'd get some coffee and aspirin as soon as he finished his meeting with Lev Kozlov. He intended to take the measure of the production manager and find out where he was during Aaron's murder.

He found Lev's office unoccupied. It was only slightly larger than any of the other offices on the floor, about twelve by fifteen feet, with no antechamber for an executive assistant. Windows covered most of the two exterior walls and flooded the room with sunlight.

A standard issue workstation setup stood to the right of the door, an upholstered swivel chair behind it. A drift of filmie schematics covered the desktop. Sample chips of metal alloy and greasy, broken gears littered the shelves of a bookcase below one window. A visitor's chair was shoved back into a corner. It was the office he'd expect a mid-level manager to occupy, not that of a CEO-in-waiting. He wondered whether this was Lev's choice or some punishment inflicted by Leon.

Rafe checked his nanocom. He was three minutes late for their meeting. He drew his ball from his pocket and rolled it between his palms while he took a closer look at an artist's rendition of the orbital station tacked to one wall. Had the blackmailer forced Leon into building it, just like he'd forced Leon to buy the mining station? It hadn't been on Leon's list of blackmailer demands.

What CEO in his right mind put a manufacturing facility on this side of the jump gate system when the raw materials, the suppliers, and the customers were on the other side? EcoMech would pay hefty gate charges to bring in every scrap of material, only to pay more charges to get the finished harvesters back through the gates to Earth. They ought to name it Leon's Folly.

What part had Lev played in the decision-making? Rafe had known the man when they were both teenagers and remembered him as a popular, good-looking guy six years older than himself. With a twinge of jealousy, he also remembered how the girls drooled over Lev, a charismatic leader, while Rafe had played the school clown, unable to control his hyperactivity.

He checked the time again. Fifteen minutes and still no Lev. No message to explain his tardiness, either. He'd be damned if he'd wait all day. He bounced the ball hard against the floor, pocketed it, and walked out. He trotted down the stairs, crossed the lobby, and pushed through the building's glass doors.

Harvest's afternoon heat slammed into him. A security guard nearby glanced his direction and nodded.

In the parking lot, a flyer eased down to the pavement on whisper quiet fans. It had the pointed nose and lean, racy lines of a jet fighter, not the typical car-with-wings shape of most of Harvest's craft. Oversized nacelles graced the ends of stubby wings fore and aft. The body was longer than Rafe expected in a two-seat model. Dual tail fins rose in a V behind the main compartment. The craft wore swirling blue and green EcoMech corporate colors. Sun glinted off the paint job, momentarily blinding him.

The flyer door opened, and Lev Kozlov stepped out. The production manager stretched his tall, muscular frame, then reached back in to withdraw a straw Stetson that he settled on his dark hair. His sleeveless t-shirt set off tanned arms and hung over well-worn jeans. His square-toed rawhide boots clip-clopped against the concrete walk as he sauntered up. He looked more like a cattle rancher just back from checking the herd than a high-level manager greeting his new boss.

"You're late," Rafe said, then wished he'd started with a softer approach. A hostile interrogation wouldn't get him the information he wanted.

A bemused smile touched the manager's lips. "I sent you a message, but I guess you didn't get it. Can't fly when the control grid's down. Alana might give me a ticket."

He bit back an angry retort to Lev's insolent excuse and walked back toward the building.

He scanned the man's attire. "Sorry if I interrupted your day off."

Lev looked Rafe up and down. "We do real work in my division, and we dress like it."

Fire alarms screamed from the building. A man and a woman in contractor coveralls pushed out, hands clapped over their ears. They brushed past Rafe and were stopped at the curb by the guard. Apparently Kama hadn't caught the hacker yet.

The manager huffed a laugh. "Guess you haven't instituted any of those fancy security measures your company's famous for. Or are you waiting for your experts to tell you what to do?"

Surprised by the quick attack, Rafe clamped his jaw shut, determined not to respond in kind. Leon's blackmailer had been patient and methodical, not someone to tip his hand with an open display of anger. Lev might not be the blackmailer, but that didn't preclude him from harboring resentment because he'd been passed over for promotion.

Lev jerked a thumb toward the parking lot. "Let's take a ride."

The flyer's two seats jammed together in the narrow fuselage, putting Rafe shoulder-to-shoulder with the older man. The body of the craft might be longer than normal, but the extra space hadn't been used to make the passenger compartment more comfortable. The bigger man's knees grazed the dash as he positioned his feet over the floor pedals.

Rafe strapped into the double-shoulder racing-style harness—which seemed overkill for a cruise around the city—and admired the brushed steel finish of the control panel. "Nice flyer."

Lev placed his hat in a hollow behind his seat and stroked the dash. "She's a prototype."

"You race?"

"Occasionally. Not like your brother did."

A twinge of guilt flickered through him at the mention of Miguel, dead seven years.

The flyer rose smoothly from the shimmering heat of the asphalt lot. Lev set their heading and waited for a response from the control grid. He didn't get one. That didn't stop him rising two hundred feet and cruising away above the campus.

"Thought you didn't want a ticket?"

"Rules don't apply if your name is McTavish." His knuckles whitened as he gripped the controller. "Or Goldman."

The flyer shot forward, pressing Rafe back in his seat. It occurred to him that the manager might be taking him for a one-way trip. No, too many people knew about their meeting. The building security guard had seen them leave together.

Lev slammed on the directional fans and banked the flyer through a corner that had the four-point harness cutting into Rafe's carotid artery.

"Leon was a piece of shit. I can't say I'm sorry to see him gone. But Aaron was a decent guy. Too bad someone topped him. He deserved better." Lev smirked his direction and brought the prototype back to level. "I hear your daddy's a 'person of interest.'"

Jump gates weren't the only way to travel faster than light, Rafe decided. Start a juicy rumor, and it would break all the rules of physics.

"It's early days."

"I expect you'll miss Aaron's guidance about how to run a great big company like EcoMech. But then, I guess your daddy can advise you."

The insult should have raised his ire. Instead, Rafe laughed. The only thing his father might 'advise' him about was when the next shuttle left and how he ought to be on it. He needed a good night's sleep before he got anymore loopy. Lev frowned and shifted in his seat.

They skimmed over the bluffs at the north edge of the city. Lev tugged on the stick to give a wider berth to a sea of six-foot tall, brick-red garraweed that waved beneath the flyer. The damn stuff was impossible to kill, toxic to herbivores, and useless for anything except spewing micro-spores that clogged machinery and choked humans. He wouldn't miss it when he returned to Earth.

"Where we headed?"

"Test flight. Time to find out what this baby can do. Unless you're worried about going along in an experimental craft."

All Rafe wanted was to return to River City and get a cup of coffee with a side dose of aspirin for his headache. Sitting up all night drowning his sorrows in a bottle of wine hadn't been his best idea, and the stress of dealing with his father and his monumental error about Kama only added to the throbbing. But he heard the challenge in the manager's voice and wasn't about to back down.

"As long as we get back for my next meeting." He hoped he'd have time to check on Kama. He had to apologize, had to get into that room and make her listen.

The manager accelerated, and Rafe felt the first telltale vibration in the craft. He gripped his armrest while the flyer made a steep ascent into the deep blue Harvest sky. It leveled off well above normal cruising altitude. Acres of red garraweed flowers rippled on golden stalks for as far as the eye could see.

"You never ran the canyons again after you wrecked your daddy's flyer." He grinned at Rafe. "Lose your nerve?"

Lev banked hard left, and Rafe bumped against the manager's shoulder. Then he smacked the door as Lev flung the craft right. He struggled to hold his anger in check and yanked on his harness to tighten it.

"I grew up—unlike three of our schoolmates. Racing flyers through the canyons was a stupid, dangerous game played by kids who were old enough to know better."

Lev gave him a wicked grin. "This baby's faster than that crate of yours."

Rafe lifted his chin. "You *might* take the Spider in a straight line race since you're running newer technology, but you won't beat her time through the canyons."

"Let's just see."

The manager shoved the joystick forward, and the nose pitched down at an alarming angle. As their speed and the vibration increased, Rafe cursed himself for not keeping his mouth shut. He wasn't a kid anymore. What did it matter whose flyer was faster? He needed to find out where Lev was the night Aaron died.

The sea of garraweed gave way to islands of bare rock. The flyer rushed toward a great rend in the ground, the closest of many etching the desolate landscape before them. A red light blinked on the dash, and a mechanical recording warned of the approaching surface.

They plunged a full quarter mile into the canyon before Lev started to pull out of the dive. The flyer shuddered and bucked while they dropped another five hundred feet through the ever-narrowing rock walls. The fans screamed as the control system trimmed the craft just above the dry riverbed. Rafe let out a breath he didn't realize he'd been holding.

The channel twisted and turned through the limestone and shale canyon. The tan and gray layers of the walls rushed past less than six feet from his window. The manager poured on more speed.

"There's the starting line. Clock us."

"I'm not here to play games."

Lev chuckled and punched a control, starting the dash-mounted timer. They raced between faded red stripes painted up the walls and thundered on through the channel past the black mouths of caverns that marked the entrance to a labyrinth of tunnels hidden in the rock. Ahead, their path split, the right path a longer but straighter and wider course, the middle a meandering run to a dead end, and the left an obstacle course of torturous curves, narrow passages, and stone arches punctuated with unpredictable debris caused by landslides. He hoped Lev had the good sense to take the right path.

The manager turned left and flashed down the shorter, more dangerous route, the fans screaming as he bounced the craft within inches of the encroaching walls on every turn.

"Your dampers can't handle the resonance oscillation," Rafe warned.

Lev replied without taking his eyes off the course. "Keep talking. I'm still gonna break your record."

They roared into the next curve. With a bump and a screech, the back left nacelle brushed the wall, slewing them sideways until the control unit compensated. The near miss didn't slow Lev.

Sweat broke out on Rafe's face despite the cool air blowing from the vents in the dash. The guy was crazy.

"Pull out or slow down. She isn't ready, not at this speed. Another brush like that and they'll be picking us up with a sponge."

The first of the stone bridges stretched across the canyon, providing a comfortable space beneath it for the flyer. Rafe glanced back at the high tail fins and wondered whether the craft had enough clearance for the later arches.

Lev hurled the flyer under the bridge without easing up on the throttle. Turbulence rattled the cockpit.

"Guess I should have brought a case of wine and a couple of broads. Then it would be like old times out here. Me chasing skirt, and you drunk on your ass."

"Take us back now," Rafe ordered, his voice tight.

"Can't. Haven't finished the test run. Two seconds under your time already by my reckoning."

The flyer shimmied through an S-curve into a short straightaway. Lev adjusted his grip on the stick and opened the throttle, his rugged face a study in grim concentration, his eyes shining like an addict's after a hit.

Ahead, another crumbling stone arch spanned the canyon as it swept around a right curve. The flyer tore under it and aimed for a landslide beyond. Lev yanked the stick back and applied braking, but the craft shuddered and responded slowly. A puff of smoke erupted from the front left nacelle.

The flyer pitched up over the slide with a rattling that shook Rafe's teeth. For one long moment, he thought the manager might try to run under the next bridge despite the loss of the left braking fan. They were moving too fast and too high to drop below it.

In desperation, Rafe reached across and gave the stick a vicious pull. The nose rose, but not fast enough. With a scream of tearing metal, the belly of the flyer dragged across the top of the bridge as it climbed out of the canyon. Lev flung Rafe's hand off the control column and fought to keep control while he slowed the craft.

Rafe slammed his fist on the dash, cutting off the timer. "What the hell did you think you were doing?"

The manager glared at him. "Taking a new flyer model for a test flight before it goes into production. We working stiffs don't spend our days boozing and screwing other men's women like you desk-bound management types. We do our jobs."

Rafe's head throbbed worse than ever. He turned away from Lev and watched the landscape roll by. It was a bad idea to punch the pilot while they were still in the air.

"When I spoke to Aaron late yesterday afternoon, he mentioned that he called you. What did he want?"

Lev went still. "He wanted to meet, face-to-face, today. He didn't say what it was about."

Rafe hadn't thought to ask Alana about Aaron's future appointments. He'd do that at his earliest opportunity.

"Give me a run-down on the orbital station."

Lev smiled. "I submit monthly reports. Maybe you should read them. Or are there too many long words for you to understand?"

Rafe's patience gave out. "Your reports are crap. Maybe Leon didn't check them against the financials, but I did. You're seventy percent over budget and months behind schedule. I don't know what *you* call that, but I call it gross mismanagement."

The manager blinked at him. He eased them past the bluffs and over the suburbs of the city before replying.

"You can blame the asshole running the company. Leon's the one who insisted we use suppliers from his list of cheapskate vendors, suppliers who couldn't deliver on time or on spec."

"Where were you last night?" Rafe nearly missed the slight widening of Lev's eyes before the man turned away.

"At the station." He faced Rafe. "Check the shuttle passenger lists if you don't believe me."

Rafe glanced at his nanocom. He was already late for his meeting with Svenson. No chance of stopping for coffee and aspirin.

"Put me down next to Building 8."

Lev brought them in low and fast over the campus to a soft landing in front of the building. Rafe cracked the door.

"You gonna fire me?"

"Give me one reason why I shouldn't."

The manager stared at him with raw hatred shining through slit eyes. "Your daddy might regret it."

It wasn't the answer Rafe expected. "I want a detailed station report on my desk by morning. And fix the goddamn dampers in this graceless piece of junk before you kill someone."

Rafe slid out, slammed the door, and strode away, blessing his legs for not shaking.

19

Kama stretched her back and hissed through her teeth. She switched Building 17 on in her campus emulator and applied system patches to prevent further access by the hacker. When they were in place, she shut off power to the building.

She'd already done the same with two-thirds of the corporate campus, but the hacker didn't know it. His commands went to the emulator, and it responded just as the buildings had. The hacker had to be in one of the buildings that still operated, but he wouldn't know the others had gone dark because of the emulations.

At one point, she thought she'd cornered the nasty little cyberpunk in Building 6. But just as Alana's people rolled up to the doors, the hacker popped up on the system again. Both the guards and the security vids showed no one left the building. He must have taken a break and not been stopped by a power outage as she'd thought.

She switched Building 23 to the emulator, patched the system, and shut the power down. Minutes ticked by. No further attacks surfaced on the network. A thrill of victory coursed through her. She checked to be sure McTavish didn't still linger in the hall and popped the lock on the door.

"Dzandarova, Building 23."

The security chief gave her an appraising look. "You're sure this time?"

"Yes! Now go get the bastard."

Dzandarova strode away down the hall, sending orders over her nanocom to rally the troops. Kama sent patches to the remaining building systems. Once they had the hacker in custody, she'd power up the campus. She stashed her gear, threw her duffel over her shoulder, and jogged out to join the arrest.

Late afternoon sun beat down, hotter than ever. Light glinted off the windows of the building across the open space, blinding her. She should have made the security chief wait for her and cursed Harvest again. Once she identified the hacker, it wouldn't take long to trace him back to Cullen McTavish.

When she reached Building 23, sweat streamed down her face, and her coveralls stuck to the back of her neck. Half a dozen security vehicles jammed the loop drive approach, and a cordon of guards surrounded the building.

Dzandarova came out through the front doors, ten contractors in her wake. Security officers removed their nanocoms, placing an evidence tag on each. A knot of men and women dressed in green coveralls stood outside the cordon, watching. They had scowls on their faces. One of them pointed to Kama.

The security chief approached and handed Kama a bag of nanocoms. "Here they are. Now give me the proof to figure out which one of these people is our hacker so I can let the rest go."

"Inside," Kama said.

They returned to the lobby. Cool air washed over her. She sat in a comfortable armchair and hooked her decrypter to the first nanocom. In a minute or two, files scrolled across the screen. The owner had spent the afternoon working on shipping schedules. She found no evidence of illegal code or the compiler software necessary to spin out the viruses the hacker used.

Over the next half hour, she tried all the nanocoms with no more success than she'd had with the first. She stared at the bag, disbelieving.

"You searched the entire building? No one's hiding? No one got out?"

Dzandarova's mouth turned down. "Are you telling me none of these people is our hacker?"

20

Rafe pondered how firing Lev could harm his father while he paused in the empty lobby of Building 8 to try his nanocom. The building was dark, and the network down. No way to reach Kama or Bob. He cursed under his breath and headed for the stairs, certain that Svenson wouldn't be in the powerless building. If the man wasn't here, he'd swing by the data center. This time, he'd smash open the door if that's what it took to get Kama's attention.

He strode down the second floor corridor to Lars Svenson's office. A pretty executive assistant with short blonde hair and a severe gray suit sat behind the desk in the dim antechamber. Had Svenson wrangled himself a full-time assistant, or was she, like Bob, a contractor ordered to wear business apparel instead of coveralls while she worked? As soon as she saw Rafe, she leaped to her feet, opened the door to the inner office, and ushered him in.

Light streamed through the windows. Svenson's office looked like an advertisement from an office supply catalog. The space was twice the size of Lev's. A mahogany desk and leather swivel chair faced the door. A bookcase stood against one wall, and a two-seat cloth upholstered couch against the other. Two comfortable visitor chairs occupied the space before the desk. An ornately framed still-life oil painting hung above the bookcase, and an impressionist water color hung over the couch. The office lacked any imprint of its occupant.

Svenson rose and reached across his desk to shake Rafe's hand. His grasp was cool and firm. He gestured to one of the chairs.

"Welcome, Mr. McTavish. What can I do for you?"

"Please call me Rafe."

"Of course."

Rafe wondered if the man had facial reconstruction gone wrong. Svenson was in his late forties, but his forehead was unlined, the faintest of crow's feet showed at the corners of wide brown eyes, and neither frown nor laugh lines creased the sides of his generous mouth. As he examined Rafe, nothing in his face moved. He was a plastic doll devoid of expression.

"Bob didn't say what this meeting would be about. How can I help you?"

"I'm making the rounds of upper management, meeting everyone. Aaron spoke very highly of you."

"Did he? He asked for my legal opinion frequently, but I hardly knew him."

Rafe was surprised by the statement. Aaron had indicated Svenson was a CEO candidate, but the chairman wasn't likely to entrust his company to someone he 'hardly knew.'

"With all the churn we've experienced recently, it's important that we maintain continuity. I'm trying to follow up on any pressing issues you may have had with Leon or Aaron. When I spoke to Aaron late yesterday, he mentioned that he'd called you earlier. What did he want?"

"My assistant spoke to him. They arranged an appointment for tomorrow. I assumed it was board business."

Rafe nodded. He wished the pretty assistant had offered him coffee, but with the power down, she probably couldn't. He suspected both she and Svenson were still here because of the lawyer's appointment with him. The campus seemed deserted.

"Anything going on in legal that I should know about?"

"Nothing out of the ordinary day-to-day items. If you'd like me to go over those with you, I can prepare a report."

Rafe already had a desk stacked with reports he hadn't read. The last thing he wanted was to add to that mountain.

"You live in one of those new high-rise condos on the south side, don't you?"

A quick flicker of surprise showed in Svenson's eyes, but his only response was to nod.

"My hotel won't be operational for another few days, and really, I need to find something more permanent. Are there any vacancies in your building?"

"Keon Mabutu is EcoMech's facilities manager. I'm sure he can find you something suitable."

Lawyers. He wanted to leap over the desk and shake the man until he said something useful. "Did you manage to avoid last night's riots?"

"Yes."

Rafe ground his teeth. "Where'd you hole up?"

"At home."

"Sensible." He thought about leaving since he wasn't making much progress. Then he reconsidered. "Tell me about Bert Gerlach."

Svenson leaned back in his chair and swept his eyes over his desktop. "What is it you want to know?"

Rafe stifled a grin. Finally, the lawyer had flinched. "Your assessment of him as a manager."

"I suppose he does his job well enough. Leon made him second in command. HR could provide you with his employee evaluations."

"I'm looking for more than the sanitized HR version." Rafe leaned forward in his chair. "I may decide to shake up the chain of command."

Svenson's brows twitched. "I see. He has broad experience at the company because he's moved around between the divisions as he's made his way up."

"Tell me something that isn't in his record."

"I'm not sure what you're after, Mr. McTavish." The lawyer shifted in his chair. "I was mildly surprised to see him moved to R & D. He never impressed me as the creative type, and he doesn't have an engineering or scientific background. But I suppose he left those endeavors to the people under him and focused on managing the division. He seems to have done that well enough."

Rafe nodded. "And Lev Kozlov?"

The lawyer's eyes snapped to Rafe's and back to the desktop. "Again, I'm not sure I'm the best person to comment on his performance. There seemed to be some ongoing disagreement—or perhaps 'feud' is a better word—between him and Leon. I recall going to Leon's office one day and Leon being…"

"In a towering rage?" he supplied.

Svenson almost smiled and tipped his head in agreement. "Lev had done something, I don't know what. I offered to look into Lev's employment contract to see whether it would be possible to let him go for cause, in which case, he'd forfeit his retirement benefits. But Leon said his father wouldn't allow it."

"Did he say why?"

Svenson spread his hands. "It wasn't my business."

☠   ☠   ☠

Rafe climbed the stairs in his own dark building. He'd been to the data center, but Kama was long gone. He wrestled his mind back to his suspects.

So there was something between Leon and Kozlov, and it involved Aaron. Why hadn't the old man told him about it? Who else might know?

Too many secrets and not enough progress.

He needed a shot of caffeine. Maybe he'd find some cold dregs of coffee in Bob's pot. His nanocom chimed, reminding him he was already late for his appointment with Bert Gerlach. Then there was the strange offer from Bose and Tang. Was it a piece of Aaron's murder puzzle, or was it unrelated?

He expected Bob to be long gone by now. To his surprise, his assistant manned his usual desk and used the screen of his nanocom to shine light on a filmie he read. When he saw Rafe, he leaped to his feet.

"Good to see you, sir. Apparently my message about your meeting with Mr. Gerlach just missed you at Mr. Svenson's office."

"The power's out and the network's down all over campus," Rafe said. "I'm not getting any messages from anyone."

"Yes, sir. That's why I sent a runner."

Rafe marveled at the man's ingenuity. Then he sniffed.

"Is that hot coffee I smell?"

"Yes, sir. I'm afraid it isn't up to my usual standards, though."

He hurried around his desk to the counter where the coffee maker usually stood. It had been replaced by a metal carafe mounted over a small can of burning fluid. Bob poured coffee into a travel cup and snapped a lid on before handing it to Rafe.

"I have a report on the state of the campus if you want to hear it," Bob said.

Rafe took a long pull on the coffee. "All I want right now are a couple of aspirins and a teleporter to take me to my meeting with Bert Gerlach."

His assistant opened his desk drawer and pulled out a packet of aspirin. He tore the top off and handed the remainder of the packet with its contents to Rafe.

"I'm afraid I don't have a teleporter, sir, but there's a company flyer waiting in the parking garage. It has the coordinates of the R & D facility preprogrammed in the autopilot. Mr. Gerlach will meet you there. They aren't experiencing any technical difficulties today. Your wardrobe is cleaned and packed in the trunk."

Rafe tossed back the aspirin and washed them down with another shot of coffee. Then he looked Bob up and down.

Bob squirmed. "Is there something wrong, sir?"

"I'm wondering where you keep the magic wand. Runners? Clean clothes? Hot coffee? All done while the campus crumbles around us. You're amazing."

The assistant beamed. "Shall I walk you down to your flyer and tell you about the campus?"

"No," he replied, heading for the door, "but you can walk me down and tell me what you learned about Bose and Tang."

Bob fell in beside him. "The outage made it impossible to get the passenger lists, but Bose and Tang arrived at their hotel at 18:30 yesterday evening."

Rafe reached the stairs and started down. "If communications were down, how did you get that information?"

"I went to the hotel during my lunch break."

They continued past the ground floor and down into the two levels of parking garage beneath the building. When they emerged from the stairwell, Rafe spotted a dark blue mid-sized flyer next to his company car.

"But we can't be sure they came straight from the shuttleport. They might have arrived earlier."

The little man glanced sideways, worry in his eyes. "The hotel wouldn't give me any information, so I bought the shuttle van driver a cup of coffee. He's a contractor, too. He picked up Bose and Tang at the shuttleport at 18:00 yesterday. He took their bags off the luggage carousel himself. I hope I didn't overstep my bounds."

Rafe grinned and clapped a hand on his shoulder. "Well done. You'd make a fine investigator."

He walked over to the flyer and opened the trunk. As Bob had said, his clothes were neatly stacked in boxes, all encased in plastic cleaner bags. He checked around the dim, empty garage to be sure they were alone, and then dug out clean trousers and a fresh shirt. He'd had enough of smelling like a campfire.

He stripped off his shirt and pants while Bob turned away, face flushed. When Rafe had the new clothes on, he stuffed the old clothes in one of the plastic bags. Bob snatched the bag from his hands before he could jam it between the boxes.

"I'll take care of those, sir."

Rafe stifled a laugh at Bob's stricken expression and closed the trunk. As he did, the lights blazed on. He hoped that meant that Kama and Alana had caught the hacker.

"If the network is up, I have another assignment for you."

"Yes, sir?"

"I want the passenger lists for all the outbound and inbound shuttle flights for the past two days."

Bob's eyes dropped to the pavement. "You want to verify what the van driver said."

"I'm checking for another passenger."

The little assistant brightened. "Is there someone in particular you're looking for, sir?"

Should he share his suspicions with Bob? Kama could probably get him the same information, but he wasn't certain she would, and he didn't blame her. He needed more than Kama's help. He needed a team.

"I want to know whether Lev Kozlov was on the station last night, but I'd prefer if word didn't get out about my interest in his where-abouts."

"He was on the station late yesterday afternoon. I called him about a missing report, and I recognized the station in the background."

Rafe opened the flyer door and slid in. "Then skip the outbound lists and check all the inbound lists from when you spoke until they stopped flying last night."

"Yes, sir."

"And be careful. We're chasing a murderer."

Bob's eyes grew round. He nodded and hurried away toward the stairs.

21

Kama brushed stray hairs from her sweaty forehead and trudged to the guard house. It had been a long, hot bus trip to the compound. Dzandarova hadn't offered her a ride, not that she'd expected one after her stinging defeat. Unless the hacker knew how to turn invisible, her plan should have worked. She couldn't fathom what had gone wrong, and she was too frustrated and hungry to go back through her data now.

She had to catch the intruder. She had to ensure that Cullen was convicted and that his son ascended to the chairmanship. She needed McTavish to build the Sharma Network, assuming he ever forgave her. Nailing the hacker would also be her atonement for her own foolish interference.

Her eyes burned from lack of sleep, and her shoulders ached from the stress of pursuing the cyberpunk. Goldman's backup files nestled in her duffel. When she'd been through them, she'd tackle the hacker again. Fresh eyes might see something new.

The big gorilla with the beer gut stepped from the guard house. If he gave her any grief, he'd pay for it. By tomorrow morning, he'd find that he'd donated everything he owned to charity.

"Ms. Bhatia, we didn't expect to see you here."

The door of the guardhouse opened, and the young guard joined his partner.

"You're not going inside, are you?"

"It's hot, I'm tired, and I don't want any hassles," she said, wondering how he'd remembered her name when he watched fifteen thousand contractors come and go every day. Maybe it was because she'd been with McTavish. She didn't expect to have his protection now, not after last night.

"No, ma'am. We know what you tried to do, and we're grateful for the help," the big man said.

So all Dzandarova's people knew about her failure with the hacker. Heat rose in her face. She nodded to the guard and stepped toward the gate.

"Maybe you want to stay at the Nighthorse place again tonight," he said, cutting her off from the gate, "after the hacker posted those vids of you."

Kama lurched to a halt. "What vids?"

The guard stuck his nanocom in front of her. On the tiny screen, she stood with Dzandarova outside Building 23 while a computer-altered voice-over called her a traitor and a spy and urged the contractors to retaliate. Then a reporter came on to recap how the video had been played over all Harvest's channels by the hacker. So far, the mystery woman in the Oasis uniform hadn't been identified, but EcoMech security credited her with chasing a cyber-intruder out of the campus network.

Shiva. Samir would go wild when the news reached him. It probably already had. He'd send an assassin for the hacker and an extraction team for her. She'd be dodging them as well as McTavish.

She wouldn't bow to the hacker's threats. She'd stay here with the rest of the contractors where she belonged. She wasn't running back to the Nighthorse house. She'd had enough of their insane family feud.

"Open the gate," she demanded.

"But Ms. Bhatia, Chief Dzandarova—"

She shoved past, flung open the gate, and marched through. When she reached her building, she jerked open the creaky door with more force than necessary and strode into the lobby. Heads turned, and a murmur rose. One woman nudged her companion and pointed. A teenage boy watched her, open-mouthed, and then hurried from the room.

Teeth clenched and chin up, Kama followed the smell of food to the dining hall. When she got there, most of the room was already empty, and the kitchen was closed. She muttered a curse and stomped the length of the room to a table illuminated by an overhead light that still worked. All conversation died for a full minute.

She pitched her duffel onto the table and fished out Goldman's stick drives. She loaded Goldman's data to her nanocom and set up queries to parse the data. While she waited to see what turned up, she searched her duffel for a protein bar. No luck. Her stomach growled so loud she thought they'd hear it on Oasis.

A few groups of contractors remained, scattered around the echoing space. They talked quietly, but she couldn't miss their unfriendly looks.

As the minutes ticked by, they filed out, a few at a time, until only two men remained sitting at a table ten meters away.

Her nanocom vibrated announcing the completion of her queries. She pulled the square of metallic fabric from her bag and spread it on the table. A quick tap on the nanocom produced streaming lists of data. She muttered another curse under her breath and modified the query.

Looking through financial records was McTavish's specialty, not hers. He was a damn wizard at it. She wondered where he was right now. *Probably looking for evidence that his father didn't kill Goldman.*

At some point, she'd be forced to remind him of his promise to look after EcoMech for Gabe. It was the only way she could think of to keep him at the helm of the company. She prayed he'd put aside his anger at her and live up to his commitments to Gabe and Oasis.

It was just as well she'd admitted her hacking to him. That's who she was, what she did. He had some romantic image of her as a knight in shining armor, a paramour he could put on a pedestal. It was exactly the mistake she'd made eight years earlier, rushing into a relationship with Thom. By the time she'd realized what a monster he was—

The two remaining men watched her. Something about them made her shiver despite the miserable heat. Maybe coming here hadn't been such a good idea. Hellfire, she wouldn't be run off by a cyberpunk. Still, she wished Dzandarova had returned her stunner.

More results spewed down the cloth, and Kama turned to them. One caught her eye. A woman named Toni Benton had received a payout of one hundred thousand credits yearly for the past eleven years. Who the bloody hell was Toni Benton, and why was Goldman paying her so much? Unlike Goldman's other expenses, this one had no notation indicating what the payment was for.

Electricity coursed through her blood. She connected to the EcoMech network. Her mailbox filled with messages from McTavish. She debated opening them. Eventually she'd have to talk to him, but she'd prefer to find the evidence she sought first. She ignored his missives and burrowed into the personnel records searching for Toni Benton. The results came back empty. A search of Leon and Amaya Goldman's personal files did no better. She thumped a hand on the table.

The fastest way to find Toni Benton was to contact Samir. His 'data analysts' were tapped into every information source in the galaxy, but he was the last person she wanted to talk to. She chewed her lip. To ask for his help, she'd also have to give him the full story of events on Harvest, including her failure to find the hacker. She wouldn't do it. She didn't need help from anyone.

The lights went out. Kama started and checked her nanocom. *Curfew. Of all the stupid—* She fumbled in her bag for her work light. A quick flash around the room showed she was alone. With the lights out, she'd lost her network connection.

Enough was enough. Why sit in the dark and heat when she could be comfortably ensconced in her workroom at her school chasing the same leads she chased here? She had a hidden account on the EcoMech network now. She could monitor remotely for the hacker and continue her investigation from a safe place.

Besides, McTavish said he was leaving. Why should she stay if he didn't? Why hadn't there been a report of his resignation? Had she missed it? Maybe the board wanted to name a replacement first. She stashed her light, grabbed her duffel, and left.

Ahead, dim lights shone in the lobby, and quiet voices floated to her. She connected to the network, contacted the shuttleport, and booked a seat on the first flight out.

Kama passed the vacant front desk, ignoring the stares of the dozen men and woman grouped in a knot near the front door. She'd catch a few winks in her room, and then she'd start again looking for the hacker. She pushed through the stairwell door and climbed, cursing Harvest and her own foolishness for coming here with every labored step.

The second-floor stairwell light was out, as were the lights on the next several landings. Dim illumination from much higher lit the darkness enough for her to continue. When she reached the third floor, the ground-floor door scraped open and clunked closed behind her. Footsteps scuffed on the treads as someone jogged upward. No, more than one person.

Who the hell runs up stairs in this heat and gravity? Another cold shiver lanced through her. She peered down into the gloom, but whoever was coming stuck to the wall out of her sight. She shrugged her bag higher on her shoulder, gritted her teeth, and bolted up the stairs.

22

Rafe landed beside the two-story R & D warehouse. The sun already dipped low on Harvest's horizon, triggering the lights around the parking lot where a lone black sport flyer parked. Nothing stirred at the other warehouses along the street, not even the hot, still air. He got out and slogged up the five steps to the warehouse door.

A light inside the door did little to illuminate the cavernous space. Rows of work tables and fabrication machines disappeared into the darkness. The faint smells of oil, hot metal, and glue tainted the air. Footsteps approached from his right. He spun to face them, and then felt a moment of embarrassment at his jumpiness.

"Mr. McTavish, I was worried that we'd lost you." A blond man in his late forties stepped into the light, hand extended. His face crinkled in a pleasant smile that lit his hazel eyes and exposed even white teeth. He topped Rafe by nearly half a foot and wore a sharp navy suit that hung well on his trim figure. "Bert Gerlach."

He took the man's hand, the grip strong. "Call me Rafe."

Gerlach smiled. "Welcome to Harvest. I would have introduced myself sooner, but you're a hard man to catch up with. Since you're here, would you like a tour of the facility?"

Rafe didn't want a tour, he wanted answers and then to find Kama. He also wanted cooperation and tempered his response.

"Maybe another time, when it isn't so late."

"Of course. You must be exhausted trying to adjust to Harvest. Maybe you'd like to discuss business over dinner? Aaron mentioned that you were a connoisseur of fine wines, God rest his soul, and there's a restaurant downtown that has a wonderful selection. I eat there often."

"If it wasn't trashed in last night's riot," Rafe replied, glad for the quick opening. "Did you get caught in it?"

"Just missed all the excitement." Gerlach opened the warehouse door and held it for Rafe. "Had I lingered over dinner as I usually do, I would have been in the thick of things, but I was home safe before it began. Never thought I'd be glad for the drudge of quarterly reports, but working on them saved my butt last night."

They walked down the steps to stand by the flyers. Gerlach's talk of food reminded Rafe he hadn't eaten all day. The manager's invitation made his stomach tighten, but he had to find Kama and beg her forgiveness.

"I'm already engaged for the evening," he apologized. "But I would like to ask about something Aaron said. He mentioned he'd arranged a meeting with you when I spoke to him yesterday afternoon."

"Yes, that's right. I was a little surprised, to tell the truth. I expected to see him Sunday anyway, but perhaps he didn't want to talk in front of the others."

"The others?" Rafe asked, his patience dwindling.

"Our foursome. We golfed every Sunday. Aaron insisted we continue despite Leon's death. Said he needed the exercise to keep his heart healthy. I assumed you'd be joining us in Leon's place."

"Ah. I don't play." He ran a hand through his hair. Aaron hadn't mentioned that he was golfing with one of their prime suspects. "Who else comprised your foursome?"

"Your father. When someone couldn't make it, Lars subbed in."

"Svenson?" *The man who said he hardly knew Aaron?*

"Yes." Gerlach gazed into the distance. "I always got the feeling that he was holding back so he wouldn't best the others, but he didn't mind trouncing me."

"Did Aaron mention what he wanted to talk about?"

The manager shrugged. "I thought perhaps he wanted to be sure I would support you, make sure I harbored no ill will for being passed over."

Rafe cocked an eyebrow. "And do you?"

Gerlach laughed. "I admit I was angry at first. But EcoMech has always been a family venture. It's not unexpected that they'd find someone with a blood relationship to take the helm. You proved yourself by building Security Partners."

The man seemed innocuous enough, and Rafe wanted to be gone. His desire to find Kama consumed him.

"Thank you for staying late to see me. I'm sorry to cut this short, but something's come up." Rafe offered his hand. "I'll have Bob arrange a proper meeting."

Gerlach took his hand with a smile. "No problem."

Rafe started his flyer and eased out of the parking lot while Gerlach got into his own vehicle. He didn't bother with the autopilot as he headed for the contractors' compound. In his mirror, he saw Gerlach's black flyer rise behind him.

They both streaked north across the river while Rafe mused about Svenson. Why would the lawyer lie about how well he knew Aaron? It didn't make sense. He put it aside to think about later, after he'd found Kama.

Below, a tangle of cars backed up for several blocks along one of the main boulevards. At the head of the line, twenty contractors milled beside a stalled bus. Three times as many people gathered on the lawn of a tiny park across the street. A giant sculpture of EcoMech's three founding fathers occupied a place of honor in the green space, and a sea of candles, bouquets, and colorful paper tributes surrounded the statuary. As Rafe passed over, someone from the group on the grass tossed something at the contractors.

"Hell," he muttered.

He cut his speed and began a circle back while tapping in a connection on his nanocom.

"Where you are you, Mr. McTavish?" Alana asked on the other end of the connection. "You were supposed to wait in your office for my security escort."

"Send everyone you have available to my flyer coordinates. We're about to have another riot." He punched in the location displayed on his navcom.

"What's the situation?"

"A contractor bus stalled, and it's getting too much attention from a group of locals. I'll see what I can do to keep a lid on until you get here."

"Don't even think about getting out of your vehicle. I'll have officers on the scene in ten minutes."

The rays of the setting sun flashed off a bottle tossed in the direction of the bus. On such a hot evening, those attending Aaron Goldman's impromptu memorial would be well-lubricated.

Rafe brought the flyer down half a block in front of the bus. When he popped his door, he smelled smoke from barbeque grills, and his stomach growled. The vigil attendees shouted jeers and taunts at the contractors, and a couple of the contractors responded with insults of their own. Many of the mourners held beer bottles and had the unfocused eyes of drunkenness. One had a baseball bat resting on his shoulder.

The driver of the bus stood by its open door talking to someone on her nanocom. Rafe approached, keeping watch on the crowd on the grass.

"Rafe McTavish," he said, extending his hand to the driver, a petite woman with a bob haircut and uniform rumpled by the heat.

Her brown eyes swung from her nanocom to his face, and then they opened wide. She stared at his extended hand for several seconds before clasping her sweating palm against his.

"Cully Wilson," she said. "I'm sorry about the bus. I'm trying to get the shop out here to look at it, but they won't come tonight."

"What do they expect the passengers to do?"

"Walk."

Rafe looked at the hot tired faces of the contractors and noticed that one of them was a heavily pregnant woman. Three or four others were teenagers barely out of childhood.

Across the street, a massive tanker truck pulled to the curb by the park, further reducing the flow of traffic around the bus. A sign on the side read *Liquefied Cattle Feed – Not for human consumption.* The driver jumped down with a case of beer under one arm, and the crowd on the grass cheered.

"It's five miles to the compound. They'll have heatstroke before they get halfway. Is that your boss you're talking to?"

She glanced down at her arm. "The shop foreman. My supervisor has gone home."

"May I?"

She swiveled her arm around so he could see the screen.

"Do you know who I am?" he asked the red-faced foreman. The man's brows drew down while he squinted at the screen. Then they shot up.

"Mr. McTavish?"

"If you don't have a replacement bus here in twenty minutes, you're fired."

The foreman's eyes opened in terror. "But, sir, I don't have any drivers."

"I don't care if the tooth fairy drives. Just get it here."

He turned to Wilson. "Lead the passengers north, but move calmly. We need to get out of this neighborhood."

Wilson looked at the angry employees gathered across the street and swallowed before nodding her head. Rafe waded into the throng of contractors standing by the bus.

"Sorry for the problems, folks. Please follow the driver." He urged people forward. "There's a restaurant a few blocks ahead where we'll get you all cool drinks while we wait for a replacement bus."

"We can't afford their prices," someone shouted.

"And they won't serve contractors," another added.

"No one serves contractors anymore."

Rafe waved his arms to still the crowd. "They'll serve me, and I'm buying."

A big, ruddy contractor removed his arm from around the shoulders of a beautiful young woman of African origin. She tracked her husband with her eyes and clasped her hands over her swollen belly. The big man shoved through the others to stand toe-to-toe with Rafe. "Why should they listen to you?"

He stuck out his hand. "Rafe McTavish. You're...?"

A ripple of talk washed over the crowd. As it did, heads turned his direction.

"Wade," the man said, staring at the offered hand without taking it.

"It's an unfriendly neighborhood, Wade, and I don't want to see anyone get hurt. Can I count on you to help me get these people away safely?"

The contractor's brow furrowed. Before he could disagree, his wife took his arm and towed him in Cully Wilson's wake. Half a dozen passengers trailed behind. More jeers rose from the crowd across the street, and a bottle sailed over the top of the bus to crash against the storefronts that lined the opposite side of the sidewalk. Wade's wife yelped. Wilson and the others ducked back.

Around the front end of the bus, the man with the baseball bat appeared. His face was flushed with anger and drink, and two more men holding empty beer bottles like clubs stood at his shoulder. "Planning to torch our neighborhood next? Or maybe you wanna murder us like you did Aaron Goldman?"

Across the street, the tanker truck roared to life.

Rafe pushed through the contractors and stood beside Wade's wife. "There's no need for trouble. Just step aside, and we'll be on our way."

Rafe glanced to the rear of bus. More unfriendly men with beer bottles and barbeque skewers blocked that escape. He and the contractors were trapped, hemmed in by the bus and storefronts with no exit except through an armed mob. He wiped sweaty palms on his pants. How long since he'd called Alana?

The ringleader slapped the bat against his palm and advanced, half a dozen of his fellows now at his back. "We'll teach you contractors your place."

Behind the group, the tanker pulled across the street and nosed onto the walkway so close to the storefronts that its driver-side mirror scraped the glass. It rumbled up behind the ringleader's band, ready to box in the contractors. Wade bristled at his shoulder.

"Come on, guys, there's a pregnant woman and a bunch of kids here. They haven't done anything to you." Rafe spread his hands.

One of the ringleader's lackeys seized Wade's wife by the arm and tried to drag her into their group. She shrieked, and Wade shoved past, his fists bunched. Rafe leaped to restrain him, but too late.

Wade ducked a haymaker and planted a meaty fist in the nose of his wife's abductor, followed by a kick to the man's groin. As his victim fell, he dragged Wade's wife down with him, and two more attackers leaped at Wade.

Rafe grabbed the hand of one and gave it a vicious twist, snapping the man's wrist. The other man's bottle connected with Wade's head, and he dropped unconscious to the sidewalk, blood running down his face. In a heartbeat, the mob exploded. The other attackers surged forward into the contractors, clubbing anyone in range. The bus driver pulled Wade's wife to her feet and dragged her away into the street. Cries of fear and pain rang out.

It would all be over in a few minutes, Rafe knew, unless he did something to stop it. He needed to get to the tanker truck, which continued its relentless crawl forward.

The baseball bat whistled by his head. He charged forward and sunk his shoulder in the bat wielder's stomach. The man doubled over and the bat was Rafe's. He blocked bottles, cracked shins and jabbed at guts, clearing a path to the oncoming tanker's hood. He sprang for the hood, vaulted the cab, and landed on the catwalk on the top of the tank.

He ran the length of the catwalk and dropped to the back bumper. With a yank, he reeled out a four-inch diameter hose and flipped on the tanker's pump. Hose in hand, he regained the catwalk and prayed that whatever 'liquefied cattle feed' was, it wouldn't do any permanent harm.

The truck driver waited at the end of the catwalk, a long wrench in his hand. Rafe swung the end of the hose and charged forward. The metal valve cracked against the man's knee. He howled in pain and tumbled to the pavement beside the truck. Driverless, the truck continued its slow crawl ahead.

Rafe aimed the nozzle at the mob at the far end of the bus and jerked open the valve. The hose bucked in his arms, and he wobbled on the catwalk. A great gout the color and consistency of thick cream spewed out like a rotting monsoon, shooting over the heads of the angry mob and drenching everyone within fifty feet of the end of the bus. Shrieks of surprise rang out, and the mob at that end dissipated.

Seconds later, an incredible stench stung his eyes. He played the hose over the backs of the ringleader's gang just a few feet in front of the truck. They were knocked to their knees. When they regained their feet, they stumbled away howling their displeasure. Over the roar of the crowd, he heard the wail of sirens. He wrestled with the shutoff valve.

Driverless, the truck veered, and the front bumper caught on the bumper of the bus. The jerk of the impact threw Rafe onto the hood. He scrabbled for something to grab onto, but his eyes watered so badly he couldn't see. He slid headfirst over the front and smacked his skull on the sidewalk.

For a moment, he lay stunned on the pavement, unable to orient himself. He rolled to his knees and reached out with a steadying hand. It met warm metal. *The side of the bus.* The sound of the truck engine filled his ears. He tried to stand, but the knock on the head left him dizzy. He was done for. The bumper of the truck made a painful impact with his shoulder. In another instant, he'd be crushed under the tire.

Before he could topple to the concrete, strong hands gripped him under his shoulders and dragged him away. Tears streamed down his cheeks. His rescuer's face was a blur. He was shoved into the alcove of a storefront doorway.

"Stay here while I stop the truck," a familiar voice ordered.

Rafe pressed his sleeve over his watering eyes, waiting for the stinging to abate. The sound of the truck motor died, replaced by approaching sirens. When he looked, he saw Bert Gerlach squeezing out of the truck's cab. The man minced down the steaming sidewalk, grabbed Rafe by the arm, and steadied him while they walked around the bus to the park.

The street crawled with security troops in riot gear. They herded contractors into one group and employees into another. A teenage boy and an older woman in contractor coveralls were stretched on the grass while two officers used first aid kits to staunch bleeding from cuts on their heads.

Down the street, an officer flagged traffic onto an alternate route. An ambulance bore down from the opposite direction. Another officer snapped pictures of the street and began collecting discarded weapons from the pavement.

"Are you all right?" Bert Gerlach's concerned hazel eyes looked into his.

"You saved my life. Thank you."

The R & D manager smiled. "EcoMech can't afford to lose another CEO."

"I told you to stay back," Alana said as she walked up behind him.

"It would have been much worse if he had." Bert gestured toward the tanker. "There are casualties under the truck."

Alana's face paled. "We have people *under* the truck?"

Rafe looked at where the truck now stood and gritted his teeth. "A contractor by the name of Wade, and the ringleader of the employees went down in that area. I didn't see what happened to them."

"You stay right here," Alana ordered.

She grabbed a passing officer and pointed across the street. He corralled another man, and they went to the truck.

"What is that stench?" the security chief asked.

"Unprocessed potato slurry," Bert replied. "It's mildly caustic, so you should get people washed off as soon as you can."

Rafe glanced down at his own smeared, stinking shirt and torn pants and was thankful that he had clean clothes in the flyer. Maybe he could find a public restroom to wash in. He didn't want Kama to see him looking and smelling like this. She was already keeping him at arm's length.

The officers returned. "Two under the truck, ma'am, both dead. The truck crushed one. Looks like the other has a caved-in skull."

Guilt and regret shot through Rafe. He should have responded faster. He should have foreseen that there would be retaliation toward the contractors. He shouldn't have fired their council in the first place.

"Well, hell. What's wrong with people?" Alana said. "Get all the contractors in ambulances and get them to the hospital. We'll question them later."

She eyed Rafe, and then her gaze lingered on the R & D manager. "You're a little off your patch, aren't you, Mr. Gerlach?"

"I was headed home from my meeting with Rafe when I saw him land at the stalled bus. I thought I might be able to help."

Alana turned a disapproving stare on Rafe.

He spread his hands in surrender. "If not for Bert, you'd have three people under the tanker."

Alana's mouth pulled into a hard line. "I'm assigning two officers to your security, and by God, you'd better not ditch them."

The last thing Rafe wanted were security officers hanging on his every word while he apologized to Kama and begged her forgiveness.

"You're overwhelmed already. You need your people here to mop up. I'll go to Shannon's." It wasn't a complete lie. After he'd picked up Kama, he'd do exactly that.

"Why don't I believe you?" Alana muttered. "I'll need a statement from you about this mess. I want it in my mail before midnight. Otherwise, I'll be coming for you, and you can complete it at the station."

Rafe ducked his head, willing to agree to anything if he could just be gone. Together, he and Bert walked to the end of the block where their flyers were parked. As they approached the flyers, his nanocom beeped. When he tapped it, Shannon's face filled the screen.

"Has Gabe called you?"

He stopped walking, dread rising. "No. Where is he?"

"I don't know. The last anyone saw of him, he was in his room. That was an hour ago."

23

Footsteps closed behind Kama, and she lunged for the sixth floor hallway door. The handle slipped through her fingers. Before she could reach again, someone yanked her back by the collar of her coveralls. The force of the jerk spun her around and sent her crashing into the opposite wall. Her cheekbone smacked the concrete and pain blossomed. She screamed as loud as she could.

A fist landing in her kidney cut off her cry. She bent her knees and smashed back with her elbow. She heard a grunt, and the weight pushing her head against the wall fell away.

In the dim light, she could see two rough forms. She aimed a kick for the smaller man's groin before he recovered from her blow to his gut. The larger man swung a right at her face. As she blocked it, her foot struck the other man's thigh, wide of her target. She screamed again, hoping someone would hear. The little guy came back at her, landing a punch in her stomach and knocking the breath out of her.

The larger man shoved her back hard. Her head impacted the wall. Dazed, she slid to the floor. Boots pummeled her legs, and then hands grabbed her hair, lifting her out of her protective curl. It felt like they ripped her scalp away from her skull. A fist landed in her ribs. She tried for a knee to a groin, but the smaller one rewarded her with another fist in the stomach.

The landing door swung open. Light blinded her. Men shouted, feet scuffled, and then her attackers released her. She fell back and slumped to the base of the wall.

The brawl ended when the two men were dragged into the sixth-floor hallway by a group who made their displeasure clear. The two louts were thrown to the floor, and their arms were twisted behind their backs. A middle-aged woman crouched beside her.

"Are you okay?"

"Smashing," Kama replied. She struggled to stand on wobbly legs. The landing spun twice before it steadied.

The woman picked up her duffel from where it had been kicked during the fight. On the stairs above, an emaciated teenage girl and another man watched from the semi-darkness. In the hallway, the group of men secured the attackers' hands behind their backs and forced them away.

"Drop them down the lift shaft for me, will you?"

"We'll deliver them to the guardhouse out front. Despite what the McTavish family thinks, we aren't all thugs and murderers. I'm Heidi."

"Kama. Everyone in the McTavish clan isn't a greedy lying slave driver, either, despite what you hear on the news."

A snicker floated down the stairs.

Kama glared up at the onlookers, embarrassed by her defense of McTavish. If he weren't so pig-headed, she wouldn't be in this mess. She couldn't get off this planet—and away from him—soon enough.

A young boy raced up the stairs.

"Mom! Come quick. Some people have been hurt."

Heidi followed her son down the stairs. The watchers from above clattered past, and Kama fell in behind them, keeping a firm grasp on the handrail while her head throbbed and trembling shook her body.

The lobby was packed with milling contractors. An arriving group wearing hospital scrubs trickled in the door, many wrapped in bandages. One heavily pregnant woman leaned on the arm of a companion while tears streamed down her reddened face.

"What happened?" someone shouted.

"Our bus stalled, and when we got off, we were attacked," a skinny, pimple-faced teen proclaimed. "They said a contractor murdered Mr. Goldman, and they'd get even. They killed her husband!"

An angry buzz rose over the lobby.

"We can't let them get away with it!" a man shouted, and others added their agreement.

"We'll march on the campus and burn it to the ground!" another yelled.

"To hell with the campus," a woman cried. "Go for the McTavish family. This is their fault."

Kama froze. Dzandarova couldn't stop a mob fifteen thousand strong if it wanted McTavish's blood. She had to warn him.

"No," the pregnant woman shouted. "Rafe McTavish saved our lives. If he hadn't been there, none of us would have survived. He fought to protect us."

Kama pictured McTavish leaping into the mob with no regard for his own safety, and goose bumps rose on her flesh. Yes, he'd do exactly that. Had he been injured? What the hell was he doing rescuing contractors? He'd said he was leaving. She squeezed her arms around herself and waited to hear more.

"Then what will we do?" someone asked. "We can't let this go unanswered."

"We'll wait," Heidi said. "We'll see whether the perpetrators are arrested. If they aren't, then we can talk about an appropriate non-violent response."

"We've tried non-violence, and where has it gotten us?"

Clamor pro and con deafened Kama.

Heidi waved for quiet. "Some of you tried violence, and what did that accomplish? Things got worse. We're law-abiding citizens of Earth Authority. Acting like rabid animals won't help anyone."

More arguing started. Kama tapped in a connection to the EcoMech network. A quick hack turned on the dining hall lights. She paced down the corridor and found a table in the center of the space.

As long as Goldman's murder remained unsolved, the board and employees would blame the contractors. More of them would be hurt. McTavish couldn't protect them all. But he'd try, and eventually he'd be the one hurt—or killed.

She'd called him a coward for running away, and now it was her who intended to leave while he seemed to have changed his mind. A horrible sense of time running out chilled her. With a grimace, she opened a secure connection to Oasis.

After several minutes, Samir appeared on her screen. His dark hair was mussed, as though he'd smoothed it with has hand instead of a comb. Sleep lines marked his olive skin, and the collar of his pajamas showed at the bottom of the screen. Behind him, she could make out the paneling of his home study. His black eyes first glowered at her, and then widened in surprise. Too late, she remembered the bruise on her cheekbone.

"I apologize for waking you, but I have an urgent request."

"What's happened to you?"

She sighed. "I tripped on the stairs. I need information on a woman."

"The woman who tripped you?"

"No."

He looked off-camera, probably to his wall screen where he displayed the latest reports from his network of spies and informants. His chest rose as he sucked in a breath, and then his attention was all for her. She rocked back under the intensity of his stare.

"What happened to maintaining a covert presence at EcoMech?"

"We've had... complications."

"That's what you call it when a terrorist broadcasts your image across the galaxy and agitates for your assault? You will not remain on Harvest."

"I have to stay. McTavish needs my help."

"You think Varun will permit that when threats have been made against your life?"

"He doesn't have to know. Censor the news feeds. You have the resources in place."

One dark eyebrow threaded with gray twitched up. "Censor *Varun's* news feeds?"

She gulped. "The woman's name is Toni Benton. Goldman's funneled money to her for the past eleven years. I need everything you can find about her. The sooner I have that information, the sooner I can leave Harvest."

A glacial coldness slid over Samir's face. "I will need access to the EcoMech network."

Kama wanted to throw her nanocom across the room. So this was his price, the access he'd chased unsuccessfully for months. What would McTavish say if he knew?

"I've already checked EcoMech's records. She's not associated with the company in any capacity."

His forehead tipped toward the camera and his hands spread. "Ah, well, if you've already looked for her without success, there's little point in having my people investigate. They're so much slower than you. And without access to the EcoMech corporate network, they couldn't cross-reference their findings."

Heat washed through her. A sense of helpless panic followed. If she didn't stop the blackmailer, McTavish could be the next to die. But McTavish would see this as another betrayal.

"All right, I'll give you access." A terrible foreboding climbed her esophagus with the words.

A glint of victory shone in Samir's eyes. "You cannot remain there. If you must involve yourself, do it at a safe remove."

If McTavish was putting himself at risk, how could she do less? Dzandarova didn't seem capable of protecting him, or he wouldn't have been rescuing contractors from mob violence.

"I need to be here. McTavish has no one to watch out for him."

"And you have no one helping you," the head of Oasis security shot back. "If you want my cooperation, then I must assure your safety. I'm sending backup."

Kama ground her teeth. She didn't need Samir's goon squad following her around like a pack of dangerous wraiths ready to kill anyone who looked at her wrong. But maybe she could use them to shadow McTavish. Lakshmi knew the fool needed protection.

"Fine. But tell them they'll follow my orders."

Samir almost smiled. It made her skin crawl.

24

Rafe flew in ever widening squares tracing the streets around the Nighthorse home, his eyes scouring the darkness below. If Gabe ran away, where would he go? Shannon admitted he'd taken his suitcase, which meant he'd probably left of his own volition and not been coerced.

On the other hand, a clever kidnapper might take the suitcase to muddy the waters. When he found the boy—if he found the boy un-harmed—he'd give him a piece of his mind.

The houses soon petered out to the east. He couldn't imagine the kid wandering into the garraweed scrub surrounding the city. If he had, they'd need infrared scanners to find him. He'd tried tracking Gabe's nanocom, but the boy had turned it off. He came around again, flying lower than legally allowed.

A block ahead, a small figure sat on a bus stop bench, something boxy at its feet. Rafe brought the flyer to street-level and cruised to a stop next to the bench. He opened his door and stepped out, ready to deliver an angry lecture.

Gabe wiped a hand across his nose, defiance shining in red-rimmed eyes as he met Rafe's glare. The poor kid looked desolate. All thought of a lecture drained away.

"Get in."

Gabe shook his head. His fists balled in his lap. "You don't want me."

His words stabbed at Rafe's soul. He closed the flyer door, walked to the bench, and sat down. He didn't know what to say. He could drag the boy away, but what purpose would that serve? Gabe would run again at the first opportunity.

"Where are you headed?"

"To the shuttleport." The boy sniffed and wiped at his nose again.

"And then?"

That earned him a suspicious look. "I'm going to Earth. My dad said that's what you did."

Rafe winced. "You're a little young to join Earth Force."

The boy frowned at him. "I know that. I'll stay with Mr. Fukiyama until I'm old enough for pilot school."

"Ah." He drew his ball from his pocket and rolled it in his palms. "Who's Mr. Fukiyama?"

"He used to be our gardener. He retired last year."

"You don't want to stay with Shannon and Ben?"

"She says I lied about seeing your dad. I have to stay in my room until I learn to tell the truth." Gabe leaned forward and peered down the darkening street, looking for the bus. "I didn't lie. I saw him."

"I believe you." He bounced the ball on the sidewalk. Something inside him warred with that assertion.

"But you're mad that I told."

Rafe ran a hand through his hair. "I'm not mad. You did the right thing."

"Then why don't you want me?"

Rafe admired the first of Harvest's two moons rising over the houses on the opposite side of the street while he thought about a reply. In Mumbai, he'd volunteered to coach soccer for at-risk youth. He enjoyed the boisterous energy of kids. But coaching a few hours a week wasn't the same as being a father. What if he weren't any better at it than his own father?

"I always thought if I ever became a parent, I'd start with a baby— and a wife. I'd have time to learn what to do, someone to back me up. I never imagined starting with someone your age. I'm afraid I'll mess up. I already have, or you wouldn't be running away."

Gabe studied the toes of his dusty shoes. "Kama said she'd adopt me."

Rafe walked his ball across his knuckles and struggled to keep his jealousy in check. He'd give anything to have her want him. She'd called him a coward, and he was. To change her opinion, he needed to change his behavior. He had to do the right thing.

"There was an accident earlier. I don't think the bus is coming."

The boy slid off the bench and picked up his suitcase. "Guess I'll walk."

He stood and put a hand on Gabe's shoulder. "Look, I can't be your father, but if you'll give me a chance, I'd like to be your favorite uncle. If you try it and decide you don't want to live with me, you can go wherever you want. You can live with Mr. Fukiyama. Or Kama."

Troubled eyes met Rafe's. "Do I have to stay at Shannon's?"

Rafe sighed. It wasn't his first choice, either, but he'd promised Alana. "Only overnight. In the morning, you can come to the office with me, and I'll find other accommodations."

Gabe shifted his suitcase from one hand to the other while Rafe held his breath.

"I guess we can try it."

Rafe took the boy's suitcase, and they both climbed in the flyer.

Gabe wrinkled his nose. "Something smells bad."

"Sorry." He cracked the windows, but it did little to ease the stench in the confined space.

As he opened a connection to Shannon, tension crawled up his neck. *Breathe, think, speak.* He needed to keep his mutinous tongue in check.

"Did you find him? Is he all right?"

"He's fine. We're headed back there now." He drew in a deep breath. "We need to talk about his situation."

"He has an appointment tomorrow with a child psychologist who will try to do something about his pathological lying. In the meantime, I'll get a tracking bracelet for him until I can be certain he won't run away again."

The thought of Gabe tagged like a criminal sickened him. His hands tightened on the controls. "There's been enough brainwashing in our family, don't you think?"

Shannon's face clouded. "He's upsetting the girls with his wild stories about their grandfather being a killer. If he's going to stay here, he'll have to apologize and promise not to do it anymore."

"It's Dad who's telling lies. He denied being in the neighborhood, and we can prove he talked to Aaron after the board meeting. Why lie if he isn't guilty?"

"Maybe he's protecting someone."

"If he didn't do it but he knows who did, he's guilty of complicity."

"I'm sorry, Rafe. I know you and Dad haven't always gotten along, but I don't know how you can accuse him of being such a monster. If you honestly believe he killed Aaron, then you aren't welcome here anymore. And if you won't allow me free rein to raise Gabe as I see fit, then neither is he."

Shannon closed the connection before Rafe could say another word. He wanted to pound his fists on the dash and rage at the universe. Before he could start the engine, his nanocom chimed.

"What?" he said, his tone sharp.

Alana's tired face displayed on the screen. "I have a squad ready to search for Gabe."

Rafe swallowed his frustration. "Thanks, Alana, I already found him."

"Good, then you'll be headed to Shannon's?"

What kind of parental example would he set if he lied in front of Gabe? But he didn't want to air the family's dirty laundry.

"We're catching a bite to eat. We both missed dinner."

Alana was silent for a long moment. "Where's that girl of yours going? If she's following a lead, I want to know about it."

Rafe blinked at the screen while his heart thudded in his chest. "What makes you think she's leaving?"

"As a witness in Mr. Goldman's murder, she's on our watch list. She booked passage on tomorrow's early shuttle."

Kama leaving? He had to convince her to stay. "Where is she now?"

Alana stared hard at the screen. "You don't know?"

Rafe's cheeks warmed. "I've been a little busy."

"At the contractor compound. You want to tell me what she's doing?"

"I would if I could, Alana. Now I need to get Gabe some chow." He cut the connection.

"Are we really going to dinner?"

"Sure. Right after I talk to Kama. What would you like to have?"

"Can we get pizza?"

"Pizza it is."

Rafe flipped on the engines and took the flyer north over the treetops. Something Shannon said nagged at him, but he wouldn't think about it now. He was finally on his way to see Kama, and that's all that mattered.

25

The dining hall door creaked open, and the shuffling of cards stopped. Kama lifted her head from where it rested on her arms. The three men and a woman playing poker near the entrance watched McTavish stride down the floor toward her. Relief rolled over her. He didn't look injured from the bus attack.

McTavish stopped on the opposite side of her table, head bowed and shoulders drooping. His dress slacks were ripped at the knee, dirt smeared his shirt front, and his hands were the color of lobsters. The most awful smell swirled around him.

She'd failed to catch the hacker, and she still didn't have the evidence she needed to prove his father murdered Goldman. Now that she knew he was okay, she wanted him to go away.

When his eyes took in the bruise on her cheek, he jerked upright. "What happened? Who hit you? A contractor?"

He looked toward the card players, posture stiffening. How could he defend the contractors against a mob one minute and accuse them the next? Her eyes narrowed.

"Channeling your father now?"

He swung back to face her. From the distress lining his brow, her comment hit its mark. She wanted to hold her nose so overpowering was the stench. Even the open sewers in Mumbai's slums didn't smell this bad.

He glanced again toward the group of contractors. "This place is too dangerous. You're coming with me."

Kama shot up, hands flat on the table. "You're the one who

shouldn't be here. Shiva, they're planning to lynch you and your murdering father."

"Is this man annoying you, Kama?"

The card players walked down the dining hall but stopped well back, their noses wrinkling. They gave McTavish unfriendly looks.

"Yes."

The men advanced another step, and McTavish shifted into a fighting stance. She toyed with the idea of letting them duke it out, but she'd seen what McTavish could do. The contractors didn't stand a chance even at four-to-one odds.

"Never mind." She walked around the table, snagged her duffel and his elbow, and dragged him away toward the exit doors. "He's just leaving."

The air outside was hot and dusty, but at least a breeze carried the horrible odor downwind. Her squad of bodyguards peered through the glass doors.

McTavish rubbed a hand across the back of his neck and took a deep breath. "I'm sorry. I didn't come here to argue. I came to apologize and to beg your forgiveness. You were right about everything. I shouldn't have allowed the board to push me into firing the council. I should have listened when you tried to tell me about the threat to the EcoMech network."

She took a step back. She wouldn't forgive him. It would only encourage his notion that she was some goody-two-shoes. He had to see her for what she was.

He spread his hands. "I was wrong to blame you for Aaron's death or the riots. I should have known you wouldn't—"

"Open your eyes, McTavish. I'm a thief and a spy, and I won't apologize for it." She crossed her arms. "I did everything you accused me of, and I'll do it again."

He blinked and thrust his hands in his pockets. "You did it because you care about people, and you're willing to stick your neck out to help them. You have a good heart, and I love you."

She threw up her arms. "I'm the girl of the month, nothing more. You've been through enough women that you should recognize the signs."

Moonlight reflected the pain in his eyes. It made her ache, and she looked away.

"Alana told me you're leaving. When I see what's happened to you… Go back to your school. Stay out of things here. I need to know you're safe. When this is over, I hope you'll give me a second chance."

The man didn't take 'no' for an answer, but she couldn't bring herself to abuse him further. He looked so forlorn.

"I thought you were leaving."

He flinched. "I have to make sure my family is safe first."

How could he still hold so much love for someone who cursed him with every breath? "Is that code for 'get my father off the hook'?"

"There's more going on than we realized. Everyone's at risk—Shannon, her girls, Greg, even Gabe."

"And you're at the top of the list." *Damn him.*

He shrugged. "I knew that when I came here."

Would he never stop risking his life for a family that didn't care if he saw tomorrow's sunrise? He seemed so depressed, so defeated. He needed hope.

"I stole Goldman's backup files from his safe. I'm leaving tomorrow to follow a lead that may identify the blackmailer."

McTavish looked poleaxed. He turned away and stared into the night sky. After a minute, he turned to her again.

"Do you like pizza?"

"Are you *propositioning* me?"

"No! I mean—" Confusion flitted across his face before his tired blue eyes met hers. "Gabe and I were on our way to dinner. I thought you could join us. Afterward, you could show me what you found."

"Gabe's with you?" Bringing the boy to the compound seemed dangerous.

"He's waiting in the flyer." McTavish gestured toward the front gates.

Her empty stomach reminded her of how long it had been since she'd eaten last. Her mouth watered at the thought of pizza. She might also get the chance to bring up Gabe's future, advocate that McTavish consider the boy's desires.

She'd steel herself against his charms and get a meal. Then she'd get on with her hunt for the blackmailer—without him. She hefted her duffel and strode toward the gate. He fell in beside her.

"What's that smell?"

Even in the dim lights from the guardhouse, she could see his cheeks redden.

"Potato slurry. Sorry. I'll clean up in the guardhouse."

"Good thing we're going for pizza and not burgers."

His brow pulled down. "Why's that?"

"Because otherwise I'd have to make a bad joke about having a McSlurry with my burger and fries."

He regarded her with disbelief. Then the black cloud of his depression rolled back and he laughed.

She waited by the flyer while he cleaned up in the guardhouse. When he came out five minutes later, water droplets sparkled on his wet hair, and he smelled of soap. Gabe shifted to the back seat, and she and

McTavish climbed in.

She stuffed her duffel between her feet. "If you're planning to use Shannon's place while we talk, I should warn you that I'm not welcome there."

Gabe leaned against the back of her seat. "Shannon kicked us out, too."

If Shannon wanted no part of the pair, perhaps Kama wouldn't need to advocate for Gabe to live with McTavish. She waited for McTavish to explain. Instead, he asked what toppings they wanted on their pizza. After he called in the order, he started the engines and pointed them toward downtown.

In fifteen minutes, they'd picked up their order and taken off again. The scent of the food filled the flyer. Kama wanted to rip open the boxes and dig in. She wondered where they were going. McTavish hadn't said a word.

They settled in a neighborhood of small, neat homes, most with curtains drawn. The light brown house they stopped at had a blue sedan parked in the driveway, wilted lawn, and some kind of dead vine climbing a trellis by the front door.

McTavish carried the boxes up the walk and pressed a doorbell. After several minutes, the porch light came on, and the door opened. Chief Dzandarova peered out at them.

"Mr. McTavish, what a surprise." Sarcasm oozed out with the words.

"With all the reporters in town and my hotel closed for refurbishing, it's hard to find rooms." McTavish flashed his rakish grin. "Since you're concerned about my security, I wondered if I could borrow your couch for the night?"

She narrowed her eyes. "I was just talking to your sister. We speculated about where you'd turn up next."

"Ah." He shifted his feet uncomfortably.

"We'll share our pizza," Gabe offered.

"How very thoughtful, Gabe. Please come in." She gave McTavish a cold smile. "Perhaps while we eat, your uncle will fill me in on what he's been up to today."

26

Rafe settled on the lumpy couch and sipped his coffee. Maybe this hadn't been the best idea, but he'd run out of options. Now that they'd demolished the pizza and sent Gabe to bed, he steeled himself for Alana's grilling and debated what to tell her.

Much of the information they'd gathered about their blackmail suspects had come through Kama's boss, Samir Ganguly, a phantom Rafe knew by reputation only. The man was said to have masterminded everything from terrorist attacks to macabre assassinations, all without leaving a shred of hard evidence. One look at the records Samir provided, and Alana would know they'd been obtained illegally.

Alana leaned back in her well-worn armchair on the opposite side of the cramped living room, a cold beer dripping sweat onto the cheap lamp table beside her. She skewered Rafe with her gaze.

"Besides trying to stop riots single-handed, what have you been up to today, Mr. McTavish?"

Kama gave him a sharp look. She wouldn't be happy bringing Alana into the investigation. The last thing he wanted was Kama angry—no, more angry—with him. Heat still simmered under her neutral façade.

"I spent the afternoon interviewing our blackmail suspects to find out where they were when Aaron was killed."

"Kali, McTavish, *by yourself?*" Kama rolled her eyes. "Moorhk."

"I could have gotten that information for you," Alana said, nodding her agreement of his foolhardiness.

"But not without raising their suspicions."

"And what did you learn?" the security chief asked.

"Bob verified that Lev Kozlov was on the orbital station late yesterday afternoon, and his name doesn't appear on any incoming passenger lists.

"Bert Gerlach and Lars Svenson both say they were at home. We have no way to verify that."

"And for this you risked your life?" Kama glared at him from the other end of the couch.

"For the moment, I suggest we focus on Lars. He lied about how well he knew Aaron. I can't figure out why he'd do that unless it was to cover up that he'd paid a social call the night Aaron died."

"You've eliminated Mr. Gerlach," Alana said. "Why?"

Rafe gave her a wry smile. "If he wanted me out of the way, he could have left me in the path of that tanker."

Kama sucked in a breath, and a little thrill coursed through him. How could she worry endlessly about him, and at the same time work so hard to drive him away? Perhaps she had commitment issues, or a previous relationship ended badly. He wished he knew more about her.

"What about your father's alibi?" Kama folded her arms. "Did you investigate that, too?"

He felt like he sat under the glare of hot lights, strapped to a chair in a room outfitted with all the latest in torture devices.

"I know Gabe's testimony seems to put my father in the frame, but I have reservations."

Kama snorted.

Alana leaned forward. "What might those be?"

"You were there that night, Alana. While we stood at the door waiting for the all clear, what could you see?"

The security chief shifted her eyes to the coffee table while she recalled the previous night. "The study door was open and light came through, although not much. I could smell paint and see that something was scrawled on the walls. Nothing seemed out of place, except for Ms. Bhatia on the floor at the far end."

"When did you realize it was Kama?"

Alana sat back and frowned. "Not until I scanned her ID bracelet."

Rafe shook his head. "I mean when did you realize it was a person?"

"You've lost me, Mr. McTavish. What's your point?"

"I knew Kama was there, and I knew what she looked like, but standing in the open door, I couldn't tell who was on the floor or even be sure it was a body."

"It was too dark," Kama whispered. "I couldn't see whoever hid on the stairs, and Gabe couldn't have recognized your father. Why did he lie?"

"I don't think he did. He saw my father later, as he got in his flyer under the street light. But he followed someone else."

27

Kama wanted to crawl under the coffee table. It was still possible Cullen McTavish killed Goldman, but as McTavish had pointed out, he had no motive. If Kozlov had an air-tight alibi, they could delete him from the suspect list. She agreed that Gerlach was unlikely to save McTavish's life if he wanted to replace McTavish. That left the lawyer, Svenson.

McTavish turned to her. "You said you found a lead to the blackmailer?"

Kama flicked her eyes to Dzandarova and back to him. She didn't like the idea of including the security chief. Bad enough that she'd had to lean on Samir. Asking for help always came at a price.

"Goldman's been paying a hundred thousand a year to a woman, Toni Benton, starting eleven years ago."

Dzandarova's brows shot up. "How'd you get that information?"

McTavish answered without missing a beat. "As executor of Aaron's estate, I tasked Kama to go over his records. I suspected that Aaron knew what Leon was being blackmailed about, but he wouldn't tell me."

"Who's Toni Benton?" the security chief asked, apparently mollified. "And how is she related to Leon's blackmail?"

"Twelve years ago, she worked at EcoMech," Kama replied. "Back then, she went by Tina Burke. She spent six months as Leon Goldman's executive assistant. Four months after she quit, she changed her name and got her first cash payment from Aaron Goldman. She was also given ownership of a bar at the Eden entertainment station."

McTavish pulled his ball from his pocket and rolled it between his palms. His eyes became unfocused. Dzandarova gave him a funny look but said nothing.

"Leon didn't think his father knew about the blackmail. And why would a woman who left the company twelve years ago make the kinds of demands the blackmailer did?" The ball walked over the top of McTavish's knuckles. "Does she cross paths with any of our suspects?"

Kama shared his frustration. She'd asked Samir the same question. "Not that we can find."

Dzandarova's eyes narrowed. "Who else is working this case?"

After a hesitation, McTavish answered. "My data analysis team at Security Partners."

"Must be nice having all those resources at your fingertips," the security chief grumbled. "If you're going to see this Benton woman tomorrow, I'm sending an officer with you, Ms. Bhatia. You're not authorized to make an arrest."

Let Dzandarova try to send an officer. She'd lose the man the minute they hit Earth Central, and then he'd discover that his name suddenly appeared on the terrorist watch list.

McTavish pocketed his ball. "That won't be necessary. I still retain my EA investigator credentials. I'll accompany Kama."

28

Alana glared at Rafe, but he wouldn't back down. Kama would never agree to take an officer. From the look on her face, she wasn't happy about having him along, either. He wouldn't let her go alone. They were chasing a cold-blooded killer.

"I'm not babysitting Gabe," the security chief announced.

He hadn't considered what to do with the boy. The whole guardian thing made life more complicated. He'd need to figure out whether to hire a tutor or enroll Gabe in a school. All that would have to wait until they moved to Mumbai.

"I'll take care of it," he said, uncertain about how he'd do that.

Alana rose from her chair, and Rafe rose with her. She bid them goodnight and left the room.

Kama glowered at him. "Stay here. Take care of Gabe. I can handle Toni Benton."

He sat down on the ancient, scruffy couch, glad for a chance to talk to her at last.

"It's too dangerous for you to go alone."

"However did I survive before I met you?" Her words dripped sarcasm.

He kicked himself for voicing his concerns. Nothing made Kama angry faster than the slightest hint she might need help. He should know that by now. She lived a dangerous life as a hacker, but it was nothing like the danger inherent in chasing a killer. He'd protect her whether she liked it or not. He just had to figure out how.

"There's something else I need to tell you."

He ran a hand through his hair while queasy anxiety tightened his gut. Kama waited, a foot tapping the floor.

"EcoMech's about to go under."

Her face went slack. "That's impossible. Oasis would have seen it coming. Varun would never have agreed to a partnership."

"Leon's been using dubious financial practices to cover his poor management. He took out loans and used EcoMech shares as collateral. If the stock price drops below a certain level, the banks can call in the full amount of the loans immediately. EcoMech has no way to pay.

"Aaron intended to lean on his old friends to get refinancing. Without his clout, EcoMech has no chance of convincing the banks to make new loans at affordable interest rates. Leon's and Aaron's deaths—along with all the labor strife and a host of quality issues with the latest shipment of harvesters—have pushed the stock price down to within ten points of triggering a default."

She went still, and her voice dropped. "There must be something you can do. Oasis needs EcoMech to build the Sharma Network."

He fiddled with his coffee cup to avoid seeing the disappointment in her eyes. "I'm the new kid. I don't have the necessary influence in the financial markets to convince lenders to bet on an EcoMech recovery."

"And your father? Can't he talk to the bankers?"

"My father has been involved in a number of failed business schemes. That's why my mother left the Madison Trust in my hands and not his. No one would lend him a single credit, much less refinance the millions Leon took on. Now with the rumors about his involvement in Aaron's death..."

Kama rose and paced the room. She stopped on the other side of the coffee table.

"There has to be a way."

He rolled the coffee cup between his hands and looked into her dark chocolate eyes. "Maybe there is. Some representatives from Caligo Corp approached me with an offer for a merger. They have the assets to cover enough of EcoMech's debt to pull the company back from the brink. The merged company could still partner with Oasis in the Sharma Network."

Kama backed away and held her hands up in defense. "No! You can't agree. Oasis could never partner with Caligo. Don't you know what they're like? How could you consider such a thing?"

Surprised by the hysteria in her voice, he stood to face her. "EcoMech's investors aren't all rich robber barons. Hundreds of thousands of middleclass workers have their life savings sunk in pension funds that hold big chunks of EcoMech stock. If the company goes, they'll take a huge loss. A hundred thousand EcoMech employees will be on the streets. It's my job as CEO to do what's right for all of them, not just for you and the Sharma Network."

Color climbed her face. "So that's it? You'll sell?"

He spread his hands. "It seems like the path that hurts the least number of people."

"Is it? I've heard the Goldman option and the Caligo option. I haven't heard a McTavish option. Or isn't that part of your job? Oh, that's right. You're just marking time until you can run home to Mumbai."

She snatched her duffel and stormed out.

29

Kama tiptoed into the living room, planning to make her escape before anyone else awoke. She'd spent much of the night tossing in her bed. If McTavish could hand EcoMech over to Caligo Corp, she'd seriously misjudged him. There were no honorable men or women at Caligo, only greedy bastards and sociopaths who would let nothing stand between them and power.

She'd done everything she could to keep the Sharma Network out of their hands, and now McTavish wanted to give it to them on a platter. And he thought she should be grateful because it would give temporary respite to a few hundred thousand investors and employees before Caligo enslaved them in the name of profits.

She wanted to shake him, to slam him into a wall, to make him see the terrifying consequences of his decision. To hell with trying to protect him. To hell with finding Goldman's killer. Mass murderers disguised as corporate executives would soon run the galaxy despite her efforts to stop them.

McTavish sat on the couch slurping coffee while he scanned a filmie. A dozen more were strewn across the coffee table, and two or three had drifted onto the floor. The pillow and blanket Dzandarova had left for him sat untouched on the little table by the door. He looked awful, eyes red-rimmed and face drawn. She gave up her stealth approach.

"Time to go." She tapped her nanocom.

He glanced at his own. "Five minutes."

He strode toward the bedrooms. When he returned ten minutes later, a sleepy-eyed Gabe trailed him. McTavish stuffed the filmies into a document case and led the way to the flyer. They rode in silence as Harvest's too-bright sun climbed over the horizon.

The shuttleport was a small glass and concrete structure with a sprawling asphalt parking lot on one side of it, and the two shuttle runways on the other. The insides of the building were divided in half by a ticket counter and security check points. The guards recognized McTavish and flagged them around the scanners.

They hurried through the empty waiting area with its rows of vacant plastic seats and into an empty concourse that jutted away from the building. At the end of the concourse, they emerged onto the tarmac and trooped through the heat to climb portable stairs into a shuttle.

The shuttle was half full at best, and they were given VIP seats at the front. Their fellow travelers were mostly men and women in business attire, but a few, like McTavish, wore casual dress. Unlike McTavish, the men had showered and shaved. In his case, his dishevelment added to his aura of the hard-partying playboy. She cursed the day she met him.

On this side of the jump gate, there was little she could do. Once they crossed to Earth Central, she'd leave him. It would be crowded there, and easy enough to get lost in the hustle and bustle. She'd already ditched the stupid tracking bracelet at Dzandarova's house.

They'd barely lifted off the runway when he opened his case and pulled out a fistful of filmies. One surreptitious glance told her they were business reports. Some displayed pie charts or columns of figures. Others were paragraph upon paragraph of dense text.

On her other side, Gabe stifled a yawn. She smoothed his hair and looked with disapproval at his dress shirt and slacks. McTavish ought to get the boy some normal kid clothes. She'd miss Gabe and wished she could tell him goodbye.

Next to her, McTavish's leg bounced in a fast rhythm while he studied his documents. She did her best to ignore it, but his calf brushed hers. Irked, she jerked her leg away.

McTavish looked up from his fan of documents. "Sorry."

Kama leaned back, closed her eyes, and began to review the records from her pursuit of the hacker. She would never get another shot at the punk, but she wouldn't rest until she understood why her plan hadn't worked.

A moment later, a cascade of filmies spilled into her lap. She jerked upright as McTavish made a grab for them. They slid away onto the floor.

"Sorry," he mumbled.

Their heads collided as they both reached down to fetch the lost filmies.

"Ow!" Kama glared at him and rubbed her head while he made another try at retrieving his documents. "Can't this wait until you're in the office?"

His cobalt eyes locked on hers. "In forty-five hours, the Caligo offer expires. I can't reject it unless I can develop a plan that saves EcoMech without a merger."

She stared at the filmies. "You're not going back to Mumbai?"

McTavish sighed and rubbed the back of his neck. "I promised Aaron I'd see that Gabe inherits the company. I can't be the kind of man who goes back on his word, and I can't guarantee Gabe's inheritance unless I stay."

"And your father?"

McTavish's face hardened. "I don't want to fight him, but if he won't see reason, I'll have no choice."

His eyes got a distant look. "There's also something fishy about Caligo's offer. I can't fathom why a pharmaceutical company wants to merge with an ag company. Why make the offer now? Their representatives seemed to know more than they should about EcoMech's finances."

She couldn't believe her ears. "You think Caligo is involved with Goldman's murder?"

"I have no proof to suggest that, but they certainly seem anxious to swoop in and profit from his death." He looked her in the eye. "Even if I do find a way to save EcoMech, there's no guarantee the company will have the necessary capital to build the Sharma Network. I want you to know that up front."

Kama squeezed his hand. "You can do it."

☠   ☠   ☠

At Harvest's tiny jump gate station, they transferred to a jump ship for an uneventful trip to Earth Central. When they reached Earth orbit, Kama pointed out the sights to an excited Gabe.

The giant terminal hung like a row of side-by-side donuts in the blackness of space. The end rings provided docking for ships. The next ring in from each end housed gift shops, restaurants, and hotels. The center donut provided housing for station personnel and administrative offices. They all spun slowly to create an environment with artificial gravity.

In the distance, space tugs and customs shuttles flitted around huge conglomerations of cargo containers. Jump ships, the locomotives that towed chains of containers through the jump gates, maneuvered to drop passengers at the station or boosted away to pick up another load headed for far-flung colonies.

When they reached the busy terminal, they disembarked into a wide concourse that circled up out of sight. Humans of every hue and in every kind of garb traversed the station's corridors. As usual, the place was packed.

McTavish kept a hand on Gabe's shoulder, and she trailed behind them, scanning the crowd. As they headed toward the inner commercial ring, McTavish glanced down at his nanocom. By the time Kama got close enough to read the message he'd received, he'd cleared the screen. He glanced back at her, and then his eyes slid past her before he turned around and plowed on.

McTavish led them to a coffee shop located amidst a group of gift shops. A big, blond woman with a buzz cut sat at a table nursing a cup and scanning the crowd. She dressed in sensible shoes, loose black pants, and a baggy tan jacket that made hiding a weapon easy. Kama recognized her in a heartbeat.

The woman jumped to her feet with surprising agility and rushed to fold McTavish in a crushing embrace, which he returned with enthusiasm. She overtopped him by a good six centimeters. There was no mistaking her for anything but a strapping mercenary despite her attire.

"RM," she said, pushing him back to arm's length, "you look like hell. Don't they have razors on Harvest?"

McTavish responded with a broad grin.

"Barb, you remember Kama? And this is Gabe Goldman." He put a hand on the boy's shoulder. "Gabe, this is Barb my sec— the new CEO of Security Partners."

Barb turned a jaundiced eye on Kama before offering her hand to Gabe. "Hiya."

Gabe's mouth sagged open. "Are you one of Uncle Rafe's spies, too? Like Kama?"

A predatory look came over Barb as she shifted her attention to Kama, and Kama smirked.

"How's Ying?" McTavish asked, oblivious to the exchange.

Barb broke into a radiant smile and thrust her nanocom in front of him. "Tired and cranky. Look at what popped out."

McTavish's smile lit his whole face. He gazed with fascination at her nanocom. "She had the baby, and you didn't call me?"

This was a side of McTavish Kama wouldn't have guessed existed. He seemed delirious with joy. She wondered again about why he shared a house with a lesbian couple. It must put a crimp in his playboy lifestyle.

"I've been a little busy running your company and putting together this mission."

"Sorry," he said, his smile fading. "I shouldn't have dragged you out here. You should be home with Ying and the little guy."

Barb slapped his back and included a quick flip of her hand, a sign so deftly given that Kama almost missed it.

"If you'd heard the lungs he has, you'd know how glad I am to be away for a few hours. Besides, what's family for?"

Two big louts also in casual dress strolled up to flank Barb. McTavish called them by name, and handshaking and backslapping ensued. Then he turned to Gabe.

"Barb and these two gorillas will be your escorts today. No wandering off, okay?"

Gabe stared up at the new arrivals, each at least another six centimeters taller than Barb. He swallowed and offered his hand. With straight faces, each of them engulfed his hand in theirs and introduced themselves, but the twinkle in their eyes gave away their amusement. When she thought about the lengths McTavish had gone to in order to provide Gabe with bodyguards, a chill swept over her. Was the boy in that much danger?

Gabe gestured McTavish aside and whispered in the man's ear. McTavish nodded and returned to the group.

"We're making a pit stop. Be right back."

With that, they threaded their way through the crowds toward the restrooms.

"Man, he's one lucky kid to have RM for a dad," Barb said.

Kama snorted. "Yeah, McTavish can teach him all the best pickup lines."

The woman lifted her chin, her lips curled up in a knowing smile. "Don't believe everything you see in the news vids."

Kama crossed her arms and lifted her own chin. "What's that supposed to mean?"

"He doesn't date."

Kama laughed. "Is that his clone twin making the rounds of the clubs with one pretty woman after another on his arm? Or did the news channels fabricate the vids?"

Barb's predatory look returned. "Not dates. Protection details. He's the face man. What you don't see in the vids are the other four squad members working the perimeter."

At Kama's disbelieving look, she chuckled.

"It's how he started Security Partners. After five years with Earth Force, he thought he'd networked with the brass sufficiently to start his own security business, and his officer buddies would favor him with contracts. Despite how impressed they'd been with his service, they told him he had to prove he could build a viable company first.

"So he made the rounds of the corporations. But all the 'ol boys' could see was a rich kid playing at toy soldiers, not the decorated Earth Force Special Ops captain and hard-working entrepreneur.

"When he couldn't make any inroads with the husbands, he crashed charity events and chatted up the wives. It was popular back then to snatch kids from rich families and hold them for ransom. Hell, it still is.

Anyway, the 'difficult' kids, the kind who liked to party hard, tended to ditch their security, putting themselves at risk. RM suggested that he could provide a security detail that wouldn't be ditched. He did it by pretending to 'pick up' his target and blending in with the brats."

"They never realized they'd been set up?" Kama asked, incredulous.

"Nope. Then one night, five terrorists hit the Mumbai Club while RM and the squad were there with a client's daughter. They weren't interested in ransoms. They wanted body count."

Kama gasped. "The Mumbai Club bombing? He was there? Dozens of people were killed. But the news only reported a single suicide bomber."

"He got his client's daughter and several of her friends out, and then he went back in to stop the bombers. If he hadn't, the death toll would have been much higher. He wouldn't allow any publicity because it would blow his cover."

"Crazy moorhk," Kama muttered.

Barb nodded and cracked a wry smile. "That's RM. Within days, word went around the society circles, and Security Partners had more business than it could handle. He didn't need to continue the escort service, and he sure didn't need to do it himself, but he did. He has a knack with the lost souls, the ones who've gone off the rails into self-destructive spirals. He never gives up on them. But he never dates. He's relationship phobic."

McTavish and Gabe wove through the crowds back to the table, and she saw him with new eyes. *Of course he's relationship phobic.* At the mining station, when he thought he might die, he'd confessed his guilt over the loss of his wife and children. She'd heard the pain in his words. Now she saw how that pain had scarred his life.

Reality shifted around her. What if she wasn't the girl of the month? What if he meant it when he said he loved her? He seemed suddenly fragile, and she had the power to shatter him. A shiver of fear pierced her chest.

McTavish and the boy chatted happily as they walked. Their warmth radiated through the station to blanket her. She pushed it away. If he knew her, really *knew* her, he'd change his mind. That meant confessing her own sins, and she wasn't ready. Might never be ready.

McTavish checked his nanocom again. For just an instant, the smile slipped. His eyes met Kama's, and deep concern flickered in the shining cobalt.

"We should push off," McTavish said when he reached them. "Remember, Gabe, you stay with Barb."

Gabe stared up at the big merc, his face frozen half in fear and half in awe. That wouldn't do. If McTavish thought the boy might be in danger, then it was imperative that Gabe follow Barb's orders without hesitation. Bonding was in order.

Kama ruffled the boy's hair. "I hear there's a great zero gee laser tag maze over on Playground 3. It's a short shuttle hop from here. Maybe you and Barb could take on the goon squad." Kama jerked a thumb at the two mercs. "She can teach you how to shoot."

Gabe turned pleading eyes on Barb. "Will you teach me to shoot?"

Barb gave Kama a withering look and smiled through gritted teeth. "If I can teach a space cadet like your uncle to shoot, I guess I can teach you. Besides, these guys couldn't hit the broad side of a battleship. We can beat them easy, but only if we stick together, kid."

Kama stifled a laugh. "And get him some new clothes, something that doesn't scream, 'Rich kid! Snatch me.'"

30

Rafe stepped from the docking bay into the main concourse of Eden. An odd perfume tingled his nose, the odor trailing from a scantily clad female who sauntered by carrying a poster advertising a gambling casino. He experienced an immediate rising desire to get intimately acquainted with Kama as soon as possible. *Focus.*

As they walked, flashes of color drew his eye to the garish neon displays along the station walls, promoting every imaginable kind of entertainment vice. A cacophony of hawkers just beyond the docking bay entrance offered pills and potions promising an assortment of pleasures. He turned his head looking for a navigation kiosk and making note of the man in the loud, floral shirt and baseball hat strolling along thirty feet behind.

"Toni's Place is this way." Kama waved at a dimly lit corridor off the main concourse.

Was Kama the type to spend time in a den of iniquity like this? "You've been here before?"

"I downloaded a map."

Which didn't answer his question. Should he probe further? She volunteered little about herself, and his data searches came up consistently empty. He hungered for more information.

"Do you frequent the entertainment stations?"

She glanced sideways at him. "I make the rounds a few times a year."

"Ah." He hoped his disappointment didn't show.

"What about you?"

What should he say? That he wouldn't be caught dead in a place like this? His idea of a vacation was wind-surfing across the bay amidst a pod of whales, or racing down an Alpine ski slope at breakneck speed.

"Once, chasing an embezzler."

Red and blue dome lights flashed in the ceiling of the hallway, and many of the doorways to other businesses sported well-endowed men and women in very little clothing beckoning them to come in for a visit. He ignored these as best he could.

"What kind of entertainment do you prefer?" He hoped she gambled and didn't come for the drugs—or the sex trade, although that seemed to be Eden's main source of revenue.

Her brows lifted in surprise, and he thought he'd overstepped his bounds. She looked away, face thoughtful. Then she gave a wicked laugh.

"I stalk hackers trying to break into the casino networks." She grinned at his confusion. "Every up-and-coming hacker takes a shot at the casinos eventually. We have layer upon layer of traps waiting for them. Most don't make it past the second level. It's fun to watch."

A sizzle of excitement shot through his chest. She'd shared with him, and that meant more than her twisted remark about watching criminals for entertainment. They'd built a fragile connection. He didn't want to break it.

"We? You mean Oasis?"

"We provide free software and the latest in network security in exchange for being allowed to monitor the casino systems and track intruders."

She steered them down a cross-corridor. As they turned the corner, he caught another glimpse of the big, brown-haired man in the baseball cap.

"Then you turn the hackers over to law enforcement?"

"If they show real talent, we hire them. The second-rate punks are watched until they try a grab somewhere else. Then their potential victims get an anonymous tip."

"Why aren't they arrested here?"

The casinos don't want that kind of publicity—it opens the door to law enforcement snooping."

"What happens if a skilled criminal doesn't want to hire on with Oasis?"

They walked another fifteen feet before she answered. "I only identify them."

She knew—or at least suspected—more, but if he pressed, they'd end up in another argument. He swallowed his questions, glad for her new willingness to share. Kama stopped in front of a sign proclaiming

Toni's Place and stepped inside.

A giant of a man barred their way. "You'll need to provide a hundred credit deposit before I let you in."

Rafe flashed the man a warm smile. "We're here to see Toni on business."

The big guy's eyes narrowed. "You think I was born yesterday? A hundred credits, or move along."

"That's ludicrous." Kama planted fists on her hips.

Rafe tapped a credit transfer into his nanocom before she could kick the man in the shins. The giant checked for receipt of the funds, grunted, and waved them through a second doorway into the main room of the establishment.

A hundred foot square area offered a bar along one wall, a huge vid screen playing a porn flick on another, and a series of larger-than-life portraits of nudes in suggestive poses spaced along a third. Couches and fake potted plants dotted the floor space, giving an almost jungle-like atmosphere to the place.

Near-naked men and women lounged on the couches, some engaged in conversations and more with what had to be customers in various states of undress. Rafe's nose detected the odd scent again, undoubtedly a synthetic pheromone meant to drive service requests up.

They took a table near the middle of the room. A scantily-clad, large-busted woman approached, sidling up uncomfortably close. Trying to keep his eyes on her face and off her surgically augmented torso, he asked to speak to Toni.

She waved toward the couches. "We don't have any hostesses named Toni. Or maybe you meant a guy? I think we used to have one, but he quit last week. What are you drinking?"

"Nothing for the moment, thanks."

Throwing him a pouty look, she sauntered away.

Kama lowered her duffel to the floor beside her chair and scowled at him. "What happened to the McTavish charm?"

"We're being followed." He nodded toward the smoked glass windows that displayed the corridor beyond. "The thug in the Hawaiian shirt and baseball cap loitering across from the entrance."

Kama barely glanced at the window. Her face gave nothing away. "How long did it take you to make him?"

Stung by her suggestion that he wasn't being attentive enough, he replied, "The squad picked him up at Earth Central."

He tapped a finger on the table and squirmed in his chair. His eyes wandered to the porn film despite his desire to keep them elsewhere.

"He's been with us since the jump gate station. Shocking field craft. His boss ought to send him back to spy school."

Something about her voice raised his suspicions. "Barb says he's following you, not Gabe or me."

"According to the blueprints, those..." Kama waved at the portraits, "failed attempts at art are doors into private rooms, except for the one on the far right. It opens onto a hallway that leads to an office. If I trigger the fire alarms, we can get back there in the confusion."

Rafe gaped at her. "A fire alarm would cause a stampede out of this section of the station. People would get hurt."

She pursed her lips. "I'll limit it to the alarms in this establishment."

"Let's try something a little more subtle first."

Rafe approached the bar. A man and a woman provided service there, both naked from the waist up. He flagged the male bartender over to him. Once again, he asked for Toni.

The bartender ogled him. "I can only talk if you order a drink."

Rafe ordered a glass of water, for which the man charged him the outrageous price of twenty-five credits, and then he repeated his question.

"Toni doesn't see customers." The bartender moved down the bar to wait on another customer. When he'd finished, he strutted back to Rafe. "Anything else I can get you?"

Kama's solution drifted into his mind. He set it aside. "A hundred credit tip is yours if you'll tell Toni that Aaron Goldman sends his regards."

The bartender gave Rafe a smile, and then he disappeared behind the far right portrait. Rafe waited impatiently at the bar. With each passing minute of exposure to the chemicals in the air, the prostitutes scattered among the couches looked better and better. He didn't dare turn Kama's direction.

The bartender returned with a near-twin to the giant at the door, this one fully clothed, including, Rafe thought, the unseen bulk of body armor. The brute patted Rafe down for weapons, glanced in his document case, and started for the door. Kama scrambled up and dropped in behind them.

At the door, the guard blocked their way.

"She doesn't come in without a search, and the bag stays out here."

Kama stiffened. Rafe jumped between them.

"You search her and the bag, and then they both come in."

The big man rooted through Kama's duffel while she watched with slit eyes. His pat down of her was quick and professional. Rafe exhaled the breath he'd been holding.

They proceeded down a narrow corridor.

Beside him, Kama muttered, "We should have used my method."

They were shown into an office not unlike those in corporations throughout the galaxy. Soft overhead lighting made the space welcoming and bright. Fresh air whispered in through ceiling vents, and beige carpet under their feet muffled the sound of their entrance. The body guard closed the door behind them but remained inside.

An attractive woman Rafe guessed to be about five years his senior sat behind a real wood desk. She was tall, blond, fair-skinned, and busty. Her blue eyes swept over both of them and came to rest on his.

Rafe crossed to the desk and offered his hand. "Tina Burke, I'm Rafael McTavish, and this is Kama Bhatia."

The woman regarded him coldly without taking his hand. "I believe you've mistaken me for someone else. My name is Toni Benton. Mike, see the gentleman out."

Rafe blurted, "I'm Aaron Goldman's executor. If you want to continue receiving payments, we need to talk."

The woman waved her hand to dismiss the hulk from the room.

"Sit down, Mr. McTavish." She pointed to a pair of chairs on the opposite side of the desk. He and Kama settled in the offered seats.

"What is it you want from me?"

"Information. Why was Aaron paying you a hundred thousand credits a year?"

The brothel owner laughed. "None of your business. Now get out of my establishment."

"You won't receive another credit until I have an answer." He sat back and steepled his fingers.

Benton pulled a filmie from her desk, tapped on her nanocom, and handed it over. "This is a copy of my contract with Goldman. You can pay me as outlined in the document, or you can pay a pack of lawyers to defend the estate from me. Your choice."

Kama snatched the document before Rafe could read it. One glance and she'd taken it in. She looked at Benton, disbelief on her face.

"A hundred thousand a year until 2047, and then a final payment of a *million* credits? In exchange for saying nothing about services rendered to the Goldman family?"

"That sounds very much like blackmail, Ms. Benton."

The woman laughed. "Prove it."

Rafe leaned forward. "Describe the services."

"If I tell you, it negates the contract. I'd be a fool to do that."

Kama looked ready to leap across the desk and throttle the woman. He put a restraining hand on her arm.

"Leon was being blackmailed. Aaron asked me to look into it. Now Aaron's been murdered. I believe the two crimes are connected and that you're involved. A word to EA will have them crawling all over your business."

He let his statement sink in. "Or you can help me now, receive the remainder of your payments, and stay off EA's radar. *Your* choice."

Benton rubbed fingertips across her bowtie lips and regarded him through half-closed eyes. "You'll put that in writing? I won't be penalized for disclosing our business arrangement?"

"Business arrangement my ass," Kama muttered.

Rafe tapped a statement into his nanocom, affixed his thumb-print, and sent it off to Benton. In a moment, her nanocom chimed. She checked her own screen, and then regarded him across the desk.

"I don't know anything about Leon being blackmailed, although it doesn't surprise me. He was a bastard. Aaron Goldman paid me to... well, it was after the fact, but he paid me to produce an heir to the Gold-man legacy."

Rafe tried to imagine Aaron hiring this woman to bear a child for him and failed. "Perhaps you could be more specific?"

She smirked. "I'm Gabe Goldman's birth mother."

Rafe stared. "That's impossible. Amaya was his mother."

"Run a DNA test if you don't believe me."

He rubbed the back of his neck and tried to take the information in. "Did Amaya know?"

The question raised her eyebrows. "Are you kidding? That bitch would have killed the boy if she'd found out. She tried to kill *me* for screwing around with Leon."

"How did he do it?"

"You mean, how did Leon fool her?" Benton leaned back in her chair. "They'd tried having a kid. In fact, they'd tried to have several kids. She carried embryos, they used surrogate mothers. Amaya's eggs were too damaged. None of the fetuses survived to full term. Or if they did, they were vegetables and died soon after they were born. Amaya wouldn't agree to use donated eggs. It had to be hers or nothing.

"Leon and I were—well, let's say we were close friends. I was his executive assistant. He and Amaya were going for another round of fertility treatments. He proposed that he knock me up, and that when it was time for his and Amaya's kids to be born, he'd see to it that one of the babies would be swapped with mine."

"He paid you for this?" Kama asked, disgust wrinkling her face.

"I'd have to leave my job at EcoMech, or people might get suspicious about who the father was when I started to show. He set up a trust fund to compensate for my lost income and medical expenses.

"Amaya got wind of our affair. Just before I left Harvest, she showed up at my apartment carrying a Samurai sword, for God sakes. Scared the hell out me. She warned me to never go near Leon again."

Rafe exchanged a look with Kama. The memory of Amaya's death threats against him still made him shiver.

"When it was time for Amaya to be induced, Leon had me meet him at a med station in Earth orbit. While Amaya was having her baby in one room, I was next door having mine. The med tech took him from me, and that was the last I ever saw him.

"But the next day, as I was leaving, I ran into Amaya in the hallway. She came snarling up out of her wheelchair and tried to scratch my eyes out. She swore she'd kill me.

"I didn't doubt for a minute that she'd come after me. Leon, that bastard, waved it off. So there I was, broke, no job, and no more help from Leon once he had his precious kid."

"So you went to Aaron," Rafe guessed. "And you told him Gabe was your son."

"Damn right. Unlike Leon, he believed Amaya was dangerous. He helped me change my name and set me up in business here. He said it was worth every credit if it meant he'd have an heir."

"You never contacted Leon again?"

"Hell no. Amaya had a way of finding out things. I wasn't about to take that risk."

"Especially when you already had a sugar daddy paying your way," Kama spat.

"Look, lady, we had a contract. No one took advantage of anyone. Goldman got what he wanted, and I got what I wanted."

"What are your intentions now?" Kama demanded.

Toni's brow wrinkled. "You mean do I want the boy? It's tempting. He'll be worth a bundle. But I signed away all parental rights, and I don't think the court would look favorably on me."

"Who knew about the baby swap?" Rafe asked.

Toni leaned back in her chair. "I wasn't involved in any of that."

"Do you remember any of the techs' names?"

She laughed. "Are you kidding? I was whacked out on pain killers and didn't care who delivered the kid as long as they got the damn thing out of me."

Kama's hands squeezed the chair arms.

Rafe leaned forward. "And you never told anyone else?"

"With this place and two point eight million credits at stake, I can keep my mouth shut." She tipped her head sideways. "You think someone else found out and killed Aaron Goldman? Why? You can't get money from a corpse."

Rafe stood. "It isn't about money, Ms. Benton. It's about power."

Kama tapped furiously on her nanocom while they walked back to the docking bay. They wouldn't be away a moment too soon as far as Rafe was concerned. He'd had a full salute in his pants since they'd arrived. If they had time, he'd hit the john and relieve the stress before they caught the shuttle out. He nearly twisted his head off watching another half-naked female pass, and ahead, a raven beauty with gorgeous, mounded breasts adorned by nothing more than tiny, glittering pasties giggled her way his direction.

Fingers snapped in front of his eyes. "Earth to McTavish. Are you listening?"

Heat climbed his face. He struggled to focus on Kama with limited success. "Sorry. I'm a little distracted."

She arched an eyebrow at him. "Where's your ball?"

He grimaced. "I... misplaced it. I don't think it would help."

She followed his wandering gaze, rolled her eyes, and took his hand, dragging him rapidly through the crowd. Her skin felt soft and warm against his. He wanted to pull her into a doorway and kiss her. No, he wanted a lot more than kisses, but they'd be the place to start. He'd kiss every inch of her until she begged him to—

"McTavish!" She shook his shoulder. "Your ID."

He didn't remember arriving at the docking bay. A bored security guard waited for him to hold his nanocom next to the scanner. He obliged and followed Kama on board a shuttle. Once he'd buckled in, his hand drifted to hers. He wanted to hold on forever. He wanted to feel her hands on him, stroking his skin...

She turned wide eyes his direction. "I can spill an iced drink in your lap if it will help."

He jerked his hand away. "Sorry."

Too embarrassed to look at her again, he closed his eyes and focused on slowing his breathing, trying desperately to find the calm center and boost his beta waves before he said or did anything else he'd regret.

☠ ☠ ☠

Someone shook Rafe's arm. He rose through the blurry fog of sleep to the sound of shuffling feet. His gritty eyes labored open to the sight of passengers disembarking. Kama pulled her duffel from under the seat and rose to join them.

As he stood, their Hawaiian-shirted watcher stepped out through the hatch, and his alertness amped up. They ought to do something about that guy, ambush him and find out who he worked for. From the size of him, he'd be a handful, and Rafe wasn't carrying any weapons. He had Kama's safety to consider, too. As soon as they disembarked, he'd contact Barb and have the squad make the approach.

They stepped through the hatch into a well-lit docking bay that wasn't Earth Central. Astringent tainted the air, and two wheelchairs and a stretcher stood against one wall.

"Where are we?"

"RockPoint Medical Center." She took a left and followed a corridor away from the bay.

He rubbed a hand over his face and felt terminally stupid. "Okay, I'll bite. Why are we here?"

"Of the five med techs listed as providing services to the Goldmans and Tina Burke during the deliveries, two received large cash deposits to their bank accounts the day Gabe was born. A few days later, one of them died. The other one, Marco Jimenez, works here now."

"Died how?"

"In an accident. The tech failed to close an anesthetic gas valve properly, and the gas ignited while the tech was cleaning, according to the insurance reports."

Kama stopped by a door marked 'Maternity Clinic' and checked her nanocom. "Our guy goes off shift in ten minutes."

Kama leaned against the wall at one side of the door, and he joined her. Patients and staff drifted past. He didn't see the Hawaiian shirt guy.

He turned to face her. "About my behavior on the shuttle—"

"If you'd get a decent night's sleep, you wouldn't drift off while people are talking to you. Then you wouldn't have to apologize." She shifted her duffel higher on her shoulder. "You better let Barb know we'll be late getting back to Earth Central."

Grateful for her disguised forgiveness, he notified Barb of their delayed arrival. Barb was as averse to zero gee as he was, and he could imagine her discomfort playing laser tag in such an environment. He'd hoped she and Kama could be friends, but the women seemed off to a rocky start. He didn't understand why.

"You'll keep Gabe?" she asked.

"For better or for worse. He said you offered to adopt him."

"He's a great kid." She scuffed a shoe on the floor. "Did you want children? I mean, after losing your family..."

He chuffed a laugh. "I thought I'd never marry, and if I did, I'd start with a wife and work up to a family. Now I've skipped the nuptials and jumped straight to a pre-teen son. My life's turned upside down since I met you."

Her jaw worked, but no words came out. When she spoke, she addressed the floor.

"I want a child someday. But I have to be certain—absolutely certain—that I'm with the right man." Longing mixed with fear in her voice.

A fluid warmth oozed through his chest. He wanted to wrap her in his arms and heal the trauma that scarred her soul, a soul as fragile as blown glass. If he squeezed, she'd shatter, and then he'd lose her forever.

A squat, dark-haired man wearing scrubs emerged from the clinic. Kama pushed away from the wall.

"This is our guy."

Kama hustled after him. Rafe jogged to catch him up.

"Marco Jimenez," Rafe called.

The man turned, and Rafe held up his nanocom, his EA credentials on the screen.

"Inspector McTavish, EA Criminal Investigation Unit. Is there somewhere private we can talk?"

Worry clouded the man's brown eyes, and he rubbed a hand over his stubble-covered jaw. "There's a coffee shop. It won't be busy this time of day."

He led them along the hall and around the corner to something large enough to be considered a restaurant, not the small shop Rafe expected. As promised, the place was deserted.

The heavenly aroma of coffee wafted in the air, and Rafe wanted to order a cup. But sharing a meal would make the interrogation too informal. Jimenez seemed the meek type who would respond better to pressure.

The tech led them to a table in the middle of the establishment, away from the shop employee working to clean and restock the order counter. He took the seat facing the door. Rafe and Kama sat opposite him.

"What is it you want?"

"Eleven years ago, you agreed to swap babies for Leon Goldman and falsify their DNA records."

The tech went still. "I didn't falsify the records. That was Smith, the other guy Goldman paid."

A tiny smile curled Kama's lips. "But you switched the babies on the way to the nursery."

"Goldman said both the kids were his, and the one his wife had didn't look like it would last an hour. I figured I was sparing her the grief of another dead child. She had a history of that. The mother of the healthy kid didn't want her baby anyway. It was a win all around."

Rafe folded his hands on the table, thrilled that their questioning was going so well. "Besides you and the other tech, who else knew about the switch?"

Jimenez shifted in his seat, and his eyes dropped to the table. "No one."

Kama leaned forward. "You're a rotten liar. Tell us the truth."

Rafe held up a hand to stop her. "Look, Mr. Jimenez, you may not have heard. Aaron Goldman has been murdered. I believe that the person who killed him did so because of the secret of Gabe Goldman's true parentage. The statute of limitations is up on your crime. You have nothing to fear. But you may be able to help me catch a killer. I ask you again, who else knew about the switch?"

"Some things went wrong at the station." The tech looked from one to the other of them, and his face colored. "If they'd come out, I would have been in trouble."

"So you traded the information about Goldman to keep someone quiet. Who did you tell?"

Jimenez shook his head. "Hell, man, that was a long time ago. I don't remember."

Kama scooted her chair around the table beside his and thrust her nanocom in front of him.

"Tell me if you recognize any of these men." She tapped her nano-com.

The tech frowned at the screen. "He looks familiar."

An angry bee zipped by Rafe's ear. A small, dark hole appeared in the tech's forehead, and then he slumped over the table. Rafe lunged for Kama, meaning to knock her to the floor, but she'd already kicked back her chair and bolted for the exit.

Rafe turned to see the Hawaiian shirt guy release his grip on a heavy-set man clad in scrubs. The man in scrubs sagged to the floor. Rafe ran straight at the Hawaiian shirt guy, hoping Kama didn't try to take him on and cursing himself for not doing something about the watcher sooner.

To his surprise, Kama ignored their watcher and dropped to examine the victim on the floor whose head twisted at an odd angle. A zip gun lay on the floor beside the body.

Rafe stopped short of the Hawaiian shirt guy, who stood a good three inches taller than him and had arms roped with well-toned muscle. His stance screamed 'fighter.'

"Dammit, Wolf! We can't question a dead man," Kama said, looking up at the watcher.

Wolf's eyes never left Rafe. "He was an assassin with a weapon pointed your direction. I did what I had to."

"I don't recognize him, do you?" she asked Rafe.

Rafe bent and examined the body. A crude dragon tattoo covered the back of his left hand.

"Prison tat. The scar on his cheek looks like an old knife wound. He's probably hired help."

A clatter came from the restaurant counter. He turned and saw a spilled tray of cups at the shop clerk's feet. The clerk gaped at the med tech slumped over the table. Rafe turned back to the assassin disguised in scrubs.

Kama unbuckled the nanocom gauntlet from the dead man's arm and slipped it in her duffel. Then she searched his pockets but found nothing. She left the zip gun beside the body untouched.

Rafe gripped her wrist. "You can't steal his nanocom. It will help security identify him."

"We don't have time to wait for EA's results," she replied.

They both stood. She glanced around the room and tapped her nanocom. In a moment, she looked up at Wolf. "We're in a dead spot. No camera coverage here. You should go."

"No, he shouldn't. Cameras in the corridor will have him coming toward the restaurant. There's a camera over the order counter that recorded us talking to the tech when he was shot, so they'll know it wasn't either of us who killed this man."

Kama frowned at him and pulled up her nanocom. "I'll erase the footage."

Wolf raised a hand to stop her. "That will make the police suspicious. Besides, the cashier has seen me."

Two uniformed security guards trotted along the corridor toward them. The last thing he wanted was to spend hours explaining what he was doing here to an EA investigator who, because of Rafe's high profile, would bump the whole mess upstairs where he could explain everything again.

It was possible that the tech had other secrets in his background worth killing for, but he doubted it. The man had been targeted because he could identify Leon's blackmailer. With both the tech and his assassin dead, they had less chance than ever of solving Aaron's murder. And with EA tramping through the investigation, the blackmailer could easily go to ground without ever giving himself away. He couldn't let that happen.

"Let me handle this." He stepped past Wolf to intercept the security guards. He glanced back at Kama and whispered, "Look faint."

At the sight of the body on the floor, both guards drew their stunners.

"I'm Rafael McTavish." Rafe flashed his EA credentials and pointed to the corpse. "This man tried to kill me."

One of the guards lowered his stunner and saluted. "Mr. McTavish. What happened here?"

He glanced at Kama, who looked belligerent, not faint. Wolf stood at her shoulder, impassive.

"My girlfriend and I were having a consultation with the med tech over there." He waved at the table where the tech slumped. "This man took a shot at me and missed. Unfortunately, he killed the poor tech."

The second officer rose from checking the killer's body. "A consultation in a café?"

"It was a private matter, off the record." He gave them a deprecating smile, slid his attention to Kama, and then down to her belly. On cue, the officers followed his eyes. Her jaw tightened. He hoped she'd forgive him.

"I see. And then what happened?"

"My bodyguard stepped in to protect me." Wolf's face remained immobile as Rafe nodded towards him. If they asked for Wolf's full name, he was sunk.

The officer pointed to the body. "Any idea who he is? Or who sent him?"

Rafe chuffed a laugh. "I've put away plenty of people who might want me dead. Any of them could have sent this hack."

"His nanocom is missing."

He wished Kama hadn't stolen the nanocom. If they searched her duffel and found it, his story would quickly unravel.

"Officers, I'd be happy to answer all your questions and sign a statement. I'd prefer that my girlfriend's name not appear in the record." He gave the men a wink, and after a moment of hesitation, they nodded their understanding.

"Her delicate condition has her feeling faint. If you wouldn't mind, I'd like my man to get her on a shuttle before the reporters arrive."

When they all turned toward Kama, she swooned against Wolf.

"Shouldn't your bodyguard remain with you?" the first officer asked.

Rafe beamed at the guards. "I'm sure I'll be safe in your capable hands."

31

Barb's two gorillas had planted themselves at Gabe's back, scanning the crowd at the departure gate, and Barb stood beside the boy doing her own perusal while she awaited McTavish. She'd been on edge since Kama's arrival. Wolf waited next to the gate, his eyes also moving constantly over the other passengers.

Kama mused on all the ways she could pay McTavish back for implying she was his pregnant girlfriend. Nothing sufficiently fiendish came immediately to mind. He jogged down the concourse toward them, barely in time for the last flight to Harvest.

McTavish pulled to a puffing halt and gave Barb a quick squeeze. "Sorry I'm late. Thanks for watching Gabe. Give Ying my best."

The big merc caught his arm. "RM, you need to take the squad with you."

"We've been over this. If I show up with bodyguards, it will alert the killer."

Kama snorted derision. "Come on, Gabe. We'll miss our flight."

She lost the last snatches of Barb's argument with McTavish as they walked through the hatch onto the jump ship, followed by Wolf, who took a seat near the back.

Gabe settled beside her, decked out in jeans and a red t-shirt emblazoned with the D. C. United's black and white eagle logo.

"Nice duds," Kama said.

Gabe turned a radiant smile on her. "Barb bought them for me. She's super nice. Did you know she was Uncle Rafe's drill instructor when he joined Earth Force? She said he was a pain in the patootie."

Kama stifled a laugh. "I bet getting him to follow orders took some doing."

"When he first got there, he was a total screw up. He didn't listen, fell asleep in class, got his butt kicked in hand-to-hand combat training."

A sickening wave roiled her stomach. *He had PTSD from finding his wife and children dead.* But McTavish hadn't told anyone, even though it could have gotten him out of the inevitable punishment for his perceived misbehavior.

"Barb says Earth Force wanted to kick him out. Everyone thought he'd be happy about that, but he wouldn't go. She says now they're glad he didn't. He saved a bunch of lives, and they gave him a medal." Gabe sighed. "Do you think Uncle Rafe would teach me to fight?"

McTavish joined them, sans bodyguards.

"You should listen to Barb," she admonished while he strapped into his seat. "You're not invincible."

"You could have told me about your watch dog." He sounded peeved.

He leaned close and spoke in a low voice. "Was it Svenson?"

"The med tech ID'd Lev Kozlov."

He scratched at his rapidly growing beard. "Did he have a chance to see the other suspects before he was shot?"

"No, there wasn't time. Records show that Kozlov's wife was at the med station at the same time that Leon and Amaya were there. She had an abortion."

His mouth turned down. "Being there isn't enough. He had to be in a position to cause problems for the med tech."

"Maybe he saw something, or overheard something."

"He has an alibi for Aaron's murder. I wonder what the med tech was so concerned about covering up. Did you find anything suspicious in his background check?"

"Samir's working on it."

"What about the assassin? Anything useful on his nanocom?"

"It was a stolen device over which a fake ID had been recorded. We've sent fingerprints and DNA to Samir, but it will take until morning to get the results."

He opened his document case and perused his filmies. In a moment, he was snapping the corner of one with his fingernail. The sound drove her crazy. She fished a gel-filled hand exerciser bag from her coveralls pocket.

"Here." She thrust the bag at him.

He gave her a puzzled look.

"I couldn't find any balls the right size."

Pink suffused his face, and he took the bag with a nod.

They rode in silence until the approach for docking at the Harvest jump gate station. McTavish put his documents away and turned to her.

"You shouldn't come back to Harvest."

"This from the man who won't agree to be accompanied by a security squad."

His look of disapproval didn't waver.

"If you're worried about me, tell Dzandarova to give me my stunner."

He glanced over his shoulder to where Wolf sat. "Do you work with him often?"

Something in his face hinted at jealousy. She nearly laughed aloud. Then she remembered Barb's assertion that he never dated. Had the story all been a ruse to keep her away from him?

"Is it true those women you're with in the news vids were all assignments?"

He turned his attention to the gel sack in his hand. "I'd prefer it if that information didn't get out."

It wasn't the answer she expected. "Because you enjoy your gigolo reputation? It goes with that 'Sexiest Man in the Galaxy' title the press crowned you with."

He grimaced. "The clients we escorted started out as just assignments, a means to an end, a way to get Security Partners off the ground. Most of them were surrounded by people who wanted something—money, publicity, influence—and they knew it. They'd lost faith in humanity. All I wanted was for them to make it home safe. They came to trust me. If they learned now that I'd been paid to be their friend..." His eyes focused on hers. "Promise me you won't tell anyone."

She looked away, struggling for a response. He'd proved himself to be a caring human being more than once, and it frightened her. Why? When she turned to him, he was glancing over his shoulder at Wolf again. She'd caused McTavish so much pain, so much trouble. The least she could do was ease his mind about her bodyguard.

"He's Samir's right hand."

His expression grew cold. "An assassin."

She laughed. "That would be Samir's *left* hand. Wolf manages Sharma family security so Samir can concentrate on other things."

"If Samir wanted to protect you, why send a senior manager? Why not send a field agent?"

Kama shifted in her seat. McTavish didn't look like he'd drop the subject.

"He's the only bodyguard I never managed to ditch. And he's also a reminder from Samir."

"Of what?" His voice held more suspicion than curiosity.

Of things I don't want to talk about. But she couldn't lie to him forever. He was serious about her, and that rocked her world.

"Not long after my mother and I arrived on Oasis, I... came to Varun's attention." The question was there in his eyes. "Okay, I hacked something I shouldn't have, and Samir caught me."

A tiny smile rounded his cheeks. "It's nice to know *someone* can catch you."

"Give me a break! I was ten and hacked Samir's personal account."

His brows shot up. "And you lived to tell the tale?"

She ignored his jest. "When Varun realized the level of my programming skill, he put me to work. It was supposed to keep me busy and out of trouble."

"I'm guessing that didn't go quite the way he expected." He grinned openly.

"Do you want to hear this or not?"

He plastered a contrite look on his face and leaned closer. "Tell me the rest."

"Samir assigned a bodyguard to me. More of a babysitter, really, and I resented it. Over the next two years, I went through a slew of them. None lasted more than a few weeks. Those who weren't fired outright quit because they couldn't stand being bested by a kid. Then he assigned Wolf, his newest acquisition."

She glanced back at the man. When she turned around, all the mirth was gone from McTavish's face.

"Wolf was eighteen and hungry for a place to belong. Samir said he could stay only if he could succeed as my minder. I was the bane of his existence. I did everything I could to lose him, to humiliate him." She smiled at the memory, but then the smile faded. "Despite that, he never quit looking out for me. Never once."

Tears threatened to spill down her cheeks. She blinked, surprised by the loss and longing rising in her chest.

"You were... involved?"

"No." She sucked in a deep breath. "He saved my life. He watched me fall from grace, and he stuck by me."

He took her hand. "Samir wants to remind you of that fall."

She nodded.

McTavish squeezed her hand. "You came here to help me find the blackmailer. When we have, will you stay? We've had our differences—"

Kama placed her fingers on his lips. "When this is over, McTavish, we'll talk."

Joy danced in his eyes and a grin split his face. "Rafe. Call me Rafe."

The clang of the docking collar halted their discussion. Kama woke Gabe, who had dozed off. They filed into the receiving area of Harvest's jump gate station, which was little more than an open room with rows of chairs secured to the floor and a business counter against one wall. The place seemed crowded, especially for this time of night.

McTavish led the way to the counter. He queued in line behind half a dozen other people. Wolf passed his nanocom over a scanner beside a door marked 'Station Ops' and disappeared through it. The line crawled forward.

"Mr. McTavish, you should have come directly to the counter. You didn't have to wait with the others." The agent, a thin, sandy-haired fellow of at least forty spoke with the breathlessness of an ice flu survivor and looked with disdain at her.

McTavish gave the man a kindly smile. "No problem. We were booked for an earlier shuttle, but we were unavoidably delayed. Do you have three open seats on the next flight?"

The agent tapped at his console. "We had maintenance issues with a shuttle earlier this evening that's caused a disruption to our schedule, but I know we can find space for you, Mr. McTavish, and I'm sure someone will be willing to give young Mr. Goldman their seat. Such a shame about his recent losses."

"What about Ms. Bhatia?"

The agent's eyes flicked her direction. "Full-time staff and business-class travelers take priority over contractors. I can put her on the first shuttle in the morning—assuming there's room."

Kama ground her teeth. McTavish blew out his cheeks and ran a hand through his hair.

"Can you at least ask whether anyone would be willing to give up their seat for her?"

"Of course, Mr. McTavish, but I wouldn't hold out much hope."

The PA system announced the start of boarding, and a line formed at the hatch. A pretty flight attendant greeted each boarding passenger while the agent scanned nanocoms and asked whether anyone would be willing to wait for tomorrow's shuttle. He got no takers.

"I'm sorry, Mr. McTavish." He shuffled back to the counter.

"Don't come to Harvest," McTavish said. "You're safer on Earth. You can find the information we need from there just as well as you can from here."

Kama folded her arms. "You sound just like Samir."

"Is there a problem?" the flight attendant asked.

"There's no room for Kama," Gabe piped up.

The attendant smiled down at Gabe before turning to McTavish. "If you don't mind riding in the crew compartment, Mr. McTavish, we can take all of you."

"Isn't that illegal?"

"We bend the rules for VIPs." As though to justify her offer, she added, "Leon Goldman rode with the crew regularly."

Gabe's eyes got big. "Can I do that?"

From the look on his face, the offer troubled McTavish. "You won't reconsider and go back to Earth?"

"If you're going to Harvest, I'm going to Harvest."

He clapped Gabe on the shoulder. "Do exactly as you're told. Don't distract the crew."

The attendant escorted a beaming Gabe onto the shuttle. She and McTavish followed and found their seats in the passenger cabin. She hadn't meant to share so much with him and wanted to forestall further questions.

"Will you tell Gabe about his real mother?"

McTavish snapped his harness in place. "Undoubtedly Aaron and Leon both wrote their wills so that Gabe benefits regardless of his parentage. But Amaya's will may have language that prevents Gabe from receiving her estate if he's not a blood relative. I'll have to notify EA and the lawyers."

He turned sad eyes on her. "He'd find out eventually anyway. Better if he hears it from me. But if I reveal it now, the murderer will know I'm chasing him. I'll wait until he's caught."

She jammed her duffel under her seat. "I can't believe that bitch. She didn't even ask about him or what will happen now he's lost all his family. All she cared about was his net worth."

"I sent Ms. Benton a message suggesting that she disappear until we catch Aaron's killer."

Kama shot him a surprised look. "You think she's a target, too."

He responded with a grim nod.

☠   ☠   ☠

At the Harvest terminal gate, they disembarked and waited for Gabe to join them. When he appeared, his face glowed with excitement. The flight crew trailed him.

The shuttle pilot, a short man with slick-downed hair and sparkling brown eyes, snapped Gabe a salute. Then he removed the rocket-and-stars pin from his jacket lapel and fastened it to Gabe's shirt. He shook the boy's hand while McTavish watched with an amused smile.

"Welcome to the crew, Mr. Goldman. You're now an official member of the EcoMech Flight Club."

Gabe grinned up at the pilot and gave his own salute.

The smile froze on McTavish's face. His eyes got that faraway look that told her he was processing something.

"Do other EcoMech executives ride with the crew?"

"Well..." The pilot ran a finger under his shirt collar and cleared his throat. "The executives frequently fly at short notice. Sometimes the observer seat in the crew cabin is the only way to meet their unexpected requests."

McTavish's brows drew down. "Doesn't EA notice that your passenger list includes more people than your shuttle accommodates?"

The flight attendant's eyes darted from McTavish to the pilot and she ducked her head. "Executives flying with the crew aren't included on the passenger list."

Kama sucked in a breath while she waited for the question she was sure McTavish would ask.

"Did anyone ride with the crew yesterday?"

With a guilty nod, the attendant replied, "Mr. Kozlov came down on our final run."

32

Rafe led them down the empty concourse, mind churning about Lev's busted alibi. They should get him in for questioning at once.

At the terminal, a phalanx of black-uniformed security guards greeted them. He stopped short.

"Mr. McTavish."

A woman in her forties, perhaps five-five, with narrow shoulders and delicate hands, stepped from the guards' midst. A thick cinnamon-colored braid hung down her back. Her buff-colored skin hinted at mixed heritage, and a large mole on the left cheek stole attention from the heart-shaped face.

"Major Balau." He placed a protective hand on Gabe's shoulder.

Anger flashed in her piercing brown eyes. "It's 'Commander Balau' now."

He acknowledged her correction with a deprecating nod. "What can I do for you?"

"This is your security detail. They will escort you to your quarters." She waved a hand at Kama. "The contractor will be taken to the compound."

Kama's eyes narrowed. Before she could speak, he jumped in.

"Chief Dzandarova will provide any protection we may need."

Balau's chin lifted. "Alana Dzandarova has been relieved of duty by your board of directors. All EcoMech security is under my control."

Rafe's hand tightened on his document case. "It's late. We'll sort this out in the morning. Now if you'll excuse us."

"Take her." The commander flipped a hand a Kama.

A guard reached for Kama's arm. In the blink of an eye, Rafe snatched the guard's wrist and twisted it into a painful position between the man's shoulder blades. The other guards drew their side arms. Kama pulled Gabe behind her.

Rafe focused his attention on Balau. "You have a funny way of ensuring my safety, Commander."

Balau's face stiffened, and she looked with fury at the guards. "Fools! Holster your weapons."

When they'd obeyed her order, Rafe shoved his captive away. "Ms. Bhatia is not subject to EcoMech's rules for contractors. As Gabe's tutor, she will accompany him at all times. Are we clear?"

The commander gave him a cold stare, spun on her heel, and strode out. Four of the guards remained behind. Rafe retrieved his document case from where he'd dropped it. He placed a hand on Gabe's back. The boy trembled, and his eyes slid away from the black-shirted guards.

They walked through the terminal to the parking lot, drawing a stare from the janitor who emptied the trash can just outside the door. While they climbed in his flyer, the Total Security guards got in their own flyer, a light-armor model, the barrel of its .30 caliber machine gun protruding from the top-mounted turret. The sight of it made him uneasy.

"Kali! Who does that woman think she is?" Kama said.

Rafe held a finger to his lips, cupped a hand to his ear, and then pointed to the other flyer. Her eyes widened for a moment before her lips drew into a hard line. She pulled a tiny black box from her duffel and switched it on.

"Have you eaten?" Her eyes never left the device's screen.

"No time. What about you and Gabe?"

She pointed to the dash. "We picked up something."

Now that Balau was here, he ought to get Kama and Gabe off Harvest. And the rest of his family, too. Greg had just started his internship at Wandermere, but he'd be back for Aaron's funeral, the day after tomorrow. He had to get the situation on the ground under control and send Total Security packing. Letting the board pressure him into hiring them was another mistake he wished he hadn't made.

※　　※　　※

Fifteen minutes later, they were knocking on Alana's door. When she opened it, her eyes went first to the escort flyer before they met Rafe's. Beat-up jeans and a baggy t-shirt replaced her security uniform.

"You're the proverbial bad penny, Mr. McTavish." She stepped back and waved them inside.

"Sorry to impose again." He herded Gabe and Kama in and closed the door.

"Gabe, you should get ready for bed," Kama said.

The boy's eyes darted to the front windows. "I'm not sleepy."

Alana took in Gabe's expression, and her own face hardened. She muttered something under her breath and followed the boy's glance to the windows.

"Let me show you the rest of the house."

Rafe thought they'd seen all there was of the tiny three-bedroom home on the first visit. She walked away toward the kitchen. They all followed.

"Looks like a storm coming, don't you think?" Alana said.

She grabbed the edge of a low cupboard and swung it away from the wall to reveal a half-height steel door. She opened the steel hatch and waved them into the darkness. As Rafe ducked through, a light came on, illuminating a stairway leading down. Before he reached the bottom, the hatch clunked closed behind him.

Rafe entered a fifteen-by-twenty foot square space under the house lit by a single bulb in the ceiling. Shelves filled with boxes lined one wall, and a narrow bed stood against another, a nightstand and lamp next to it. An old braided rug covered the floor. A recliner, the twin to the one in the living room, was pushed back under the stairs.

Alana followed them down and swung a hand around the space.

"Nothing like a good storm cellar to keep you safe." She gave Rafe a wink. "It's soundproof, too."

She dragged the recliner away from the wall and opened two folding lawn chairs that had hidden in the shadows of the steps. She arranged the seating in a tight circle at the opposite end of the space from the bed.

Kama peered around the space, a smile twisting her lips. She helped Gabe into the bed, gave him ear buds, and transferred a movie from her nanocom to his. Watching her easy interaction with the boy gave Rafe a warm glow.

What event in her past gave her such pain? Would she ever trust him enough to tell him? He'd wanted to hug her when her eyes filled with tears, but he sensed a defensiveness that kept him at bay. He needed time with her, but they never seemed to have any. After a kiss on Gabe's forehead, she joined them at the chairs.

"Have you seen the news?" Alana asked before they'd settled.

"Commander Balau told us that you'd been replaced. Otherwise, we're in the dark."

"She's a piece of work." Alana settled in the arm chair. "She arrived not long after you left this morning. By midday, she'd ordered all the contractors back to the compound, and then her goon squads started searching rooms there. They turned up an assortment of weapons and several caches of drugs.

"When your father heard what they'd found, he fired me and put

Balau in charge. She spent the day deporting contractors. Anyone who protested went, too. Three contractors have been hospitalized with serious injuries from clashes with her people."

"Good God!" He ran a hand across the back of his neck.

"I'll admit we have some drug problems here, but nothing on the scale of what she found. And we've never had weapons slip by us." Alana's face became grim. "I think the guards who conducted the search planted what they found."

"You can't let her get away with that." Kama sat forward. "Fire her. Kick them off the planet."

"Their contract includes hefty penalties for early dismissal," Alana said. "You can't get rid of them unless you can prove incompetence, negligence, or deliberate criminal activity."

"Balau is too crafty to get caught at anything that would void her contract."

Kama cocked an eyebrow at him. "The two of you have a history."

He sighed and sat back in the squeaky lawn chair. "At EA's request, I investigated allegations that her Earth Force Peacekeeper unit was brutalizing Peruvian villagers to get information about eco-terrorists. Everyone I questioned was afraid. I couldn't get enough evidence to press charges, but I passed on my suspicions. She was reassigned to desk duty in Europe, and her career ground to a halt. A year later, she left Earth Force and has worked with various mercenary outfits since."

"Shiva!" Kama muttered. "And now she's set her pack of jackals on you."

"In retaliation for the arrests at the compound, the hacker overloaded the electrical circuits in three campus buildings and started fires. Because of all the false alarms yesterday, no one thought today's alarms were real. Six people are suffering from smoke inhalation, and one poor fellow had a mild stroke brought on by the stress."

"That's not possible." Kama's brow drew down. "I applied patches to the systems. He couldn't have hacked in again."

All her attention went to her nanocom. In a second, she was pulling equipment from her duffel, oblivious to him and Alana.

"What did you learn today?" the security chief asked.

Rafe rubbed his hands on his pants. "We found someone we thought could identify the blackmailer, but he was killed before we finished our questioning."

Alana rocked back in the recliner and the color drained from her face.

"But at least we know now what Leon was blackmailed about." He checked to be sure Gabe wasn't listening. The screen of the nanocom still flickered with images, but the boy's eyes were closed. "Amaya wasn't

Gabe's birth mother."

The security chief huffed out a breath. "Doesn't surprise me. The kid's too nice to be related to either of his parents."

"We also learned that Lev Kozlov was on-planet at the time of Aaron's murder. We need to question him, but I don't want to alert Balau."

"I've been keeping tabs on everyone today." At his raised eyebrows, she laughed. "We're like one big family here, Mr. McTavish, and we aren't fond of outsiders. Mr. Kozlov is on the station tonight, and Mr. Svenson and Mr. Gerlach are tucked up safe at home.

"But before you set your sights on Mr. Kozlov, you should know that Mr. Svenson lied about his alibi."

"Svenson, too?" Any sense of progress slipped away. "Where was he?"

"We don't know for sure. We were reviewing traffic camera footage trying to identify more of the contractors who may have participated in the riots. We picked up Mr. Svenson's car headed north across the river just after the riots started, but we lost him when he hit the residential neighborhoods. He returns half an hour later."

"We'd better have him in for questioning."

"You'll need to do something about the contractors." Alana's eyes dropped to the old rug. "They say that if we haven't made any arrests in the bus assault by noon tomorrow, they'll go on strike."

Kama looked up from her nanocom. "The stock price has fallen another two points."

33

Kama sipped her morning tea and squirmed in the upholstered visitor's chair carefully placed so that Balau's spy camera wouldn't pick up her nanocom screen. She'd already knackered the camera and microphone in McTavish's inner office. If she tampered with the ones in the outer office, Balau would know they were onto her.

At the assistant's desk, Gabe read a book on his nanocom while a noisy children's cartoon played on the monitor. From the way his eyes darted to the door every few minutes, she didn't think he was reading much. Their 'security escort' loitered in the hallway.

She turned her attention to her nanocom. How had the hacker overloaded circuits in the campus buildings? Her surveillance bots hadn't been tripped, nor could she find any evidence of the punk's activity anywhere on the EcoMech network.

The hacker worried her. Was he part of Caligo's plan to weaken EcoMech? Or was he working for Aaron's killer? His invisible access to the campus meant he could surface anywhere at any time, putting McTavish at unacceptable risk.

Her focus drifted to what she'd learned about McTavish on their trip to the entertainment station. She'd made a horrible mistake before rushing into a relationship with a man she hardly knew, and McTavish surprised her at every turn. She'd broken the law, worse than anything he suspected. How could he love her when he didn't know her?

But she couldn't help imagining what life would be like with him. And with Gabe. The boy would be part and parcel of any future relationship with McTavish—as would Cullen and Shannon be. She pushed the uncomfortable thoughts of the McTavish family away and got back to work. McTavish had to be kept safe. Sorting out everything else could wait.

She went through the lists of people coming and going from the buildings and matched it against video footage. There were no overlaps in visitors between the buildings that experienced fires. She gave her duffel a sharp kick.

Lars Svenson entered the office. He gave Gabe a puzzled look before turning to Kama. A hint of disapproval colored his expression.

"I have an appointment with Mr. McTavish."

She tilted her head at the closed inner office door. "In there."

As the lawyer entered the inner office, Kama switched to a feed from her own audio and video bugs planted in McTavish's office and popped in ear buds. Svenson stopped short when he saw Dzandarova sitting in one of the visitor chairs. McTavish rose and waved at the other chair. Svenson closed the door and took a seat.

"You know Alana." McTavish sat and folded his hands on the desktop. His eyes gleamed as he focused on the lawyer. It made Kama shiver.

The lawyer nodded a greeting. "I'd heard you'd been dismissed, Ms. Dzandarova."

"Alana retains her EA law enforcement credentials—as do I."

The security chief returned Svenson's nod, her face blank. Kama wouldn't want to play poker against her.

"What can I help you with?" The lawyer focused on McTavish.

"You can tell us where you really were the night Aaron died."

For a beat, Svenson froze. "I was at home, as I told you before."

McTavish tapped his nanocom, and the vid screen mounted on the far wall came to life. It displayed Svenson at the wheel of his car, a date and time stamp at the bottom indicating it was captured fifteen minutes before Aaron's death.

"Perhaps you want to revise that statement," McTavish said. He picked up a stylus and rapped it against the desktop.

Kama grinned. *Let's see him weasel out of this.*

The faintest sheen glistened on Svenson's forehead. "I forgot. I did run out for groceries."

"There's a store six blocks from your apartment," Dzandarova said. "Why were you videoed on the other side of town?"

"The local store didn't have what I wanted."

"Which store did you go to?" McTavish asked.

"The Food Fest on North-South Five."

McTavish let silence stretch while he watched Svenson, but the lawyer was too crafty to fall into the trap of unprompted blabbing.

Kama dove into the corporate system and navigated to the store accounts. Maybe she could provide more ammunition to break the story. A few minutes digging turned up Svenson's purchase—a two-credit packet of biscuits. A quick check of the store nearest his apartment revealed stocks of the same item.

The door to McTavish's office opened, and Svenson strode by, face frozen. When he'd passed through the outer office, Kama joined McTavish and Dzandarova.

"He's lying. There's a transaction in the system for the biscuits he purchased, but his local store had them, too."

"I'll order the store surveillance footage." The security chief hurried out.

☠   ☠   ☠

Kama glanced at the closed door to McTavish's office where he labored to save the company. She had a theory about the building fires, but to verify it, she'd need to examine their circuit boxes.

McTavish wouldn't like her roaming the campus, especially if the security escort followed her. When she told him where she was going, he'd protest.

She could say she was going to a cafeteria, but she needed to be straight with McTavish. She owed him that.

Kama tapped on his door and opened it. He spun away from the window and scrambled to his feet.

"Come in. I was just..." A blush of guilty color crept up his cheeks.

She closed the door and put her back against it while he floundered to finish his sentence. When he went silent, she walked to his desk.

"You're allowed to take breaks, you know," she said.

Chagrinned, he came around the desk to face her. "I was daydreaming about us. About making you dinner."

"Something vegetarian, I hope."

"Ah." His face fell. "My mother's pot roast, actually. Comfort food."

Kama laughed. "When I couldn't solve a programming problem, my father made bread pudding."

His expression became serious. "Thank you for telling me about Wolf."

She studied her right foot, scuffed it on the carpet. "My past isn't pretty. I made mistakes, terrible mistakes."

When she looked up, his cobalt blue eyes shone with kindness. Too bad she had to shatter it.

"I gave Samir access to the EcoMech corporate network."

McTavish blinked as though she'd spoken in a foreign language he didn't understand. Then his face twisted into... horror? Disgust? He stepped away to stare out the window, his back stiff, his shoulders hunched.

"I'm sorry. It was the only way to get the information about Toni Benton." Kama took a step closer. "I did it to protect you."

"It wasn't the only way." He turned to her, his cheeks hard, brow furrowed, eyes clouded with betrayal. "Barb could have checked her out."

Do the crime, do the time. It was the only path to inner tranquility. She'd learned that lesson the hard way, but her trade was justified.

"Goldman's killer has had years to find her. If we'd taken the time to do it the legal way, Toni Benton would have been dead by the time we got to her. Samir's identification saved her life."

Uncertainty flickered in his eyes. He returned to gazing out the window. "I can't condone what you've done."

"When we have the murderer, I'll clean up the network and block Samir's access. I'll purge his files."

McTavish exhaled a sigh and faced her. "Don't bother with the purge. Oasis is our partner, not our rival. If Samir wants to wade through millions of files to see how badly Leon ran the company, let it be his punishment for snooping."

Kama closed the space between them. "I'm sorry. I had to keep you safe. If anything happened to you—"

McTavish tipped his head forward and waited for her to finish the sentence. Her throat closed, and her words died unspoken.

He took her hand and squeezed it. "I understand."

Tears sprang to her eyes. She blinked them away and drew in a deep breath. "I'm going to the cafeteria."

"I could use some coffee. Gabe and I will come with you."

She put up a hand to stop him. "No, you won't. I'm using the trip as an excuse to check the buildings that caught fire yesterday."

Worry lines rippled across his brow. "You shouldn't go alone."

"I don't want Balau's goon squad looking over my shoulder. There's a good chance they'll stay here with you and Gabe."

"It's Alana's job. Leave it to her."

Kama stiffened. "If Balau thinks we've found something, she'll swoop in and grab it. I can move around without being tracked. Alana can't."

His mouth opened, closed. She didn't need to be a mind reader to know he wanted to object.

"Besides, I won't be alone. Wolf's keeping an eye on me."

"Ah." A struggle between concern and relief played out on his face. Eventually he nodded. "Good. Bring back coffee."

☠   ☠   ☠

Building 19 was hot and dark and smelled of smoke. Kama used her nanocom to light the way and thanked Lakshmi that they hadn't started cleanup yet. She stood before the scorched door to the power room on the first floor of the parking structure.

It took a hard jerk to get the warped door open. She didn't hold out much hope of finding evidence, not in a fire as hot as this one. When she stepped inside, the tang of fire retardant stung her nose.

The cramped space was lined with breaker boxes and racks of compact batteries, all of it charred but recognizable. The flames had eaten through the ceiling, and faint light shone from the lobby above.

One by one, she examined each breaker. In the last box, an alligator clip attached to a short length of melted wire hung from a contact point. A little thrill shot through her. She pointed her light at the floor beneath the boxes and made her way back to the starting point.

Two more clips lay in the debris on the floor. She pulled her sleeve over her hands and gathered the evidence.

"What are those?"

She started at the unexpected voice. Wolf stood in the doorway.

"You're supposed to be watching McTavish."

"No, I'm supposed to watch you." Wolf stepped into the cramped room, plucked the bag from her hand, and peered at the contents. "Not your doing?"

"Arson isn't my thing." She grabbed the bag from him and stuffed it in her pocket. After a last look around, she exited into the parking garage.

"Samir wants everything you have on the hacker."

Kama bunched her fists, and her face warmed. "It's a waste of his time. He needs to focus on the assassin."

They walked through the darkened section of the parking structure toward the distant light under another building. Wolf studied her profile for a long minute before returning his attention to their surroundings.

"He's already identified the assassin. Evan Nelson, a small-time hood with a record for hijacking electronics shipments and trafficking in stolen property."

"He doesn't sound like the type who would move up to murder for hire."

Kama paused at the edge of the lighted area, just outside the range of the security cameras that covered the parking area. She tapped her nanocom and switched them to a prerecorded loop, and then she advanced through the garage on her way to the cafeteria in Building 9.

"A neighbor says he received a package day before yesterday. A search of his apartment turned up two kilos of rhodium in a bolt hole in the floor."

Kama stopped and stared at her escort. "Two kilos? That's an outrageous price for a hit. It shouldn't have cost more than a tenth of that."

Wolf paused, glanced around, and then continued. "It covered two hits, not one. Before he left for the med station, Nelson took a flight to

Chicago. While there, we believe he killed Milo Demasi, an investigator who worked for Trans-Atlantic Insurance."

"What's the connection between Demasi and the med tech?" She stopped at the exit to the parking garage and switched the security cameras back to a live feed.

"He investigated the accident that killed the med tech's colleague a few months after Gabe Goldman's birth."

From across the garage, the lift dinged to announce its arrival, and the doors slid open. Wolf drew back into the shadows of a support pillar, and Kama joined him. A well-dressed woman stepped out and clip-clopped on high heels to her car at the other end of the area.

When she'd gone, Wolf continued. "He was also an investigator on the Mars Development tunnel collapse."

Kama's pulse quickened. Finally they'd discovered the missing link between the blackmail of Leon Goldman and the events on the mining station. "Any connection between him and Gerlach, Kozlov, or Svenson?"

"Not so far."

He fell in beside her as they headed through a long, narrow passage to the next building. The air was hot and dusty, but cooler than on the surface. Kama manipulated more security cameras to cover their passing.

"Samir wants you off-planet today. Commander Balau ran a background check on you last night."

The news sent a chill over her, but she wouldn't let him see her worry. "She's more interested in McTavish than me."

Wolf eyed her. "You're very protective of him."

She looked away. "EcoMech is an important part of the Sharma Network."

"He does nothing to protect you, yet you are the more valuable asset."

Kama's spine stiffened. "He's doing the best he can with the resources he has."

"Bull shit," Wolf replied with a dismissive wave. "He owns a security company, and yet he's here without competent bodyguards. Or even *incompetent* bodyguards."

Kama's doubts about McTavish's lack of bodyguards swam to the surface of her consciousness, but she wouldn't speak them to Wolf. "He doesn't want to tip his hand that we're onto the blackmail scheme."

"Little late for that, isn't it?"

"You make it sound like he doesn't have a plan."

Wolf laughed. "No, I think he doesn't have a clue. He'll get both of you killed."

"He's smart and determined. He'll get to the bottom of Goldman's murder, and he'll help build the Sharma Network." Or at least she hoped he would.

They walked in silence for a minute before Wolf said, "He has a reputation for partying—and womanizing."

"You think he's cast a spell on me? His public behavior is a façade. He's not like that."

"You thought you knew Thom, too."

She stopped and faced him. "McTavish risks his life for others. He's a good man and nothing like Thom."

Wolf watched her, impassive. She muttered a curse and walked to the parking area for Building 9, home to a first-floor cafeteria. Wolf stopped at the perimeter of the space while she continued toward the lift shaft in the center.

"Be careful, Kama," he called.

34

"You're sure this information is reliable?" Rafe asked, rocking back in his chair. A drift of filmies cascaded off the side of his desk.

Alana gave a grim nod. "When the contractors hear the evidence from the bus assault has been lost, we'll have another riot. Balau is already concentrating her forces near the compound. She hasn't allowed any of the contractors to return to work this morning."

Rafe swore under his breath and glanced at the wall where the video screen showed a steady downward trend in EcoMech's stock price. Another five points would trigger automatic default on EcoMech's loans. Once that happened, there'd be no putting the cat back in the bag. Other creditors would pile on.

He had to do something to avert more conflict. He tapped his nano-com, and Keon Mabutu, EcoMech's facilities manager on Harvest, appeared on the screen. The man listened while Rafe made his request.

"'Bout time," Keon murmured in his soft-spoken voice. "Give me thirty minutes."

Rafe placed his next call to the PR department.

"I'm holding a press conference," he announced. "Get as many reporters as you can to the contractor compound. I'll be there shortly."

Alana watched from the other side of the desk, disapproval in her eyes.

"At least let me get you a reliable security escort, not those Total Security bozos."

He rose and walked around his desk. "Showing up with a large security contingent makes it look like I don't trust the contractors. Trust is a two-way street. If the contractors don't think I trust them, why should they trust me?"

Alana stood and followed him to the door. They nearly collided with Kama, who carried two cups of coffee. From the smug excitement on her face, he was sure she'd learned something on her refreshments run, but he didn't have time to talk now.

"Stay here and keep an eye on Gabe." He took one of the cups and brushed past her.

"Where are you going?"

"You don't want to know," Alana said.

☠   ☠   ☠

Rafe brought the flyer down a block from the contractor compound. He couldn't get closer. The approach to the gates was clogged by three blue EcoMech facilities vans, a semi pulling an empty flatbed trailer, two buses, and dozens of cars. Fifty feet from the gates, a bulldozer idled. Five more buses parked in the surrounding neighborhood.

Reporters milled around the vehicles, and twenty Total Security guards looked on, rifles at the ready. Inside the fence near the buildings, a few hundred contractors watched.

As Rafe walked toward the compound, Commander Balau stepped into his path, six burly guards at her back. Alana circumvented the guards and walked on.

"Mr. McTavish, our intelligence indicates that the contractors plan a protest. I can't allow you to remain in the area."

The assault rifles the guards carried made the hair rise on his arms despite the late morning heat. They'd mow down the contractors like a harvester in a wheat field. With fifteen thousand lives in the balance, he'd better get his next move right.

"I'm here on corporate business. My legal department tells me that if you impede business, you'll be in breach of your contract."

Balau's eyes narrowed. "And if I don't ensure your safety, I'll also be in breach of my contract. Therefore, I order you to return to your flyer."

"And if I don't?"

The commander nodded to her men, who quickly circled around Rafe.

"Then for your own safety, I'll be forced to remove you." A smug smile touched her lips.

Half a block ahead, a cry of "It's McTavish!" went up among the reporters. En masse, they jogged between the traffic jam of vehicles and bore down on Rafe. Balau turned to look, and Alana, who brought up the rear, gave her a cheery wave.

Hatred gleamed in the commander's eyes when she faced him. For a moment, he expected her to draw her pistol and shoot him. He tipped her a polite nod and stepped past to intercept the mob of reporters.

"Have you caught Aaron Goldman's killer?" one shouted.

"Do you expect more contractor riots?" another called. "Will there be arrests in the bus attack?"

Rafe plowed through them until he reached the flatbed trailer. Keon Mabutu stepped up and shook his hand. The last time Rafe had seen Keon, he was a scrawny fifteen-year old. While the facilities manager hadn't gotten much taller, the stocky black man had doubled in weight and looked strong enough to wrestle a tiger to a standstill.

"Let's do it," the manager said, excitement shining in his dark face.

Rafe walked up the trailer ramp and smiled down at the group, waving his hands for quiet.

"I'd like to thank you all for coming at such short notice." He turned to the PR department spokesman, who wormed his way through the crowd. "Are you ready to broadcast?"

"Fifteen seconds," the man replied, then spoke into his nanocom in a low voice.

The number of contractors watching from the compound grew. At this distance, he couldn't read their expressions, but their body language screamed hostility. He hoped he wasn't making a mistake. The PR spokesman gave him a nod.

"As you all know, in the recent past, EcoMech has experienced difficulties in our relations with our contract employees. I'm here today to announce changes to our employment policies as they affect contractors.

"First, I'm cancelling the curfew for contractors. I trust our contractors to behave appropriately and see no reason to restrict their off-hours movements.

"Second, contractors will no longer be required to live in the compound, although they can remain there if they wish. Any contractor who prefers alternate living arrangements should contact the HR department. Families with children will be given first priority for placements in available housing.

A murmur rose from the reporters. The contractors' ranks swelled further. They watched the broadcast on their nanocoms.

"Third, EcoMech coveralls will be optional attire. Office workers may wear corporate casual attire. All other workers will wear clothing appropriate to their jobs, including any required safety equipment.

"Finally, over the next two weeks, ID bracelets will be replaced with normal corporate credentials to allow contractors access to necessary resources. In the meantime, we'll shut down ID tracking."

"What concessions are you asking for from the contractors?" the canary lady shouted.

"Our contractors are valuable members of our staff. We couldn't succeed without them. I see no need for concessions. All I ask is that they do the best job they can and if they have issues or concerns, they bring those to me."

"Why should they believe you?"

"You mean how do they know this isn't all empty rhetoric? My mother taught me actions speak louder than words."

With that, he jumped down from the trailer and strode to the bulldozer. The driver looked up in surprise as he mounted to the cab.

"Straight through the gates," Rafe ordered.

"But they're closed," the driver said.

Rafe grinned. "Don't let that stop you."

The driver gave him a dubious look, shifted the dozer into gear, and crawled forward. The double gates crumbled before the blade of the machine. With a little maneuvering, the driver deposited the mangled steel and wire to one side of the opening.

"Good man!" Rafe slapped the driver on the back and jumped down. He flagged the three blue vans inside. The pack of reporters trailed the vehicles. Behind them, a work crew began disassembling the remaining compound fence.

Rafe walked to the growing throng of contractors where he was joined by Keon. The contractors' reactions ranged from suspicion to joy to outright disbelief. The drivers of the vans got out and waited beside their vehicles, nervous eyes watching the contractors.

Rafe pointed to the vans. "These folks are here to fix the climate control systems. I'd appreciate it if you'd give them any access or assistance they require."

He clapped a hand on Keon's shoulder. "Mr. Mabutu will prioritize additional repairs. I'd like a volunteer from each building to draw up a list for him."

Suspicion dropped like a curtain, and everyone fell silent. Finally, a middle-aged woman he recognized as one of the group guarding Kama in the dining hall stepped forward. Her arms were folded over her chest, and her brown eyes stared straight into his without flinching.

"Will charges be brought against the people who attacked the bus?"

"Yes, but the bus passengers will have to help identify those involved."

Someone a few rows back called, "A contractor's word against a full-time employee? You're having a laugh."

A stir of agreement rippled through the group.

"What happened to the evidence?" the woman asked.

"I don't know, but I won't let its loss stop me from prosecuting those involved. Will you help?"

She swiveled left and right, taking in the consensus of those around her. "We'll do it."

"Thanks." He offered his hand. "We haven't been properly introduced. Rafe McTavish."

She shook with some reluctance. "Heidi Lowe."

"I'd like to get folks back to work. But before they do, lunch is on me. Contractors eat free in EcoMech cafeterias today. Buses are standing by to transport workers."

"What about all those security guards?" a woman deep in the crowd asked.

Rafe turned and saw at least thirty Total Security officers blocking the opening where the gate used to be. When he looked at the contractors, fear played over their faces. He needed to turn the tables on Balau.

"I'll be riding the lead bus. They're going to make sure we all get to campus without incident. Will you join me, Heidi?" He offered his arm.

She took a long minute deciding before drawing a deep breath. "Thank you, Mr. McTavish. I believe I will."

He grinned. "Rafe. Call me Rafe."

The reporters parted, and a river of contractors flowed behind Rafe as he strolled to the gate. Balau stood in the center of the guards, hands on her hips, lips pulled into a hard line. He stopped before her.

"Commander, your forces will provide security for the contractor buses. I expect them all to arrive at their destinations without incident."

He didn't wait for a reply, just stepped forward. For a moment, Balau held her ground. Then she melted away. Rafe led the contractors to the buses. Alana joined him there.

"You have more guts than brains, Mr. McTavish," she whispered.

He grinned. "That's no way to talk to your boss, Alana."

"At the moment, you're not my boss." She gave him a wry smile. Then her face hardened. "Balau's a dangerous woman. Watch your back."

Rafe glanced at his nanocom. News of his press conference was spreading quickly through the financial markets, and as he'd hoped, the stock price was creeping higher. Now if he could just hang onto the gains and find Aaron's killer, perhaps he could pull the company back from the brink.

35

Kama trailed McTavish and Dzandarova into his office. McTavish moved with renewed energy despite his obvious fatigue. Watching the broadcast of events at the contractor compound had sent a thrill of admiration through her, although she wished he'd find less dangerous ways to make a difference.

McTavish turned on the wall display. The image was a rerun of the bulldozer crashing through the gates, and the announcer recapped his actions at the compound. At the bottom of the screen, a chart of the EcoMech share price showed a peak followed by a retreat. His shoulders slumped.

Kama stared. "Why is the stock dropping again?"

He blew out his cheeks. "Could be triggered by profit-taking."

As they watched, the stock lost another point.

"Or not." McTavish tapped his nanocom. After a long interval, his call was answered.

"RM, what you doing? EcoMech stock up down like yo-yo. With baby, I no have time to make trades every five minutes. How I earn fortune so I be rich like you? Baby need new shoes soon."

Despite their grim circumstances, McTavish smiled at the mention of the baby. Then the smile dropped away.

"Sorry to interrupt, Ying, but I need to understand what's happening in the market. I thought some good news about EcoMech would bolster the share price, and it did briefly. Now it's dropping. Why?"

In the background, an infant wailed, and Kama wondered again about the relationship between Barb, Ying, and McTavish.

"I shouldn't have called," McTavish said. "I'll find someone else to ask."

"Who you going to call? No financiers owe you favors. No one tell you market gossip. Barb change diaper while I talk to contacts. I call you soon."

The connection died.

"Is she another of your Security Partners data analysts?" Dzandarova asked.

"She's my—. She's Security Partners' chief financial officer." McTavish pulled his ball from a desk drawer and rolled it between his palms. "What did you find on your 'coffee run' that has you so excited?"

Kama tossed a bag filled with the clips and wires onto the desk. "The fires weren't the result of system hacking. Someone physically sabotaged the breaker boxes."

McTavish sat back in his chair. "Then it could have been done by anyone, including Balau's people."

"No, it's our hacker."

"How can you be sure?" the security chief asked.

"The only way the hacker could have escaped me was by moving unseen from building to building. The same is true for whoever rigged the electrical fires."

"Do you know who it is?"

Kama chewed her lip. "I don't even understand how it's being done. The cameras don't show a single person—or even the same couple of people—moving between affected buildings. The ID system verifies that. The building blueprints don't indicate any utility tunnels except for those that carry plumbing pipes, and those are too small for a human. Besides, I'd pick up the ID bracelet moving."

Dzandarova pocketed the evidence bag and heaved to her feet. "I'll get one of my guys to take these to the lab. Maybe we'll find something that will help."

Knuckles rapped on the office door, and it cracked open. McTavish's assistant stuck his head in.

"Sorry I'm late sir. Can I get you anything?"

"Come in and close the door," McTavish ordered. When the assistant complied, he continued, "The office has been bugged by Total Security. We've disabled the devices in this room. They're still operational in the outer office."

Understanding lit Bob's face. "That's why there's a children's movie playing on my display. But why is Total Security spying on you, sir?"

"That's what we're trying to find out," Dzandarova replied. "In the meantime, don't open any sensitive corporate documents or discuss anything connected with Mr. Goldman's murder while you're out there."

The assistant swallowed hard. "Yes, ma'am."

Bob slipped out with the security chief. When they were gone, Kama dropped into one of the visitor chairs.

"There's been another murder." She updated McTavish on the information she'd received from Wolf, but didn't tell him about Balau's interest in her.

"So the dead insurance investigator has been feeding damning information to our blackmailer while telling the insurance company that there was no wrong-doing." McTavish rolled his ball through his fingers. "And the cleanup must have started within hours of Aaron's death. Why?"

"Perhaps the blackmailer saw through Goldman's crazy plan to bait him with a phony story."

McTavish's nanocom chimed.

"Boss, you in big trouble," Ying said. "Rumors say EcoMech owe money to banks, can't pay."

"Do you know where the rumors started?"

Ying chuckled. "They called 'rumors' for a reason. But my guy at Galactic Traders heard it from his guy at First International Bank. EcoMech owe them money?"

"Not as far as I know." McTavish walked his ball across his knuckles. "What can I do to turn this around?"

"You better flash cash and squash rumors before panic selling hit."

He sighed. "The rumors are true. EcoMech doesn't have any cash."

Kama balled her hands into fists. First International was practically a subsidiary of Caligo Corp.

After a long pause, Ying said, "I tell Barb you come home soon. She too busy with baby to be big boss at Security Partners."

McTavish chuffed a laugh. "Thanks, Ying. I appreciate your support." He ended the call.

"What will you do?" Kama asked.

"Find Aaron's killer," he replied, eyes roving over the disorganized stacks of filmies littering his desk.

Kama left, mind racing. Caligo had offered a merger, and now they were torpedoing EcoMech's finances. Fury welled up. McTavish's positive actions toward the contractors had turned the share price around once. Maybe all he needed to beat Caligo was more positive news.

"Loo run," she said as she swept past the thugs in the hallway.

In the ladies' room, she opened a connection to her step-father. As always, he was dressed in an impeccable black suit, his gray hair swept back from a widow's peak. His dark eyes seemed to look into her very core. He frowned at her, something he never did.

"Kama, are you all right? Samir tells me conditions on Harvest have become dangerous."

She forced a careless smile. "Samir exaggerates. McTavish has things under control."

"I've seen no sign that he has things under control. Quite the opposite. I've seen a terrorist encourage others to take action against you, but Samir tells me McTavish has done nothing to provide for your security." Varun shook his head, disapproval plain in his voice. "I expected more of him."

"He's doing what he can, but he needs time to make changes."

"He's employed Total Security. They'll make the situation worse. As a security professional, he should know that."

"Hiring Total Security wasn't his idea. The board forced him into it." She regretted her words the moment she'd said them. They made McTavish look weak.

Varun's frowned deepened. "I'm reconsidering our offer of a partnership in the Sharma Network. Rumors of EcoMech insolvency are rampant. There's little point in having EcoMech join if it won't have the finances to participate."

A cold knot formed in her stomach. "Caligo is the source of the gloom and doom about EcoMech's finances. They're pressing for a merger and want to drive the price down, back McTavish into a corner where he's forced to sell."

Varun's brows rose. "A merger?"

Kama leaned over the screen. "Caligo wouldn't be interested in EcoMech if it weren't for our offer to share the Sharma Network with them. Without Caligo's pressure, McTavish would have no problems."

Varun's long, thin fingers tapped his lips. "With Caligo as a partner, there would be no question of having sufficient resources to build the network."

Kama shook with anger. "Caligo would squeeze the network dry. It would never allow Earth's poor to migrate away from the filth and pollution created by greedy corporations. They'd be left behind to die."

Varun spread his hands. "If your McTavish remained at the merged company, he could mitigate Caligo's behavior."

"Kali! You can't allow Caligo to force EcoMech into a merger."

"What is it you want me to do, Kama?"

"Announce the Sharma Network partnership now. It will bolster EcoMech's share price and give McTavish a chance to turn things around."

Varun's eyes narrowed. "Your mother and I would like you to return to Oasis. You've had eight years to sow your wild oats. It's time for you to take your rightful place at the head of Oasis Development."

Kama sucked in a breath and held it.

"It's what your father would have wanted," Varun murmured. "He sacrificed his life for it."

"I have my school," she stammered.

"Pah! You conduct half your classes remotely. You can do that from Oasis."

"I can work for Oasis remotely. I already do."

"Samir feels we can better ensure security of our new technologies if we restrict knowledge of them to Oasis. As you've proved in the past, it's too easy to hack a data stream. We can keep both the technology and you safe and secure here."

"But McTavish needs me"

Varun's eyes went hard. "The Sharma Network and Oasis need you more. If you want me to help him, then you must agree to return to Oasis. You must break off with McTavish. He attracts danger, takes foolish personal risks, and he does nothing to protect you."

Prickles crawled over her scalp, and her voice came out in hushed tones. "I take care of myself. I don't want McTavish's protection."

"To McTavish, you're an expendable tool, a way to reach his goals, nothing more. We shield you—regardless of your wishes—because we care about you." Varun leaned toward the screen. "You must make a choice."

The room spun around her, and her limbs grew numb. Her lungs felt clogged and refused to draw air. Her fantasies of a future with McTavish vanished like air out a hull puncture. She had no choice. She couldn't allow McTavish to fail. She couldn't allow Caligo to wrest EcoMech from him.

She cleared her throat in a useless attempt to dislodge the lump caught there. "I'll come home—but not until we've found Goldman's killer. Will you make the announcement?"

"Leave it to me," he said, the glitter of victory sparking in his eyes. He closed the connection.

36

Bob scurried into the office, closing the door behind him. He gestured at the wall display.

"Some kind of important announcement coming, sir. They mentioned EcoMech."

Rafe looked up from the fistful of filmies he held and sighed. He might as well watch the news. He wasn't getting anything useful done, and really, what was the point if he couldn't save EcoMech anyway?

On the display, a press conference was just getting underway. Oasis' chairman, Varun Sharma, stood behind a podium with Clara Dubois, chairperson at Wandermere Consortium. Rafe's pulse quickened. The camera showed a mob of reporters clustered before them. It zoomed in on Sharma.

"Thank you so much for coming on this auspicious occasion." Behind the wily chairman, an enormous screen came to life, the words 'Sharma Network' writ large over a picture of the Milky Way. Rafe sat up and sucked in a breath.

"It's my pleasure to be here with Chairperson Dubois to announce a joint venture between Oasis, the Wandermere Consortium, and EcoMech. I had hoped that EcoMech CEO Rafael McTavish could be here also, but recent events on Harvest have prevented him from joining us.

"As you all know, galactic growth has stagnated over the past fifteen years. Earth Authority has not had the means to build new jump gates or even to maintain the gates it built to the smaller colonies seeded before the ice flu epidemic. Because of the enormous costs involved, corporations were equally unable to afford new gates.

Sharma gave his audience a radiant smile. It still reminded Rafe of a cagey shark.

"Today, all that has changed. Oasis has developed technology that will greatly reduce the cost of gates and begin an explosive phase of human expansion into the galaxy. The gates will connect colony worlds directly, with no need for a diversion to Earth orbit first. New worlds will be opened for a fraction of the previous investment."

"Will EcoMech have the finances to invest in your network?" a reporter called over a hubbub of excited voices. "Word on the street is that they're about to go under."

Rafe's stomach burned like a fire pit. How much would the announcement of the Sharma Network help if investors didn't think the company would last until it was complete?

Dubois stepped to the podium. "Wandermere has a long history working with Rafe McTavish for our security needs. We have complete faith in his ability to steer EcoMech toward increased profitability."

Sharma smiled at her before turning to the reporters again. "EcoMech stock has become the bargain of the century. Now that our partnership has been announced, it frees Oasis to enter the marketplace and purchase shares. After all, who doesn't like a bargain?"

At the bottom of the screen, the stock ticker jumped up. Rafe pounded a fist on the desk, whooped for joy, and then rounded the desk to hug his startled assistant.

Kama burst through the door, and he gave her a hug, too. Without thinking, he pressed his lips to hers. It felt good. No, it felt *wonderful.* His grip on her tightened.

Bob cleared his throat. With a jerk, Rafe let go. Heat crawled up his face. Her eyes were wide and her face flushed. Her fingertips grazed his cheek.

Then her expression clouded. She stepped away and turned her attention to the wall display. Hatred flashed in her dark eyes. "Gotcha, you bastards."

His joy fell away. Just for a moment, she'd opened herself to him, but now she seemed filled with regret. Why? Had he pushed too hard? Frightened her off?

He stood beside her, watching the slow crawl of the stock price. "I still can't promise to participate in the Sharma Network. I can only say that I'll do everything I can to make it happen."

"Thank you. I know you can do it." The corners of her mouth pulled up in a smile that didn't reach her eyes. A streak of worry coursed through his muscles. There was something she wasn't telling him.

Kama and Bob left the office. Rafe moved behind his desk and tapped his nanocom. Ivy Tang answered his call.

"Mr. McTavish, how nice to hear from you." The tension in her face belied the tone of her greeting. "I hope you have good news for us."

"I'm sorry to disappoint you, Ms. Tang, but we don't think it's in EcoMech's best interest to merge with Caligo. However, if you would like to engage EcoMech consultants, we'd be happy to help Caligo with its terraforming challenges."

The woman produced a stiff smile. "You're sure this is the right course for you and EcoMech? The stock price has experienced substantial fluctuations over today's trading. We both know they are not real changes but only changes in perception. Should brokers and analysts hear more bad news, EcoMech's fortunes could change again—and yours with them. A merger with Caligo would put you in a strong position, safe from the whims of the market."

Rafe had a momentary twinge of guilt. He should have informed the board about Caligo's offer, but he couldn't chance them accepting it. He hoped he wouldn't regret his decision later.

"Thank you for your concerns, Ms. Tang. I believe EcoMech can weather any temporary churn in the share price."

"As you wish, Mr. McTavish."

He closed the connection and checked the time. A knock sounded on his door, and Bob announced Lev Kozlov's arrival. Rafe didn't bother to rise while Bob showed the man in.

Today, Lev wore a sport shirt and slacks, but the insolence was still there in his body language. The man didn't bother with a greeting. He eased his lanky frame into one of the visitor chairs.

"No HR lackey to document our meeting?"

Rafe leaned back in his chair. "Alana may join us later, but her presence isn't necessary. I'm still a deputized Earth Force investigator."

"If you want to fire me, go ahead. But if you think you can show cause by proving that I engaged in illegal activities, I wish you luck. I won't be the fall guy because the company is on the rocks and the man responsible is dead. Hell, I wasn't even the second lieutenant. Go after Gerlach."

"Believe me, if I want to fire you, I will." Rafe sat forward, hands on his desk. "Where were you the night Aaron was murdered?"

Lev's mouth drew into a hard line. "You won't hang that on me, either. I was on the station."

"Bullshit. You rode down in the crew cabin on the late shuttle."

Lev went still. "So I made a mistake about the nights. What of it?"

"Eleven years ago, your wife had an abortion at a med station in Earth orbit. You were present."

The manager's face purpled. "My ex-wife's medical records are none of your damn business. Just because you're a McTavish doesn't mean you can run roughshod over the law."

"Leon and Amaya were there at the same time."

"Who gives a fuck! We're done here." He stormed out the door.

Rafe rose to follow. Bob stepped in and blocked his path.

"Sir, I think you need to turn on the news."

"Not now, Bob."

Kama joined Bob and said, "Now, McTavish. Balau's arrested your father for Aaron's murder. The stock price is already down three points."

37

Kama's eyes stared at her nanocom without seeing it. Her limbs weighed a quintal and her mind refused to focus. Her fingers strayed to her lips. She replayed the moment when McTavish had given her the impulsive kiss. She had to tell him soon that she couldn't stay. It would strike like a laser through his heart.

Shannon swept into the office and slammed the door in the face of the security guard who followed her. She glanced at Gabe, still occupying Bob's chair, and crossed the room to confront Bob.

The little assistant scrambled to his feet. Kama pretended to tune out the disruption and continue her search for the hacker. She couldn't leave Harvest without catching the cyber-criminal, not if she wanted to assure McTavish's safety when she was gone.

"I want to see Rafe."

Bob spread his hands. "I'm very sorry Mrs. Nighthorse, but you just missed him."

Shannon glanced at the closed door to the inner office. She frowned, walked to it, and threw it open. Her face took on a lovely shade of pink.

"Maybe next time you should call ahead," Kama quipped.

Shannon's blush deepened. "I did. He's not taking my calls."

"He's been very busy this morning. Would you like to wait?" Bob offered the visitor chair he'd used. "Can I get you a cup of coffee?"

McTavish's sister crossed her arms and chewed her lip. Her eyes wandered to the outer door, and her frown deepened. "Why are those gorillas following me everywhere? Did Rafe order it? They frighten the girls."

Gabe glanced at the door, his face pale and worried. He hadn't said two words all morning.

Kama gritted her teeth. Scaring kids! It was unforgivable. She ought to give Balau a piece of her mind. Better still, she ought to erase the woman's identity. Nothing to put a kink in the day like being undocumented.

"Can you help me?"

Kama dragged her attention back to Shannon. "Do what? Prove that your brother framed his father?"

"Sometimes he is the most stubborn, pig-headed—" She took a deep breath, and her shoulders loosened. "He listens to you. Tell him I need to talk to him about dad and this business with Aaron."

Kama sat a little straighter. They shouldn't discuss this in the office with Balau listening. She gave the woman a hard look. "I think I left a pair of coveralls at your place the other night. If you have the time, maybe we could go get them?"

"In the guest room? I didn't find—"

Kama grabbed Shannon's elbow and steered her to the door. "I'll be back in a bit, Gabe. You stay here with Bob."

The guards in the hallway broke off their chat. The one who'd followed Shannon to the office fell in behind them. He was a surly brute who hadn't bothered to shave. A few crumbs of something white clung to his black shirtfront, and one was stuck in his untidy mustache.

Kama stood square in the middle of the lift for the trip to the parking garage, ensuring that he was crammed in a corner. His booted feet shifted on the carpeted floor while he dodged her duffel. She hid a smile.

Shannon led her to a dark green van. Once inside, she swept for bugs but found none. The guard slid into a patrol car and followed them onto the street.

"What's this about missing coveralls?" Shannon headed northeast away from campus.

"The office is bugged, but your car's clean."

The woman's mouth fell open. "Corporate espionage? Do you know who's behind it?"

Kama jerked a thumb over her shoulder. "Our friends at Total Security. Caligo's trying to pick up EcoMech at fire sale prices and doing all it can to stir up trouble."

"More of them are stationed at the house. Are my girls in danger?"

McTavish had told Kama his family was in danger, and she hadn't listened. He would do anything to protect them, and Caligo would do whatever it took to wrest control of EcoMech from him. That made Shannon and her children targets. She should have asked Samir for more backup. There were too many assets to cover.

"Your brother has thrown a spanner in Caligo's plans. They retaliated by arresting your father, and now he's at the police station trying to get him released. Remain alert, and keep the girls close."

Shannon's face paled under her tan. They wove through light traffic as they left the business district.

"So Rafe doesn't believe dad killed Aaron?"

"I don't think he ever did." Kama gave herself a mental kick over her lack of trust in McTavish's judgment about his father. She'd failed him when he needed her. She wanted to make it up to him, but she'd never get the chance. "You two were too busy rehashing the past to see you were both on the same side."

Shannon drove in silence for the next five minutes. "It's because of Gabe's testimony that Total Security arrested dad. If he hadn't lied—"

"He didn't lie. He chased the killer, but he couldn't keep up, which is probably a good thing when you think about it. The first person he saw clearly was your father in a neighborhood where he didn't belong, and he jumped to the conclusion that your father was the man he followed." Kama shifted her duffel to the floor. "What do you know about Aaron's murder?"

Shannon's pale face turned toward her. "I'd rather discuss it with Rafe. If you could let him—"

"He's busy trying to get your father out of jail and save the company. Tell me."

"I won't air the family's dirty laundry with a stranger." Shannon pulled away from a traffic light faster than necessary.

"Don't lose your escort."

The woman turned puzzled eyes on her. "Why not? He gives me the creeps."

"Better to lull them into a false sense of security. Makes losing them later a lot easier."

"You learned all this spy craft stuff as part of your teacher training?" Shannon eased off the accelerator and glanced sideways. "You work for Rafe, don't you? You're one of his operatives."

Kama laughed. "Not in this lifetime. Or any other. Why was your father parked three blocks from Aaron's house?"

She drove another half-kilometer, hands clenched on the wheel before she answered. "He was seeing a friend."

"A friend he won't name and who won't come forward to provide an alibi. Is this friend a married woman by any chance?"

Shannon tossed her an angry look. "He's a gentleman. He'll never tell."

"A *gentleman*? Then why's he screwing another man's wife? Does he realize this is a murder investigation?"

"I'm sure he's worried about how her husband might react. He wouldn't want to put her in danger."

"Then he shouldn't have fooled around in the first place!" Kama shook her head. "Vishnu, did he really think no one would ever find out? Who is she?"

"I can't tell you. And I won't tell Rafe, either."

Kama bit back a curse. The whole trip had been a complete waste, and she'd left Gabe alone in the office with only Bob for protection. She could have used the time to chase the hacker. But McTavish needed ammunition to shoot down Caligo's plans, and an airtight alibi for Cullen would help.

"Caligo will use anything they can against your brother, including the safety of you and your kids. You can help him rescue the company and keep your family from harm, or you can save your father's reputation and risk being Caligo's next target."

Shannon glared at her. "You're trying to scare me."

"Yes. Caligo plays to win. They won't care about the lives it costs."

Horror and uncertainty caused tension lines across Shannon's forehead and around her eyes. Her knuckles went white, and a tremor shook her arms.

"What if she won't come forward willingly?" Shannon asked in a small voice.

Kama kept the smile from her face. "We won't know until we ask."

☠   ☠   ☠

Half an hour later, they pulled to the curb in front of an upscale house three blocks north of Aaron Goldman's place. The security car pulled in behind them.

"Okay, who is she?" Kama asked, her gaze on the white façade.

"Vanessa Kozlov."

Kama goggled. *McTavish's father was banging Kozlov's wife? Talk about a motive to take control of EcoMech.*

"How long has this been going on?"

Shannon looked down at her hands. "It's not something my dad and I discuss, but I heard the rumors six months ago."

Kama noted the street light just one house away. The idiot hadn't even had the sense to park around the corner. Lev had to know. But what was the connection to Aaron's murder? It was blind luck that Gabe had come forward to identify Cullen McTavish.

A woman Kama's age answered their knock at the house door. Red rimmed her bright blue eyes. Blond hair tumbled to her shoulders in a messy, seductive way. A tiny, upturned nose perched above pouty pink lips. Ample breasts showed under a tight t-shirt that accentuated her narrow waist. Lean legs ran down to sandaled feet.

"What do you want?" she asked, her voice low and husky.

"It's about Cullen. He needs your help," Shannon said. "May we come in?"

Vanessa peered over their shoulders to the security car. "There's nothing I can do. Please go away."

Kama jammed a foot in the door. "Your lover is going to prison for the rest of his life—which won't be long if he's sent to Bliss. You'll be as guilty of killing him as if you'd stuck a knife in his chest. Can you live with that?"

Tears spilled down Vanessa's cheeks, and she disappeared into the house. Shannon gave Kama a disapproving frown and followed.

The inside of the house was cool and dark, all the windows heavily tinted to block the sun. Steel and glass seemed to be the theme, from the heavy glass coffee table before the leather couch to the chrome-tubed lamp tables at each end of it to the shelves displaying objet d'art along one wall.

Shannon placed a comforting hand on Vanessa's shoulder. "Help my dad, and he'll take care of you. You won't have to hide your relationship anymore."

Fear flared in the woman's face. "You don't know Lev. He's insanely jealous. If I tried to stay here..."

Kama glanced at her nanocom. This was all taking too long. The stock price continued its slow death spiral. "We'll give you bodyguards. And when you've testified, we'll give you a new identity."

Vanessa wiped her tear-streaked face and glanced at a suitcase standing by the door. "I have to leave now, while I can."

Shannon placed a pleading hand on the woman's forearm. "At least make a statement to security before you go."

"And give Lev proof of infidelity? What kind of fool do you take me for? I'd never be able to claim any of his property."

Kama ground her teeth. So the woman was little more than a gold-digger living off Kozlov while chasing the McTavish money. And because of her unwillingness to come forward, Kama had bargained away her own freedom. Muscles knotted in her neck.

"How much cash would it take to convince you to give a statement?" Kama asked.

Shannon's mouth dropped open. "You can't pay her for her testimony. The court would throw it out."

"Only if they could find the money—or prove the connection between it and her statement," Kama muttered.

Vanessa walked into the bedroom, and Shannon and Kama followed. A second suitcase lay open on the bed. From what remained in the closet, two suitcases wouldn't begin to accommodate the woman's wardrobe. Lev might be a jealous husband, but he wasn't stingy.

"You have to help Cullen," Shannon pleaded. "He cares about you. If you leave like this, you'll break his heart."

Vanessa stopped packing long enough to glare at Shannon. "Better his heart than my head."

Kama wanted to wrap her hands around the bitch's neck and choke the life from her the same way Varun had throttled her life away from Oasis. She thrust her bunched fists in her pockets and stormed outside.

On the porch, Kama swung her arms and shrugged her shoulders, working out the tension burning there. Vanessa might be right about the danger she faced. After all, if Lev was behind the growing string of murders, he wouldn't flinch at killing his cheating wife.

But if McTavish was going to beat back the accusations against his father and stabilize the stock price, Vanessa had to speak. Or did she? What if her story leaked to the press?

Kama tapped her nanocom and switched to one of her many fictional personas. She composed a short message and addressed it to three news organizations. Before she clicked to send it, she stopped.

She should tell McTavish first. Kama opened a connection to him and gave him an update.

He groaned. "That explains Lev's threats. He knows Vanessa's cheating on him with my father. There's no point in her denying it."

"She won't come forward on her own."

"And my father hasn't named her, or Balau's people would be there already."

She heard the frustration in his voice and said, "I can release the information to the press. Given her state of mind, she'll snap under the pressure and admit what she's done."

"That's just wrong on so many levels," he replied.

"We're out of options, McTavish. You can't shield your father from his monumental mistake and still save the company. You have to choose."

After a long silence, he sighed. "Do it."

38

Rafe paced the lobby of the security building, fingering the ball in his pocket. Somewhere in the warren of offices, a video conference between Balau, an EA prosecutor, a judge, and his father's attorney was taking place. With luck, the prosecutor would dismiss the murder charges.

Forty-five minutes later, a security guard escorted his father to the lobby and handed over an envelope of belongings. His father snatched the envelope and strode across the space between them, his face contorted with rage. Rafe's muscles drew taut.

"Come to gloat?" his father whispered while staring down through slit eyes.

Before Rafe could stop himself, he blurted, "If you'd told the truth about where you were, you wouldn't have been arrested."

His father bared his teeth and lifted his fists. For a moment, the old man stood stiff and shaking. Then he stepped around Rafe and stalked to the station door.

As he reached to open it, Alberto Cobo pushed in. The board member registered surprise. Cobo gave the barest of nods to his father and walked across the room. His father followed. The board member glanced back, frowned, and stopped in front of Rafe.

"We're having an emergency board meeting tomorrow morning following Aaron Goldman's memorial service. You'll be expected to justify your actions toward the contractors and convince us of why we should keep you."

Rafe gritted his teeth to prevent giving a response he'd later regret.

He'd be in a stronger position if EcoMech had a peaceful night. Perhaps that would mollify them—at least until he told them about EcoMech's financial state.

"About time," his father said. "I told you he was the wrong choice. We should have hired Gerlach—"

"I intended to tell you in private, Cullen, but since Rafael will hear soon enough anyway, I may as well say it now. The board thinks it's best if you resign immediately. If you don't, we're prepared to remove you."

His father puffed up. "On what grounds do you propose to remove me?"

"You're under investigation for murder, for God's sake. Isn't that enough?"

In the entrance to the back hallway, Balau looked on. A smirk curled her lips. She lifted her chin and turned away to disappear toward her office.

His father responded with angry threats, but Rafe didn't hear them. It all became surreal. If the board pulled its support for the man now, it would look as if his father was guilty after all. Caligo had outflanked him again.

"Enough," Rafe said with quiet detachment.

Both men turned on him.

"My father has a solid alibi for the time of Aaron's murder. He was with a woman who, because of her marital status, is reluctant to come forward."

"How dare you," his father said, his face livid.

"So the gossip is true. One scandal to excuse another?" Cobo said. "All the more reason for your father to resign."

Rafe drew in a deep breath. This wasn't the time or the place to cross swords with Cobo. He needed the man on his side if he wanted the board to accept his recovery plan, something he'd have to tell them about soon.

"Let's not make hasty decisions," Rafe advised. "The case could break open at any minute. Once Aaron's killer is named, interest in my father will quickly wane. How would the board's decision look then?"

"And is an arrest imminent?" Cobo asked. "If so, why arrest Cullen?"

Rafe shrugged, unwilling to take the board member into his confidence.

"I want Total Security fired immediately," his father demanded. "They're incompetent."

Rafe resisted the urge to laugh. "We're stuck with them for another ten days. We can't afford the penalties if we cancel early. But we should reinstate Alana."

"Then the *board* will look incompetent," Cobo said. "Like we can't make up our minds."

"Perhaps we can put the matter on tomorrow's agenda?"

Cobo gave a grudging nod.

"It would help if we all went out together and presented a united front to the press," Rafe suggested.

His father's jaw worked back and forth. Rafe took that for tacit agreement. Cobo led the way out the front door into a ravening pack of news reporters.

"Mr. McTavish, we heard you've been released on bail," one of them shouted. A cacophony of questions rang in the stifling air.

Rafe waved for quiet. "The investigative team made an error. My father will be completely exonerated in due course."

The canary-dress reporter pushed to the front of the pack. "We heard you lied about being at the house. That there's an eyewitness who places you inside at the time of the murder."

His father took a step forward. Rafe dodged to intercept and gave the harpy his most disarming grin.

"Perhaps you and I can have dinner soon. You can fill me in on where you get your juicy gossip. Or do you make it up yourself?"

The other reporters chuckled. Rafe turned to address them.

"Make no mistake. We *will* find Aaron Goldman's murderer and bring him to justice. Now if you'll excuse us, we have a company to run."

With that, his father and Cobo pushed through to Cobo's car, waiting at the curb. The car swept away. Seconds later, Alana's car pulled up. Rafe climbed in front. His security escort scrambled for their own vehicle.

Kama huddled in the back seat. She had no greeting for him. She stared out the window, a little crease between her brows, the same crease she had when she mulled over telling him something important. He needed to find time alone with her, to see if he'd done something, said something he shouldn't have, something that was driving a wedge between them.

"All right, Alana. Let's find Lev."

39

Kama stared out at the parking garage walls. How would she tell McTavish she was leaving? He'd think she'd strung him along to get the Sharma Network built, and that would crush him. She couldn't do that to him, but she couldn't think of a kind way to break the news.

They pulled into a no-parking zone beside the elevator and got out of the car.

"At least let me call a couple of my guys for backup." Dzandarova slammed her car door.

Kama checked behind them for their escort. A hundred feet down the garage, the three goons who comprised the McTavish protection detail sauntered toward them.

"Let me handle Lev. You two stay out of the way. And try to keep the security escort from overhearing." McTavish pushed the button to call the lift.

Kama counted the seconds until the lift arrived. She'd like to drop their followers down the lift shaft, preferably from the top floor. One hand rested on her nanocom. The lift pinged, the doors slid open, and the three of them stepped inside.

Footsteps jogged toward the lift. She tapped her nanocom. The doors slid closed, the floor indicator panel went dark, and the lift rose. McTavish glanced her direction, but kept his face neutral.

Dzandarova frowned at the indicators, and then at the control panel. "What's wrong with the elevator? I better call maintenance."

"I wouldn't bother," McTavish said. "It's probably a temporary glitch."

"It's an elevator," the security chief replied. "Glitches, even temporary, are a safety concern."

Dzandarova opened a connection and reported the issue.

On the tenth floor, McTavish led the way to Kozlov's office. The manager shot up from his workstation.

"What do you want, McTavish?"

Even under the dress shirt and slacks, Kozlov's trim physique shone through, and every muscle was pulled tight. Maybe Dzandarova was right and they should have brought some of her people.

"Answers, and this time, you'll give them to me," McTavish said, voice low and firm. "Where were you the night Aaron died?"

"And if I don't, are you gonna sic your women on me?"

McTavish lowered his head and kept his stance relaxed. "I'm sorry about your wife. No one wins when a spouse cheats."

Kozlov planted his knuckles on his desk and leaned forward. "You know that because you screw married women, too?"

"I'm not my father." There was a tiny catch in his voice, the only indication that he was bothered by the man's accusation.

"Bull. You rich guys are all alike. Think you can do whatever you like and get away with it. This time I'll have my pound of flesh."

Alloy samples and crumpled filmies spattered off the wall as Kozlov cleared the desk with an angry sweep of his arm, and launched himself at McTavish. The two men grappled against the bookcase with a slew of grunts, growls, and muttered oaths.

"Testosterone spill on ten," Kama muttered. But her torso tensed. All it would take was one misjudged block and McTavish could be seriously injured.

At Kama's side, Dzandarova looked on, frowning. There wasn't much sign of the usual decisive, efficient law-woman. Presumably her big book of Standard Operating Procedures didn't include a section on 'Boss Has Ball-Kicking Contest.'

"We should do something." Dzandarova said.

She ducked a broken chunk of gear that whistled past to clatter on the hallway floor. Anger at McTavish surged. Varun was right. McTavish took too many risks.

The two men staggered across the carpet and reeled against one of the windows. Kozlov was far larger and a solid block of muscle, but McTavish was his usual slippery weasel self, ducking and deflecting most of the bigger man's angry haymakers. For all his muscle, it didn't look like Kozlov knew much about fighting.

Dzandarova took an uncertain step forward, and Kama stopped her with a hand on the arm and gritted teeth.

"Step in there and you're just asking to get your clock cleaned. That

Kozlov guy's all martial and no art."

"But he's choking my boss!" Dzandarova objected.

"Knowing McTavish, he's probably enjoying himself," Kama said, and gestured to the action, where McTavish spoiled her point by having his head bounced repeatedly off a pane of toughened glass.

Dzandarova threw up her hands and scurried away, doubtless in search of reinforcements. Kama couldn't blame her. To an onlooker it probably seemed like McTavish was getting the worst of it, but she'd spotted at least three moments he could have dropped the bigger man with a blow to the throat or back of the neck and chose not to. He was biding his time and letting Kozlov wear himself out.

"Hurry up, McTavish," she called. "The goon squad will be here soon."

There was a muffled grunt from McTavish. "Working on it."

Kama reined in her anger and focused on her nanocom, where she restored the lift to normal service. More crashing drew her attention. The workstation display screen lay broken on the floor. A twist of the hips, a wrench on a flailing arm, and McTavish had the bigger man in a choke hold. Kozlov's face purpled as he strained to free himself.

Kama stepped through the door. "Finally. Now that's over, perhaps we can—"

Someone barged past her, and her head cracked painfully into the wall. A security guard's meaty fist sunk in under Kozlov's ribs as his two companions hauled the fighters apart. Kozlov doubled over from the blow, and then fell under the black-clad goons' retaliatory rain of blows from fists, feet, and rifle butts.

"Hey!" Kama hollered. She seized a rifle barrel and yanked the weapon out of unsuspecting hands. The owner turned on her. She had just enough time to remember her sage advice to Dzandarova all of ninety seconds earlier before a fist smacked into the side of her head and carpet approached her at speed.

The rifle clattered away out of reach, and her breath rushed out as a boot found her ribs. Kama's world contracted to a point. She waited for the next blow, hoping that they weren't kicking the crap out of McTavish as well.

The blow never arrived. Instead, swearing, a crunch, and several loud thuds followed. Kama hauled in an uncooperative lungful of air and rolled onto her back.

One of the Total Security goons lay against the bookcase with his legs stuck out and his left arm twisted at an irreparable angle. Another was wedged under the desk. The third sprawled beside her, his legs in the office, chest in the hallway, and face mashed into the floor. McTavish bent over her, expression full of worry.

"Kali, McTavish. Balau isn't going to like this."

Kozlov struggled to his feet and blinked down at the unconscious guards. His eyes went to McTavish. His mouth opened, closed. He wiped the back of his hand across blood-smeared lips.

"You could have put me down in the first five seconds," he said at last. "Why didn't you?"

"He doesn't like to show off." Kama's gaze swept the room. "Mostly."

"Let's find a vacant conference room—before these guys wake up."

McTavish put a protective arm around her shoulders and steadied her down the hallway. She accepted his help, enjoying the feel of him next to her.

"You know Balau will flip when she hears what you did to those guards."

His brow creased. "Tomorrow after Aaron's service, I want you to take Gabe to Mumbai. You can stay with Barb and Ying until I've gotten rid of Balau."

He didn't know she wouldn't be coming back. She couldn't jerk the rug out from under him now, not with so many obstacles still to overcome. Alana's people could escort Gabe to Earth.

"We'll discuss it later."

McTavish's jaw set in that brook-no-arguments way he displayed when he gave orders, but his eyes searched her face. He could always tell when she tried to keep secrets.

Once they were seated at the conference table, McTavish turned his attention to Kozlov.

"Tell me about the abortion. The medical records show it was an elective procedure. Mother and fetus were both healthy."

Kozlov's face closed down. "It's ancient history and none of your damn business."

"Why couldn't Leon fire you?" McTavish asked. "Were you blackmailing him?"

The manager showed a flash of surprise, and then the insolent smirk returned. "Because I'm good at my job. And his daddy wouldn't let him."

"Why would Aaron protect you?"

Kozlov slammed his fists on the table. "For the same reason you won't fire me."

Kama frowned, trying to suss out what the manager meant. Maybe the knock on her head was worse than she realized. Beside her, McTavish straightened.

"It was Leon's child, not yours."

The breath caught in her throat as pieces fell into place. Kozlov had every reason to hate the Goldmans and to want to bring down EcoMech.

He'd been at the station when Gabe was born. He must have overheard the plan to switch babies.

"I'd been sent to Earth to help get the Omaha factory online. I hadn't been back long when Cindy told me she was pregnant." Kozlov frowned at the table. "We'd been trying for a while..."

He looked up and his eyes narrowed. "At our first checkup, they said the fetus was at least two months old. I'd only been back a month. I confronted Cindy, wanted to know who knocked her up.

"She spun a story about Leon raping her. Said she didn't report it because she was afraid I'd be fired. I'd seen her flirting with him at a company party. Hell, she flirted with every man she ever met."

Kozlov rubbed the back of his hand across his mouth. "She said she loved me, pleaded with me not to divorce her. I agreed, but only if she got rid of the baby."

"What happened at the med station?" McTavish asked.

"Cindy nearly died. The med tech was high when he did the procedure, and he botched it. They said she could never have children."

Kama glanced at McTavish. Did the manager's story dredge up memories of his own dead children? He looked pale under his tan, and little tension lines formed around his lips. She wanted to take his hand, show her support, but this wasn't the time.

"Did you see Leon?"

Kozlov laughed. "I did a lot more than see him. I planted my fist in his nose. He was livid. He filed assault charges."

The manager looked puzzled. "I never understood why Aaron intervened. Sure Leon cheated with my wife, but... Maybe he felt sorry for us. It just seemed like he made more of it than I expected."

"Did you ever think Cindy might have told the truth?"

"That Leon raped her?" Kozlov shook his head. "He was a prick, but he wouldn't have gone that far."

McTavish ran a hand through his hair. "When Shannon was seventeen, Leon came by and asked her to go with him on some errand to the test fields. He'd been drinking. She thought he wasn't safe to fly, so she agreed to go if he relinquished the controls.

"It was all a ruse. At the test fields, he got her into a maintenance shed and ripped her clothes off. He told her since they were supposed to get married eventually anyway, why wait?"

A shiver ran up Kama's spine. She'd known his family was a screwed up mess, but this was beyond the pale.

"Leon raped Shannon?" The disbelief was thick in Kozlov's voice.

"No, but only because Ben Nighthorse showed up. He'd come back for a part for a broken weed burner. That's how he and Shannon met."

Kozlov sank back in his chair. "Shannon never reported it?"

McTavish looked Kozlov in the eye. "Aaron and my father swept it under the rug as a prank by a drunken teenager. They didn't want a scandal to taint the company name."

"My God. Then Cindy—" Kozlov's face darkened, and he went silent, eyes unfocused.

McTavish let the manager stew a minute. Then he asked, "Where were you the night Aaron was killed?"

Kozlov straightened and his expression hardened. "Hiding down the block from my house, making a video of your daddy dropping in on my wife."

"Did you see anyone on the street?"

"No, but I couldn't see much of my side of the street."

"You didn't see Gabe?" Kama asked.

"He'd be 'anyone' wouldn't he?" the manager said, sarcasm threading his voice.

Kama bristled. The guy was a bona fide jerk. No wonder Vanessa had an affair. McTavish should fire his ass. But she had to admit, with his secret uncovered, Kozlov seemed less like a candidate for Goldman's murder.

McTavish rose.

"Do I get to clear out my office before Alana escorts me out?" Kozlov asked.

"Did you submit a resignation?"

The manager shrugged. "When I threw the first punch?"

McTavish pushed unruly hair off his forehead. "You missed. Close only counts in horseshoes and hand grenades. I want that station report today, no excuses."

☠   ☠   ☠

They met Alana in the parking garage, where two uniformed officers stepped out of an EcoMech patrol car.

"Where's your escort?" Alana said, looking behind them.

McTavish replied with a straight face. "They've been detained upstairs. I need to borrow your car. Can you catch a ride with your people?"

"What about your interrogation of Mr. Kozlov?"

"He's clear. I'll fill you in at the office."

"Do you promise not to lose us?" Alana asked, suspicion in her voice.

McTavish made an X on his chest. "Cross my heart."

He held the passenger door for Kama. A little niggle of irritation squirmed through her thoughts at the gesture. It must have shown on her face. He gave her a deep bow, an over-gallant sweep of his arm, and an impish smile. She stiffened her back and climbed in.

He drove at a sedate pace, checking his rearview mirror before turning away from the office.

"Where are we going?" Kama asked.

"The long way," he replied. He glanced her way and drew in a deep breath. "Something's worrying you. Will you share?"

Ice formed in Kama's blood, and she clutched her duffel to her stomach. He'd know if she lied.

"When we catch Goldman's killer, I'm going to Oasis," she said, her voice rough.

McTavish stared straight ahead. "For how long?"

"Forever," she said, choking on the word.

The car decelerated for half a block before it regained its speed.

"I apologize if I said something, did something—" His hands squeezed the wheel, released, squeezed again.

"It was Varun's price to announce the Sharma Network early." Kama focused on her duffel, black like her future, like her heart. Her fingers ached where they gripped the fabric. If she let go, she'd float away into the darkness. "I had to stop Caligo from taking over. I had to be sure you won."

They drove another block in silence before McTavish said, "I know long-distance relationships are hard, but we can make it work. I can come to Oasis—"

"No. Never to Oasis," Kama breathed. "Never anywhere. Varun doesn't approve of you."

McTavish's head jerked toward her. "He can't hold you prisoner!"

"I gave my word." She turned away and looked out the window. "I'm sorry."

40

Rafe stared out Alana's kitchen window and sipped coffee without tasting it. Morning light shone through the glass, bright and hot, but it did nothing to melt the cold lump in his chest.

Nine days until he could dismiss Total Security. Four hours until he sent Kama away with Gabe to the safety of Earth. She'd fight to stay, of course. He wouldn't risk it, much as he wanted to share every possible minute with her.

Once Total Security was gone, he'd turn EcoMech around, no matter what it took. He'd prove to Sharma that he was a sharp, successful businessman, a solid partner, and a worthy suitor for Kama. He'd force the wily old chairman to release her from her promise, even if it took years. Would Kama wait?

Alana walked into the kitchen, trailed by Kama, who had dark circles under her eyes and a pale, pained expression. From looking in the mirror this morning while he shaved, he knew he didn't look any better. He wanted to sweep her into his arms and hold on tight.

"What's the status on the evacuation buses for the mourners attending the viewing and service?" he asked.

"They'll be in position in half an hour," Alana replied, "Six blocks north of the conference center."

"And the flyers for the VIPs?"

"Four with the buses." Alana poured herself a cup of coffee. "We have a hiccup. Balau sent thirty of my people out to a research station west of town. There's been a suspicious explosion. She blames it on contractors."

"Anyone hurt?"

"Hell, boss, there isn't anyone *at* the research station most of time. But she claims to have intelligence that a terrorist cell is gathering there. What would a terrorist cell do in the middle of nowhere?"

Rafe massaged the ache developing in the back of his neck. "Then it's a diversion. She wants your people out of her way."

"You think she'll try to incite the contractors again, like she did with the compound search?" the security chief said.

"Looks like. Put everyone on high alert, and make sure you have plenty of manpower available to keep a corridor open for the buses."

"I'll do what I can. She's already jailed a dozen of my senior officers on trumped-up corruption charges and dismissed at least that many field staff for insubordination."

Kama hissed through her teeth. "That woman is pure evil. You should cancel the service, or at least postpone it until she's gone."

"My father would never allow it. Besides, if we cancel, we're as much as saying we don't have Harvest under control. That'll put the stock price into another tailspin and play into Caligo's hands."

He thumped his mug on the counter, and coffee spilled. "I'm done playing her game. Alana, be ready. As soon as the VIPs have gotten to the shuttleport, I'm firing Total Security."

Alana rubbed her cheek. "If EcoMech is broke, how will you pay their penalty?"

Rafe strode toward the bedrooms to get Gabe. "They can stand in line with the rest of EcoMech's creditors."

☠   ☠   ☠

A black-garbed security officer flagged Rafe's flyer toward the second level of the parking garage under the conference center. The place was already packed with vehicles, but spaces near the elevator had been reserved for him and the board.

Rafe pulled in beside Bert Gerlach's black flyer. The man gave him a nod and joined Lars Svenson, already waiting at the elevator. His father cruised into the space next to him, and Shannon parked in the next space along the row. Rafe gritted his teeth and stepped out.

Lev Kozlov strolled up. At the far edges of the parking space, his shiny prototype glinted in the artificial light. His father glared at Kozlov, his jaw working back and forth before he strode to the elevator to join the others. Kozlov kept his hands in his trouser pockets, an air of cool confidence surrounding him.

Shannon alighted from her flyer, her three daughters in tow. Her husband, Ben, and son, Greg, were conspicuous by their absence. Rafe couldn't help think that they were lucky to miss the family reunion about to take place. With a sigh, he shepherded Gabe to the elevator.

Shannon appeared beside him. "I'm worried about Greg. He should have arrived last night, and I can't reach him. Have you heard anything?"

Rafe stiffened. He stroked back his cuff to expose his nanocom and punched in a connection to Greg. While he waited for a response, he said, "Where's Ben?"

"In the middle of nowhere on a water survey. There wasn't time for him to make it back. Besides, he had no love for Aaron." She bit her lip. "Are my children in danger?"

"The board is meeting right after the service and will select a re-placement CEO," Cullen said in a voice loud enough to be heard across the parking garage. "Bert, I'd like you and Lars to be there in case they want to conduct interviews."

Lars remained silent, expression giving away nothing while he nod-ded his acquiescence. Bert glanced at Rafe, embarrassment showing in his eyes, before he assured the man he'd be available. Lev stared at the older McTavish in momentary disbelief before turning his gaze on Rafe.

Rafe gritted his teeth, his face warming. He wanted to shout at his father for his stupidity and callous disregard toward the contractors. Wanted to tell the man how hard he'd worked to save the company, a company he couldn't care less about. How he'd given up his comfortable life to come to this hell hole to protect his family even though they didn't give a damn about him.

Greg didn't pick up.

The elevator door opened, and Bert, Lars, and his father got on. Lev held back and gestured for Shannon to enter.

Shannon shooed the children in and stepped away. "Go with your grandpa, girls. I'll be up in a minute."

Lev brushed past and boarded the elevator. The door slid closed on his father's irritated look.

Shannon glanced at Gabe. She took Rafe's arm and dragged him ten feet away.

"You shouldn't have come back."

His gut twisted. "You hate me, too."

"What? No, of course not." She dropped her hand from his arm. "When you left, it was the best thing for both of you. You'll never make Dad love you, and it causes you so much pain. I want you to be happy, but you can't do that here."

"I don't understand. Why does he hate me? I know I was difficult—"

"Oh, Rafe, it's not about you. It's about Mom." Shannon blinked back tears. "Do you remember when you were thirteen and you broke Mom's crystal vase?"

He'd been goofing off, practicing his soccer footwork in the living room, something he'd been told a million times not to do. The ball had gotten away from him, bounced into the shelves, toppled the vase. But it was only a vase.

"He hates me for that?"

"When he got home and found what you'd done, he was furious. He'd given that vase to Mom on their first wedding anniversary. He slapped you. You had a bruise on your cheek for a week."

His hand strayed to his face.

"He's always had anger management issues. He's worked very hard to maintain control. He loved you, but your ADHD brought out the worst in him. He was afraid that next time, he wouldn't stop until he'd killed you.

"He told Mom he wanted to send you away to boarding school. She wouldn't hear of it. So to keep you safe, he moved out. He figured in a few years, you'd be grown and gone. Then he'd patch things up with Mom, and they'd spend the rest of their lives together." Shannon stared across the parking garage, eyes brimming with tears. "He loved her more than anything in the world."

"But she died a year later," he whispered.

His sister nodded. "In his mind, you stole what little time they had left together, and he can't forgive you. He'll never forgive you.

"Go home, Rafe. Take Gabe with you and make a new family, one that appreciates the fine man you've become. Find the love and happiness you deserve." She squeezed his hand. "Don't let him hurt you anymore."

Time seemed to stand still. He couldn't take it in.

"I can't leave. The company's a mess, and I promised Aaron."

"None of that matters—"

"Yes, it does. I'm sorry if it causes Dad pain, but I have to stay. I have to find Aaron's killer. I have to keep you and your children safe. I can't let the company fail. Millions of investors and thousands of employees would be hurt." He looked down into her green eyes. "I can't run away from him again."

Shannon's face fell. "No, of course you can't."

His sister walked to the elevator and pushed the call button. He glanced at his nanocom. Greg should have responded by now. Where was the boy? He opened a connection to Alana.

"I know you're swamped," he said, "but can you check the shuttles to see if Greg Nighthorse is on one? He isn't responding to calls."

"Ms. Nighthorse asked me to check earlier. We haven't found him."

A cold chill walked Rafe's spine. "Keep trying."

41

Kama opened the front door. The security guards had followed McTav-ish away from Alana's house. A black sedan pulled up at the curb, a tight-lipped Wolf at the wheel. She jogged to the car and slipped in.

"Take us to Building 13."

He glanced her way before steering the vehicle onto a main thor-oughfare leading to the campus.

"Samir says you're coming home."

Kama stared straight ahead, willing her face into a neutral mask while her stomach turned to cement. In her head, the minutes until she and McTavish would be separated forever ticked by.

"Not until we've caught Goldman's killer."

He looked at her again. "McTavish doesn't look after you. If he did, he wouldn't involve you in a murder investigation."

Kama snorted. "Getting involved was my decision, not his. But Mc-Tavish respects my choices even when he doesn't agree with them—un-like Varun. He's taught me things..."

"Do you love him?" he asked in a low voice.

"What does it matter? When we leave here, I'll never see him again."

She cleared her throat, trying to dislodge the ball of cotton wool stuck in her windpipe. Wolf drove to the campus in silence.

"Did you receive the new credentials Samir sent for the hacker?" He turned down the ramp of the parking garage under Building 13.

"Yes." She chewed her lip. Would the hacker agree to join Oasis? Few had the courage to say no to Samir. Still, he liked to perpetrate the illusion that they joined voluntarily. It helped morale.

What would McTavish say if he knew Samir planned to spirit the hacker away? She'd heard the disapproval in his voice at the entertainment station.

The building lobby was deserted. Full-time staff would either be attending the service at the conference center or watching at home on their vid screens. Only contractors would work today.

She and Wolf took the lift to the second floor. Her nanocom displayed plan and elevation views of the building, and a blinking red spot that marked her quarry. A shiny new stunner—a gift from Samir— bumped gently in her coveralls pocket. She hurried down the corridor.

She stopped outside the ladies loo. A janitor's cart blocked the door. On the blueprints, the red dot flashed on the other side of the wall. Kama grinned.

"Wait here," she said.

She pushed the cart aside, slipped her hand into the pocket with the stunner, and opened the door.

The emaciated teenage girl she'd seen in the stairwell when she'd been beaten jerked her head around and dropped her cleaning rag in the sink. White heat surged through Kama. Without this girl's meddling, what future might she have had with McTavish? She would make the girl pay.

A quick glance told Kama they were alone. She moved a step closer.

"Game over, Emelia. I win."

Emelia's eyes flared open for just a moment. Then she laughed, an uneasy sound that betrayed her nervousness.

"I don't know what you're talking about." She backed away but ran into the wall.

"I give you points for cleverness. Porking up before you came to Harvest, and then losing thirty kilos after you were fitted with your ID bracelet was a damn smart way to ensure you could ditch it later without opening the clasp and setting off its alarm."

"I did nothing." Her eyes darted about. Kama blocked her only escape.

"You picked the wrong target. You should have left EcoMech alone."

The girl's fists bunched. "Traitor. You spy on the contractors and work for the power brokers, the men with the money. And what do you get? Not even their respect. That man, McTavish. He leaves you in the filthy contractor compound while he lives in luxury."

Kama's spine stiffened. She took a step forward. "McTavish isn't like that. He's trying to improve things, but it takes teamwork and cooperation."

"You believe that drivel? I thought you were smarter. He's just like all the rest of the rich, greedy bastards. He won't stop until he owns the galaxy. With my last breath, I curse them."

"Let's hope you won't be taking that last breath anytime soon," Kama said in a threatening tone. "Tell me how you moved from one building to another without being seen."

Emelia's eyes narrowed. "I admit nothing."

"Okay, if that's your choice. It'll cost you at least a year in prison."

"For what?" the girl asked. "You have no proof I did anything wrong."

"There's your phony identity for starters. It's a tissue of lies that unravel under close examination. Tell me what I want to know."

Emelia plucked the cleaning rag from the sink and twisted it in her hands. "You've been brainwashed by McTavish. Open your eyes. He's made you his watchdog."

"Tick-tock, Emelia."

The girl took a step closer. "Or are you his bitch? Does he screw you on his desk?"

"That's it." Kama raised a fist. "Tell me—"

The girl lunged forward, tossing the wet rag in Kama's face and dashing past. Whatever cleaning fluid was on the thing stung her eyes like buggery. She cranked on the nearest faucet and rinsed the vile liquid away.

Wolf pushed the girl through the door, one arm behind her back. Terror shone in Emelia's expression. Kama waited a long minute before nodding at him to release the girl.

Kama crossed her arms. "We can do this the easy way or the hard way. Your choice."

The slightest of frowns creased Wolf's brow. He expected her to extend Samir's offer, but Kama couldn't betray McTavish by letting Emelia get away. The girl stared at her, and she stared back.

"Fine." Kama gestured to Wolf. "Break her arm."

Surprise and confusion washed through Wolf's body language. He recovered and reached for Emelia, playing along with Kama's ruse.

"Wait!" Emelia shrieked. "I used the utility tunnels under the buildings."

"No you didn't. I've seen the blueprints. They're too small." A little sneer curled the girl's lips, and Kama smacked her hand to her head. "You altered the blueprints. How do you access the tunnels?"

"From the lavs or the parking garage." Emelia pointed to the stall in the far corner. "There's an access hatch in the ceiling. Go through it and you'll see the shaft for the water and drain pipes."

Kama walked to the stall and looked up. There was the hatch. By standing on the toilet, she could push it open. She pulled herself into a cramped space between the suspended ceiling of the loo and the next floor above. The light from her nanocom faded into the distance before reaching the outer building wall.

As the girl had said, a meter-square shaft carried the pipes up through the building and down to the utility tunnels buried below the parking garages. Ladder rungs were embedded in one side of the shaft. She had to admit Emelia had balls if this was how she'd gotten around the campus.

Back in the loo, Kama slapped the dust from her coveralls and nodded at Wolf to dismiss him. "You can go."

For a moment, she thought he wouldn't obey. He backed up a step, turned, and stepped out. Emelia's eyes followed him.

Kama tapped her nanocom, sending Alana all the proof she needed to arrest Emelia. "You could have done so much with your talent. Instead you chose to create chaos and destruction, to hurt others instead of help them. What a waste."

42

Rafe glanced around the conference room. Aaron's rose-draped casket dominated the front area, an impeccably clothed and groomed Aaron nestled in its red silk. Velvet roped corridors ran up each side wall, channeling the thousands of now departed mourners past the display. It reminded Rafe of his mother's funeral and left him queasy and disoriented.

A pair of black-shirted guards flanked the casket, automatic rifles slung on their shoulders and pistols holstered on their hips. Two more pairs guarded the exits at the front and back of the room. Where were the stunners and batons, weapons appropriate for use against unarmed civilians? Uneasiness wormed in Rafe's gut.

Two dozen chairs occupied the center of the room. The front row contained EcoMech's VIPs. Shannon and her children sat with his father and half the board on one side of a center aisle. He and Gabe had been ostracized to the opposite side of the aisle, along with the remainder of the board, which suited Rafe just fine.

Occasionally the cameras that beamed the service around Harvest and across the galaxy panned over them, the broadcast mirrored on large wall screens. He noted that Bert and Lars were seated near his father, while Lev shared his side of the room.

The next rows held the leaders of industry and government who'd attended in person, something infrequently done these days and a testament to Aaron's importance in the business community. He recognized Dieter Schloss, the chairman of Schloss Financial, one of the largest banks in the galaxy and a major creditor of EcoMech's.

Schloss had requested to meet him later in the afternoon, probably to ask about the rumors of EcoMech's insolvency. Rafe still didn't know what he'd say, assuming he hadn't been fired by then. At least the stock price had stabilized. Now if it just didn't drop again.

Next to Schloss sat Sung Woo, an influential EA economic advisor. Farther along, Lalani Troi smoothed the front of her jacket. She was EA's agricultural undersecretary and rumored to be considering a run for EA president. She'd received substantial campaign contributions from EcoMech and hoped that the company would continue to support her.

Somehow, the canary press vulture had talked her way into the room and sat in the last row. Today, she was dressed in a somber, dark blue pantsuit, but her sharp eyes scanned the gathered crowd.

Elsewhere in the building, another thousand upper-level managers, EcoMech retirees, and assorted friends and neighbors of Aaron's filled the large conference rooms to capacity. Rafe had glanced in one as they'd passed. The cloying scent from the hundreds of wreaths and bouquets on display had left him gasping.

The minister finished his remarks and stepped back from the podium to allow his father access. Rafe typed a short message to Alana querying her readiness. He received a quick reply. Alana was at the buses with ten officers, ready to ferry away mourners and fly out the VIPs should protests develop.

She noted that Balau's people were concentrated to the south, between the conference center and the bulk of the campus buildings. That left plenty of opportunity for protestors to make an end run around the forces and flank them. Alana thought it a serious tactical mistake. She'd called back the officers sent on the wild goose chase to the research station despite concerns about how Balau might react.

Rafe's father droned on, delivering Aaron's eulogy while Rafe chafed with his forced inactivity. He adjusted his tie for the twelfth time and struggled not to tap his fingers on his leg.

A whisper of voices started at the center of the room. Rafe scanned the crowd. Everyone was looking at their nanocoms, and he did the same, but he needn't have bothered. The wall displays lit up with the identical scene that his nanocom showed.

A blurry shot through a shop window to a River City street outside filled the screen. A man dressed in contractor coveralls waited on the curb at a bus stop. A security car pulled up, and three black-shirted officers got out. There was no sound, but it was clear they'd requested the man's ID.

The contractor extended his arm to show his bracelet. The smallest of the guards grabbed the arm and twisted it savagely into a wrist lock. The contractor fell to his knees, mouth open in a silent scream. The other two men used their gun butts to club the contractor until he fell unconscious on the pavement. Then one of them moved to the window through which the video was made and shattered it with his rifle butt.

"Jerrod Oakley is dead!" letters on the screen proclaimed. "Contractors revolt!" The video looped to the beginning and replayed.

His father frowned at the video display, the eulogy stopped in mid-sentence. Then he glared at Rafe. A murmur of excited voices filled the air. The guards unsnapped their pistol holsters.

"Please calm down and remember where you are," his father said. "We're gathered here for the remembrance of a great man."

His father began again to speak about Aaron. He was interrupted by Balau's appearance on the wall screens.

"This is Commander Balau. Early this morning, contractors set off a bomb at a research station outside River City, destroying it. These terrorists now shelter on the corporate campus, where they agitate for others to join them.

"By the power Earth Authority grants me, I place Harvest under martial law. All contract staff are ordered to gather in the lobbies of their buildings and await transportation to housing, where they will remain until the terrorists are captured. Full-time staff should evacuate immediately to their homes and remain there until further notice.

"Certain elements of EcoMech security are sympathetic to the terrorists and have disobeyed orders to apprehend the criminals. Until I can determine the extent of the issue, all EcoMech security officers will turn themselves over to my people and stand down. Any who don't comply will be shot on sight."

"Remain calm and cooperate fully with my officers until this crisis is resolved."

The breath caught in Rafe's chest. This was no bluff. It wasn't even a police action. It was nothing less than a hostile takeover of EcoMech. With the company under her control, Balau could do whatever she wanted and destroy or fabricate evidence as necessary to back up her actions. He had to stop her.

The giant wall screens went dark, and the lights went out, taking network access with them. Emergency lights flashed on, creating an eerie tableau in the room. Faintly, shouting came to him, and then the sound of shattering glass and the pop pop of pistol fire. Everyone came to their feet.

"Remain calm," a soldier with a sergeant's chevrons yelled over the chatter that filled the room.

More shots rang out, closer and louder. The panicked stampede of a thousand pairs of feet running past the doors shook the floor and rattled the walls. A loud boom reverberated through the building. *Flashbang*, Rafe's ears told him, not a grenade. Someone in the group cried, "Bomb!"

"Evacuate to the roof," Rafe shouted over the noise. "Flyers will pick you up there."

He gripped Gabe's hand and steered others toward the doors to the hallway. His father abandoned the podium, joined Shannon, and lifted her youngest into his arms. The VIPs threaded between the chairs and moved with purpose to the exit. The guards blocked them.

The sergeant, a squat man with a deep sunburn, held his rifle across his chest. "No one leaves the room."

Rafe worked his way past Lars and Bert to stand beside Lev in front of the officer. "We're going to the roof. The stairwell is fifty feet to the left. You'll need to clear the doorway so we can get through. Redirect people to the front of the building. Buses will pick them up there."

"I have orders to hold all of you here until transportation arrives. Step back."

Rafe clamped his teeth and growled under his breath. His father pushed Lev aside and glared first at the officers and then at Rafe.

"This is your fault," Cullen said, color rising in his cheeks. "You gave in to the contractors, and now they're rioting."

"This is their fault," Rafe replied, pointing an accusing finger at the sergeant, "for using unnecessary force against an unarmed man." He swept an arm at the board members gathered round. "And your fault for relieving Alana of her duties."

His father stiffened and loomed over him. "But you're blameless, of course. You never do anything wrong."

Rafe stepped closer. "Oh, hell, no. I'm no innocent. I should have refused to bring in Total Security. I should have negotiated with the contract staff my first day on the ground, after I saw that concentration camp where you incarcerate them. I should have worried more about saving EcoMech and less about saving your butt."

"Stop it!" Shannon forced her way between them and pulled her frightened daughter from her father's arms.

Rafe glowered at his sister. The angelic child in her arms buried her head against her mother's shoulder and sobbed. The white heat of his anger cooled. He glanced at the audience around them and deeply regretted his impulsive outburst. He took a deep breath, let it out, and stepped back.

"We can discuss my failings later," Rafe said. "Right now, we need to get everyone to safety."

His father spun to face the sergeant, rage redirected. "How do you plan to get us out of here?"

"I'm not at liberty to discuss that with a civilian," the sergeant replied, the hint of a smirk visible behind his visor.

"Don't take that insolent attitude with me. I'm your employer and therefore your superior. Answer my question."

"Sit down," the sergeant ordered, his voice tense.

Shannon placed a hand on her father's arm. He looked at her, his jaw working back and forth, a sure sign of his struggle to compose himself. At last, he put an arm around Shannon's shoulders and guided her to the chairs. The others followed.

Rafe waited while the minutes ticked by. The muffled sound of the mob rushing to the parking garage continued unabated.

The sergeant's head jerked a fraction, a tell that he'd shifted his attention to his heads-up display. He motioned to the other men, and they advanced on the VIPs.

"Come with us," the sergeant said.

He walked around the chairs to the door at the front of the room, still manned by a pair of guards. Rafe thought it led to kitchens and a service area. He was damn sure it didn't access the roof.

"No," Rafe said. "We're going up."

Before he could turn around, something hard slammed against his back. Pain and momentum toppled him over a row of chairs. A chair was flung aside, and a boot found his midriff, knocking the air from his lungs. Two soldiers hauled him up to face the sergeant, who now leveled his rifle at Rafe's chest.

Shannon had one hand over her mouth. The other hugged her daughters to her side. The faces of the VIPs showed stunned surprise. Even his father gaped, mouth open.

The sergeant surveyed the VIPs and pointed his rifle at the ceiling. "An armored van is meeting us at the loading dock. It will transport all of you to a secure location. Your cooperation is appreciated."

The man jerked his chin toward the rear exit. One by one, the VIPs queued up to follow orders. Lev gave the officer a black look, placed a hand on Gabe's shoulder, and guided him to the door. The two guards holding Rafe shoved him in that direction and loosed their grips on him.

Where was Balau taking them? He'd seriously misjudged her, and now his family would pay the price. The stinging pain of his error hurt worse than his aching gut and bruised back.

The sergeant led them through a short, narrow corridor to a shining kitchen. The sound of the mourners fleeing the building dropped away. Their footsteps echoed on the tile floor. They passed refrigeration units and a storeroom and bunched up at an access door in the rear wall.

The sergeant swung the door open. Bright sunshine blinded them. The guards shoved them stumbling forward before Rafe's eyes could adjust.

They were herded past the sergeant into a barren loading area behind the building. Nearby, a siren screamed, and shouting voices carried through the air. The hum of hundreds of vehicles trapped in traffic jams played under the cacophony of panic.

The door slammed shut behind them. The clicking of a lock followed. Rafe pulled on the handle. It didn't budge.

"Well, what have we here?" a taunting male voice called.

Rafe waded through the milling VIPs and faced fifteen hard-looking men dressed in contractor coveralls and wielding lengths of pipe. There was no sign of the promised armored van.

43

Kama watched another replay of the contractor beating looking for signs that it might be staged. She saw none. Her head grew light.

"Emelia released the video," Wolf said, voice flat. He started the car.

"No. I cut off her network access. This is Balau's doing. She's deliberately provoking a riot."

The beating video transitioned to a news announcer. "This word just in. The conference center appears to be the focus of a spontaneous contractor demonstration. Thousands of contractors have left their stations to join in a march toward the center, where we have unconfirmed reports of gunfire and an explosion."

Wolf pulled out of the Building 13 parking garage onto streets clogged by fleeing full-time workers in vehicles and grim contractors on foot. Kama tapped her nanocom, trying again to raise McTavish. When that failed, she tried Gabe. She got no response.

"We need to get to the conference center," Kama said.

"No way," Wolf replied. "That'll be ground zero. When we clear the campus, we're headed to the shuttleport. EcoMech security can take care of McTavish."

"Dammit, Wolf! I can't abandon him. And what about Gabe? He's eleven."

"What will you do to stop thousands of contractors? Use your mini-stunner?" He tossed her a fierce look. "This is a bigger problem than you can fix."

He was right, but acknowledging her powerlessness didn't make her feel any better. Dzandarova and her security officers were McTavish's only hope. She tapped on her nanocom, opening a connection to the security chief. The woman didn't answer. Kama tapped into the EcoMech system and flagged her message to open automatically. Dzandarova still didn't answer.

A chill swept over Kama. What if Balau had done something to the security chief? Without Dzandarova, there would be no flyer rescue of the VIPs. Kama traced Dzandarova's nanocom to a location two block north of the conference center, exactly where it should be.

The car crept forward, stopped. They were no more than half a kilometer from Dzandarova, but at this rate, it would take half the day to reach her. They didn't have half a day.

Kama popped her door and leaped out. Wolf shouted in surprise, but she ignored him and jogged back the way they'd come. Before she reached Building 13, Wolf was at her side.

"What do you think you're doing?" he asked.

"We'll make faster progress if we use the utility tunnels." Kama turned down the parking garage ramp.

"Faster progress to where?"

A half-height metal plate in a concrete pillar near the elevators gave them access to the tunnels. Kama hurried down the slippery rungs to the bottom.

The tunnel stretched away in two directions. Overhead fixtures threw puddles of light on the floor at evenly spaced intervals. Water and drain pipes lined one wall and sweated in the stuffy air. The place smelled of dust and damp.

Kama opened the tunnel schematics. Wolf's soft boots thudded on the floor beside her. After examining the diagram, she took a step toward the left end of the tunnel.

He grabbed her arm. "Tell me what you plan to do."

Kama jerked her arm, but he didn't loosen his grip. "You're right. It will take EcoMech security to rescue McTavish. But Chief Dzandarova isn't answering. I want to know why."

Wolf hissed through his teeth. "You have to promise you'll stay out of trouble."

She looked into his brown eyes. "No. I'll do whatever I can to help McTavish beat Balau."

His brows drew down. "Time was you would have lied, told me what I wanted to hear. You've changed."

"Blame McTavish."

She pulled her arm free and ran through the tunnel. Wolf followed close behind. By the time she reached the next building in the chain, she was breathing hard in the close, spore-laden air. Sweat soaked her chest and back. They reached a three-way junction. Kama turned right.

The next stretch of tunnel brought them to Facilities Maintenance, located near the north edge of the campus. Wolf pulled her back and climbed out first. Kama emerged behind him in a dimly lit parking garage littered with vans, trucks, mowers, bundles of pipe, and crates of equipment. They wove through the chaos, trotted up an access ramp, and dodged behind a bush to observe the street in front of the building.

Six buses parked in a row at the curb. To the north, four flyers shared a vacant lot with a tanker truck, more mowing equipment, and pallets of building materials. From a distance, the faint sounds of sirens carried through the blistering heat, but here, nothing moved.

"Where is everyone?" Kama whispered.

"There," Wolf replied. "Third bus."

Through the tinted glass of the windows, the shadows of heads and shoulders moved, as though the occupants were on a trip and admiring the view. The red dot on Kama's nanocom indicated that one of those shadows was Dzandarova.

"The flyers should have left already. What are they waiting for?"

The barrel of a rifle held by a black-shirted arm leaned into view on Kama's left. Someone watched the buses from the shade of the doorway ten meters away. Kama put a finger to her lips and then pointed. Wolf's face grew still.

"Balau's people aren't supposed to be here," she said.

"We should leave." Wolf took her arm to lead her way.

Kama dug her heels in. "Not until I know what's going on. Do you see anyone else?"

Wolf surveyed the area. "Not out here. There could be whole platoon inside. Let's go."

She chewed her lip. "You reconnoiter inside. I'll wait here. If that guard is the only one, I'll distract him while you slip out through the front doors and..."

Wolf stared. "If I find a platoon inside?"

"We'll steal the flyers and go after McTavish ourselves."

With a shake of his head, Wolf slipped away. Kama chewed her lip and kept an eye on the doorway. She heard low voices, but she couldn't make out the words. After two minutes, Wolf sent a message. Two guards at the door, no one else in the building.

Kama hitched her duffel up her shoulder and walked on a diagonal that would take her across their line of sight five or six meters from their position. Her heart thumped against her ribs, and sweat dripped in her eyes. Every step felt like she walked on adhesive. She pursed her lips and whistled the theme from her favorite musical, Into the Woods.

"Halt!"

Two of Balau's men pointed their rifles at her. She stopped and spread her hands low at her sides, as much puzzlement as she could muster in her expression. The soldier on the left stepped out of the shade towards her.

A flicker of movement behind the glass door caught her eye. The door snapped open, Wolf stepped in behind the man who'd hung back, and Kama hit the deck. A shot rang out, followed by two thumps.

One guard lay by the door, neck broken. Wolf moved quickly to the other, who writhed on the ground and grabbed at his leg. Too late, the guard realized his mistake. He reached for his rifle, but Wolf plunged his knife in under the visor, just beneath the jawbone. Blood burbled out onto the grass.

Kama got to her feet and turned away, bile climbing her throat into her mouth. When she picked up her duffel, her hands shook. No one from the bus came to see what happened despite the shot. She heard the unsnapping of holsters and the clatter of rifles as Wolf collected their weapons.

"This one has his nanocom set to a countdown," Wolf said. "Two minutes left."

Kama turned and frowned at the body. Then cold terror climbed her spine and walked across her scalp. The shadows inside the bus moved with frantic jerks, but none of them left their seats.

"They've set a bomb!"

Kama sprinted to the bus. She struggled with the door. Wolf grabbed her arm and flung her to the sidewalk. Her hip collided with the concrete, and white hot pain shot through her

"Get away!" he said. He bulled the door open and mounted the steps.

Kama got to her feet and limped up the steps. Dzandarova and two dozen of her officers filled the back rows, their hands fastened to the seats in front of them by plastic ties.

Wolf walked the aisle, his knife flashing. The freed men and women raced for the door. Kama stepped aside to let them pass and dug in her duffel for her utility knife. With it in hand, she raced down the aisle, the seconds ticking off in her head.

"Give me that," Dzandarova said, snatching the blade from Kama's hand. "Help Julio. He can't walk."

The chief turned away. In the seat beside her, slumped against the window, a semi-conscious officer turned glazed brown eyes on Kama. Blood soaked his shoulder, ran down his shirt, and dripped off his hand. His face, pale beneath his tan, contorted with pain.

Kama reached for his good arm, dragged him across the seat, and then slung his arm across her shoulder. Together, they staggered to the door. When they'd stepped through it, Wolf's strong hands lifted Julio onto his shoulders. Kama marveled at his ability to run carrying the weight.

They made the corner of the building. A thunderous roar knocked them forward into the dirt, the force rattling Kama's organs and leaving her deaf. She looked over her shoulder.

Bits of smoking metal and burning plastic rained down on the street. Smaller explosions scattered more debris when the other buses caught. The heat scorched Kama's face, even at this distance.

Her hearing returned. The roar of the bus fires sounded like they come from under water. Wolf was speaking to her. From the movement of his lips, he asked whether she was hurt. She shook her head.

Dzandarova was helped up by an officer who'd been farther from the blast. She worked her jaw, pressed her ears, then checked on the health of the others. Two officers tore Julio's shirt into strips and applied a makeshift bandage over the gunshot wound in his chest. He didn't look good.

Kama stepped up to the security chief. "What happened?"

"Balau's people showed up. We were outnumbered and outgunned. They shot Julio to make their point. When we surrendered, they loaded us on the bus. Balau came by to gloat. Said we'd make a nice addition to the terrorism perpetrated by the 'contractors' during the riots."

"You have to get the flyers airborne. There's been shooting at the conference center. McTavish needs help."

Dzandarova pivoted away. "Flyer pilots, to your flyers. Move!"

44

These men might wear contractor coveralls, but they weren't contract staff. They moved forward with slow purpose, spreading in a line to enclose the VIPs. Rafe could make them pay for their attack, but he couldn't stop them all.

"Look," Rafe said, "you don't need to harm these people. I'm the one you want. Let them go."

His father moved to stand on his left. "What are you doing, you fool! You can't negotiate with terrorists. Where are the guards? Everyone get back in the building."

"The door's locked." Rafe kept his eyes on the leader, a tall, spare man with sinewy muscles and a smile on his lips, but from the corner of his eye, he saw his father's stunned expression.

"Don't worry, McTavish," the leader said to Rafe. "We'll take special care of you. But the rest of them? They'll be collateral damage."

Where were the buses? Where were the flyers? Alana's officers should be here by now. His nanocom chimed to notify him that he had a network connection. He hoped Lev, Bert, or Lars would call for backup, although he doubted that anyone would arrive in time to rescue them. Balau would see to that.

Lev stepped to Rafe's right. A surly grin curled his lips, and his hand held an open pocket knife. An electric jolt danced through Rafe's muscles. The man must have a death wish if he thought he could take on these thugs with his puny weapon.

"Let's do this," said a heavyset man at the right end of the line. Sweat glistened on his brow, and he smacked his length of pipe against his palm.

The leader tossed him an angry look. "Not until we have the signal."

To the north, a thundering explosion split the air, and flames shot into the sky. The leader glanced over his shoulder. His head lifted, and he gave Rafe a toothy grin. Smaller explosions followed, but the man ignored them.

"And there it is. That'll be the end of your security chief and that band of losers helping her," the leader said. "Make sure no one escapes."

The shock of Alana's death froze Rafe in his tracks. A sense of surrealism, of floating in time washed over him. Despair drained the color from his surrounding. His family would die because of him.

Rafe's training kicked in. His pulse doubled. He dropped into a relaxed fighting stance, hyperaware of the men before him, how they carried themselves, where their weaknesses lay. The group of attackers took their first steps forward.

A sea of contractors swept around the corner of the building and into the loading area. With the raise of her arm, Heidi stopped the swelling mob ten feet short of Balau's men.

"Put down the pipes, boys," Heidi said. "This'll be a non-violent protest."

Rafe looked out at the contractor faces before him and saw barely contained anger. Heidi might think she had these people under control, but they were ready to explode in a rush of violence.

"Hand over your weapons," Rafe said to Balau's men. "You can't murder women and children in front of all these witnesses."

The leader stood, indecisive, caught between his quarry and Heidi's band of a hundred or more men and women. His eyes took on a crafty expression, and he pointed at the VIPs.

"These are the people responsible for murdering the contractor last night, the people who've treated you worse than animals. This is your chance to pay them back," the leader said.

"These people," Rafe took a step forward and swept his arm at the VIPs, "are innocent. I'm the one responsible. I hired Total Security. If you give me a chance, I'll see that the people who killed Jerrod Oakley are brought to justice."

A few members of the group responded with catcalls and jeers. Most murmured to their neighbors, their body language telegraphing indecision. A glow of hope ignited in his chest.

"Heidi, I need your help," Rafe said in a quiet voice. "The children need your help."

Heidi's brown eyes tracked to Shannon's girls. She crossed her arms, and the corners of her mouth pulled down.

"Mr. McTavish has done right by us. We'll give him a chance. But until the killers are caught, one thousand contractors will hold vigil out-side his office building."

Rafe moved forward and offered his hand. Before he reached Heidi, the heavyset thug at the end of the line raised his pipe and charged the VIPs. Rafe darted to intercept. He never made it.

The protestors surged forward, and Balau's men disappeared under the force of their advance. The unstoppable tide of human flesh rolled over the VIPs, knocking everyone to the ground, as those in the rear pressed forward to see what had happened.

The high-pitched screams of children's voices reached Rafe in the midst of a tangle of bodies. A few feet away, his father thrashed, loos-ening the knot of contractors who pinned his legs to the asphalt. Far-ther away, something hard connected with flesh and bone, and a man screamed. The thugs were using their pipes on the contractors.

Surprised protests sounded, followed by angry shouts and more cries of pain. Rafe clamored up and fought to maintain his balance. Through a gap in the horde of contractors, he saw the leader of Balau's thugs overwhelmed and disarmed. A man lay nearby groaning, blood streaming from a wound on his head.

Rafe turned away, grasped his father's wrist, and dragged the man to his feet.

"The children!" Rafe shouted over the roar of the crowd. His eyes darted to where Shannon had last stood, but the army of people between them made it impossible to see her. His heart leaped into his throat.

His father plowed ahead, forcing a path through the mass. Contrac-tors and VIPs who'd lost their balance in the rush forward struggled to get up. At least no one was throwing punches. The only battles raged between Balau's people and those nearest them. Rafe was delighted to see the contractors winning.

Against the building wall, the linked arms of a line of contractors maintained a barricade around Shannon, her girls, and Gabe, preventing them from being crushed by the throng. Heidi braced in the center of the line.

"What's wrong with those idiots?" she asked, using her chin to indi-cate the thugs. "Why are they attacking us?"

"They're Commander Balau's men, sent to kill the board and place the blame on contractors."

Heidi stared, open mouthed. The fighting ground down, voices gradually stilled, and the assembled contractors eased back to give them room. Balau's men, relieved of their pipes, were in the grip of battered escorts.

"Get off the campus," Rafe said in a loud voice so all could hear. "Don't go back to the compound. Disperse into the city in small groups.

Hide. Don't give Balau a target."

The contractors exchanged looks of disbelief. No one moved.

"You heard the man," Heidi shouted at last. "Total Security's gunning for us. Let's go!"

"There's more of us than there are of them!" a voice deep in the crowd called. "We can take them out, just like we did these jokers."

Cries of agreement joined in. Rafe raised a hand for silence.

"I appreciate the offer, but this isn't your fight. Think about your loved ones, those who count on you to bring home a paycheck. Take care of yourselves for their sakes, and leave Balau to me."

The mob thinned quickly, dragging the prisoners with them. The VIPs gathered in a knot near the door. Rafe's nanocom chimed, and Alana's face appeared on his screen. Relief rushed in a torrent through him, loosening the constriction in his chest and blowing on the embers of his hope.

Before he could say a word, the building door opened. A soldier emerged, asking "You guys done yet?" as he took his first steps forward. His gaze swiveled over the group, and surprise stopped him short. A second guard halted in the doorway, the open door propped against his foot. Both men raised their rifles to fire.

Rafe lunged at the first guard even though it was a useless gesture. The second guard would mow them down like so much overgrown lawn. His hands forced the barrel into the sky, and his foot planted on the guard's kneecap. A burst of rounds shot harmlessly into the air and drowned the guard's screams of agony.

Rafe leaped over the man, jerking the rifle free and up as he went. He focused on the second man, expecting his life to end in a second. His finger eased pressure onto the trigger.

Shannon hit the back side of the door like a charging rhino. The guard never saw her coming. The force smacked him sideways, and the door slammed shut. His rifle fired wide of its mark. Before he regained his balance, Rafe flipped his weapon on full auto and unloaded the clip into the guard's chest.

The guard jittered back against the wall. By the time the lifeless body thumped to the ground, Rafe had discarded his empty weapon and wrenched the dead man's rifle from him. He took pistols from both bodies and thrust them in his belt.

"My God!" Bert swore.

Rafe turned. Bert crouched next to Lars who lay on his back, blood boiling from a hole in his chest. The lawyer coughed once and went still. The rest of the group stood transfixed, faces pale.

A burst of bullets from inside riddled the door but missed those standing outside.

"Run!" Rafe said, and pointed north through a line of trees. He fired at the door, hoping to delay the troops grouping on the other side.

The VIPs sprinted off. His father scooped up Shannon's youngest. Shannon took the other girls' hands and dashed after them, just behind Lev and Gabe. Rafe followed, making backwards glances to check for pursuers.

At the edge of the trees, he took cover and watched the building. The door cracked open, and he fired a burst. He counted to five and fired again.

Bark shattered beside his head, and a bullet ruffled his hair. He dropped to a kneeling position and shifted his focus to where three soldiers sheltered at the far corner of the building. He switched to single shots. His first round hit one of the men in an exposed foot. They pulled back.

"McTavish!" Alana shouted from his nanocom. "What the hell's going on?"

"Pick up the VIPs in the meadow just north of the conference center. We're under fire from Balau's men, so make it snappy."

Rafe abandoned the tree line, leaped a low hedge, and ran across a grassy knoll to the door of Building 4 where he caught Shannon. They plunged through into the cool, dark lobby, and Rafe wiped sweat from his brow. His father's face glowed red, but the older man seemed to be taking the run in stride, which was more than Rafe could say for others in the group.

The canary dress reporter braced her hands on her knees and sucked in great gulps of air. Dieter Schloss, who had to be in his seventies, sank onto a couch and looked faint. Alberto Cobo used his discarded jacket to wipe his dripping face.

"Keep moving," Rafe ordered. He shed his own jacket and loosened his tie. His damp shirt clung to his back and chest. "Out the back. EcoMech security will meet us in the meadow."

With a sluggishness that made Rafe want to scream, the group moved down a hallway toward the back of the building. Bert took one of Schloss's arms, and Lalani Troi took the other. Between them, they pulled the financier into a staggering jog.

Bullets shattered the lobby windows. Suddenly everyone was running full tilt. Rafe stopped at the junction of two hallways to return fire before continuing. How would they safely cross the open ground of the meadow with Balau's troops so close behind? With only one rifle, two pistols, and no spare ammo, he couldn't hold them off.

45

Kama's chest refused to inflate. Over Dzandarova's open connection, McTavish shouted directions. Gunfire punctuated his commands, each burst making her jump.

"They'll be sitting ducks in the meadow," the security chief muttered.

"Shouldn't we call in EA?" a young officer asked. A trickle of blood oozed from a cut on his cheek, and fear glazed his hazel eyes. He gave a nervous glance at the flaming buses before his attention settled on the dead Total Security guards.

"Already tried. The damn gate's down," Dzandarova said. "We're on our own."

Wolf kept a straight face, but Kama saw the truth in his eyes. He knew about the gate, and he hadn't told her. Heat boiled up in her gut.

"Send your people to help them. It isn't that far," Kama said.

"We have no weapons," Dzandarova replied. "They'll cut us down along with the VIPs."

"We have weapons," Kama countered, pointing to the two rifles Wolf held. "And we can get more off Balau's soldiers."

Dzandarova's brow furrowed. "Assuming we can get close enough to kill them before they kill us."

"We can if we come from behind them," Wolf said in a voice so cold and calculating that it made Kama shiver.

"And just how do you propose to do that?" the security chief asked.

Kama's heart jumped. "Through the utility tunnels. Where is McTavish now?"

"They've just exited Building 4."

Wolf stepped to the corpse of the man whose neck he'd broken and stripped off the Total Security uniform. He shed his baseball jersey and jeans while Dzandarova looked on, skeptical.

"We'll harvest weapons as we go," Wolf said, pulling on the dead man's clothes. "Body armor if there's time."

The EcoMech security officers surrounding them exchanged glances and waited for Dzandarova to issue orders. Wolf was already striding toward the building doors.

Dzandarova shook her head. "I want six volunteers to accompany Ms. Bhatia and her friend in a rescue mission."

Every officer's hand shot into the air. A look of pride flickered over the security chief's face before it hardened again.

"Be safe," Dzandarova said, selecting six men and women.

Kama ran after Wolf, the officers close behind. They caught him as he started down the shaft to the tunnels. He led the group at a flat-out run until they reached Building 4 a kilometer away. She had no time to question him about the gate failure. They climbed to the ceiling of the ground floor.

"We'll come out in the restrooms. Wait there for further instructions," Wolf ordered. He turned to Kama. "That includes you. These men will shoot first and ask questions after. No heroics."

Without waiting for a response, Wolf slid the ceiling tile aside and dropped from sight. One by one, the EcoMech team followed. Wolf had already departed by the time Kama hit the floor.

The room was crowded, and the smell of sweat and fear tainted the air. So did the odor of cleaning chemicals. A janitor's cart like the one Emelia used stood in a corner, abandoned by the contractor using it.

Kama pawed through the six bottles of various cleaners reading their contents. She emptied four into a sink and ripped up a cleaning rag. Then she carefully poured some of the contents of the remaining two bottles into each of the empty bottles. She stuffed each with a strip of rag.

"Anyone have a lighter?" she whispered.

She received blank looks. With tobacco consumption banned, no one carried lighters these days. They were such convenient little devices. She dug matches and a strap from her duffel. She hang the bottles from the strap like a bandolier across her chest.

"Molotov cocktails?" a woman asked, her worried blue eyes staring at the bottles. "Have you seen what those can do to a person?"

"Have you seen what an automatic rifle can do?" Kama replied, anger rising.

Wolf pushed through the door. He carried two sets of extra weapons.

His gaze flickered to Kama's wardrobe addition, but he said nothing. She didn't want to think about how he'd acquired the arms.

"They're organizing an assault on the meadow. Our objective is to distract them from their target and give our people time to get away. Shoot and run is the order of the day. Questions?"

"You," he said, handing a rifle to the woman who'd spoken with Kama, "get up to the third floor and shoot down on them. As soon as you've taken a shot, move to a new window."

The woman grabbed the rifle from his hands and trotted out. Wolf handed over the other rifle, pulled spare pistols from his belt, and distributed them to the remaining officers.

"These won't pierce their armor. Aim for arms, legs, and feet." He pointed to two men. "You two work the west end. You three take the east side. Kama, you take the entry doors. I'll go east and close on their flank to obtain more weapons. Don't shoot me. Fire on my mark."

Instructions completed, they dispersed. Kama resisted the urge to run after Wolf and instead worked her way to cover near the rear entry. The place was a mess. Broken glass crunched under her boots. Clumps of stuffing from a grouping of chairs erupted from the upholstery like dandelion heads. Thinking of all those bullets aimed at McTavish chilled Kama to the bone.

Outside, fifteen meters from the building, a line of twenty black-shirted guards hid behind a waist-high hedge, a grassy expanse visible beyond. They were crouched and awaiting orders to charge. Eight under-armed men and women against twenty armed and armored soldiers. A trickle of doubt iced Kama's nerves.

Foliage blocked her view of McTavish and his party. That the Total Security force hadn't rushed after them already spoke to McTavish's skill with the rifle. She rested the barrel of the pistol on the edge of the window and took aim at an ankle.

"Go!" said Wolf's voice on her nanocom.

Half a dozen weapons fired, and Kama snapped off her first shot. The gun bucked in her hand, and the report made her ears ring. Up and down the enemy line men turned. A few grabbed at arms or legs where they'd taken hits. One toppled to his side and didn't move again. Her target, unhurt, spun and pointed his rifle at the building.

Kama scurried to the corner of the room and dove behind a planter from which a monster ficus grew. A hail of bullets whistled through the area and pocked the wall behind her. Bits of plaster vaporized to hang in the air, and torn leaves rained down. Her stomach clenched, and she swallowed hard. Sweat poured down her body.

She peeked out. A soldier sprinted toward the door.

Toward her.

Her mouth went dry. Three shots rang out in quick succession, the first two plinking against the man's helmet, jerking his head to the west. The third pierced the armor, and red exploded against the inside of the face plate. He fell forward, carried by his momentum to skid against the door. Only Wolf could have fired from that angle.

Enemy weapons returned fire toward the east end of the line. Kama sprang back to the window, took aim, and hit her target. A soldier dropped his weapon and grabbed his ankle with a howl of "I'm hit!"

"Fall back!" Wolf ordered.

Over the connection, his rifle sounded as loud as her pistol, each shot fired individually to conserve ammunition. She fired twice more, grazing an arm and missing another target. She swore at her poor marksmanship and withdrew.

At the other end of the hallway, feet crunched through debris. Kama froze. A gruff voice organized men into search parties. She tapped her nanocom.

"We've got company in the lobby," she whispered. She swapped her pistol for matches and ran toward the invaders.

46

The explosion of rifles behind him made Rafe duck. It took him a second to realize that the firing wasn't directed at the VIPs. A grim smile curved his lips. The cavalry had arrived. He'd wrest the board away from Balau and destroy her plans yet.

The first EcoMech security flyer coasted down to the grass in the center of the meadow, its fans kicking up a noxious cloud of dust and garraweed spores. Alberto Cobo was the first to reach it. He wrenched open a door and threw himself in.

Rafe charged past the VIPs. He reached in the flyer and dragged Alberto out. The man screamed invectives and ordered Rafe to unhand him. Other board members pressed forward, vying for a place in the vehicle.

"Women and children first!" Rafe shouted over the scrabble around him.

Lev grabbed the shoulder of a board member, cocked a fist, and hit the man in the face. His victim dropped to the grass holding a nose that gushed blood. The manager dragged Gabe through the knot around the door and shoved him inside. Rafe's father ruthlessly knocked people aside to deposit his granddaughter next to Gabe.

A second flyer landed fifteen feet away. Those on the fringes around the first vehicle broke off and rushed for it. Bert handed one of Shannon's girls to Rafe's father, and Lev cleared a path for Shannon and her remaining daughter. The canary-dress reporter bulled past and piled in.

The ear-splitting shrill of fire alarms echoed from Building 4, followed by the muffled sound of shots.

"Ms. Troi," Rafe called, reaching for the undersecretary.

She shook her head and guided Schloss forward. "Take Dieter. He needs medical attention."

The elderly financier gasped through an open mouth, a hand clasped over his heaving chest. Naked fear showed in his eyes when they met Rafe's. Rafe hesitated. Troi's lips drew into a straight line, and he handed the old man to Shannon.

"Get him to a medical facility," Rafe ordered the officer in the pilot seat.

Rafe slammed the door. The flyer's fans screamed against the load it carried, and the craft lumbered away to the north slowly gaining altitude. An overburdened second flyer rose in a storm of swirling dust that blinded him, and a third flyer arrived. A fourth flyer hovered a hundred feet up, waiting for room to land.

"McTavish!" Lev placed a hand on his shoulder and pointed into the southern sky with the other.

Total Security's armored flyer swept in over the tops of the buildings, closing fast on the meadow. Dread throbbed in Rafe's head.

Rafe spoke into his nanocom. "Alana, order your pilots into the parking garages. Balau's flyer is here."

He grabbed Troi and dragged her to the third flyer. She sprang in. The flyer rocked as it lifted, and Rafe smelled the burning of overheated fans. Only his father and Bert Gerlach remained on the grass. The fourth flyer rose higher to avoid the drunken zigzag path of the third flyer leaving the meadow.

At the hedge, a dozen guards vaulted the shrubs and brought their rifles up, but they didn't advance. Rafe could think of only one reason they'd hold position. He raised an arm to flag off the fourth flyer.

A blazing streak cut across the meadow, and the fourth flyer exploded. The shock wave knocked Rafe back. He threw up an arm to shield his face from flaming debris.

The Total Security flyer bore down on them, three missiles still cradled beneath its belly. Shannon's flyer was just visible on the horizon, diving toward the pavement and the safe haven of a garage. The second flyer had dropped from sight somewhere to the west. The third vehicle wobbled east, thirty feet off the ground. The armored flyer pivoted toward it.

Rafe sucked in his breath and tapped his nanocom, one eye on the troops by the hedge. A connection opened. He flagged Bert and his father to run with him to the west and the safety of Building 6.

"You missed me, Balau. You never could shoot worth a tinker's damn."

In the background of the connection, the whine of flyer fans nearly drowned Balau's reply. "Make no mistake. I'm coming for you, McTavish."

As he'd thought, she piloted the craft, the epitome of a killing machine. The flyer changed direction, pointing its deadly machine gun and missiles his way. The line of soldiers at the hedge opened fire. A bullet grazed Rafe's shoulder, and he dropped his rifle. No great loss since he was out of ammo and unlikely to get more.

"Hold your fire! He's mine," Balau screamed over the connection. Then it went dead when she switched to her tactical frequency.

Rafe angled away from Bert and his father and ran a zigzag pattern for the door of Building 6. Balau's strafing caught him before he gained safety. The .30 caliber machine gun stitched a line in the dirt inches from his legs and zipped by perilously close to his father.

The rumble of Balau's fans grew louder. Hot air buffeted Rafe's back, and dust swirled around him. He adjusted his course and pounded toward the side of the building thirty feet to the left of the door. His lungs burned.

Fifty feet from the concrete and glass wall he dodged left. The machine gun erupted in a deafening rat-a-tat—to his right. He pulled a pistol from his belt and fired three shots at the window he approached. The glass shattered, and he dove through, rolling on the carpet and colliding with a desk.

More bullets screamed over his head. On hands and knees, Rafe scrambled to the corridor. He rose and ran toward the lobby. Behind him, the corridor walls splintered and cracked as Balau tracked his heat signature and continued firing.

Bert and his father crouched in a hallway off the back of the spacious lobby. Rafe pointed at the stairwell.

"Parking garage!" he gasped.

The two men joined him in a mad dash down the stairs. Seconds later, they were blasted off their feet and tumbled to the bottom. The lights went out, but dim illumination filtered through from somewhere above. Chunks of concrete smashed to the steps and rolled down in an avalanche. Thick dust hung in the air

Rafe's head throbbed. Sharp pain radiated from his right hip and shoulder, but not enough to indicate breakage. Despite the ringing in his ears, he heard groans. The human ones came from Bert. The nonhuman ones came from the top of the stairwell—or what was left of it—where slabs of wall tilted at an angle creaking ever closer to collapse. Flames crackled in the lobby, and smoke thickened the already unbreathable air.

Rafe rolled to his hands and knees. His father struggled to a sitting position. Bert staggered to his feet and looked up.

"What the hell was that?" the manager asked, his voice a hoarse whisper.

"Missile," Rafe replied. He coughed and rose. "Let's go."

He offered a hand to his father. The man glared at him and got up on his own.

Rafe tugged on the stairwell door. The force of the explosion had warped the frame. He coughed again, looked up at the crazy cant of the walls above, and headed down another level, all the while expecting the building to cascade down on them.

His nanocom chimed. He wiped a coating of dust from the screen and saw Kama. Thick tendrils of hair had come loose from her ponytail and framed a face streaked with dirt and sweat. She panted, he thought from exertion, and fear widened her eyes. A strap with rag-stoppered bottles attached to it draped across her chest. It sent a zing of worry racing along his nerves and explained the fire alarm in Building 4.

"McTavish, are you all right?"

"Balau needs target practice," he replied. The explosion of the flyer flashed in his mind, and he winced at his attempted levity. "Where are you?"

"Coming to your rescue. Wait for us near the east end of the garage."

Rafe pushed open the stairwell door and exited into the parking garage. Despite Balau's instructions to evacuate, half the parking spaces still held cars. He jogged down the board aisle to the east, expecting to see Balau's flyer or perhaps her troops swarming down the entry ramps. Unless Kama brought a whole regiment of soldiers and armored tanks, they'd be trapped here.

Near the end of the garage, his father grabbed his arm and pulled him to a stop.

"Why is that Balau woman trying to kill us?"

Rafe gave his father's hand a pointed look, but the man didn't let go.

"Caligo wants to acquire EcoMech. Balau's mission is to drive us into bankruptcy."

His father snatched a pistol from Rafe's belt and pointed it at his son.

"Bullshit. This is all some takeover scheme of yours gone wrong." His father reached in and took the second pistol, handing it to a Bert, who received it with obvious reluctance.

Rafe balled his fists. "Someone wanted Leon's job. He blackmailed Leon into making bad business decisions so the board would fire him. That's why EcoMech is on the brink of ruin. Aaron hired me to block the blackmailer's scheme."

His father loomed closer, and drops of spittle sprayed Rafe's face as he shouted at his son. "That contractor hussy of yours killed Aaron."

Rafe shook with barely contained anger. He leaned in. "The blackmailer killed Aaron to protect his identity."

His father pressed the pistol against Rafe's chest. The flames of naked hatred burned in the man's eyes. Rafe drew a shallow breath, sure it would be his last.

His father's brow twitched. The hatred changed to uncertainty. The pressure of the gun eased. The uncertainty became dawning realization. Slowly his father's head twisted to face Bert.

"You were on the street that night, coming from the direction of Aaron's house."

Bert's face twisted into a cruel smile, and he raised his pistol. "I appreciate how hard you've worked on my behalf to convince the board I was the best candidate, Cullen."

"At the bus incident, you saved my life," Rafe said in disbelief.

"Your father had already assured me I'd be the next CEO when the board fired you. Better to play the hero," Bert replied. He pointed the pistol at the elder McTavish. "Too bad you won't live to see me appointed."

Rafe lunged, grabbing the pistol with both hands and shoving it sideways. It discharged. Bert's fist connected with his temple. The parking garage spun, but Rafe clung to the gun with his left hand while he stabbed his right elbow in the manager's gut. It was like connecting with a steel plate.

Bert took a second swing at Rafe's head, but Rafe ducked, and the blow glanced off. While the man was off balance, Rafe lowered his shoulder and plowed the manager backward until they slammed into a car hood. The gun spun away. A vicious left hook connected with Rafe's jaw, driving him off the manager.

Before Rafe could rush in, a gun barked. Blood blossomed on Bert's chest. His gaze went to the wound and up to Rafe's father, who stood with the gun aimed and ready.

"Aaron Goldman was my best friend," his father said, his face an ugly purple.

He pulled the trigger again. Rafe jerked with the report, and put up a hand in a stop motion. Bert sank to his knees and toppled to his side, dead. His father fired three more shots at three-second intervals. Rafe watched in frozen surprise. He no longer recognized the monster holding the gun. Shannon's words came back to him. *He was afraid that next time, he wouldn't stop until he'd killed you.*

Finished with Bert, the monster faced him, gun raised.

47

Kama crawled through the access hatch into the parking garage of Building 6 and thought they were too late. Nearby, a gun fired, steady, repetitive, like an execution. Fear burbled up in her chest, stopping her breath. She ran silently toward the noise.

The lights had gone out. Dim emergency bulbs illuminated the aisles, but they did little to push back the eerie shadows surrounding the cars. The place could be full of black-shirted troops.

Kama cut through a row of vehicles and stopped with a jerk. McTavish stood frozen, staring at his father. Gerlach lay a meter away, unmoving. Cullen McTavish pointed a pistol at his son. Wolf stopped beside her. He leveled his rifle at the men.

"McTavish!" Kama called.

As though awakening from a spell, Cullen turned to look at her. His face lost its horrible rictus. McTavish sagged. He took a few steps and scooped up a pistol from the floor.

The rumble of flyer fans echoed off the walls. The sound came from the west end of the parking garage. From the east, dozens of booted feet ran down the access ramp.

"This way." McTavish started for the tunnel leading to another garage.

"No, this way," she said. Wolf was already backing toward the access to the utility tunnels, his face tense.

Cullen looked down at Gerlach as though seeing him for the first time. Then he stared at the weapon in his hand. What the hell had gone on down here?

McTavish snagged his father's arm and dragged him a few steps. The older man came to his senses, jerked his arm free, and jogged beside his son. The flyer fans hummed louder. A search light flashed their direction. Kama picked up the pace.

Wolf waited by the pillar, his rifle at his shoulder, his focus on the east ramp.

"Down," Kama said, pointing to the open hatch.

Cullen reared back, giving her a mutinous look.

"Fine. Die here, you pig-headed—"

Wolf snapped off three shots. The incoming Total Security troops ducked for cover behind vehicles. A second later, the flyer-mounted machine gun sprayed a wall of hot lead into the pillar and the surrounding cars.

Cullen dropped into the access shaft. McTavish grabbed her arm in a brutal grip and pushed her through next. He followed. Above her, Wolf let off a short burst of rifle fire before he appeared on the ladder. They rushed to the bottom.

Kama pulled a bottle from her bandolier and placed it on the floor under the access shaft. She dug a match from her pocket.

"Give me that," McTavish said, "and get out of here."

"My matches. I stay," she said, putting her fists on her hips.

"We don't have time to argue," McTavish said. He reached for the match.

Wolf crouched beside the bottle and flicked his lighter. A little flame danced in the still air. "Go."

She and McTavish both glared at him. McTavish grabbed her hand and pulled her away. He broke into a jog. Cullen stumbled along behind them.

"Where does this lead?" McTavish asked, motioning ahead.

"Building 4," she said. "But we can't get out there."

"I heard the fire alarms." While he jogged, he tapped his nanocom. "Alana, what's your status?"

Wolf's shoes slapped on the floor behind them. Muffled voices shouted, Kama's incendiary device went up in a whoosh, and men screamed.

"Thank God. You're alive," Dzandarova said. "What about your father?"

"He's with us," McTavish said. After a pause he added, "Bert Gerlach didn't make it."

"I'll inform your sister. The VIPs are en route to safe houses. With the weapons Ms. Bhatia's friend provided, we're assaulting the security building. If we can get to the armory, maybe we can make this a fair fight."

"Any ETA on backup from Earth?" McTavish asked.

"The gate's down. We're on our own."

McTavish stopped and closed the connection. He whirled on Kama. "Why did you take the gate down?"

Kama opened her mouth to speak, but Wolf beat her to it.

"She didn't. A Total Security ship carrying five hundred men and half a dozen armored vehicles arrived at the Earth-to-Harvest gate to reinforce Balau. There wasn't time to create sufficient red tape to deny them entry."

"So you sabotaged the gate." McTavish ran a hand through his hair. He didn't look like he believed Wolf.

Kama squeezed his hand. "If I'd known, I would have told you."

His eyes softened, and he gave a tiny nod. He faced Wolf. "Is there anything else you've neglected to inform me of?"

Wolf's jaw tightened.

Kama arched an eyebrow. "Spit it out."

"Your nephew, Greg Nighthorse, is a guest in the Sharma household on Oasis."

Kama tapped her ear, uncertain that she'd heard him correctly. McTavish blinked at them both.

"He was followed from Wandermere to Earth Central. Because you'd failed to provide prudent protection—much like you have with the rest of your family and Kama—Samir interceded to keep him out of enemy hands." Wolf's eyes had gone cold, and his voice was threaded with steel. "We'd better get moving."

Wolf slipped around them and trotted away. McTavish didn't move. His hand went to his pocket and pulled out his ball. He rolled it across his knuckles and back while his eyes became unfocused.

Wolf stopped and walked back. He started to speak, but Kama held up a hand. Cullen stared at his son. She wondered what he saw. The old man hadn't said a word. Maybe he was in shock.

McTavish pocketed the ball. "How do I get to the conference center?"

Kama crossed her arms. "You can't go there. Balau's troops surround the place. We need to get outside her cordon."

"We can't beat Balau as long as she has that armored flyer."

"You don't need to beat her. In a few hours, the gate will return to service, and EA forces will arrive," Wolf said. "You can hide in the city until then."

"How many will die while we hide?" McTavish asked. "Any loss that could have been prevented is unacceptable."

Kama threw up her hands. "And you're going to do something about the flyer."

"I have to," he said in a quiet voice. "Which way?"

Kama clamped her mouth on the protest she wanted to make. She showed him the tunnel map.

"We're here. Follow this tunnel to Building 2, and then take the junction south to the conference center. The utility shaft runs beside the restrooms. There's access from the ceiling."

"I'm only interested in the parking garage." His cobalt eyes met hers, and he laid a hand on her shoulder. "Take my father to safety. I'll find you when this is over." He opened a connection to Alana and hurried off, speaking to her as he went.

Kama's fingers curled into fists. He'd play hero, risk his life to save others, probably get himself killed. She couldn't let him go alone. She took a step and stopped to face Wolf.

"I have to go with him," she said, her heart seizing in her chest.

Wolf's lips thinned. He looked first at McTavish fast disappearing down the tunnel, and then at Kama. He nodded and said, "Be careful."

Kama raced after McTavish. Although she ran as quietly as she could, when he slowed to turn at the junction, he must have heard her approach. He waited, face dark.

"I told you to stay with my father," he said, voice icy.

Far down the corridor, boots clattered on ladder rungs. She and McTavish both looked. At the bottom of an access shaft, flashlights played over the walls. Wolf and Cullen had vanished.

McTavish grabbed her sleeve and pulled her after him into a new tunnel that angled south. They ran, light-footed and breathing hard, until they reached the shaft leading up to the conference center.

"What's the plan?" Kama asked.

"I go up first to reconnoiter. When you come up, we make our way to the south end of the garage. Then we make sure we're seen, and we flee in a flyer."

Kama goggled. "That's the plan? You want to play tag in the sky with Balau for a couple of hours until EA arrives?"

"More like hide and seek. If she's busy chasing me, she won't think too much about what else is going on, and she won't use that flyer to counter Alana's attack on the armory."

"Unless she's already shot you down," Kama pointed out. She slapped a hand to the side of her head. "And I thought you were a smart guy."

The hint of a grin brushed his lips. He pulled the clip from his pistol and examined it. With a sigh, he slapped it back in the gun and reached for the ladder.

"Here," Kama said, pulling her pistol and a spare clip from her pocket.

He frowned. "You may need to defend yourself."

She laughed and tapped one of the bottles on her bandolier. "I'm more the grenade type."

McTavish looked thoughtful. "Be ready with those."

He stuck the spare pistol in his belt, jammed the extra clip in his pocket, and scrambled up the ladder. Kama followed. He eased open the access hatch and stepped out.

Kama's hands shook. She squeezed the ladder rungs and took deep breaths. No sounds came from the parking garage. When McTavish stuck his head into the shaft, she jumped. He gave a quick wave, and she climbed up and out. McTavish hid behind the pillar that housed the access shaft and looked out toward the center of the space.

Like Building 6, the conference center operated on emergency power. Unlike Building 6, the garage was almost empty. Kama joined McTavish and peered into the gloom. The VIPs' flyers waited near the elevators at the center of the facility. Kama looked them over, trying to discern the fastest and most maneuverable.

Voices drifted to them. McTavish drew her behind the pillar.

"Two guards by the elevators," he whispered.

"Can you shoot them from here?" she asked.

"Two at once?" he said. "I'm good, but not that good."

"I can draw them out," she said. The very thought made her quiver.

"No need. We'll go around."

She cocked her head. "But don't you need one of the flyers?"

"Not one of those," he said. He pointed around the opposite side of the pillar. "*That* flyer."

Kama leaned around the pillar the other way. At the far end of the garage, next to the exit ramp, light glistened off something blue and green. A vast open space yawned between their position and the flyer. The hair on her neck stood up.

"They'll see us before we get there," she said.

"We'll stay in the shadows next to the wall and move slowly so we don't attract attention."

"I thought you wanted attention?"

He grinned. "Not yet, although..."

He stripped off his tie and plucked one of her improvised fire bombs from her bandolier. With the aid of the tie, he lengthened the fuse by half a meter.

"Match," he said, sticking out a hand.

"Why don't I get to play pyromaniac?" she grumbled. "After all, they're my fire bombs."

McTavish hid the bottle behind the pillar and laid the fuse on the floor. He motioned Kama toward the darkened back wall of the garage. She walked with swift, quiet steps, angling to avoid emergency lights. The scrape of a match striking sounded. She glanced back.

The fuse seemed impossibly bright, and Kama checked to see if it had attracted the guards. They seemed oblivious. McTavish strode across the floor, a man on a mission. Her breath caught in her throat, and regret for her promise to Varun stabbed at her.

They were fifty meters from the flyer when her bomb ignited with a bang. Light flared and danced behind her. Smoke and chemicals tainted the air. The guards shouted. Their running footsteps echoed on the concrete. She abandoned her careful walk and sprinted for the flyer.

McTavish pelted past and swung around the front of the machine to get in on the pilot's side. Kama leaped in the passenger seat and jammed her duffel between her feet. She fumbled for the shoulder harness. The hum of power vibrated her seat, the fans purred, and they lifted off.

Kama took in the sleek nose, the enormous high-speed front fans, and the glowing control console. "Bloody hell, McTavish. You know how to pick 'em."

The guards, alerted to their escape by the sound of the engine, charged their direction, rifles firing. Pain lanced through Kama's thigh, and she jerked. Too startled to cry out, she placed her hand on the area. Warm moisture spread on her palm, and hot fear flooded through her.

She flicked a glance at McTavish, who focused on the unfamiliar controls. If he knew she'd been hit, he'd abandon his plans to stop Balau. She couldn't let that happen.

48

Rafe goosed the flyer toward the exit ramp. He heard impacts, and ducked involuntarily. He prayed they hadn't hit anything vital.

He slewed into a tunnel, scraping the belly on the deck before zipping out of sight of the guards. The controls seemed overly sensitive. Maybe it was his nerves. He forced himself to relax and feel the flyer through his body. An arrow painted on the wall was overlaid with a sign for Buildings 15, 16, and 17.

"Now what?" Kama asked, voice tight.

Rafe glanced at her. She stared out the windshield, the knuckles of her left hand going white where they clutched her harness. He grazed the sidewall and cursed, snapping his attention back to his path out.

"We convince Balau we're escaping. Then we lead her to a parking garage where Alana has a little surprise planned. Can you hack into her command frequency?"

Kama grunted and pulled her duffel into her lap. She extracted a black box, switched it on, and shoved it back in the duffel. He heard her tap her nanocom. In a moment, confused reports played in the cabin.

"She's lost us," Kama said, her voice thin. "She's ordered her people into the utility tunnels to search."

"Good. That will keep them busy. What's Balau's position?"

Kama called up new data. "She's waiting at the meadow."

Rafe opened a connection to Balau. "Commander Balau, it's over. Your reinforcements have been stopped at the jump gate. You've lost your hostages. Order your officers to stand down, surrender now, and I'll request leniency at your sentencing."

"She's traced your signal. She's headed to Building 15."

They emerged from the tunnel into a triple length parking garage. Knots of soldiers gathered at the utility tunnel access points for the three buildings rising overhead. Rafe veered away, aiming for a ramp to the surface. Automatic weapons fire sounded behind them.

An excited voice reported their presence. Rafe broke out of the dark parking structure and into open sky. He blinked against the harsh light and scanned for Balau's flyer. It appeared high and to his left, coming fast. He banked right and aimed for the cover of another cluster of buildings. Windows in the wall of glass and concrete nearest them shattered, bullets walking a path toward him.

Rafe pointed the flyer's nose down and opened the throttle. Acceleration forced him back in his seat. Telltale vibration told him Lev hadn't fixed the stabilizers.

At the last possible minute, Rafe pulled the control harness back hard. The fans screamed and a mechanical voice warned of an imminent crash. The flyer leveled off inches above the ground.

He dove into a parking garage, cutting his speed to maneuver down the ramp. When he'd cleared it, he roared to a tunnel that lead away to another building, but not before noting that guards maneuvered vehicles to block exit ramps and tunnel mouths, an unwelcome development.

They raced through a mile of tunnels. His hands were sweat slickened, and his mouth dry. He wished Kama hadn't come with him, although her presence gave him courage.

He switched communication channels. "Alana, are you ready?"

"We're a go," came the terse reply from the security chief.

"Where's Balau?" Rafe asked Kama. In the open air, the commander could move more quickly and directly than he could in the tunnels. He didn't want to pop out to discover her sitting on his rabbit hole.

"She's... She's approaching on an intercept course."

Kama's voice was indistinct and her information unhelpful. Rafe risked another quick glance at her. She watched her nanocom, but she seemed half asleep, like a pilot who'd pulled too many gees.

He steered the flyer up another ramp emerging in front of Building 30. Fist-sized craters appeared in the asphalt ahead of them, the result of Balau's machine gun. His hands gripped like a vise on the controls, and he heeled the craft over. A bullet pinged on metal, a fan shrieked, and a puff of smoke spit from his right front fan. The flyer shivered and slowed.

He keyed Balau's channel.

"Alana, we're hit. Is the access to the city tunnels open under Building 1? Balau's closing on us." He counted a silent three, swore aloud, and closed the connection.

Rafe pulled the flyer's nose up, rocketed away from the tree line, and made a sweeping turn over the conference center heading toward Building 1. It jutted above the landscape a mere six stories, EcoMech's first permanent office complex. Beside it, the campus's only above-ground parking structure rose three levels. An EcoMech security car parked on the grass next to the building.

Balau opened fire, the sound of her gun so close that it froze Rafe's blood in his veins. He zigzagged down, aiming for the opening to the ground floor of the garage. The flyer handled like a drunken elephant, listing on the right front corner and wobbling off course. Balau's flyer filled his rearview screen.

He zipped through the entrance, narrowly missing the side. The right front nacelle grazed the pavement, throwing the tail up to drag against the ceiling. For one frozen moment, Rafe feared the craft might cartwheel and end up a skidding pile of scrap metal with both of them trapped inside. Then it leveled.

A bright square of light shone through the exit at the opposite end of the building. Beyond it, a grassy hillock stood, its slope landscaped with ground cover and a row of saplings outlining its crest. He ought to slow down, but he didn't dare. The side walls of the garage went by in a blur.

Before he made the exit, a deafening boom shook the flyer, sending it down to smack the pavement when he needed it to climb. He yanked the control harness back. The flyer lifted, cleared the slope by mere inches, and topped the sapling.

Rafe banked left and looked over his shoulder. A smoking pile of rubble occupied the space where the garage had stood, Balau's flyer trapped beneath it. He whooped, punched a fist in the air, and turned to Kama to share the joy of their victory.

Kama's head lolled toward one shoulder. Skin drained of color shone through a film of sweat. Her eyelids drooped closed. Her right hand covered a spreading red stain on the leg of her coveralls. He couldn't see her breathe.

"Kama!"

49

Rafe strode along the hallway toward the boardroom. Afternoon light filtered through open office doors to throw intermittent squares of illumination on the carpet. He'd meant to take aspirin for his throbbing head and bruised back. He'd forgotten, overwhelmed by demands for his attention, not the least of them this command performance ordered by his father.

Alana leaned against the wall near the door. She looked like road kill, her face drawn, her uniform creased from her sleepless night directing the roundup of Total Security stragglers. She straightened when she saw him and nodded a greeting to the two security officers who trailed in his wake.

Rafe swept a hand at the door. "Did they summon you, too?"

"I hoped you'd have a few minutes to help me finish my paperwork," she said. She lowered her voice. "I have some questions about Mr. Gerlach's death."

"Ah." He shoved his hands in his trouser pockets and glanced at the door to the lions' den. "I shot him in self-defense."

Alana nodded, her eyes never leaving his face. "Is that what your father will say, too?"

He hesitated. "You'll have to ask him."

The security chief pursed her lips. "He's a very busy man now that he's chairman. I wouldn't want to bother him."

The tension in Rafe's shoulders eased. "What's the status on our prisoners?"

"The last of them shipped out fifteen minutes ago. We identified the men involved in Jerrod Oakley's beating death. An EA prosecutor is filing separate charges against them." She frowned. "I informed Heidi Lowe about the charges, but that mob of contractors is still squatting outside your office building. Your assistant had box lunches delivered to them. It looks more like a rowdy party than a protest."

"Give them a chance to savor their victory. They'll disperse soon enough, and we'll need all the cooperation from them that we can get while we rebuild," he said.

"We made a discovery about Svenson, too. He made a 'cookie run' the same night every week. Surveillance tapes show he 'bumped into' the same couple of contract company reps each time. When we showed them the tapes, they admitted they were being extorted for kickbacks in order to get their workers hired."

Rafe ran a hand over the back of his neck. "So that's what he was hiding. Nothing suspicious came up when we ran his financials. When you have the time, search his apartment. The money has to be somewhere."

"Your girl ID'd the hacker, but we can't find her."

An electric shock buzzed through Rafe. "She's awake?"

"A couple hours ago." Alana gave him a wry smile. "I wouldn't want to be her doctor. She's..."

Rafe grinned. "Full of fight?"

"Something like that."

Rafe's nanocom chimed, and the grin fell from his lips. He wanted to go to Kama, to hold her tight and never let her go. He'd come perilously close to losing her forever. Instead, he opened the boardroom door and stepped inside.

All the familiar faces were in their usual places around the table, although more than a few sported bruises and black eyes from their fight over the flyers. The hubbub of their conversations died with his appearance. He took his seat at the end of the table opposite his father and focused on deep, slow breathing.

To his surprise, Alberto Cobo was the first to speak.

"We've read your report... or perhaps I should call it a confession? Failure to inform us about the merger offer, deliberately hiding EcoMech's financial state." Cobo settled back in his chair. "We'd replace you today if we could. Because of this unfortunate business with Total Security, there are no satisfactory candidates for the position."

Rafe recalled Lev's punch to Cobo's face and suppressed a smile. Lev would never become CEO as long as the present board remained in control.

His father focused on him with slit eyes and steepled fingers. They hadn't spoken since Gerlach's shooting. Rafe didn't know what to say, realized that he didn't know the man at all.

"We've decided to give you another chance," Alberto said. "You'll follow Aaron's recovery plan to the letter. Any deviations must be pre-approved by the board before you make them. You'll send detailed weekly status reports. Essentially, you're on probation. If you demonstrate that you can behave appropriately, the board will consider retaining you."

Around the table, board members nodded agreement. All except his father. Rafe tapped his nanocom.

"I'm sending you an offer for refinancing of EcoMech's debt. The rates are highly favorable, better than the company would get from any other source. Refinancing is a critical first step in EcoMech's recovery."

The men checked their devices in silence. After a lengthy pause, Alberto scowled and turned his attention to Rafe.

"This offer is contingent on you remaining as CEO for the next five years."

"Dieter Schloss was very grateful for his rescue," Rafe said. "He also found my vision of EcoMech's future to his liking."

Alberto leaned forward. "You have our permission to accept Dieter's offer."

Rafe plastered on a regretful smile. "I'm sorry, gentlemen, but your terms for my employment are unacceptable."

His father's eyes widened a fraction and his hands moved to his lap. The other men exchanged looks and waited for Alberto to respond.

"What is it you want? More salary? A larger bonus?"

"We'll follow my roadmap to recovery, not Aaron's. I'll keep the board informed and listen to your suggestions, but I will make autonomous decisions about EcoMech's policies and operations."

"This is extortion!" Alberto spluttered.

"It's a negotiation. It would be extortion if I reminded you that I control thirty percent of EcoMech's voting stock and informed you that I'm willing to start a proxy fight to gain a controlling share."

As one, the men leaned back in their chairs and averted their eyes from their chosen spokesman. Alberto turned to Rafe's father for support.

The elder McTavish regarded the man with contempt. "I warned you about him."

To his son he said, "You give us no choice. Do what you will, but don't expect us to applaud."

Rafe waited for the burn in his stomach, the sense of failure that always accompanied confrontations with his father. Instead, he felt as though he'd lost half his mass, as though he sat at a table on Earth's moon instead of on gravity-heavy Harvest.

His father checked the time on his nanocom. "That's it for today."

Just one thought filled Rafe's head: *Kama's awake.* He shot from the room.

50

Kama stood by the hospital bed and dug through her duffel, taking inventory to be sure all her valuable—and illegal—tools were in their proper places. Wolf waited outside her room door, ready to drive them to the shuttleport. The thought of what lay ahead closed her throat and made her hands fall still.

"Shouldn't you be in bed?"

Kama started at McTavish's voice. He stood in the doorway, Wolf glowering behind him. With a glance over his shoulder, he stepped in and closed the door.

"I've been discharged," Kama said. At his incredulous expression, she joked, "A little synth blood, a little speed heal, and I'm good as new. We're taking the next shuttle out."

In truth, the wound in her thigh ached like buggery, but she wouldn't admit that to McTavish. She'd intended to avoid seeing him before she left. Quick and clean, that's the way they should separate.

But it wouldn't be quick and clean no matter how much she wished it so. The pain that constricted her chest radiated from his eyes, cascaded from his tired, slumping shoulders. In a rush, he closed the distance between them and took her hands.

"I thought we'd have more time. Can't you stay another day?"

She pushed an unruly lock of hair back from his brow and stroked her hand down his cheek. "It's hard enough. I can't bear dragging it out."

His jaw tightened and steely resolve replaced the pain in his face. "This is only temporary. I'll do whatever it takes to make Varun release you from your promise. I'll turn EcoMech around, build the Sharma Network, blackmail him if necessary."

Kama took a step back. Her heart wept for him. "Then you'll be just like Varun and not the man I've learned to trust. You can't let that happen. Forget about me. Find a woman to love, to be a mother to Gabe and carry your children, to share your life, your success."

"I've already found her," he said, closing in again and taking her hand in his. "And I'm not giving her up. I'm coming for you, Kama. I love you."

The door burst open and Wolf took two swift steps in. "We have to go."

Kama released McTavish's hand and glared at Wolf. The naked fury on his face sent a tide of tension rushing from her feet to her head.

"What's wrong?" she asked. The words quivered as they left her throat.

Wolf gave McTavish a look that could melt steel. "Varun's been attacked. He's in critical condition."

Time stopped for Kama. She put a hand on the bed, afraid she might topple. *Attacked.* The word echoed on and on in her head. She had to get to Oasis. Nothing else mattered.

McTavish took her elbow. "My flyer's outside. I'll take you to the shuttleport. When you know... anything, call me."

The walk to the flyer and the trip across the city went by in a blur. Kama's heart slowed and the tightness in her chest loosened. She wondered whether Wolf blamed her, blamed McTavish. He should have been there, watching Varun, protecting him, not here involved in EcoMech's struggles.

McTavish landed next to the terminal entrance and walked with them to the door. Wolf passed through.

Kama didn't know what to say. McTavish seemed at a similar loss, lips parting to speak and closing again. Eventually he threw his arms around her and crushed her to his chest. She squeezed him as though her life depended on it. Then she jerked away and ran after Wolf without a backward glance.

51

Rafe stood on the pavement unable to decide what to do next. He should get out of the heat. Already his shirt was sticking to his back. But his feet didn't move. He looked through the tinted windows of the terminal hoping to catch a final glimpse of Kama.

He didn't have a picture of her, he realized. She had to be on campus surveillance footage somewhere. He'd ask Alana to locate it.

A picture. It was his mind's subtle way of avoiding his fear. What if Varun died before he'd secured her release? Would she stay on Oasis, or would she be free to join him on Harvest?

With heavy steps, he walked back to his flyer. His nanocom chimed again, as it had three times during the flight to the shuttleport, all of which he'd ignored. A rush of anger shot through his chest. Could he not have even a half hour to say goodbye to Kama?

He stroked back his cuff. The screen displayed Shannon's name, and also that she'd been the one calling earlier. His anger deflated, replaced by a pinch of worry and a double dipper of guilt. She'd offered to mind Gabe for the day while he focused on EcoMech's immediate needs.

"Shannon," he said, as his sister's worried face appeared. His own concern flared. "What's up? What's wrong?"

"It's Greg. I don't know what to do." Her words rushed out in a jumble. "Ben won't be back until tonight. I can't leave the children."

"Slow down. What about Greg?"

"He's on Oasis—I still don't understand what he was doing there. He said it was a mission for you, and he'd be home today. I was just so grateful he wasn't here while—"

Rafe's back stiffened, and his heart went cold. "What's happened to Greg?"

Shannon's face shattered. Tears leaked from the corners of her eyes. "He's been arrested. They say he tried to kill Chairman Sharma."

www.ingramcontent.com/pod-product-compliance
Lightning Source LLC
Chambersburg PA
CBHW060053150626
46556CB00017BA/135